PRAISE FOR RUPERT WONG

"My favorite urban fantasy this year... Very fun, fast, quick read,
and the protagonist's voice amused me."
Silvia Moreno-Garcia

"Speaking of fun... a high-octane fantasy and murder mystery.
It's got a near-perfect first chapter, and I'd love to
see more in that world."
Lavie Tidhar

"If Rupert Wong doesn't become the God of Rapidly
Extemporised Plans, it won't be through lack of trying. Or
possibly God of Great Personal Jeopardy. Whichever seat in
whatever pantheon he finally attains, he deserves it, because
reading *Rupert Wong* is a divine experience."
Jonathan L. Howard

"*Rupert Wong, Cannibal Chef* is one of those books that
you have to pick up when you find it, if only to see
whether or not the title is screwing with you.
Bottom line: if you can handle the profanity and grotesque
content, you just may find this one to your liking..."
Manhattan Book Review

"Isn't 'good' an illusion? Isn't Rupert doing the best he can, and
shouldn't we applaud him for that? The answer is, of course, no.
And it's a no that the novella weaves expertly...
It is fun and funny and charming, but it is also subversive
as hell and exquisitely pointed."
Nerds of a Feather

"Refuses to let Rupert off the hook, refuses to let him be
the hero riding in on a silver horse. It fits, and it unsettles
in a way that I think is important."
Quick Sip Reviews

GODS & MONSTERS

Unclean Spirits
Chuck Wendig

Mythbreaker
Stephen Blackmoore

Snake Eyes
Hillary Monahan

Drag Hunt (Novella)
Pat Kelleher

FOOD

OF THE

GODS

An Abaddon Books™ Publication
www.abaddonbooks.com
abaddon@rebellion.co.uk

Collected edition published in 2017 by Abaddon Books™
Rebellion Intellectual Property Limited, Riverside House
Osney Mead, Oxford, OX2 0ES, UK.

10 9 8 7 6 5 4 3 2 1

Editor: David Thomas Moore
Cover art: Sam Gretton
Design: Sam Gretton, Oz Osborne and Maz Smith
Marketing and PR: Rob Power
Editor-in-Chief: Jonathan Oliver
Head of Books and Comics Publishing: Ben Smith
Creative Director and CEO: Jason Kingsley
Chief Technical Officer: Chris Kingsley

ISBN: 978-1-78108-519-6

FOOD
OF THE
GODS

CASSANDRA KHAW

ABADDON
BOOKS

*To anyone who ever despaired of
publishers who will publish
Southeast Asian heroes.*

PART ONE
RUPERT WONG, CANNIBAL CHEF

ONE

"YOU CAN'T UNIONISE. If you unionise, you'll—" I feel jaw muscles tighten from the impending awkwardness. "You'll make demonic-undead-baby-ness look viable."

I slump. The words hang like the absence of applause at the end of an ill-considered comedy routine. Luckily, my audience isn't the type to heckle. Instead, they stare, a violence of gold-green eyes dangling from the ceiling. Unblinking, uncurious. I used to wonder if death kills your sense of humor. It does. At least, when it comes to the kwee kia. I've never heard any of these ghost kids laugh.

"Why not?" The voice is wood rot and maggot bodies convulsing in ecstasy. Heartworms boiling out of an old junkyard dog. "You said to protect our own."

I scratch the back of my neck, shrug, and make pointless noises. I neither need nor want to be splitting hairs with them. In two hours, the boss is expecting a feast to end all feasts. Which means I'll need to very quickly figure out how to process obese Caucasian while organizing the refreshments. Guan Yin forgive me, but the first actually galls me less than the second. Meat is meat by any other name. Plus, the excess of available lard means I can put Penang delicacies on the menu, something that will no doubt delight the guests who keep halal. Human is very similar to pork, after all.

(I know, I know. Religious pundits say that cannibalism is forbidden in the Quran anyway. The *ghouls* say that this isn't *quite* the same.)

As for the beverages, I can't say I'm looking forward to the process. The blood will need to be segregated and decanted into custom Swarovski vials, cross-checked against autopsy records and attractively labelled—the boss abhors bad handwriting—to ensure no one confuses the selection. It's all tedious busywork coupled with the vague risk of infection. I blame it on the fad burning through the northern penanggalans. They've made HIV into the 'It' flavor. It's a bloody mess.

(Ha. Get used to it, ang moh. The juicy hot dog of life is best enjoyed between two puns.)

"Yes. But unionising is going to encourage those Taoist priests and bomohs and what-have-yous to make even more of you," I tell them as I sift through the spice rack. Cardamon. Is cardamon an anathema to any of the guests?

"Genetic diversity is good," declares one of the kwee kia, his voice like a hornet's nest, humming with importance. "We need to consolidate resources against larger threats."

"Only if you breed. Which you shouldn't do. Because you're underaged and shit. Also, dead." I'm tripping over my tongue and my thoughts, but I can't help it. Tact isn't my forte. "And where did you even learn—"

Their glittering stares tell me everything.

"Oh. Oh, right. *I* taught you that. Right. Shit." I press the heel of a hand into my left eye where a dull ache is taking root behind the socket. "Anyway, tell you what. Let's talk later. Tonight, even. Come find me."

I peel my sleeve back and expose my wrist. There's a patch of skin on the inside still naked of demonic tenants (I'll explain that later), proof that I'm not completely drowning in the red. The kwee kia don't hesitate. One by one, they detach moth-silent from the ceiling to land on my forearm. Say what you will about these little bastard sons and daughters of the grave, but they're amazingly courteous. No one jostles for access. No one tries to drain me dry. They all consume exactly one small mouthful of blood; just enough to keep my scent in their noses. The last even goes as far as to lick the opened vein close. So polite. Their mothers would be proud.

Having acquired their thimble of bodily fluids, the kwee kia disperse, scuttling through gaps in the masonry and openings in the roof. They're like cats in that respect, capable of navigating spaces you'd think were too small for their decay-plumped bodies. A bomoh friend of mine said it has something to do with how they are made. By nature, fetuses lack the tensile skeletal structure that adults enjoy. Mix that physiological quirk in with some blasphemous juju, the natural consequences of putrefaction, and you get some, well—you get those guys.

Still, they were legion, and I am but one: Rupert Wong, superstar chef to the ghouls and liaison for the damned of Kuala Lumpur. By the time the air stops reeking of frangipani, I'm giddy from blood loss. My fingers tingle; my head swims. But these are just inconveniences, minor obstacles to be overcome in the pursuit of the month's rent. Speaking of which...

I pick up the tools of my office—bone saw, cleaver, garden shears for those hard-to-crack ribs—before wobbling unsteadily towards the walk-in freezer. Inside, a three-hundred pound tourist and his generously proportioned wife await.

Day jobs. *Love* them.

* * *

"SAYANG, YOU'RE LATE."

The world is made up of rituals. From the way you brush your teeth to how you show obeisance during religious ceremonies, it's an endless list of interlocking behaviours seared into your unconscious self, charms against the madness of reality. Minah and I have them, same as anyone. I come home the exact same way each day: hours too late and smelling abattoir-sweet, my clothes speckled with gore. Minah then reprimands me the same way she has every evening since we moved in together: softly and without malice, her voice like the sunlight piercing the belly of the monsoon rains. I invariably follow up with a smile, sometimes an apology, before locking the door and checking it thrice.

It's an unusual door, with bolts and padlocks to keep the meth-heads out, yellow paper talismans to keep Minah and her boy in. I'm not trading in hyperbole when I say I check it thrice. I really do. Once for habit. Twice for caution. Three times for love. Minah still has nightmares about picking tendons from her teeth, about her bloodlust flinging her over a shoulder and running off to an orgiastic frenzy of people-eating. She can't sleep if the wards aren't in mint condition.

"Sorry, kitten," I say, tired, turning around to pick my way to the kitchen. "It was dinner for thirty today."

Our home is neither large nor lavishly appointed. In another life, it might have been called Scandinavian chic, with its armament of IKEA furniture, austere color scheme, and Minah's one signed poster of Alexander Skarsgård. But right now, there's just too much clutter, too many pieces of magical paraphernalia littering the walls and the floor, for it to be called anything but 'liveable.' To be fair, most of it is concentrated around the doorway to our guest-bedroom-turned-office, but it's impossible to walk three feet without stumbling over a prayer book or a ba gua mirror.

"You've worked with thirty before," Minah replies quietly.

"Yeah, but not with fat white people." I lean against the doorway, cross my arms and waggle a finger. The air is thick with spices: turmeric, cumin, sauteed garlic. "I cooked *American* today."

Minah turns from the stove. She looks about nineteen. She *was* nineteen, when they put her in the ground, belly ripe with child. Six months later, she clawed her way free of the earth and stalked down her cheating wretch of a spouse. Then, she gobbled him up, bones, balls, and all. Him and the bitch he poisoned her for.

She spoons a lock of dark hair behind an ear and smiles, lips a curved bow with no teeth. "And—?"

"Um." Damn it. Minah always knows when I'm holding something back. "I—"

Something on the ceiling lets loose a mad little hiss, half lizard and half wasp, all feed-me-your-liver-with-lima-beans. Minah glances up, serene, mouth touched with apology. It's been five and a half years, but she's still beating herself up over our ineptitude at domestication.

"And how's my little dude?" I raise my arms.

It drops like a coconut, and I catch it between my open hands and hold it as far from my face as I can manage. It scratches at the air and hisses again, louder this time, blind fish eyes twitching. Minah's baby is a tragic anomaly. Because it died in her womb, it is irrevocably tethered to her existence, as much a part of her being as her fingers and toes. Because it died before it could even be born, it's... *broken*. Bad.

"He's a little hungry, I'm afraid."

"Ah." I say, careful not to express anything that could be construed as strong emotion. Feeding time is awkward enough as it is. "Okay. I gotcha. No worries."

Over the years, I've gotten good at being a surrogate father-slash-demon-child-wrangler. I wait for Minah's baby—in my brain, its name is George—to become distracted before I make my move. When a wail from the kettle grabs its attention, I pull George to my chest and wedge its head beneath an armpit, careful to keep its limbs tightly pinioned. It squirms *ferociously*, anger pouring off its wet little body, but it doesn't fight me for long. When I present my wrist, biology takes over. George sinks its needle-teeth deep into a vein and begins suckling blood like it was ambrosia from Zeus's tit.

"What about you?" I look up from the sanity eradicating tableau that is George's bedtime snack. "You need, um, topping up?"

Minah shakes her head, voice stiff. "I'm not a glutton."

"Okay. Just checking," I reply, adjusting the distribution of weight in my arms. If I squint hard enough, if I fight hard enough against my mind's objections, George can almost, *almost* pass for a normal infant.

(The lies we tell ourselves, ang moh. Honestly.)

Minah and I find an old silence together. I settle into a chair, still cradling George, and fidget with the old-fashioned radio on the dining table. She fusses over dinner. Under Minah's skillful hands, the aromas condense into identifiable names. Yogurty chicken korma and stir-fried paku pakis drenched in belacan. Confections summoned from coconut milk and pandan extract. We don't talk, only listen to the noises that domesticity make. Led Zeppelin joins in after a squeal of static, singing about heaven and ways to buy redemption. And for a little while, my world borders on normal.

But then the air fills with frangipani again, sweet and cloying like gudang garam cigarettes, and all that tranquility goes away. I jolt upright and scan the seams of the building for the telltale flicker of tiny fingers, the flash of yellow-green eyes. None emerge, but I can feel the crush of their attention.

"Sayang?" And so can Minah, it seems. "Are you expecting guests tonight?"

I nod as I detach George from my wrist. It comes off with a *slorp* and a gasp, its complaints reduced to aggressive burblings. I leave George on the table and bind the wound with a kitchen rag, fingers compressed over the serrated wound. The checkered fabric blooms crimson.

"The kwee kia want to, um, unionize."

Minah raises an eyebrow. It's remarkably expressive.

I raise my hands, abashed. "Don't say it. I shouldn't have read them those business manuals. I know, just. I'm learning to be better about doing stupid things. I swear."

Deliberately and silently, she returns to her cooking. I wilt under the weight of her disapproval, but there's no time to court her forgiveness. Guiltily, I skulk out of the kitchen and into my office, where it is dark and rich in bright, unblinking eyes.

"You're late, Mr. Wong." whispers one of the kwee kia.

"Yeah, well. Bite me." A heartbeat passes before I realize what I've just said. I raise my index finger. "Metaphorically."

TWO

LET'S TAKE IT a step back, ang moh. Let's talk about what I do in the evenings. You already know I cut up tourists to make splendiferous banquets for ravenous abominations in custom-fitted Armani suits. But why do I waste time with undead babies when I could be making sweet music with my darling Minah?

(I'm sure there's a crack to be made somewhere in that last sentence. Don't take the bait, ang moh. You're better than that.)

The answer is simple: mutual benefit.

I did some bad things in my youth. Real bad. Like, rob-your-mama-and-stab-your-cousin bad. All of which came to a head when I turned twenty-four. I was up to my neck in unhappy ghosts, each and every one of them saddled with complaints so heavy I remember being shocked I could stand upright. One night, after many, many sleepless nights, I gave in and called a priest.

And what he said, well. It was a lot like being told you have cancer. Somewhere, somehow, on a primal level, you knew something is dangerously wrong; but you try to ignore it. The lump in your right testicle. The invasive mole. The inexplicable sudden weight loss. You let yourself pretend that borrowed time isn't borrowed unless you publicly admit it's a loan. But then the voice of reason cuts through all your delusions. The ugly truth gets yanked out like a tapeworm from the brain. And you cry. You wail at the ugliness of it, the unfairness. The shock of being mortal. But deep down, though? None of it really surprises you. You always knew this was how it had to go down.

The holy man didn't tell me anything I wasn't already expecting. He said I had an express pass to all Ten Courts of Hell. I would be there for a thousand years, if I was lucky. Longer, more likely. I wasn't just damned. I was *fucked*.

After pickling myself in cheap liquor, I did what any reasonable guy would do. I called up Diyu—I'll tell you how some other time, ang moh—and asked if there was any way I could negotiate to get time off for good behaviour.

17

They said yes.

So now I'm working off my karmic debt through community management. I mediate arguments. I listen to complaints. I exorcise stubborn ghouls. I push pencils on hell paper and do the books every Hungry Ghost Festival.

And sometimes, I listen to dead fetuses expound on the necessities of a government-sanctioned union.

"LOOK, GUYS. YOU'RE forgetting one very important thing here. You're not free agents. Under, let's see"—I rifle through a grimoire, try to ignore the chicken-skin texture of human leather against my palms—"yeah. Okay. Under article 3.152, you are contractors under independent enterprises. Unless you get explicit permission from your employers, you cannot establish a union."

The kwee kia exchange fish-eyed stares. They blink, moist and loud. "That is where you come in, yes?"

"Me?"

A buzzsaw symphony of assent. "Yes."

I put the tome down. Rub a knuckle into an eye, and work on pretending I'm still an indomitable professional. No, the food doesn't concern me, and I'd much prefer the kwee kia's company to the lukewarm embrace of my loving langsuir. Why do you ask?

I square my shoulders and fold my arms. "No."

Outside, gray collects smog-thick across the city skyline, a haze of moisture veined with flashes of lightning. I count the seconds under my breath. Eight, nine, ten. Thunder purrs. The kwee kia exhibit no concern. One slithers closer, head twisted at an eye-watering angle.

"Why?" Its cranium revolves further. "Are you not our representative? Are you not our liaison—"

"Yes, and yes. But that isn't the point."

Another plunges from the ceiling, loose draperies of skin flapping, to land atop the antique table lamp presiding over my desk. "We must unionise. It is the only way. Foreign competition is seeking to invade our market. If we do not present a united—"

My hands jump up in defense. "No, no, no. No. Wait. No. First of all, *what* foreign competition? That doesn't make any sense. Diyu won't allow it. And I *know* the Jade Emperor isn't going to sign off on a refugee plan."

"*We must consolidate!*" the kwee kia shriek in disharmony.

"You keep saying that, but I don't think you understand the words—" My voice cracks into something undignified.

But the kwee kia aren't having any of it. Without warning, the kid on my lamp lurches into the air, knocking it over so that it detonates into a million terracotta pieces. The rest follow, exploding in every direction, a frenzy of distended bellies and poison-bright gazes. Darkness hits like a fist.

Now, they're screaming, voices tangling, mixing into a slurry of punctuations and half-coherent exposition:

"We must consolidate!"

"The dog-women lie. Not kind. *Not kind*. They come to eat and feast—"

"So old. So *powerful*."

"Tear out our hearts. Eat our livers. Drink our blood. Punish us. Punish us for the sins of our father. We will not allow—"

"*We must consolidate!*"

Before I know it, one of the kwee kia propels itself into my face. Dirty nails dig gutters across my cheeks and my nose, grime-encrusted toes claw for purchase on my lips. I stumble backwards, stubbing my toe against the desk, and scream into moldering flesh. Terrible, *terrible* idea. A foot jams itself into my mouth, and I splutter as I try to rip the beast from my sideburns.

Then, as quickly as it began: stillness.

Nothing moves. Nothing speaks. Nothing so much as twitches a membrane. The kwee kia freeze, their attention riveted by the window. Even the one on my head presents no objection when I detach its grip and deposit it on my desk, only rocks there like a discarded voodoo doll, still and stiff. *Something comes.* The thought is cigarette-burn hot, sudden as infant death. It hums under my skin like an itch.

I suck in air. "What—"

The kwee kia scatter, squirming into the cracks in the walls and the gaps in the ceiling, their eyes blinking out one after another.

I glance over my shoulder, every hair on my body quivering on end, and take stock of the turbulent cloud formations, and how they churn and writhe; amoebic, snarling, *hungry*. The city is very, *very* dark now, the storm practically smeared across my—

The world implodes with a muffled *whumph*. The window crunches inwards, screams as it breaks. Silver glitters through the air. Fog boils through splintered glass; too dense to be natural, stinking of incense and salt and the smell of dead, drowned things. I throw myself over the desk and burrow into the alcove beneath before curling armadillo-tight, arms over my head. Forget machismo. Cowards live to breed to another day.

A muscular shadow worms through the, out of the sky and onto the ceiling. There's a fusillade of claws. *Clack. Clack. Clack. Clack.* A sound like a heartbeat. Ceaseless, systematic. *Clack. Clack. Clack.*

I peek out. Up.

"Shit. Shit, fuck. Kanasai diu—"

DRAGONS ARE EVERYWHERE in Chinese mythology: sinuous, slithering beasts with magnificent whiskers and incongruously stubby little limbs. Totally ridiculous-looking next to their colonial cousins. What purpose, after all, could four fat legs serve on a six-hundred-foot long serpent? None, obviously.

Except to make them a little less terrifying to their devotees.

Real Chinese dragons are nothing like their literary depictions. *Real* Chinese dragons have faces that could launch a thousand traumas. They're fire-breathing, lightning-swilling centipedes with mouths full of knives. Mile-long komodo dragons with scales and an attitude like a lungful of acid.

Primordial monsters. Lovecraft's Elder Things squeezed through a lizard-shaped mold. Pre-*pre* B.C. shit.

And one of them is now dangling over my head.

"Rupert Wooooong." Its voice is the song of the anglerfish. The rasp of the ocean storm. The moan of a sperm whale as it is ferried into the abyss, insides unspooling, slurped down by indescribable abominations.

"You know—" I wet my lips. Hysteria feeds chemical courage into my veins, double-dose of adrenaline. "I am never, ever getting my deposit back on this place. Couldn't you have just knocked on the door like everyone else?"

"If you please us, you will never want for anything again," Us. Not me. *Us.* The bottom of my abdomen opens and my entrails plummet through, yanking my throat tight. Horrified epiphany crawls up my vertebrae. "Serve us, and we will reward you."

"Your Highness—" My mouth is dry, dry, dry. This isn't *just* a dragon. This is a Dragon *King. The* Dragon King of the South Sea. Dolphinfucking Ao Qin himself.

"You are as good as they say you are, Rupert Wooooong." Foghorn laugh that sinks, halfway between that drawn-out syllable, into something that verges on human. "You haven't wet yourself. We are impressed."

I look down. No point explaining it was timing and not courage that held my bladder in check. "Sure."

The fog recedes, as does the stench of deep waters. Oil-black Berlutis peep into view. I scuttle out from hiding as a foot begins to tap, my smile dangling like a loose eyeball. Soundless, the Dragon King has gone from nightmare to billionaire Bruce Wang, trading claws for cufflinks, arm-length teeth for an armory of pinstripes. Ao Qin folds his arms as I straighten, before he nods with all the gravity of a god whose existence has never been in doubt, his eyes raking over my Tesco-bought wardrobe.

"So, uh. To what do I owe this magnanimous visit?" Despite my best efforts, my attention frays, skipping from his patrician visage to the water-logged ruins of my office. This is going to cost thousands I don't have.

"We wish to hire you." Even in human form, his voice is strange and low, a heartbeat in the marrow. "We wish to borrow your services for an important duty."

"Uh-huh. Sounds good," I rub my neck, skin pimpling under his yellow search-light stare. (Here's a trick to remember, ang moh: the supernatural can and will never completely hide who they are.) "And this comes with all the money I could possibly want for the rest of eternity, right?"

He grins. There are mandibles in the dark behind his teeth.

"Yeeessss," Ao Qin croons, gliding closer. "All the treasures of Atlantis. All the wealth rotting in the South China Seas. All of it is yours if you find what we want."

"Okay. Uh-huh. Sounds good. I'm thinking about it," I gnaw on the inside of a cheek. I'm clenching and opening my hands, only half-consciously. "Yeah. *Definitely* thinking about it. But, you gotta tell me what you want first."

The air crisps with burning ozone.

"Nooooo. We will not-t-t-t-t-t-t—" Ao Qin unwinds that last letter like a cartoon snake, spits each repetition with a resounding click. "We have already shown you *great* favor by not devouring your heart. We would not normally tolerate this show of disssssrespect—"

Hindsight is always so incandescently clear. In retrospect, I probably should have kowtowed or curtsied or, better yet, crawled on my belly until Ao Qin expounded on the proper way to exhibit respect in the countenance of omnipotence. I gulp and try not to disgorge my intestinal tract one swollen loop at a time.

"—but we have heard *such* great things about you." He dusts his shoulder with a pale, elegant hand, takes another step nearer. We're practically in sexual harassment territory now. Gods have no concept of personal space. "Rupert Wong, Seneschal of Kuala Lumpur, you have been called by Heaven to participate in an investigation of unparalleled importance."

Dimly, my breath clogged with salt and reptilian musk, I catch myself wondering why Minah hasn't come knocking. She *must* have heard the din. Had Ao Qin ensorcelled the room? Did he do something—

"Repeat after me: I, Rupert Wong, pledge to forfeit eternal respite if I fail at this task, for there is no peace for those who fail Heaven's will."

I lick my lips again, ricocheting back to the pants-wetting present. "I, Rupert Wong, pledge..."

(You don't say no to a six-hundred-foot-long dragon, ang moh. Ever.)

THREE

"ARE THOSE CHICKEN feathers?"

Ao Qin narrows his lambent gaze and chuckles, the noise gargling in his throat, almost loud enough to disguise the ticking of his mandibles. "Always the comedian, Wooooong. Yes. We desire that you seek a chicken worthy of us."

"Ah." I run a nervous tongue over my molars and then try for a grin. It comes out a tortured rictus. "Okay."

He holds his position. I really, really wish he'd blink.

The silence lengthens and lengthens, stretching like filaments of mucus, so heavy with expectations that you could asphyxiate a small pony in the tangle. Ao Qin is *clearly* waiting for me to arrive at some important epiphany, and delighting in the fact I don't even have a postcode in mind.

I look back down at the box in his hands. Inside, three massive feathers on a bed of crushed velvet. Nothing else. No personal effects, no disembodied appendages, no letter of incoherent farewell. The only clue is the rust-brown blood congealed in the plumage.

"Murder most fowl?" I ask, careful to emphasize the last word. Irreverent humor is the last bastion of the beleaguered bureaucrat.

Ao Qin says nothing.

"Crane?"

The corners of his mouth twitch a millimeter upwards.

"Phoenix?"

He cocks his head like a lizard, jerkily.

I inhale until my lungs sting. Then, in one spaceless burst, the words mangling together: "Angel? Fenghuang? Garuda? Griffin? Sphinx? Thunderbird? Pegasus? Cannibal flying unicorn?"

Ao Qin sighs, an infuriating little sound, somehow both condescending and long-suffering. Honestly, you'd think it was *his* office that was gutted and maimed, *his* windows that were chewed up by a localized climatic holocaust. He dips taloned fingers into the box and extracts a feather, holds it up to the pale light of the evening. His face changes then. Softens. The can't-be-fucked-with-you-mortals arrogance, the mannequin alienness, even the anglerfish glow of his eyes—it all dims, drowned in a bone-deep, heart-pulping anguish. The sight of it braids ice around my spine.

What could possibly hurt something like *him?*

"Erinyes."

"Oh."

The chill spreads and suddenly, I can't breathe, because I can see my future and it is written in claret. Greek mythology isn't exactly my forte, but anyone who knows anything about the supernatural know about the Furies.

The Kindly Ones. The Gracious Ones. The motherfucking matrons of vengeance.

"Oh," I repeat, mushing my face with a hand. "You want me to—"

"—find out why they killed our youngest child."

His voice is so soft, so *human* that it roots me in place. There is something universal about the language of hurt, something about it that makes it impossible not to ache in echo. I look up, mouth filling with half-considered platitudes, in time to see the Dragon King extend a finger and prick the dead center of my forehead.

My vision detonates.

A JIGSAW OF body parts: legs split and sucked clean of marrow, arms gnawed down to the white of their tendons, finger-bones scattered like dice. I can't look away, won't look away. My throat fills with copper, salty-sweetness that brims as pain saws through my tongue. I bite down harder. A foreign thought hammers against my temples: I am a king. I cannot break.

Ao Qin's memories permit only a moment's sliver of personal autonomy, enough to register what is happening. Then they descend again, waves boiling, choking.

His rage is volcanic, primal, acid in the arteries. He/I run our fingers along the arc of an exposed spine. The smell is her. He—I—We would recognize it anywhere. This is our child, our youngest, our mate's sweetest and most beloved.

We follow the vertebrae up to the flayed line of the throat. To her jaw, the serene bow of her mouth. Eight centuries since we've seen her smile, and we find it now. Still luminescent. Still beautiful in death.

Dimly, we register the bloodied detritus that was her husband. His face wears its terror. His lips still scream. Strange, so strange. Why did he exhibit his pain but not our daughter? Perhaps it was her royal lineage that gripped her composure tight as her ribs were cracked open, her chest emptied of lungs and nerve. Perhaps, perhaps, perhaps...

We stop ourselves. Such contemplations are merely auxiliary to this horror, this nightmare that we can never remedy, no matter the offerings we heap upon the absent Jade Emperor's lap. Our daughter is dead.

Our daughter is dead.

Our daughter.

Is.

Dead.

Dead.

Dead.

"My lord," a voice seeps through the thundering mantra of our grief. "You may want to see this..."

"I'm sorry," I slur the words, gorge rising as the borrowed memory is devoured by the present. Everything is too bright, too loud, too... *everything*. A sensory deluge so acute that even the throb of my pulse overwhelms. My knees buckle and I sag forward to vomit today's lunch into a waste bin.

(You have to understand, ang moh. Ignoring the fact that it is absolutely jarring to be forced into someone else's mind, butchery and violence are not synonymous. There's a difference between being able to prepare a Scottish rump roast—yes, it's exactly what you think it is—and being dragged through a stew of phantasmal gore. One is a systematic ecosystem of parts; order translated into cold-cut meats. The other? Far less orderly.)

Ao Qin's voice unfurls. "We do not require condolences. We require justice, Mr. Wong. We require *blood*."

Nasal cavities aflame with stomach bile, I wipe my mouth on a sleeve and stand. Push up and unbend, one wobbling leg at a time. The world swims dangerously, but my balance holds. Hysteria quickens my speech. "Look, I'm *not* going to kill a Fury for you. I *can't*. Not because I don't want to, because Guan Yin knows I'd like nothing more than to keep razor-mouthed gods like you happy, but there is absolutely no physical way I can—"

The Dragon King makes a strange, high noise. Over and over, stuttering like a broken VCR, until the sound transmutes into a tooth-grinding wail. It takes me a moment to realize he's laughing. "We do not expect you to kill them, Mr. Wong. We expect you to gather evidence. Ineluctable proof that they performed a crime. We require these materials before we can confront the Greeks."

A little better, but nothing close to ideal. No one likes being treated like a petty criminal. (Personal experience goes a long way, ang moh.) I can't imagine the Furies would appreciate me poking my stubby nose into their business. "But. Boss. Your Highness. *Sir*. With all due respect, the Furies aren't exactly the kind to act on impulse. History shows that they—"

"*They killed my daughter.*" Ao Qin slams his palms on the table. Wood splinters under the impact. More terrifying than his introductory exhibition of power, than the price tag of his wardrobe, than the hate with which he builds each quiet word, is the absence of the royal pronoun. This is *personal* for him. Personal in a way I never thought gods could do.

"Okay," I say again, raising my hands slowly. "I get you. Fine. So, just get in, get whatever you need, get out, and... get paid?"

"Yes."

"Okay," I say, for what feels like the hundredth time today. I close my eyes and squeeze the flesh along my nose bridge. "And, what if I don't actually find something?"

"You will."

"Or what?" The words escape before I can throttle them in the crib. I freeze, as does Ao Qin. We're both equally shocked by my audacity, I imagine. "Your Highness. I understand that you, uh, see your daughter as a paragon of virtue. But hear me out here: what if, *hypothetically speaking*, the Furies have a close-and-shut case? If that were the case, what happens to me?"

Something squirms under Ao Qin's smooth plaster-white skin. Down through the slant of his left cheekbone, down his nose, down his throat where it bulges perversely before vanishing from sight. Silence follows, noose-tight and pregnant with menace. Without altering expression, Ao Qin clicks the box shut and slides it across the table.

"If that were indeed the case," He begins, gauze-light, his enunciation cotton-edged, like someone speaking through the membrane of a dream. "We would be forced to act as though you had failed us."

"But—" An argument about fairness bashes against the back of my teeth, but common sense prevails for a change.

Ao Qin's gaze deepens. "We assure you that we thought long and hard about this. Our daughter is faultless. Our daughter would never do anything to incur their wrath. You will find the answer we desire. We are certain of this."

"I—" Monosyllabic protests seem to be in vogue this conversation.

"If we had the option, if we could ask one of our own to undertake this quest, we would have. But that isn't possible. Not without risking a war with the Greeks. It has to be you, Rupert Wong."

Unspoken: human scapegoats are all the rage. "Okay."

We trade stares. Ao Qin crosses his hands behind the small of his back, eyebrows slightly arched, and nudges the air with an upward thrust of his head, as though rolling a ball into my court. Unwilling to commit just yet, my skin blistering under his scrutiny, I stoop down to harvest bits of smashed pottery, broken glass, and tattered papers. The sloughed-off flesh from the kwee kia—formaldehyde can only do so much for these acrobatic tykes—I leave for the vacuum.

We maintain this rhythm for a while: me, cleaning. Him, observing. A few minutes into my housekeeping, I hear a discreet *thud*. I look up. A paperweight has been mysteriously returned upright.

The unexpected act of nominal charity kindles a weird anger. You can push me around. You can dick with my life. You can raise my rent. But don't pretend you actually *care* about my well being. Especially not now, not here. That fury quickly transfigures into ill-guided inspiration. A plan clicks into place and I stand, giddy with the knowledge I'm about to say something breathtakingly idiotic again.

"By the by, Your Highness. I was *thinking*," I draw a circle in the air with a finger, my other arm looped around the waste bin, its bowels acrid with the stomach bile. "Theoretically speaking, if I went to Diyu and told them that you were press-ganging one of their representatives into unsanctioned service, wouldn't that annul my oath and get you into incredible amounts of legal trouble?"

The Dragon King cants his skull. "Are you threatening me?"

"I'm not threatening you," I say, as I deposit my container on the desk, all the while thinking to myself: *Yes. Yes, I am.* "I'm just expressing, in a roundabout way, my desire to not be enslaved by a verbal contract. As much as I'd like the fortune you've promised and to avoid the certain death you've been implying, there is no way this is happening. I'm not—I'm not risking those Furies."

"Not even for me?"

Minah peels from the doorframe, a monochrome palette of what little is good and beautiful in my world. Her feet make no sound, no sound at all (the langsuir, ang moh, are very good at levitation) as she picks through the wreckage, eyes half-shuttered, baju kurung rustling like the waters of a midnight lake.

"Minah," I swallow. "Sayang, you shouldn't be here—"

She ignores me. Her attention belongs wholly to Ao Qin, who watches her sinuous approach with a mix of repulsion and wonder. I wonder if he sees a little bit of his daughter in her corpse-pale face, her scar-kissed arms. Eventually, Ao Qin nods, slow and boneless, spine bending serpentine-supple. "We can grant that boon, dead little girl."

"Wait, what are we—"

In reply, Minah, still stoically ignoring my endeavours to make eye contact, laces her hands about his and bows low, lips pressed reverently to the Dragon King's fingers. "There are no words to convey my gratitude, Yang Pertuan."

"Excuse me? Someone? What are we talking about here?"

"We will even personally escort you to Meng Po," continues Ao Qin. "But *only* if Mr. Wong completes his task."

My ribs immediately become three sizes too tight. Minah was a good girl in life. Pious, even. The kind who prayed five times a day, who paid her zakat without complaint, and eschewed the temptations of bacon and expensive liquor. But all that virtuous behaviour means nothing when you've suckled on the marrow of your ex-spouse and drained his lover's heart like it was some succulent fruit. Heaven has long ceased being an option for Minah; but reincarnation? That was still a possibility.

A dim, distant possibility, like a childhood daydream half-remembered, but still an achievable solution. It would require wading through a storm of red tape, of course, and innumerable court appearances. But it could happen.

Especially if you have the backing of an antediluvian deity.

"Thank you," Minah says, her voice so rich with hope and want that I know I've lost before even she turns to fix her beautiful gaze on me. I would do anything for this girl. Anything, at all. And they both know this. Fuckers. "We shall be in touch."

I smile weakly and nod. There was nothing else to be said.

FOUR

THE SKY BURNS blue as we slouch through the gridlocked highway, the distant city of Kuala Lumpur a conundrum of skyscrapers, post-colonial architecture, and verdant green jungle. Someone punches their horn furiously. Another car replies with a loud bellow, like a beast answering a challenge.

The air conditioning coughs. Once, twice. Six times. The mechanical hacking eventually weakens into a background rattle even as Feng Mun lowers the temperature. Warm air blasts through the vents, smelling of chrysanthemum and exhaust gases. Roar as it might, the cab's emphysemic A/C is obviously losing its battle against the wet, torpid heat.

As the sun beat down through the right window, I scoot a bit closer to the left, trying in vain to melt into what little shade exists.

(Don't know why I bother, ang moh. It never works.)

"So, boss," Feng Mun begins, coy, gap-toothed smile gleaming in the rear view window. "Have you talk to my wife recently ah?"

"Sorry. Haven't had the time." I mumble, in between arranging a plate of offerings and fighting my lighter. I fumble and lose my grip. The char siew pau bounces onto the floor, gathering dirt and whatever else has collected on the carpeted floor. Hopefully, its recipient won't care too much. I don't want to deal with the competition.

My cab driver twitches a shoulder, still obnoxiously sunny. "Okay loh! If you got time, ask her if she have enough money. If not, I can burn more."

Feng Mun is the poster child of modern mínghūns. Where his predecessors married for desperation or to continue a family line, my ex-colleague (no one stays in the triads forever, ang moh) married his ghost (I'm being literal again, yes) for love. According to rumour, all it took was a single black-and-white photo and then six of years of bush-beating, nail-gnawing, long-distance courtship.

If this were a Shakespearean performance, Feng Mun would have killed himself for her ages ago, possibly while ululating about his affections, but the two are practical, earthen folk. (His wife, Sue Lin, was a prodigal accountant.) Such a transgression, she pointed out, would have doomed him to a lower strata of Diyu, invalidating the whole gesture. So, they're both waiting for his natural demise, trading messages through mediums, and affection through willing possessees. (Yes. I know, ang moh. Very unsettling. But they're happy and the mediums get paid. Who are we to judge?)

"Okay." I drain a bottle of mineral water in a single motion, chuck it onto the floor as I ignite a trifecta of red joss sticks. The air immediately clots with the smell of sandalwood, nauseatingly dense. But the God of Missing People mandates such excess. Anything else and you're asking for papercuts.

At least, that's my assumption. My comprehension of Taoist sorcery is only very minimally superior to my grasp of animistic magic, which is to say I really, really should be chaperoned by an adult at all times and kept away from the complicated ideas. I have no aptitude for the mystic arts, only pig-headed resolution and a vague certainty that knowing how to contact the people I work with is a valuable trait. It gets you somewhere. Far, unfortunately, isn't one of those destinations.

"Is it okay if I roll down the—" I clutch the lever in anticipation. Feng Mun's car is a geriatric embarrassment in every way, except for the engine purring beneath the bumblebee-yellow hood.

Feng Mun's voice booms, bright and boisterous, only slightly damaged by the scar rippling from mouth to clavicle. "Caaaaaaaaaaan! For you, anything also okay!"

"Er." *Squeak squeak squeal-crunch.* The contraption jams. "Um."

"Push harder laaaa." He chortles. On the radio, Taylor Swift's static-mauled voice rises in volume, imploring listeners to shake it off, shake it off.

I throw my shoulder into the motion, just as a torn-out scrap of newspaper glides through the pinprick gap between window and door frame. Another follows. Then another, and another. Another. Missing people notices. Kidnapping reports. Public entreaties to return a beloved son, a cherished daughter. An entire river of cheap newsprint washes into the cab, swilling together into a vaguely humanoid shape.

"Don't block my mirror, can or not?" Feng Mun shoots glibly, immune to the strangeness. Outside, the driver of a passing Proton Wira gawks, slack-jawed, until I stare him down.

Eyes—all the black of the darkest inks, all young, all excerpts from lives interrupted—narrow as they flutter past. Mouths gape, hiss like cats.

"Really, Rupert?" They grumble in perfect unison, their Cantonese accented and musical. "Of all the places in Kuala Lumpur, of all the happening joints you could have invited me to? You had to call me *here*?"

"Eh, what's wrong with my taxi, ah?" Feng Mun drapes an elbow over the back of his seat, and cranes a look backwards. He waggles a finger. "I clean it every day, you know?"

"He does." I pinch the bridge of my nose. "Look, I—can we argue about this later? I'm trying to do business here."

The God of Missing People lounges back in its seat. The faces on its skin—too young, much too young—murmur among themselves, their gazes darting this way and that, a gaggle of gossiping relatives at Chinese New Year. Seconds later, they stop, all at once, and focus on me.

"Fine." Hundreds of eyes, some visible, some walled up behind text-scarred creases, roll with teenage extravagance. "First: let's see the goods."

I wedge a smile onto my mouth and try to maintain eye contact with the countenances papered around its head, a feat complicated by their reluctance to do the same. My mood lifts, however, when a corkscrew-haired girl of about sixteen shares a wink. Good sign. Definitely. Definitely maybe.

Impaling the joss sticks on a doughy char siew pau, I nudge the offerings forward. The response this time is unmistakably favorable. The God of Missing People, cooing in chorus with itself, trails fingers of cheap paper around the spread, round and round in languid figures of eight. Over and over and over. With every orbit, the food begins to gray, rotting from the inside out. Mold settles like muslin over the decay, and the deity sighs orgasmically to itself.

"*Delicious,*" It croons. "You never fail to impress. You have no idea how many people call me up without even sparing a thought about what I want, or what I like, or—"

The god stops. Despite the tropical sun, I feel the ambient temperature drop several degrees, sinking to somewhere between 'reasonable chance of doom' and 'unequivocal disgruntlement.' I pluck at my collar.

"Yes?" I extend the word like an olive branch, half in wistful fatalism. It's obvious that there's no hand waiting to receive it, just a colony of hornets. But optimism is stubborn.

The God of Missing People doesn't answer. Not at first. I watch with growing unease as its mouth works in furious silence, like an old woman in mortal conflict with a glob of toffee. Eventually, it discharges a wad of hair and gum and chewed-up plastic wrappers into a cupped palm, before presenting the offending bezoar for examination.

"Not my fault." The exclamation bubbles out before I can stop it; I sound like an obtuse toddler. I'm too busy squashing the temptation to ask about the exact logistics of what just happened to be properly tactful. Somewhere between all that, a manic thought arises: It wasn't as though the deity had actually *eaten* the char siew pau...

"You'd think, Rupert," The god says, almost hyperventilating at this point, every word swaddled with venom, every sentence an octave above the last. "You'd *think* that you, of all people, would understand the importance of curating an offering. It's not like I asked for much. Not like your *old* gods with their virgins and golden calves."

"But, I—"

"*More excuses?*" Now its voice is vibrating. "You should be down on your knees right now, thanking me for being so benevolent. Why, I can't imagine how—"

A sigh whooshes free before I can reel it back. There's no hope for it. Persnickety gods don't stop once they've started steamrolling down their preferred tangent. I wait for an opening to riposte, misguided as that notion might be, and finally find one as Feng Mun eases us into a three-lane stalemate.

"I'm really, really sorry." Hardly the most macho rejoinder, but humility is never a bad place to start. "It was entirely an accident. I did not mean offense. If there's any way I could—"

"You could ask someone else to be your bloodhound." It sniffs.

Damn it damn it damn it damn it. "We'll be even after that?"

The God of Missing People twists its head, arms crossing, every visible face puckered with low-key distaste. Something nasty feeds into its body language; this is probably not going to be something I appreciate. "Yes. But only if you let me watch."

Nope.

"Cruelty is next to godliness," I mutter under my breath, but I extend my hand palm-up, wrist bared. With more practice than I care to admit, I slide a razor from its expertly sewn—Minah has a dreadful amount of free time—pocket in my inner sleeve. The blade itself is nothing terribly noteworthy. A plain wedge of stainless steel about the size of my thumb. Nonetheless, it suits its purpose.

I mumble a string of homemade incantations beneath my breath, spitballing new flourishes to the beat of my own breath. Contrary to pop culture, magic prefers invention to ritual—so long as you adhere to the fundamentals, that is. You can't grill a steak without meat, after all, or pull ghosts from the road without a tribute of blood. Failure to get the basic tenets right invariably results in... *stickiness.*

Anyway.

Halfway through the polysyllabic maelstrom, I stab the blade into my forearm.

Pain fountains and for the second time in twenty-four hours, the world fractures into a Daliesque painting, all melting colors and insane configurations, shapes eating shapes, faces bleeding into faces and car hoods and anorexic monstrosities with too many limbs. Images begin to flicker at the edge of my vision: television-static outlines, incandescent enough to imprint afterimages on the eyeballs, jumping in and out of reality. I catch the cracked slope of a pregnant stomach, the grimace of an old man, an ocean of eyes, hands reaching, skin crisping, crackling, sizzling, subcuticular fat smoking, fragrant as an open-air barbeque and—

I tense. The cab is now glutted with ghosts, accident victims and traffic prey. They stick to every available surface, head and limbs contorted, cracked in places, smashed in others. Bent, broken, bleeding. Bloated with water, with pus, with blood. Every variety of smashed-up a vehicular accident can possibly conjure. Ectoplasmic brain drips like rooftop rainwater.

Speak-speak-speak-speak. A susurrus of overlapping voices. *Feed-feed-feed-feed.* Warning slithers between every vowel, thick and wet. Unlike gods, who are irrefutably mood-swingy but still generally of orderly mind, the dead lean towards simple-minded violence.

FEED.

The psychic tantrum is practically an assault at this point, a sledgehammer of pure demand. I wince and thrust my arm up in fine imitation of Freddie Mercury. The ghosts don't wait. They pour forward, mouths unhinging, and it's all I can do to stammer through a hastily considered ward; barely sufficient to keep them from emptying me of everything.

A frictionless eternity later, the tide slackens, oozing to a persistent trickle. I crack open a bleary eye. My vision crawls with microscopic life and necromantic traversities, a smear of lines throbbing to a 90mph heartbeat. I'm exhausted. Spent. Gone. But it's over, except for one persistent apparition, a middle-aged Chinese woman with a face like burnt pork rinds, who refuses to detach. The rest have withdrawn, and are squatting like cats in the corners of the cab.

Speak-speak-speak-speak.

"Did any of you see the Dragon King's daughter?"

Yes-yes-yes-yes-yes.

"Did you see who killed the Dragon King's daughter?"

Whispering, too low for human hearing, as the spirits consult among themselves. In retrospect, it might have been better to provision a name, but Ao Qin, in his eternal wisdom, ignored all my tactful attempts at acquiring it.

The murmurings segues into stuttering assent: *Yess-ssss-sss-sss-ss...*

Huh. *Interesting.* An external party was definitely involved in the deaths. I mull over my options. Convenient as the alternative might be, I don't want to out the Furies. Ao Qin might not have *explicitly* stated that I couldn't share details about the case, but casual disclosure seems like a universally horrible idea, regardless.

The other issue is that traffic ghosts generally have god-awful vocabularies; something about lowest common denominators. More than one syllable a challenge.

The God of Missing People leans forward, hands planted onto the seat, one behind the other, looking for all the world like a cat prepared to lunge. My skin immediately prickles with portents of disaster. It's beginning to feel like I'm missing an important memo somewhere, the one titled, *Please RSVP to not be sacrificed horrifically.*

After some consideration, I make my play:

"If asked to testify in a court of Hell, will you agree to truthfully identify the killers if they are brought in for examination?"

The air pressure drops, fast enough and low enough that my ears go pop and Feng Mun yelps. Before either of us can articulate a coherent word, the ghosts exit en-masse, sucked back out into the coiling traffic, their eyes huge and haunted. They leave their fear in the air, however, solid as a tumour, poisonous.

The God of Missing People slides back, drapes itself across the back of the cab like some young starlet.

"Happy?" I demand through clenched teeth, coiling a bandage around my arm. Blood is unfortunately an important part of being a black magic man.

"Beyond my wildest dreams." It slithers forward again, presses its cardboard tongue against the red webbing my skin, and coos. "Now, what can I do for you?"

"Find her for me."

"Find who?"

"The—" This really is awkward. All of it. The lack of the name, the God of Missing People lapping at my wound like a docile kitten. I hunch into my shoulders and extend my arm further, placing as much distance between the two of us as possible. The spectral auntie finally departs, throwing us both dirty looks as she goes, imprecations sprouting like egg sacs under her analogical breath. "The Dragon King's daughter."

The deity raises its head, hands locked around my wrist and elbow. "I would have appreciated more input than that, but fine. Hardly a big deal at all. I'll find your girl for you and I expect a proper offering for the effort."

"Only the best."

The God of Missing People throws back its head and guffaws rancorously, before it erupts into a storm of papers, swirling around the interior of the taxi before it pours itself out of the window. The suddenness of the feat isn't without consequence. Feng Mun, already on edge, loses control of the taxi.

Impact.

Metal screeches as my head punches against the back of Feng Mun's seat and then boomerangs away. A starburst of agony, magnesium-white. I can hear shouting, doors slamming, a clatter of junk like mahjong tiles. Pain scrawls jagged spiderweb patterns along my neck, flowing from the front of my skull, down to my shoulders where it bites into muscle.

Groaning, I sit upright and roll my neck, triggering a fusillade of arthritic cracks. This will hurt tomorrow. And the day after, and the day after that.

"Wei, Rupert?"

"Mm?"

A burly man with meat-bricks for fists pummels on Feng Mun's window, his face a rictus of pure fury.

"...you got insurance ah?"

FIVE

Unsurprisingly, Ao Qin's men smell of fish.

Not unpleasantly, to be fair. Less rotten catfish, more belacan, subtly spiced and heavily salted, a scent of careful preservation, and only obvious from about a foot away. But even if they did stink of decaying ocean life, I can't imagine anyone in Chee Cheong Kai noticing.

Chinatown, Chee Cheong Kai, Petaling Street: all names for the rotted apple planted deep in Kuala Lumpur's eye. It is fecund with odours both nauseating and tantalizing, a duality of butter cream crabs and dried urine, fermented bean curd and roasting chestnuts, sewage and sweat and all the other fine accoutrements you can expect to find in a bloated tourist trap. There are a hundred reasons to part with your money here: roasted duck carcass, pirated DVDs with strategically comical sleeves, cheongsams like wisps of flame, and if you look carefully enough, mouths painted with conspiratorial promise.

"'Sup." I step between two competing storefronts, their owners growling like hounds in competition, and doff an imaginary cap at a tallow-skinned man in front of the stairwell. He stands about a head taller than me, arms crossed over a chest you could build a grand piano around, flanked by two equally grim-faced individuals.

He glowers over the rims of his tinted bifocals. His eyes are the mother-of-pearl of an oyster's entrails, and there's something about his body language that says *shark*, the same way the one on his left screams *eel*. "You're late. We've been waiting for you."

I can feel my armpits dampen under his scrutiny, but I don't tell him I had no clue, or that I spent the better part of my morning trying to convince the boss I *needed* to come to Chinatown because the ingredients I wanted to procure can be found nowhere else. Better to pretend authority than to admit ignorance, especially when wading in unfamiliar waters. So I nod. Curtly. Just a slight bobbing of the jaw in gruff masculine acknowledgment.

The three take their time to size me up, now that they've established I'm the Rupert they're looking for. They don't blink. But then again that isn't common of their genus, is it? Which leaves me to wonder if they've really transformed into humanoid form, or if I'm talking to levitating fish.

"You going to let me through?" I prod, after a minute, my head swimming with morbidly hilarious images. "We're a bit conspicuous out here."

We're not. Between the DVD merchants, cocaine-gaunt and still impossibly enthused despite the advent of high-speed internet and torrents, the posturing schools of teenage lowlife, the sunburnt tourists, and the occasional triad affiliate, we fit right in. At least, until you squint at our tattoos too long. Like mine, the ink on Ao Qin's underlings, a hodgepodge of primordial symbolism too old for anything but cephalopods to understand, disdain staticity.

"You're a lot less impressive than the others," remarks Eel, his nose twitching. He smiles; his mouth reveals too many incisors and a grotesque underbite. *Moray Eel. M. Eel. Eel for short.*

"Say what?"

"Like I said, Mr. Wong," interrupts Shark, scooping one broad arm gently, but very insistently, around my shoulders. "Please. This way."

"Wait, what others—"

Patience doesn't appear to be one of Shark's virtues. Push transitions to violent shove, as he knocks me forward with appalling effortlessness. I stumble, stub my toe on the first step, bite down a curse, but don't crash. Shark lumbers in behind me, eclipsing the glare of the noon sun, and not-so-surreptitiously blocking my exit.

"Up." As with all muscle, Shark is economical with words.

The stairwell ahead is only periodically lit. Naked bulbs dangle and sway from the ceiling, fizzing at irregular intervals, coughing like old men. Posters, pasted over the bones of a hundred other advertisements, turn the walls into a mosaic of broken dreams. The floor is lined with trash: someone's dinner, fossilized remnants of someone's dinner, and what generations of cats have dragged in, chewed up, and spat out. I toe carefully through the mess.

"So, what's it like working for Ao Qin?"

Silence. *Clomp. Clomp. Clomp.*

"How are you liking Kuala Lumpur?"

More silence. *Clomp.*

"Dry land doing okay for you?"

Clomp. Clomp. Pause.

"You talk too much." *Clomp.*

I shrug. Fair enough.

Midway to the fourth landing, I give up on the banter, if for no other reason than it feels ridiculous to wheeze for conversation, while Shark drives on like an Olympic athlete. My thighs are burning, my hips straining. It's ten years too late for so much exercise, honestly.

"Here," says Shark, interrupting my misery.

I push away from the railing and straighten, squinting through a fog of exhaustion, breathing perfectly controlled, expression perfectly uneven. An unimpressive door squats before me, its wood bloated from moisture and splintered from abuse. The peeling paint is an indistinct shade of digestive-fluids-green.

Shark doesn't wait for me to compose myself. Stopping at the top step, he reaches over me and raps on the door with sausage fingers. It swings open, and I'm instantly bludgeoned by a charnel stench.

I clamp a sleeve over my nose as I limp into the room: a dirty loft with equally filthy floor-to-ceiling windows, naked of any furniture or distinguishing feature save for the slaughterhouse tableau. Someone has moved the two bodies since I last glimpsed them through Ao Qin's head; the tatters of their arms have been gathered and crossed over their chests, their legs pushed together with a sense of decorum. What I think was Ao Qin's daughter is garnished with a bouquet of irises, white as teeth, unnervingly vivid against the onset of decomposition.

our daughter is dead our daughter is dead our daughter

Strange how expertly memory can dilute truth. Ao Qin's recollections were steeped in iron and burst intestines, but they had nothing on the actual crime scene. *our daughter is dead our daughter our daughter.* The smell is—

"Rupert?"

To my surprise, there's a man there, bald head gleaming like a boiled white egg. How did I—

"Er. You've got the advantage on me." I bare my teeth at him, arm lowering, even as I frantically endeavour to attach his wan, round face to a name. "I'm afraid I don't—*Hao Wen?* What are you doing here?"

"What are *you* doing here?" His forehead rucks. Hao Wen is a doughy-looking man with a middle-aged paunch and the cheeks of a toddler, deceptively soft. As always, his outfit seems calculated for unobtrusiveness; an off-color shirt, with off-color slacks, battered sneakers of no recognizable brand. If you ignore the unnaturally red mouth, Hao Wen looks utterly forgettable, utterly unremarkable.

(He's not, though. *Obviously.* Hao Wen is one of the rare Sak Yant masters who works directly with the soul, human and otherwise. He's hideously powerful, as a result. If you ever have the chance to meet him, ang moh, be sure to ask Hao Wen for a Mahaaniyohm. You will never be short of sexual partners again.)

"Fulfilling a duty?" I circle around him, shuffling like an injured boxer in the fight of his career, careful to make no sudden moves.

Hao Wen purses his mouth, nodding. "Mmmmmm."

"You?" I don't take my eyes from his hands. His tools of trade—bamboo-capped needles, in every size—dangle limply from his fingers.

"The same, the same. Mmm." Hao Wan bobs closer, serene. Up close, his presence is enormous. Room-eating. "Ao Qin asked me for help. Mmm."

"Me too." I try to laugh, but it comes out a nervous, high-pitched hiccup of a noise. "Seems like we will be partners then, eh?"

"Mmmmm." I've never been able to identify the reason for that sound he makes. *Mmm. Mmmm.* Happy or sad, it's always *mmmm*.

I drop into a crouch beside the bodies, arms draped over my knees, and tilt my attention partway down. Now, this is interesting. Ao Qin's memories, reasonably enough, were so consumed by unimaginable horror that they left no space for fine details. Details like the neat little cut outlining the underside of his daughter's jawline. It's a shockingly clean injury for its size. The wound travels from ear to ear, and is deep enough that I'm genuinely surprised her head hasn't rolled off her neck.

Yet, at the same time, there's no sign that a struggle had taken place. Sedatives—magical, I imagine, although I can't figure out why the Erinyes would need it—must have been involved. Or something worse. My gaze skitters over the pulped mess of the husband's face. Unlike his wife, this one went down screaming. Maybe they took him first. Maybe they made her watch...

"Any leads on your end?"

"Mmmmm." Hao Wen paces around the radius of the crime scene and, much to my extreme discomfort, comes to stop right behind my shoulder. "A few. You?"

"Mm," I mimic, a bit sarcastically. That sound is shaving at my nerves. "A few. I thought we could, maybe, consolidate what we know"—so I don't have to cross-check this nightmare—"and then, maybe divide up search zones, and—"

"*Mmmm,*" There's an uncanny edge to his constant vibrato now. "You don't know, do you?"

I sigh. "Probably not. No one tells me anything."

"There can only be one, Rupert." The tiniest *schink* of steel-on-steel as Hao Wen sighs, low and sad.

"Are you quoting *Highlander*?" The hairs on the back of my neck are standing at attention. I try rocketing onto my feet and sidling away at the same time, and end up rising in an undignified waddle.

I don't get far. Something sharp lances between my vertebrae, right above where my neck meets my shoulders. I stiffen. The needle plunges deeper, deeper, until I can almost feel a pinprick tickle against my windpipe.

"Don't move. Mmm? Mm. It will probably end very badly for you."

"You've made your point rather clear." Ha. I launch a panicked look in Shark's direction. He's clearly aware that something is going down. Unfortunately, my misfortune appears to be a spectator sport rather than cause for intervention.

Hao Wen, still *mmm*-ing thoughtfully away, dips to his haunches so we're both eye level. He shutters his eyes and begins mashing his generous jowls with his free hand hand, plucking at the flab in a way that makes him look suspiciously like a sleeping trout.

"You and I are not the only ones that Ao Qin summoned to the duty."

"Uh-huh? Crowdsourcing has its virtues."

"Yes. Mmmmm," sighs Hao Wen. "But the problem is that he's going to award only *one* person the prize."

"And the others?"

"MmMMMMMM." Nothing good can come of the tone he's using. He cuddles the sound like a pet, stroking it, teasing it, before finally, in a feathery murmur, explaining: "They die."

Uh oh.

Hao Wen snakes an arm forward and around my neck, a fresh needle clasped between his fingertips. "No hard feelings, mmm? I'm just trying to minimize the competition. Mmmm."

As he reaches down, tiny hands rise from my skin to clutch his—

FREEZE-FRAME.

So, here's the deal: being alive is awesome. It's better than being in Heaven, which I hear is endlessly dull, and certainly miles ahead of accommodations in Diyu. Unless you're keen on the bliss of non-existence, what you have right now, ang moh, is the best you'll ever get. Unsurprisingly, life, for all of its torments and unpredictabilities, is a habit-forming vice.

It is the rare soul who undertakes cosmological migration without complaint. Most buck when confronted with the notion of being separated from the material plane, although they usually concede after some initial grumbling. Not all, though. Some cling to physicality like a drug, a grudge. These spirits eventually become refugees: ghosts, poltergeists, and in some cases, yaoguai of considerable malevolence.

Diyu, of course, is responsible for containing these specters and has been authorized by the Jade Emperor to use any means necessary. Which means one of two things for the vagrant revenants: certain annihilation, or the need to be very, very clever.

And that brings us to my point for this tangent. The savviest spooks use bureaucracy to their advantage. Instead of milling aimlessly through the Earth, they negotiate tenancy agreements. Rental contracts with willing mortals.

Like me.

Oh, come on, ang moh. You didn't really think all those tattoos were for fun, did you?

HAO WEN'S EYES flare open. "What—"

I don't need to look to know what is tendrilling out of my flesh: two-dimensional arms, thin as bone, fingers too long and too warped; a face made out of teeth. "You could have stopped the first thing too."

Bob (of course they have properly foreign names, ang moh, but names have power; call a dragon a duck, and you instantly bring them closer to your level) hisses exultantly in reply. Out of the corner of my eye, I can see Bob scrabbling for purchase on Hao Wen's shoulder, every motion boneless, fluid as kerosene, pulling himself upwards, fist after fist.

The Sak Yant master moans when Bob's grip finally locks over his face, and kicks free with a yelp, scrabbling backwards on his hands. Needles spray across the floor. Bob croons his disappointment like a lovelorn girl. The commotion has agitated the other tattoos; I can feel them unfurl and swell, rheumatic from dreams of sensory gluttony but eager to awake, to capitalize on this opportunity to devour and tear and *hungry what is this light what is who are where are you delicious tired get out of my space what are you doing*

More hands stretch, more faces press against the film of my skin.

"Guys, a little help here?"

The needle impaling my spine clatters free.

I rise and backpedal away from Hao Wen, much to my renters' dissatisfaction; they like conflict. But bravado really isn't my jam. Reading my fear, the tattoo artist looks at me appraisingly, and then snarls and belches a word of old power, mountain-language, bone-speak, so potent that the air itself quavers like an exposed lung.

Half my tattoos drop dead.

Yeah. Time to go.

With one last hopeful look at Shark, who *still* hasn't budged from the exit, I stab an elbow into the window behind me. Glass erupts and empty air yawns. I glance over my shoulder: no fire escape. Clearly, the building planners weren't proponents of public safety. Below, the road swarms thick with life and plastic canopies, an artery choked with ants.

I turn back to Hao Wen and shrug helplessly.

"Been real, but I, uh. Later, Hao Wen." I flash him the one-finger salute of the rude and, biting down on my terror, pitch myself backwards into the open air.

SIX

THERE COMES A time in every man's life when he finds himself flabbergasted by the choices he's made. For some, that occasion arrives in the twilight of his years, when all he has left is a bounty of slightly wilted dreams.

For me, it's right now.

I've regretted many things over the last thirty-seven years. Flirtations with recreational chemicals, second-degree murder, an ex-girlfriend with an alarming propensity for strap-ons. But I don't think I've quite regretted anything as much as trusting Bob to whisk us away to safety.

My digestive system wasn't manufactured for high-speed rooftop chases. It might be a different matter if the pursuit involved only a single axis of horizontality, but it doesn't. As Bob violently seesaws from one precarious handhold to the next, Chinatown transforming into a stop-motion blur of post-colonial shophouses, we strain against the definition of forward motion. Up, down, upside-down. Whiplash turns at forty-five degree turns, aerial cartwheels.

My stomach heaves as we wheel around a street sign, and I narrowly, *narrowly,* escape unloading what little is left on passersby.

"How about I promise to not solve this case?" I shout as Bob latches onto the underside of a balcony, no longer even aping normalcy. His limbs have splintered into a hydra of groping fingertips. They wave like seaweed in the periphery of my vision. "Ao Qin could save you the trouble of killing me!"

Hao Wen doesn't reply, but continues doing that frightening thing where he sort of *blinks*, almost casually, from perch to perch, jolting closer whenever I peel my eyes away. Closer, closer. Steel burns in the sunlight for a twentieth of a heartbeat; a needle just about misses my ear as it whistles past.

"Get us out of—no, wait. Get us down!"

Bob sibilates his incredulity, weaving in place, clearly unwilling to take my order at face value. Smart yaoguai.

"Trust me! I have a plan! Get us down!"

Another uncertain hiss before he capitulates and we plummet, headfirst, into the alley behind a fishmonger. Bob manages to *barely* avoid snapping my neck, but I do make contact with the asphalt cheek first. I breathe a lungful of fish juices as I clamber onto my feet, spitting slime and dirt. I don't turn to look for Hao Wen, instead stumble headlong into the crowd that is, of course, milling in the wrong direction.

I free a crumpled handful of papers from my pockets, yellow talismans inscribed with shaky cockerel-blood calligraphy. One day, I'll have a proper Fulu Pai practitioner make me a batch instead of enduring my own questionable handwriting. Until then:

"Come on, come on..." No time to sort the unnecessary ones; I drop them as I jog-shuffle forward, leaving a trail of parchments that loops and twists like a cartographer's nightmare. Ah. *Here we go.*

"Uncle! You want to buy—" a salesman ventures, gesturing at a rack of knock-off Adidas goods.

I almost stop to argue about whether I qualify as an 'uncle' yet, but wave a hand and wobble forward, shouldering through a pair of tanned Caucasian men, their smiles broad and wondering behind gleaming aviator glasses. As they pass me, I tap them each on a shoulder, sticking a pair of amulets to their sweat-soaked shirts.

I then fasten another charm to the edge of a merchant's table, plant a fourth on a round-bellied auntie, a fifth on a punk with an aqua-blue mohawk and a dense constellation of piercings. This goes on until I run out of relevant phylacteries, at which point I dash into a side street through a spill of diners.

If all goes as intended, Hao Wen will waste at least the next twenty minutes looking for me where I'm not, making all the paperwork I will invariably have to fill out (Diyu is notoriously strict about use of their triangulation talismans) worth the drudgery.

The passageway dilates into a proper street and I emerge, a little out of sorts, almost into encroaching traffic. A passing motorist zips past, flipping me the bird as he goes. I dance back onto the pavement, and crane a look up. The buildings here are old and unimpressive: dreary gray, a knuckle of dodgy hotels, and dime stores fenced by a coil of taut-shouldered pedestrians.

I inhale exhaust in giddy relief. Still no Hao Wen. With luck, he's getting incarcerated right now for assaulting a random innocent. Feeling fractionally more optimistic about my chances of survival, I skitter down the walkway towards Bukit Bintang. No reason to invalidate the last fifteen minutes by chucking myself back into Hao Wen's path. If the Sak Yant master wants my hide, he can wait for it. Besides, the person I'm hoping to interrogate won't be around till midnight.

Do you know what an aging ex-mobster moonlighting as a gastronomical genius-for-hire does for fun, ang moh?

He plays *Dance Dance Revolution*.

Honestly, I'd have preferred *DotA* to hopping about on an illuminated square in eyeshot of disbelieving teenagers, but Bukit Bintang no longer has any decent cybercafés.

...What?

THE SKY NEVER truly darkens here. Light pollution stains the night a moody indigo between the gaps in the skyline. Foot traffic ebbs, alters in tone; itinerant families become replaced by rougher crowds, drunken revellers and hard-eyed women in skyscraper heels.

No one attempts conversation as I inch my way to Petaling Street, which is both good and bad. On the one hand, I'm too tired to deal with another sapient being right now; I've bled enough today to merit the eternal disapproval of the Red Crescent Society, who no doubt would have something to say about such a reckless waste of valuable blood. On the downside, the silence is giving me room to think.

Ao Qin betrayed you, growls a voice in my head. Well, maybe, mumbles another. Technically, his only crime was misrepresenting the scope of the project.

A third voice: are we really talking like marketing strategists these days?

I shake myself free of my moody contemplations. The Dragon King's frankly homicidal approach to employee motivation has definitely changed the playing field. What troubles me, though, is the fact he saw fit to alert Hao Wen to this valuable kernel of data and not I. Why? Neither Minah nor I spend enough time in the ocean—I can't even swim—to have caused accidental offense. A political thing, perhaps? A bitter rivalry between his kingdom and Diyu?

No matter how you slice the quiche, there's nothing good to find here. Ao Qin clearly has, at best, limited interest in keeping me alive. I turn a corner, and adjust the drape of the plastic bags over my shoulder as I go so that they don't cut quite as deeply into my battered flesh. Occultism isn't anywhere near as glamorous as some people believe, and about six times as heavy. (Career exorcists, by the way, tend to be repugnantly muscular. Just in case you were wondering, ang moh.)

Paranoia takes over from low-level anxiety as I jangle under the chintzy Chinatown arch, a gaudy monument to the country's intrinsic faith in the white man's ability to spend. Petaling Street, home to bargains so good, they had to write its name thrice. The place is quieter at this time of night. The stalls that choke its arteries have mostly dispersed, leaving only a few obstinate entrepreneurs and rows upon rows of eateries, furtively occupied by half-awake locals and nervous tourists. The air glitters, toothsome, hungry. Eager.

Despite the unconscionable number of rubes who visit during the day, I much prefer Petaling Street during the hours of sunlight. Easier to vanish into a body of hundreds than to be incognito on an empty, trash-haunted street. Luckily for me, Hao Wen is a no-show and after a few minutes of stalking furtively between pillars, I scoot towards the crossroads.

The trampled asphalt is green here, made eerie by the tinted glass that stretches over Chinatown like sheltering arms. In a puddle of filth, the moon is a bone-white sneer. I squat down and empty my bags, trying in vain to look like a purposeful eccentric rather than a vagabond rooting through rubbish.

Most of my paraphernalia is uncommon, but not... *unusual*. Resources to erect a shrine. Offerings. Joss sticks. A monochrome portrait of an unsmiling boy, his eyes disarmingly flinty even in their cage of photographic film. Triangles of sponge cake, tangerines for color, a currypuff. The black cockerel, though, unconscious from a strategic blow to the cranium, is considerably more arresting. Similarly, I suspect more than a few passersby might see the cleaver, pitted and marked by decades of use, as cause for alarm.

Right on cue:

"Mommy, what's he—" a little British boy flutes.

"Keep moving, dear. Don't make eye contact."

I whip my head around in time to see his mother, a stout woman with salt-and-champagne hair shield his eyes, and wrench him forward by the elbow. Her husband glowers balefully, arms fanned out into plump barricades.

Right. Time to speed things up. I wait till the family drifts away before I begin set up, a process that quickly devolves into martial combat with the rooster, who awakens seconds prior to decapitation. Shrieking and slashing, squirming with the ferocity of a captured warlord, he scores a dozen wounds before I finally pin his neck under a knee, and begin hacking through gristle and bone.

It's messy. And loud. By the time I'm done, I'm soaked to the skin, my nails pebbled with unmentionable substances.

The butchery isn't all bad. For one, it serves admirably to keep onlookers away. No one really wants to talk to an apparent axe-murderer, and those who do tend to either converse from the attention-grabbing end of a gun barrel or have the professional courtesy to wait till the madness is concluded. More importantly, I now have enough blood to summon Jesus at this point.

That's not who I call, though.

The spirit of Petaling Street is an old one, older than the capital itself, a relic installed by immigrant miners suspicious of new opportunities. A child interred alive in the soil, mouth stuffed with coins to buy Diyu's forgiveness, completely beggared of traditional funeral accompaniments to circumvent any dream of escape.

"What do you want, Rupert?"

Innocence doesn't keep. Especially not after decades entombed in the choking black earth, restless, enslaved, alone save for the company of worms. The spirit—Jian Wang; forgetfulness—rasps in a voice like construction; ponderous, deep, brimming with warning.

I don't answer, and continue instead with the runes, adding sigils of binding, patterns of stasis; rows upon rows of instruction, of warning; clauses for every situation, precautions for any eventuality. The cockerel twitches once, severed windpipe expunging a last bubble of blood. I keep painting.

"Rupert."

The bitumen is saturated with writing now.

"*Rupert.*"

"Mm?" That should be enough. I look up, wipe the blood from my jaw with the back of a hand, and then untwist and climb to my feet, dusting myself off as I go. Jian Wang stands with his arms crossed, a boy of about eight, button-up shirt hanging too loose on an emaciated frame, stomach inflamed with the memory of parasites. His mouth is small, sharp with displeasure.

"I had questions."

"Speak." Under the demand, at the periphery of hearing, a growling tangle of *we hate you live feed devour eat hate.*

I can feel him examining his restraints, muscle writhing, straining. Jian Wang's gaze narrows. I don't realize I'm holding my breath, every muscle rigid, until his lips slither into a smirk. (There are two kinds of ghosts, ang moh. The ones who wither from existential despair, and the ones who grow immeasurably dangerous from decades of rage. I'm sure you can guess which one Jian Wang is.)

"You're afraid of me." *Eat eat eat feed rip your limbs eat eat tear bite chew eat.* "I haven't seen so many wards in a long, long time."

I wet my lips, taste rust. "I have a healthy respect for your power."

"What do you want?" *Eat eat eat hate hate hate hate eat.*

His Mandarin is archaic and elegant, untarnished by exposure to adjacent dialects. From the look on his bloodless face, it's clear he expects communication in kind. Which is problematic because I can barely get through a sentence in Mandarin without pausing to think.

"Help?" I say in Cantonese, hopeful.

Jian Wang's mouth broadens. There's no teeth, no tongue; just a circle of featureless black sucking at my eyes.

I palm my face. "I need, uh. This is hard. I need—"

SEVEN

"So, IT REALLY was the Furies?"

Jian Wang shrugs and sips from his cigarette, the cherry blazing a lurid blue. He exales octagons of smoke; everyday physics has no authority over the dead. "Bodies like midnight, hair filled with bite. Hound's breath, and wings of the bat."

I champ on the impulse to critique his poetry, pitching my weight from one foot to another. While hardly the most inspired recitation, Jian Wang's impromptu rhymes are, as he has haughtily noted, still volumes better than my slaughter of his mother tongue.

"I'll take that as a yes?" I sluice Dettol over my forearms and wince as the antiseptic fluid sears across my injuries.

Jian Wang smiles thinly and hooks skeletal fingers under his right knee, towing his leg closer, cigarette now dangling between his teeth. He is sitting, improbably balanced, on the summit of a fire hydrant.

So far, the ghost has refused to acknowledge any attempt at explaining my linguistic shortcomings (public schooling, errant parents, adolescent certainty that Shakespeare would disrobe any woman, no matter how svelte), choosing instead to throw my shame in my face by demonstrating his adroitness with Cantonese, if not poetry.

I throw a cagey look over a shoulder, hunting for evidence of Hao Wen—or worse, the attentions of a well-meaning police-man come to see why a blood-drenched lunatic is talking to himself in the middle of Chinatown. Thankfully, no one emerges from the gloom.

"Right. So do you know *why* the Erinyes killed Ao Qin's daughter?" My skin throbs. It's a long shot, sure. But there's nothing that passes through Petaling Street that Jian Wang is unlikely to see.

The revenant drums fingertips across his lower lip, one corner of his mouth rising. He transfers his cigarette into a hand, drinks deep. "The Gracious Ones only venture where they are summoned; creatures of responsibility, unlike *certain* commoners."

Burn. On a more positive note, Jian Wang is no longer broadcasting low-frequency loathing in my direction, his speech reduced to one-dimensional boredom.

"Who summoned them, then?"

His eyes—bottomless, the black of rot—flash with laughter. "No one of matter, no one loved. Just a broken little dove."

Tension knits my ribs tight. *He knows something.* "What does that even—"

Jian Wang tuts an objection, an admonishing finger raised as he hops onto his feet. The ghost oils forward. "Eye for an eye, hand for a hand. Knowledge is yours, when I have what I demand."

He's baiting me, it's clear. What really unsettles me is his confidence in opening a new channel of negotiation. The spell should have him trussed so tight, he'd need permission to speak. I work my nails into my palm, and force my mouth to maintain its amiable rictus. "Fine. *Fine.* What do you want?"

"Freedom."

For the tenth of a nanosecond, I can see Jian Wang as he was, rather than what he has become: a child, frightened, suffocating around a throat stuffed with metal, dying incrementally. The world closing above him in bursts of dark loam. Alone, for however many decades he's been buried here.

"Look, I only push pencils. I have no influence over Diyu—"

"But you can fast-track my application."

That brings me up short. "I can?"

"I've checked." Jian Wang sniffs, head bobbing, all pretenses of intimidation and nicotine addiction discarded. "You have the authority to *at least* push it to the attention of middle management."

"*I do?*"

"You do."

The fact that Jian Wang knows things about my position that I don't, that he knows complex bureaucratic privileges that I wasn't even aware existed, disconcerts me in ways I can't even begin to articulate. I clamor hopefully for an intelligent rejoinder. "Since when?"

Before I can get my answer, a new voice intrudes, bassy and roughened by hard use, the words couched in lowbrow Malay. "Boss, what you doing so late?"

I spin in place, nearly tripping over my own feet, excuses cycling across the tip of my tongue. A flashlight cast lines of white up my legs, my torso, which gather on my face. I shade my eyes, catch the glint of a badge in the glare.

"Just cleaning up," I tell him absently, already aware that this is really just a show of cordiality at this point. There's absolutely nothing I can say, I'm sure, that will make any of this look okay in the incredulous eyes of the law.

The policeman sways closer, body reeking of cologne and the sweat of a fourteen-hour shift. Although his uniform strains over a rotund belly, sleeves slicing into pillowy arms, his face is hard, his gaze clear and alert. If he spends any time behind a desk, it isn't of his own volition.

"I can see that," he booms. A name tag reveals his name as Muhammad. His torch dips from my countenance, glides across the platter of offerings; lingers on the rooster, and its nest of feces and eldritch scrawlings. "Black magic?"

I shuffle back, arms behind my back, fist locked over wrist. His forwardness surprises, but not as much as the matter-of-fact delivery. "No lah," I demur, lapsing back to creole. "Only good magic lah."

"You sure?" Muhammad seems unconvinced. When he speaks, his tone is easy, a pitch calculated to disarm and reassure. It chuckles: *Ah-ha-ha. We're all friends here.* It's a voice I recognize from a different life. Muhammad hasn't committed to an interpretation of me yet, meaning I have about five minutes before I'm walked off in the direction of a balai.

"Of course lah." I say, a little too quickly. *You're getting soft*, sneers a voice in my head. "Business not doing so good, so got to ask god for help loh."

The officer strokes his armament of chins as he limps forward, flashlight wedged into a loop at his belt, spare hand braced against a cane. "I see. But normally, people use roast duck, or hell money, or fruit. Not blood."

"Um." I retreat a step. "You've got a point."

"Do you need help, Rupert?" Jian Wang inquires, mildly.

It takes every molecule of self-control to not jump out of my skin. I'd somehow forgotten about Jian Wang, who seems deeply amused by my oversight. Muhammad, perspicacious as always, follows my wild gaze to the vacant space visible to mundane eyes.

"Am I interrupting something?" He says, every word selected with elaborate care. Under the manufactured concern, I hear the real question: *how high are you right now?*

"No?"

Chink. A snap of metal. Handcuffs catch the glow of the streetlamps, circles of orange steel. I take another step backwards. Muhammad's gait elongates, smooths out, discloses a muscular strength that promptly puts me on high alert. "Tell you what, how about we go down to the station, check in with my friends, and then we can all go to the mamak, hm?"

"I can help you, Rupert," Jian Wang purrs. "You just have to let me."

"I'm... I...." My eyes oscillate between the two, death and flab, a ghost and a cold cell. I try to sidestep the policeman, circle around to the other side of Mount Muhammad.

He shifts quickly despite the cane, intercepting me, still wearing his congenial smile although his eyes have grown mirror-blank. "Don't make it hard for either of us, yah?"

"I'm not trying to—" I'm really not. Muhammad has the advantage of bulk, but I'm fairly certain I can incapacitate him before he can retaliate in kind. And if not, there's still the cleaver, an enticement sprawled seductively within arm's reach. Maybe. He is pretty fast. The muscles in my jaw convulse, and teeth click. "There's nothing to worry about here."

"Uh huh." He chucks the act. Officer Friendly vanishes, replaced by steely resolution and the growing certainty that Muhammad might be my martial superior. "Come on."

"Rupert."

I don't want to hurt Muhammad. I've got a natural soft spot for embattled professionals, being a card-carrying member of the tribe myself. Men like Muhammad and I, we just want to do our jobs and go home. Under other circumstances, I'd seriously consider allowing him to apprehend me and then paddling through the paper trail home. Unfortunately, I can't afford to hemorrhage any more time.

"Okay, Jian Wang." A tickle of rawboned dread, a whisper in my mind that sounds very much like *What are you doing, Rupert?* I ignore it. "Do your magic."

And he does.

Jian Wang rips through the air, silhouette blurring halogen-bright. I watch as he leaps onto the man's shoulders, faster and more fluid than anything humanoid has any right to be, and squat down to watch. He braces small feet between Muhammad's clavicles and rams his fingers into the policeman's mouth, grinning derangedly the whole time. Down, down, he reaches, until he is embedded shoulder-deep. Pausing long enough to leer at me, Jian Wang then begins pushing his head between Muhammad's lips, which contort grotesquely, a loop of meat like a misaligned scarf, almost comical in appearance.

"Whhh—" The cop gurgles, a death rattle noise. His eyes bulge. Air wheezes through the slit of his mouth, and it keeps going and going, even when it no longer seems possible for his lungs to squeeze out more.

His shoulders snap back, chest protruding. His sternum pops. Muhammad rises onto his toes like a fish on a hook, head canting backwards. His mouth dilates, the skin of his cheeks unstitching, turning red and white as muscle fibres unravel and tear, ivory gleaming wetly beneath yarns of pink. An arm suddenly lunges from between his teeth, fingers balled in triumph. Something gray and weak struggles within the hand's grip, dribbling black gunk. Muhammad is making new noises now, feather-fragile, confused, a feeble, whining *ay-ay-ay-ay-ay-ay.*

"Such a small man for such a big shell." Jian Wang tsks, as he slicks free, glistening like a newborn, features pliant as a balloon, re-inflating as they reenter the humid air. *Ay-ay-ay-ay-ay-ay.*

"I think I'm going to be sick," I announce, blearily.

Snap. Muhammad collapses into a heap, a discarded puppet.

"Fuck." The word tears free. I jam a knuckle into my mouth, dancing back. Great. *Perfect.* I'm a cop killer by proxy now, or at least, the only visible suspect in a ten-metre radius. "Fuck-fuck-fuck-fuck-fuck. FUCK."

Jian Wang fixes me with a look of cool reproach, closing his fingers around his acquisition as it flutters and thrashes against his skin. He brings it to his face, and his hand clenches. The thing, whatever it was, erupts into a foul-smelling smear.

"What did you do?" The words uncoil, even though I know the answer, know it would only be met with scorn. Creatures like Jian Wang don't care about creatures like us.

"Stopped him," he replies, petulantly. "Wasn't that what you wanted?"

"Most people don't help someone else by killing a person. Equivalent force. Equivalent force, damn it!" I fling my arms at the corpse, which is already somehow loosening its stranglehold on its bowels. "I didn't want him *dead*."

"You should have said so," Jian Wang counters smoothly.

"Fuck," I repeat for the umpteenth time.

Lights flare. A shiver of voices; movement. Large shapes mill in the penumbra outside of the street lamp, resolving into dark blue uniforms, concerned faces. Muhammad had friends. I raise my hands at the warning click of safeties being thumbed back. Someone, voice trembling through each staccato-gasped word, calls for back-up. They've seen Muhammad's body. They're making the logical conclusion. I'm so screwed.

"Rupert." Again, that tone: knowing, predatory, smug.

I look over at Jian Wang, hands still in the air. "Mmm?"

"I can help you. Just say yes."

So, so screwed.

In range of a firing squad, tottering at my wit's end, I say yes. Yes, as a nasty thought dislodges itself from a miasma of awful thoughts. *Isn't this all a little convenient?* But I'm not given room to entertain its unpleasantness. A weight crushes into my spine, even as shadows rush over my vision, sounds dimming to an underwater roar, and I drown.

EIGHT

THE INTERSTICE BETWEEN seconds tastes like money and is viscous as treacle, with a moist heat that clings tar-like to the lungs so that every breath scrapes and drags. If the dead are condemned to occupancy here, it's no wonder they're perpetually depicted as hostile.

I hobble through the thick film, shoving past the bodies of the living, ash-gray silhouettes that are only mostly solid. A thought intrudes: walking into someone else's skin, taking over someone else's existence, could be the easiest thing in the world. All I had to do was *put it on*—I force it down, pivot around a corner, and swallow a paroxysm of nausea as the universe flattens into a vertical canvas. In the last instant before I am compressed into two-dimensionality, a curiosity rears: *where did that idea come from?* But it doesn't last.

Purgatory, or at least this choking image of it, has one redeeming quality. For all of its lurching, stomach-frothing perils, it permits near instantaneous transportation, if you know which alley to access—which I do—and how to navigate its inconsistencies—which I also do. (If you go gambling in Diyu as often as I do, ang moh, it would be true for you as well.)

Under my breath, I count the cobbled stones, the succession of vine-smothered banyan trees. Turn right once at a traffic light when it gleams yellow, then left again when it changes to blue. Up hills, down past the churning, mud-brown river weaving through Kuala Lumpur, past the colony of dead construction workers who live still in the bones of Times Square.

Through it all, the pressure on my spine continues to mount, becoming heavier with every step, until motion itself is torture.

Have to get out have to get out.

The thought sears through my system, a knife in the brain, amplified by every shudder of my pulse.

Have to get out have to get out.

It fills my head, my veins, my chest. There's no room left for anything else.
Have to get out have to get out.
I break into a sprint.
Have to get out get out GET OUT—
Air.

I crash onto the stoop in front of my apartment, gulping breath like I'm drowning, every muscle and tendon singing with fire. After a long moment, I squeeze into a ball, and begin inventorizing my list of hurts. It doesn't take long; five seconds into the exercise, I reach the logical conclusion that *everything* hurts.

Especially my shoulders, which feel inexplicably like they've been carrying mountain ranges for a lifetime. My shoulders are wound *tight*. Rolled-up power cables, vacuum-packed and sealed into sardine cans tight. If they ever relax again, I'm building a temple to Guan Yin.

At least, I'm alive.

Groaning, I roll onto my feet and pick my way up the steps home.

THE SMELL HITS first: a cocktail of pus and bile and waste matter, pheromonal stink of terror, a glazing of metal. Gunpowder smolders. Somewhere in between, a thread of burnt-black meat. They must have come when Minah was cooking.

"Minah!" I burst through the door and instantly slip on a pool of red. I smash chin-first into the apartment floor, nearly biting off my tongue in the process. Stifling a whimper, I inch forward on my elbows, too dazed to consider the logistics of being upright, too scared to contemplate pausing and assessing the situation. If I keep moving forward, I won't have to think about what might have happened. "Minah? Kitten?"

"I told you not to bring your work home." Her voice, gently daggered, floats into hearing.

Soundless, Minah drifts into the living room and kneels beside me, her thoughts unreadable behind glass-smooth eyes. She extends a hand. Our fingers lace and just for that heartbeat, when I breathe in, I'm breathing her frangipani perfume and the promise that everything is fine, that everything is alright, that I'm with someone I love and *it will all be okay*. Then, she lets go and I'm left with the realization I'm lying on a carpet of warm gore.

"I—"

"People came to the house," Minah announces, distractedly, as though the evidence wasn't still steaming on every piece of furniture. Her baju kurung is in tatters, the hems brocaded with red fingerprints. One arm gleams with naked bone, with striations of yellow fat. "Luckily, George and I heard them come up the stairs."

"Uh." I crawl into a cross-legged position. "George is—"

"Eating."

"Okay." I nod, stupefied by pain, torn between parental instinct and instinctive horror. "Your arm. Um. Are you—"

"I think some of them actually came over for dinner before..." Minah resumes, volume raised ever-so-slightly, enough to let her swallow my question. Her tone is heartbreakingly gentle, demure. Her fingers trail up her forearm and close over the elbow, disguising wet tendon. "Sayang, why did this happen?"

"Ao Qin," I start. Flinch around the realization of how tired I am. "Ao Qin... didn't tell us everything about his plans. He—this quest is a bit like a reality show. Many people come in, only one person leaves."

"Ah," Minah breathes. Her eyes, normally so warm and vital, remain impenetrable, black as the countryside night. They travel upwards, scouring my face, move higher and then stop.

"Jian Wang." In her mouth, the name bristles like the hackles of a dog. "What are you doing here?"

"Ask Rupert," replies a sly voice from above my head, its Malay immaculate and couched in palace vernacular. "He's the one who invited me in."

Oh. Oh, right. *That* explains the ten-ton albatross around my neck. Revelation glissades into a second panicked epiphany. *What I have done this time?* Heart pushing against the roof of my mouth, I stretch an investigative arm upwards and grope through the air. Something cracks across my knuckles: a boot, a rod? I yelp regardless, snatch my hand away.

"Jian Wang?" I repeat.

It's shocking how slippery the undesirable is, how effortless it is for the eyes to cascade over things they don't want to see, like homeless vagabonds or ghosts riding pillion. I wrench a shoulder back. A shadow puddles over the floor in front of me, delineating the presence of a small child, skeletal in composition, its legs straddling my neck. Cold fingers grasp the underside of my chin, stroke my attention upwards so I'm looking into a mouth like a void, black eyes buried deep in the hollows of a dead boy's face.

"Hallo, Rupert," whispers the spirit of Chinatown.

"Aaaagggh."

"You need to leave," Minah growls. Actually full-on *growls*, an animal noise too throttled with violence to be construed as anything but a portent of bloodshed. Her lips curl back, and I glimpse fishbone teeth, crowded so closely together you could mistake them for ivory lace. "You don't belong here."

"Please." Jian Wang sniffs. "Is that any way to talk to a sister-wife?"

Minah stiffens. "I—"

"We're not married. Yet. I'd need to convert to Islam, but that's—" I thrash my arms, trying to swing back onto my feet, landing instead on my rump atop a pile of, of... *no, don't want to think about it.* "That's not even the point here. When did I agree to be your—your taxi?"

"You didn't."

"I—I, what? I didn't?"

Hands shovel in my hair, an intimacy I already find enormously unsettling. "You said you needed help."

"I... did?" I hesitate, inundated with guilty relief. Yes! Something I actually know! I bob my head vigorously. "I did."

"You didn't specify what kind of help, so I'm obligated"—you could spread the relish in his voice on toast, honestly—"to stay until you cease needing help."

Wait. Heat prickles up along my vertebrate. "With what?"

"Anything." Jian Wang's reply is full of teeth.

I jam my thumb against the underside of a canine, regretting it instantly. Intestinal tissue has no business being sampled raw. *Try not to think about what you're on try not to think about*—"That makes no sense. There have to be limits. You... you can't just hang around being a 'supportive'"—airquote, airquote—"'presence' *forever*."

"Why not?"

I stammer to a halt. Already, I have a nagging suspicion I've lost this battle, but optimism, however stupid, is the reason to live another day. "Because I said so."

Neither Minah nor Jian Wang are terribly impressed. Jian Wang laughs like a jackdaw. My beloved shakes her head, disgust bruising her features, and sways upright. Her gaze stays trained on Jian Wang, bright with carnivorous intensity, mouth peeled slightly open in threat, as though to say, 'I could hurt you any time I want.'

Polite, controlled: "You need to get rid of him, sayang."

"He needs me." Effusive, arrogant.

"I—" I'm about to object when I realize he's right. Jian Wang is my single best bet for locating the Furies, and possibly surviving the entire fiasco. More crucially, if Jian Wang is with me, he can't be anywhere else. "Sayaaaang."

"Don't," Minah snarls, the black of her eyes already radiating into the sclera. Hissing like a cat, head lashing from side to side, she paces into the kitchen, nails lengthening with every swing of her arms. "Use that tone with me."

"But sayang." I clamber after her. My stride is longer than hers; it takes no time at all catch up, to cup a palm around her shoulder. "Sayang, come back here. You don't understand."

She whirls on me, inhumanly fast, flattens her palms on the walls. Ink whorls lap at the apex of her cheeks, which are falling already to rot, attenuating to knife-edge bone. Minah growls again, deeper this time, lacerating my monkey-brain with fear. It's suddenly very hard to ignore the fact she is, in practice, a cannibalistic corpse with a dietary predisposition for the small intestines. "What. Do. You. Want?"

"It's only going to be for a little—"

"Yang, no. No, yang, no." Minah softens, mouth pursing in the tiniest of frowns, brows furrowing endearingly. "Listen to yourself. This is not how any of this ends."

"It'd be fine." I move forward and try to scoop her chin into my hands, try to push my forehead to hers. The first, Minah allows. The second causes her to recoil, gaze snapping wide open. Oh, right. She probably doesn't want contact with Jian Wang's crotch.

I shuffle backwards and stoop my head in apology, even as the child-ghost emits a rude noise. Minah pins her attention to a photograph on the wall— my last birthday; we're ringed by other contractors from Diyu, all beaming drunkenly while an amused Minah sips a cup of tea—slightly skewed and speckled with handprints. "We've got this one in the bag. Be patient with me. It won't take long. I just need a little bit of time."

"No." Her eyes find mine. In the distance, sirens glimmer red-and-blue, distorted by the smoke-glass windows. Then, softer yet: "No."

"Why?"

She caresses my cheek. "I... the matter with Ao Qin—I have no jurisdiction. I cannot tell you to do anything. It is my fault, at least in part. So, who am I to make demands there?" Grief, raw as an exposed vein. I ball my fists around the urge to hold her, to comfort. "But Jian Wang cannot stay."

"But he—"

"He is not your ally. He is not anyone's ally." Minah glances up, lips contracting into a dissatisfied moue. "If you let him, sayang, he will devour you whole."

"Now, you're being cruel," Jian Wang huffs.

"Nothing that is dead and lives is a thing to trust, and nothing exists that cannot be broken," she intones, ignoring Jian Wang, in the singsong lilt of a woman reading from a scripture. "I'm... I—call me, when you've sorted this out."

"Where are you going?" I'm burbling like an abandoned puppy, tail between my legs, but I can't stop myself. The implications tangling between each word frighten me more than Ao Qin's displeasure.

"Away." Sadness constricts around her, so tightly that I lose sight of the woman I adore. Her voice shakes.

"But—"

"Go, sayang." Minah vanishes into the kitchen, finality resting heavy in the last loving whisper, her hand ice on my wrist.

I watch her through the doorway, a sylph of a girl digging through a man's opened ribcage. *Slorp.* She frees a familiar bundle of pink muscle. It screeches, tiny hands fastened around a loop of intestine. *George*, I think, inhaling the abattoir reek, a weird affection suffusing my chest. They're *my* family, even if both of them eat unprocessed Soylent Green.

I take a step forward.

The *Ghostbusters* iconic synth-funk jingle squeals from a pocket. I snap a frantic look down, then fumble for the phone, nearly dropping it several times as it keeps squeezing free from my viscera-slick palms. Finally, after the ringing subsides and restarts at least once over, I pop it open and jam the device against my cheek. "Hello?"

"Rupert." The boss's voice is cream and caramel, decadently smooth.

I freeze. *Crap.* "Boss."

"Come to the manor when you've a moment, won't you?" The boss (my employment contract involves very clear non-disclosure clauses) never talks in definites, only suggestions that mandate immediate obedience. "We missed you. Our palates missed you. You promised us a unique feast, one worthy of surrendering a half-day off to you. What *happened*, Rupert?"

"Got sidetracked, boss." You don't argue with the boss. You don't do anything but express meek acceptance. "Sorry, boss."

"We will see you in two hours?"

"Yes, boss."

"Perfect." *Click*.

NINE

MINAH WAS RIGHT. Jian Wang really is abominable business.

"Get off." I prod at his foot. The stench is becoming nauseating: an alphabet of acute bromodosis, damp earth, and sour milk.

"No."

I prod harder. It's hard to be sure in the tenebrous cocoon of the backseat, but I think Jian Wang's legs have fused with my chest. Toes writhe under threadbare gray socks, half-submerged in my chest cavity. "Get. Off."

"No."

"Why?" My attention jolts automatically to the rear view mirror, where I can see a sliver of Feng Mun's narrow face, his eyes turgid with caffeine, or more controversial compounds. If he noticed my exclamation, he makes no outward indication of it. I relax.

"Because I can't."

Outside, Kuala Lumpur fades into a bleak chiaroscuro, street lamps blending into a wash of amber. Feng Mun's replacement cab is more well-appointed than his usual. There's a stereo embroidered with ruby LEDs, a built-in GPS system that is being cheerily ignored, and air-conditioning that actually works, possibly too well.

"What do you mean you can't?" My teeth chatter. I can't tell if it is from the effort of remaining calm, or the freezing temperatures. Clearly, I should still be screaming, gibbering in unparalleled mortification. But my lungs won't summon the requisite noises.

Jian Wang shrugs. "I can't."

Modern buildings recede into a stubble of aging shophouses, their walls tangled in black vines. The road grows pockmarked, uneven, which doesn't stop Feng Mun from driving over every bump and pothole. I trail my fingertips down to my phone where it sleeps on my lap, screen blank. I'd sent a flurry of messages to Minah: apologies, ill-thought-out pleas to reconsider the situation, even a dribbling of platitudes. Anything to provoke a reply. None come.

Kanye West replaces Madonna on the radio, a moody celebration of his own grandeur. I sigh. Over the last two hours, I've tried everything. Banishing spells, express ritual sacrifice, loud threats of amputation. A perfect storm of solutions equating in nothing but desultory mockery. I'm stuck with Jian Wang, even if I won't admit it to him.

"You okay ah?" Feng Mun asks, his voice a little higher than normal. "Got trouble with Minah, is it?"

Good old Feng Mun. He never asks about my imaginary friends. Still, it doesn't keep Minah's name from hurting. It takes a minute to frame the lie, unhook the ache embedded in my ribs. "Yeah."

"Mm." Neither of us believe me, but Feng Mun doesn't call me out on it.

We sink into quiet, Jian Wang singing gently to the electronica, his voice childishly sweet, the words completely alien. Slowly, Kuala Lumpur submits to palm trees and open road. Blackness crowds around us. I straighten in my seat. We're getting closer. The boss and his family, despite their urbane connections, prefer more pastoral haunts. Easier to put together a dinner party without unsympathetic neighbours snooping about the grounds.

The manor soon cuts into view, gaudily imposing, dressed in a rash of gothic steeples and an unnecessary number of buttresses.

"Eh, boss," Feng Mun stumbles, slurring into the next breath. "Is it okay—"

"It's fine," I say, as the taxi rumbles to a pause. I pat his shoulder reassuringly, then slap a wad of bills into his palm. "Go home."

He hesitates, bless his generous heart. "How you want to get home le?"

I feel fingers in my hair, a sharp upward tug. I follow the motion towards the sky, craning my head out of the taxi, to where Jian Wang is eagerly gesticulating at the stars, a glittering torrent poured over a featureless black night. The kneejerk irritation slips. This is probably the first time Jian Wang has seen the constellations in a hundred years.

But he's also growing roots in my flesh.

Moving on.

"I'll be fine," I promise Feng Mun again, as I bend down to share a smile. He doesn't reply, at least not verbally, nodding in time with the rap music now blasting through his speakers. Giving the roof of his taxi a resounding pat, I straighten and begin trudging up the route towards the boss's abode.

THE MANOR, UNBELIEVABLY enough, is even more chichi on the inside. The walls are lined with crushed velvet the deep scarlet of Pinot Noir, the carpeted floor adorned with a dazzling recreation of the Sistine Chapel's ceiling. Gold-leaf portraits, each housing some regal figure in exorbitant finery, watch the house from every doorway. My footsteps make no sound at all, sinking deep into the wool.

"Nice place," Jian Wang whistles.

I make a noncommittal noise, attention scrolling from corridor to vacant corridor. A musty, funeral-home stillness pervades the air. It's like the concrete is holding its breath. While the boss's immediate family is not very large—extended relatives are stored in the crypts—there is usually more than a smattering of domestic helpers lurking in shouting distance. Not tonight, though. Weird, and very worrying.

"What are we doing here?"

"Quiet, I'm trying to think," I hiss, swatting at the air. The front door was unlocked, the security system deactivated; clearly, they were expecting me. But if the boss has summoned me to enforce discipline, it deviates massively from his usual modus operandi.

"But this is *boring*."

Moments before I tell Jian Wang where he can shove his discontent, a voice cuts into hearing, feminine and nationless in accent. "Sir desires your company in the audience hall. Please proceed to the antechamber for instruction."

"Thank you, Sara." Like every other housekeeper in the boss's employ, she's gorgeous. Six feet tall, svelte. Hair like champagne, eyes like the Maldivian seas, contours like every teenage fantasy distilled into one moist wish. In sharp contrast, her clothes are austere: over-the-knee gray skirt, sensible clogs, starchy buttoned-up blouse; clean functionality over gross exhibition.

She nods again, smiles, the expression never quite reaching her eyes, which are abstract and fogged. Silent, liquid, she turns and prowls away, back straight as a line, chin slightly raised. The cloth on her sleeves ride up, revealing a litany of old tooth marks and healed incisions.

"She's pretty," Jian Wang whispers, sly. "Prettier than Minah, don't you think?"

"Eh."

We follow her to a pair of mahogany doors, the wood inlaid with intricate designs, a centuries-old diorama cobbled from the family's myriad accomplishments, and their most beloved meals. I run my fingertips over carved faces; every inflection of dismay is captured with exquisite detail, right down to the glazed acceptance of a deep-fried ending.

Sara raps thrice on the door, and someone responds in thunderous counterpoint, three precise explosions. The doors oil apart and frangipani blooms through the air.

"Rupert." The boss. "We've been expecting you."

I wince at the theatrical delivery, percussive, powerful and obnoxiously exaggerated. I knew I should have never introduced him to *The Addams Family*. Hesitating at the doorway, I steal a glance at Sara, who offers neither encouragment nor foreboding, only passionless attentiveness. No help there.

I step forward. The boss sits at the head of a Victorian banquet table, flanked by his wife and husbands, the former crocodile-sleek, the latter like a cluster of polished ivory carvings. The dining hall rises several storeys into the air before opening into a massive glass ceiling, hexagonal window-panes giving the room the feeling of a vast hive.

"Boss," I say, coming to a halt on the opposite end of the table. I barely resist the temptation to click my heels together.

He crooks a finger. "Come here."

And I do. His spouses ignore me, either too preoccupied or too refined to acknowledge a commoner, silverware tinkling against bone and porcelain over that thick, choking quiet. As I slope past, Husband Number Three slurps the marrow from a miso-glazed wrist before dividing radius from ulna, fingers groping for lengths of sweet tendon. I look away.

Despite their dietary predilections, the boss's family is virtually indistinguishable from any other members of the local gentry, if you overlook the telltale odour of frangipani.

"Rupert." The boss pushes himself up from his seat, daintily tapping at his mouth with a napkin, voice that made-for-television friendly that every politician dreams of mastering. "Rupert. Rupert. Rupert. How *are* you?"

"Uncomfortable."

His eyes gleam, mouth curling into something radiant. "You didn't tell me you were bringing a *guest*."

Jian Wang speaks up, before I can intercept the question. "We only recently became an item."

The boss laughs—no, *chuckles*. His amusement is crystalline, flawless, pitched exactly right to convey warm familial delight and a hint of budding affection. When he stops, though, he stops cold. No giddy tapering, no trailing off. Only an intent silence. "What an interesting acquisition."

I feel Jian Wang go rigid. "There was a bit of a, uh, kerfuffle. He"—I roll the words on my tongue, repulsed by the content, but they're the closest truth I can wield at this moment—"*helped* me escape. Unfortunately, we became entangled in a contractual obligation that neither of us desired. And..."

"Spare me." The boss waves a many-ringed hand, every knuckle in competition for gaudiest ornament of all. "All I need to know is if you enjoy his presence."

"No."

"Hey!"

"Excellent." The boss daubs at his mouth with a monogramed napkin and nudges his plate back with a finger. Almost at once, a blonde-haired woman materializes to collect the detritus of his meal. Like Sara, like everyone else in the boss's immediate employ, her forearms are a wasteland of hideous scars. "If you get this one thing done for us, we'll get rid of him and consider all your debts paid. How does that sound?"

"Terrible," Jian Wang spits, half-choking on indignant rage.

In reply, the boss authors a sigil in the air with a raised pinky, a jagged hieroglyph that glistens lipid-yellow for the sliver of a moment. Jian Wang emits a strangled noise, low and keening. My employer tuts his rebuke, expression bored, index finger ticking from side to side. "Children are to be seen and admired, not tolerated."

Black eyes dart back to mine, with a hint of a shark's smile. "Where were we? Yes. Complete this task, and we'll permanently rid you of Jian Wang. Deal?"

This is too easy. Something is up, he's planning something, he—I scratch behind my neck, breath held tight in my ribs. "Um."

"*Wrong reply*, Rupert." The friendliness withers; warning flashes a fin. "The correct answer would have been, 'Yes, boss. Absolutely, boss. Looking forward to fulfilling your desires, boss.' Or any variation thereof. We've been over this. I cough. You jump and *then* ask how high."

"Yes, boss."

"Excellent, excellent!" That calculated boardroom laughter erupts again, catching strange echoes in the corners of the hall. His husbands and wife do not look up. "Right. Your task is simple: we're having guests this weekend, and Fury needs to be on the menu. Catch one of the Erinyes, prepare her however you please, and serve her for our culinary pleasure."

I—"What?"

"Kill, defeather, and roast a Fury. Murder, process, and broil a Fury with pickled shiitakes and spicy miso. Execute, unrobe, and make Fury rendang. The possibilities are endless." The boss twines his fingers, drops his chin atop of them. "All I need, at the end of the day, is a Fury in our gullet."

"But—"

His voice gentles into lethality. "You missed a day and a half of work. And then *lied* to us. Taunted our appetites, filled us with hopes that would never be fulfilled. But I didn't bring that up, did I? Sayang, did I accost our employee about his absences?"

"No, sayang." His wife flicks a disparaging look in my direction, before returning to her meal.

"Lied to us." The boss repeats, slowly, each word slathered with cold gravitas. "I've *never* allowed anyone to—"

I find a gap between one breath and the next (ghouls don't need to respire, but they do require air to talk; honestly, ang moh), and lunge through. "Ao Qin."

"Pardon?"

Briefly, my pulse thrashing in my throat, I contemplate redacting my confession, but it's too late. The jangle of tableware ceases, as do the eddies of polite conversation. I raise my gaze to find myself impaled by a coliseum of eyes.

"Ao Qin," I repeat, hoping the name would function as a deterrent. Realistically speaking, the Dragon King is probably better at dispensing unparalleled levels of raw physical agony, but he's not the one sitting two feet away, a lazy smile balanced on his lips. "Ao Qin needs me to find the Furies and—"

"Oh, we know all about *that*. Don't we?" The boss cups a cheek in his palm; his smile gracious, nonchalant, terrifying. The others nod in perfect unison, not a single wasted motion between them. "Finish the job, and we'd make it all go away."

"But—" I close my teeth over my tongue, the rest of the sentence rattling like dice in my head: *but you're not a god.*

Then, another thought tugs urgently on the sleeve of my subconscious: *how the hell did he know?*

"Rupert." The boss's voice snatches me from my contemplations, leaves me completely off-balance. "What do you say?"

"Thank you, boss," I declare, head thronging with a hundred worries, each more outlandishly awful than the last. My only consolation is that Jian Wang has gone completely silent, leaving me to interact with my boss without interruption.

"Good." He discards the amiability the way another man might throw away a spoiled jacket. As one, his family members return their attention to the food. "Now, get out."

"Yes, boss."

TEN

WE WATCH IN silence as the paper blackens, flashing blue before it finally disintegrates into ash, signalling successful reception. One day, I'll convince the administration in Diyu to install a desktop.

"What happens if you accidentally burn something else with a delivery?" Jian Wang asks, animated, eager, his vigour restored now that we're miles from the boss's manor. The breeze, rain-sweetened, teases the debris from our cul-de-sac. Rats bicker and squeal. In the distance, I can hear the first ululations of traffic, and the clanking of storefronts being stirred from slumber.

I'm prepared this time for the spasm of fatigue, which arrives dulled by repeated exposure, cushioned by the soft, shapeless soreness percolating through my muscles. When was the last time I slept? Fits of unconsciousness, robbed from Feng Mun's backseat, can only sustain a man for so long.

"Uh." Reality judders through my musings. I sift through tactful explanations, a yawn intruding after each word, and settle for an ambiguous: "Mild confusion."

To my astonishment, and considerable apprehension, Jian Wang presses no further. Instead, he drapes an arm around the circumference of my skull and pitches forward, coiling about my head like an innocent child, and not a murderous revenant with potentially fatal designs.

A silhouette lengthens over the entrance of the alley. I spin around and try to project guilelessness as I stroll forward, arms and legs metronoming with forceful jauntiness.

"Morning." I nod at the middle-aged woman dragging a trash bag towards the dumpster, her apron crusted with animal fat, hair and face pinched back into a humorless bun. She scowls. When I pass her, she mutters a prayer to protect her against stupidity.

"Jian Wang," I hiss, the moment we're no longer in earshot. "*Jian Wang.*"

He stirs, petulant. "What do you want?"

"Your end of the bargain fulfilled, obviously. Tell me what you know about the Furies."

The ghost swings himself upright. Over the course of the night, his lower abdomen has completely liquefied into mine, leaving only a disembodied torso protruding from my shoulders. Jian Wang insists that this is simply nature, a consequence of prolonged contact rather than a deliberate act of malevolence. Nevermind, of course, that our contract was illicitly engineered and he tricked me into agreement without first allowing me to come to an informed decision. Oh, no. *That's* just splitting hairs.

"I know that their feathers are all the rage in Djinnestan."

"Keep going."

Rain foams across the city. It rolls down buildings, trails fingers across windows, glazes each and every road with quicksilver reflections. I breathe deep. The lashing waters feel good on my skin, a reprieve despite the knowledge that every droplet is brimming with pollutants. Then the cold seeps through, and with it a jerking acknowledgement:

"Wait. Why?"

Jian Wang barks a taut laugh. "Because the locals believe the feathers can bestow the ability to take revenge on those who have done them wrong."

"Must be expensive," I reply, absentmindedly, hunching into a popped collar, a flimsy defense against the monsoon as it tumbles over me, soaking me to the marrow.

"Not really," the ghost-child replies. "It's not like they're in short supply."

I furrow my brows as I squelch towards the lip of the pavement, my sneakers growing soggier by the minute. Traffic is beginning to pick up, tangling in the junctures between streets. Vehicles trumpet in impatient frustration. Steam ripples from exhausts, hissing.

"I—what?"

"Oh, didn't you know?" Jian Wang purrs, imbued anew with that malignant impishness, secrets gleaming like bones under the gravel of his voice. "The Furies have an entire supply chain set up in Djinnestan."

A truck roars past and a puddle geysers. It paints my jeans to my skin, paints it black and freezing. I throttle back a curse, dribbling water and the tang of mud, palming the grime from my cheeks. I need to focus. None of this is going where I expected.

"Wait. *A supply chain?* They're *franchising?*"

"No. Nothing so uncouth. The Furies are... entrepreneurs. They supply feathers. Customers supply them money. Then they supply Chee Cheong Kai with money in exchange for luxuries."

"Ah." I chew on the revelation, zigzagging unlawfully through traffic in true Malaysian fashion. Three streets down, Chinatown's ostentatious signage looms, criminally bright, its pillars already teeming with bargain hunters. Neon raincoats and impulse-bought umbrellas jounce unevenly together in commiseration. "So, wait. Stop. I—I should have known about this? Why didn't I know about this? I should have seen their immigration papers. I, mean. You know."

"Because you're terrible at your job." Jian Wang snorts. "The Greeks are part of the visa waiver, you know?"

I grunt incomprehensibly, stung by his mockery, and lengthen my stride. I'm being played—that much is clear—but what remains frustratingly obtuse are the stakes at risk. Everything keeps going back to the Erinyes, and I still don't know why.

"Do you know where the Furies are hiding?" I ask as we snake into Chee Cheong Kai, sticking to the sidewalk, which is marginally less damp than the open sky.

"No. But I know who you can ask."

THE BONES OF a city—down below the living world—no matter how large or how small, are porous, full of places that can be chiselled into rent-controlled housing and shops, reflections of the material plane and all of its grubby pleasures. The only real difference is that the environment is adaptive, capable of being unspooled into panoramic auditoriums or collapsed into mouse holes. Demons, yaoguai, household gods, the kind bound to terrestrial duties, are all united in their need for such amenities.

Jian Wang is gentler about transference this time. I barely notice, outside of the way momentum crooks a fish hook around my diaphragm and yanks, hard enough that it bisects my lungs, a single thread of acid, and I'm left gasping as we rock to a halt.

Banbuduo, Djinnestan, Domdaniel: successive cultures have assembled a fortress of names for this place, each as useless as the last, because no one who lives here addresses it as anything but *home*. I knuckle disorientation from my eyes and look up.

The heavens glimmer, eluding focus, a watery restlessness like gazing at the skin of the ocean from far below. Occasionally, shapes float into view, indistinct but unmistakably massive.

Blink.

Silence becomes avaricious commotion. This world's Petaling Street, previously hollow of life, erupts into entropy. Traders with bizarre skin tones hawk an assemblage of goods, some strange, others mundane; char siew and clandestine recordings of trysting deities, heavenly peaches and Panasonic televisions, Coca-cola bottles and an entire range of silk dresses shitted out by Anansi himself.

"Crossroads," Jian Wang announces, abruptly, rigidly, conveying the exact depth of his enthusiasm for this place.

Obviously, I'm completely sympathetic. "I bet you can't wait to make your way back there. See all the old rocks, check out the puddles."

The ghost withholds rebuttal.

We drift through the kaleidoscopic crowd, which is every color except human, a biosphere of predators muzzled by the Jade Emperor's orders. Heaven protects what it has an economic interest in, after all. Contradicting Jian Wang's information, evidence of the Furies' presence emerge long before we reach the center, which is a full ten minutes further than it should be, thanks to the weirdness of the space.

"*Merchandise?*" I demand, incredulous. I plant my shoe in the base of a pickpocket's spine and shove. Somehow, despite only having just arrived, we've been accosted six times already.

"The Furies are very popular," comes the prim reply.

An understatement, in every shade of the world. Streetside artists promote voluptuous caricatures of the Erinyes, while medicine men lure passersby with oils blessed by the foreign goddesses. There are even fried chicken stores advertising flavor tie-ins, a slightly tasteless endeavour that nonetheless succeeds at amassing long queues hungry for cultural immersion. Everywhere I look, I see feathers strung up to bangles, to rings, to necklaces like webs of cold brass, all alleging one hundred percent authenticity

"You don't say."

We pierce the crowd. I sidestep a rickshaw laden with obsidian-scaled women, their eyes massive, their clothes expensively utilitarian. Their driver looks almost human until he turns, at which point the face, amber-skinned and luridly grinning, on the back of his head reveals he is anything but.

Polite applause billows. I swivel to see an old man on a canopied dais, arms extended to invite further applause. The structure he occupies is calculated to intimidate: calcium and granite interleaved with supernatural precision, a tarp sutured from flayed eyeballs. In the middle, a conspicuous opening in the platform, just large enough to accommodate a small child.

He drops lithely into a bow, fist against open palm; Chinese courtesy despite the mahogany of his skin, the breadth of his eyes, the attributes that mark him as Malay. While unmistakably human, he exudes an easy, thoughtless puissance, like an aftertaste from a dream.

"Who is that?"

"Tunku Salleh," Jian Wang whispers tensely, voice failing as he says it, diminished by dread. "The Furies' host."

I contemplate pushing, but it's vividly clear that he has no intention to say any more. So, naturally, I push. "And?"

"And what?"

"And what's your deal with him?"

"What's my deal with who?"

I count to ten under my breath. My work only tangentially relates to the affairs of Banbuduo, rarely crossing over save for emergencies, so I tend to be rusty on its internal politics. "That Tunku fellow."

Jian Wang tautens into steel, cautious and juddering with ill-suppressed emotion. "He bound me."

Ah. My jaw clenches shut around his explanation. There's no comeback for that, really, no way to proceed without first bungling through a reluctant apology. I'm saved from my tactlessness, however, when a voice dredges itself into my awareness, calm, coarse and frayed from time's courtship.

"Jian Wang." Tunku Salleh rolls the name on his tongue like a bead. "We've missed you."

"I've been assisting the Seneschal with his duties." Beat. "We're here to visit *your* Furies."

Slight emphasis made all the more peculiar by Jiang Wang's absence of intonation, his speech mechanical, divested of feeling. *Your* Furies. A clue, perhaps, or an expression of hostility. Who knows? I'm not permitted room to ponder. Tunku Salleh advances, bonelessly graceful, wrists and knees rotating disconcertingly. Maybe, not as human as I first thought. He chuckles, as though seeing the thought, snags my hand in his and shakes it firmly.

"Tunku Salleh bin Mohammad Zain. But you knew that, Seneschal. Chinatown is blessed by your presence." A heady charisma, borderline chemical in timbre, permeates each word. I suspect only some of it is natural.

"Um. Thanks." I release his hand, resist the temptation to scour my palm against my jeans. His powdery skin feels fragile, brittle, calling to mind eggshells or insect carapaces.

He continues, gracious. Periodically, someone will untwine from the crush of people to brush fingertips against his sleeve or kiss his hand, their veneration bordering on worship. "I am happy to report that the Erinyes are being kept in the finest living conditions. They want for nothing, Seneschal. No thread of silk, no rind of precious fruit—all they desire, they are given."

"Um," I repeat. Well. This is awkward. "Actually—"

"If you seek an audience, I would be more than happy to direct you to the Erinyes. I'm certain they'll appreciate the opportunity to converse with someone closer to their level." You could write books about his aptitude for flattery, the tonal intricacies of his delivery, the way his body language expresses great humility without straying into obsequiousness. He tips his head, chuckles again, as he takes a step backwards, palm tipped face-up.

I conceal my uncertainty behind a shrug and a raised chin. If nothing else, it means an opportunity to get warm. "Sure. Why not?"

Another quiet laugh before Tunku Salleh wends into the crowd, the mouse-bones on the tassels of his belt chiming a backbeat. "By the way, if I could be so bold, you're very generous to take on a problem child like Jian Wang."

"Mm?"

"Treacherous little pup." Tunku Salleh reveals betel-darkened teeth, and reaches above my head. I feel Jian Wang squirm in wordless objection and then slump, nerveless, his weight diffusing. "We found him standing over his brother's body the day he was to be sacrificed, screaming we didn't need him anymore."

"...what did you do?" I crane a look upwards.

The old Malay man brings a papier mâché figurine into view, a humanoid figure clenched into a fetal position. Its limbs are threaded with barbed wire and slivers of vegetal green. "Something to help Jian Wang sleep. The Furies need not endure him."

I wring the hems of my shirt, disquiet billowing along my spine. Too many revelations and far too little sleep. "Appreciate the assistance, sir."

"Small matter." Tunku Salleh grins again, dark. "When you are done with whatever you are doing, however, I would appreciate it if you returned Jian Wang. Chinatown is so lonely without his ceaseless whimpers."

ELEVEN

"Weren't there supposed to be three of you?" I ask with my usual tactless abandon.

The two Furies move in balletic unison; autonomous in thought, perhaps, but not in act. Every gesture is either complemented or mirrored, every expression paralleled. They exchange looks, heads tilted, evaluating.

"Yes," says one, at last, lapping slowly at the English words like they were an alien flavor. "We were three."

The Furies look more human than I expected. Mythology depicts them as monstrous, befouled by their grim labours, their hair knotted with serpents, their visage canine in structure. But they're not. If anything, they're more polished than me. Cigarette-slim, the Furies are impeccably dressed, blue-black skin striking against white pantsuits, their hair voluminous haloes and their faces unlined. Surprisingly wingless, and anywhere between twenty-eight and two thousand years old, identical in every respect.

"I. Um. I'm very sorry for your loss." I rally behind the optimism that civic duty will protect me from certain expiry. I slip a tape recorder—an actual tape recorder, a hideous artifact from the early '90s—from a pocket and hold it forward, a finger on the record button. "But I'm here on official business. My name is Rupert Wong. I'm here to question you about your involvement in the death of His Highness Ao Qin's daughter."

Three days into this investigation and still I'm addressing the deceased as an extension of her parent. Very progressive, Rupert.

"The contract was legitimate," says the second Fury, pouring tea into her sister's earthenware cup. The steam smells astringent, floral. "We made sure of that."

"I—" The words stick in a clump. *Click.* Roll tape. "I have no doubt of that, Kindly Ones. But I need to know who requested the—the..."

I trail off and scan the room. The decor is understatedly opulent. The furnishings are Nordic, 1960s grandeur revitalized by artisan hands; the massive television in the corner, thin to the point of immateriality, a luxury even Luddites would understand. Behind the Furies, opened windows lead to an extravagant balcony, its perimeter thronging with exotic flowers.

"Xiao Quan, of course." The first rucks her forehead, mouth dimpling into a frown.

I tense. "Who is—"

The second Fury sooths their shared expression into one of quiet professionalism. "Ao Qin's daughter."

The information hits like an out-of-control bus, staggering all breath and reason from my breast. It isn't until the Furies avert their gazes, polite half-smiles gleaming, that I realize that I've been gaping. I cough, and straighten into an illusion of decorum. "Ao Qin's daughter... asked to be euthanised?"

"Not exactly," says the first Fury, glancing at her sister. "Alecto?"

"Of course, Megaera." Alecto dips her head, mouth pressed to the lip of her cup. Awkward quiet seeps in, interrupted only by her deliberate slurping and the tapping of my feet. The Fury eventually relents, raising her gaze to mine.

"Xiao Quan was not happy with her marriage. She hadn't been happy with her marriage for a very long time."

"Centuries," her sister whispers. "Centuries upon centuries."

"Yes. Her husband took advantage of her innocence and her father's disregard. When Xiao Quan ran to him, begging for succor, he told her to endure."

Magaera husks her voice into a surprisingly accurate imitation of the Dragon King's own. "'You are a wife. Act like one.'"

Her attention wraps about me, hungry, suffocatingly rapt. "Do you believe in that, too, Rupert? Do you believe wives must be wives and nothing else?"

"I—"

"Hush, sister. Don't tease. Anyway, Xiao Quan did as she was told," Alecto continues, uncurling from her seat to stride lithely towards the balcony. The sun corsets her in a geometry of shadows and for an instant, I catch the reflection of glittering scales, bejewelled eyes. "But even the strongest woman has her limit. She tired, that Xiao Quan. Tired of the beatings."

"The lies."

"The other women."

"Don't forget the other men as well."

"Mm. The way he adopted command of her name, couching his desire as hers, donning power without consequence."

"The cretin," Alecto snorts. "Anyway. After thousands of years, she eventually convinced her husband that they needed to return to her ancestral home. So that she could see her father and discuss, perhaps, a way to deify her husband."

"Of course, that was just a ruse," laughs the other Fury, her humour razored with scorn. "What she really wanted was a way to be rid of him—"

"—forever."

"Which was when she contacted us."

I shudder, shaking off their hypnotic voices like a flea-bitten mutt. "You mean she summoned you?"

"No," corrects Alecto. "Contacted. We've been here for a very long time, Mr. Wong."

The other: "Guests of Kuala Lumpur's finest gentry."

Click. The pieces clamp together, fitting jigsaw-snug, even as my suspicions sharpen into high-definition. I dig my nails into my palm and sip air until my heartbeat steadies. The Furies re-equip their bland, reptilian smiles.

"Do you mean—" I begin.

Megaera shakes her head as she thumbs through an iPhone, glass surface glimmering with notifications. Already, I've been dismissed. "No."

"She's not being coy." Her sister paces from the balcony, hands locked behind the small of her back, eyes lidded with amusement. "We were invited here from Las Vegas under the pretense of a new trade agreement between the pantheons."

"I—" I reconsider the angle of assault. "Under the pretense of a new trade agreement? I'm assuming that wasn't—"

"We don't know," says Alecto, apologetic. "Nothing has happened yet. We've been here for months, but no one has stepped forward to announce themselves as the enterprising Samaritans responsible for the invitation."

"And the feathers?" I'm not really interested, but Chinese courtesy demands a nominal interest in someone else's entrepreneurial pursuits.

"A side business that came about after we fulfilled Xiao Quan's request. The desperate will make their own myths. Why not capitalize on them?" She shrugs. "Speaking of which, and I hate to be a bitch, but it's time to leave. We have business to attend to."

I sketch an extravagant bow. "Thank you for your co-operation, Erinyes."

"You can return me to Tunku Salleh now."

The panic in Jian Wang's voice is unmistakable. I roll the crushed effigy between my fingertips, thoughtful. The queue to the Furies' suite spills around the corridor; who knew there were so many avenging spirits in a developing third world city?

"Really," insists Jian Wang. A woman, seven feet tall with a scribbled-out face, fires a dirty look as she lumbers past. "It's all right."

"You know, that's funny. I could have sworn that you were trying to get out of it before." Two feet away, a young man in fuschia clears his throat with great emphasis. I ignore him and cross my arms instead, trying in vain to maintain a measure of dignity. "You were practically extorting me, if I recall."

"Things change." Jian Wang tugs at his legs, but they've long welded to my clavicles, mere undulations under the flesh. Skin pulls uncomfortably, but nothing breaks. "I can go now."

"No. Not until you tell me what you know." I slap his hand in admonishment. Reckless bravado is the magician's best friend. Blink and you'll miss how it displaces your attention, steers you from inconvenient truths. Like my utter ignorance as to how to unknit Jian Wang from my own tissues.

"I—" The ghost's petulance thins to a knife edge. I jerk in place, cautious, senses bristling with warning. Fingers dig cracks into my skin, more purposeful this time. Pain spiders in waves across my shoulders.

"Hey! Hey! Ow! Ow! What are you—hey!" I spiral in place, clutching at Jian Wang's hands. His grip is iron, and growing more unbearable by the moment. At this point, it's clear that the spirit has decided on an exit plan. He's going to dig himself out, something I'm totally not comfortably with.

So I smash and roll into a wall, hoping to jolt him loose. But Jian Wang proves more insistent than a tick. Hissing, he tightens his hold further, and I feel muscle yowl in objection at hairline tears, widening with every leap of my pulse.

"Let me go!"

At this point, I've lost the plot. And possibly the collective respect of Banbuduo, who most likely wasn't expecting to see the local Seneschal flailing quite so vigorously. Panic overrides common sense. I claw at my back, at his wrists, at his face, all the while pinballing between surfaces, swearing in every language my mind can conjure. Agony rapidly supersedes any other concern. Animal instinct presents that age-old binary decision: fight or flee.

I decide on both.

I'm abysmal at magic. I've no illusions about that. Summonings work seven times out of fifteen, and all telecommunications with Diyu invariably include gross misspellings. But there's one piece of wizardry I can perform faultlessly, one enchantment I know like breathing. I can send myself to Hell. Not in any figurative sense, but a bonafide ability to instantly relocate into the bowels of Diyu.

(Trivia time, ang moh. The Egyptians were right about a lot of things, including the idea that souls have weight. Karma does, in fact, affect your spiritual buoyancy. In my case, I've more than enough sin to send me plummeting hellwards at record-breaking speeds upon the moment of expiry.)

My mouth dries. Lungs flatten, breathing deregulates into wet spasms. The agonal phase hurts, no matter how times you've endured it. Ventricles begin to spasm shut. My vision strobes. One by one, organs shutter into failure, and I hit the ground hard as biological death, malodorous and cold, descends to claim the real estate. My last thought before unconsciousness takes over is that I probably should eat better: the reek of my slackening bowels is quite appalling.

An indeterminate moment later, non-existence is replaced by a juddering of vertigo. Colors glimmer into rivulets, converging, too quick to parse or separate into individual hues, from loam to subterranean shadow to the auspicious shades of Youdu. Somewhere in between, I register the squeal of my own voice as it climbs into the highest register.

Crunch. The impact would kill me were I not already dead. I rock onto my feet, fingers clasped around the bottom of my skull. "Nrrggrrh."

I pound the heel of a hand against the side of my neck and cartilage wrenches sullenly into place. I take a deep breath, sulphuric air shuddering through my lungs, and immediately choke. Diyu was not made for humans, even those here on voluntary terms.

"Where are—"

"Hell," I groan.

Sinew unknits from sinew, cartilage from bone. I feel the slithering of Jian Wang's muscles as he tests the limits of his restraints. We both arrive at the same conclusion at pretty much the same time. He bolts. Except he doesn't get very far. My tattoos have limited mobility on the earthly plane, constrained by entire battalions of provisionary clauses. Here, though, they can go anywhere.

They shriek free. A forest of hands and teeth and forked tongues, quivering into eye-watering two-dimensionality. I'm struck, for a moment, by their number. Who knew one man's skin could house so many spirits of semi-legal status? Then the moment passes when Jian Wang screams in panic, even as the tattoo-spirits overtake him, papering themselves over his chest and his back. On the rim of hearing, I catch threats and promises of violence. Obviously, they didn't appreciate how he had enforced their silence.

"Good job, er, men." I stride over to where Jian Wang lies writhing amid his captors, all of three feet away. I squat down. "So. Jian Wang. I see two solutions here. First, you tell me what's going on. And second—you tell me what's going on after security beats it out of you. Both options work. I really don't care."

The only answer is vigorous squirming, and the rhythmic thump of Jian Wang endeavouring to worm away from me. I grab his foot.

"Kick once for yes, twice for no."

He doesn't reply. Feeling mildly vindictive, I stretch up and begin dragging Jian Wang along behind me, trailing spirits like a frayed umbilical cord. It's an unappetizing sight, but Diyu isn't a place for the squeamish at the best of times.

TWELVE

As FAR AS gods go, Yan Wang is pretty swell.

"No, you're not interrupting anything. We're just playing chess. Come! What news do you bring?" the Lord of Hell booms as he rolls from his chair, each mammoth step raising tiny shockwaves. I reconfigure into a meek kowtow and grit my teeth, my head rattling against volcanic rock with every tremor.

"Oh, stand up. You needn't stand on ceremony with me. We're old friends, are we not?" Yan Wang stoops to collect me in a palm. He's absolutely massive, of course. Primordial forces, especially those housed in their own environments, tend to grow that way. His amiability clashes with the ferocity of his face, which is a sunburnt claret and perpetually contorted into a grimace. As per legend, his eyes bulge alarmingly from within the frame of his colossal beard.

"'Friends' is a word I'm"—I spread my arms to steady myself, wobbling onto my feet—"not worthy of using, I believe."

"You're too harsh on yourself." Yan Wang stomps back to his chair and sprawls over the gilded structure, setting me atop a table piled high with scrolls. A glance reveals millions of names, written in neat handwriting, each prefaced by a seemingly random number. I don't ask. Jian Wang, hogtied, remains wisely quiescent. "You've been excellent in your job. A few more decades and you'll no longer be in debt."

I incline my head. Discussions about my hellbound status, however tactful, tend to make me uncomfortable.

"But I'm digressing. How can Diyu help you, Rupert?"

Glancing sidelong, I jab a thumb in Jian Wang's direction. "I think someone's trying to cause a war."

"Jian Wang?" The King of Hell opens his eyes even wider, an impressive feat by any measure of the phrase. "I am surprised. That is quite ambitious for—"

"No!" I reel from my own enthusiasm. I cough into a fist and then continue, pitching my voice low and respectful. "I mean, no, Your Majesty. I don't think Jian Wang is, um, responsible. I think he knows who."

The titan lowers his bushy brows, mouth bent in his trademark scowl. My tattoo-spirits recede, worming back into the shelter of my skin, all the while prostrating themselves, performing tongueless obeisances. Jian Wang struggles loose from his restraints, and immediately crumples into a kowtow. "This one intends no harm. This one is not worthy to speak to you. This one—"

"Jian Wang." A warning note clips between the child-spirit's babbling.

"This one—" Jian Wang looks up, gaze round with terror. "They promised they would let me go. All I had to do was hinder Rupert."

"Who promised?"

The specter of Chinatown licks pale lips once, before lowering his forehead to Yan Wang's palm again. In a whimper, so soft that it might have been illusionary, he gives a name. A family. The boss's family. *My* boss's family. I breathe out, sharply. I hadn't realized I had been holding my breath till then.

"Why?" I ask.

Jian Wang glances over his shoulder, shrugs. "You don't tell your knife what you're cooking, do you?"

He had me there. Before I could reply, Yan Wang interrupts, face lining with thought, his eyes shrewd. The King of Hell rumbles deep, a sound that digs through the marrow. "The heavens have been troubled of late. Rumours abound, of houses toppling, of offices abandoned, of dissolution in the West"—a disparaging curl of his lips—"and even dissent in our ranks. Lately, the Chinese and the Malay pantheons have been jostling for superiority. This could be a coup by the Malay."

No shit. "Have... tensions really been that bad?"

Yan Wang shrugs to potent effect. I topple over, and barely succeed in turning the collapse into a messy kowtow. Jian Wang remains on his belly. "All gods are competitive."

"But Islam—" I hesitate. "Islam is a monotheistic religion allegedly overseen by a benevolent entity of immeasurable power. It shouldn't, you know—" The words clatter behind my teeth: *it shouldn't come to violence.* (A truth to take back to your country with you, ang moh. Not every Muslim is an abomination. In fact, very few are. The rest, much like most atheists and neo-druids, are lovely individuals.)

"The ways of the world are mysterious," Yan Wang replies, tone disconcertingly sly, more appropriate in the mouth of a drinking buddy, as opposed to an omnipotent deity in charge of—actually, nevermind. Omnipotent deities do as they want.

I gnaw on the inside of a cheek and try to retain my calm. "Of course."

Yan Wang is having none of it. He erupts into full-bellied guffaws that carry throughout his antechamber. As far as such places go, the nook is rather modestly appointed. Volcanic rock connects floor to walls to ceiling, a smooth gray interrupted by tributaries of pale gold. Ornaments are few and far between here: an antique dresser, a map of Diyu, a mirror the size of a stadium ground, and the corner that Yan Wan uses for cerebral entertainment. Ignoring scale, this is more a space for an everyman scholar than a puissant monarch. Which is probably why Yan Wang keeps it this way.

"You're much too serious, Rupert." His laughter smooths into a low chuckle. "Live! There are so many years for you to accomplish that."

"I'm trying—I—Yes, Your Highness."

"Pantheons will fight and they will bicker. Such is the way of siblings. It's a small matter. Don't think too much of it."

I weigh my protests on the tip of my tongue. Yan Wang doesn't get it. He can't. He exists on a different scale from the rest of us, both figuratively and literally. So, I bite down on my argument and lower my forehead to his palm again. Even if I can't have the King of Hell lumber up to terra firma and solve my problems for me, I know exactly who I need to talk to, to finally close this sordid loop of lies.

"Your Highness?"

"Mm." He sounds like he's still threading through the waters of his own contemplation.

"If it's not too much problem, would it be okay for you to send me topside?" I flick a glance at Jian Wang, still inert, still in a pose of abject submission. "And, um, for me to leave the kid with you."

An emphatic nod that knocks me back onto my knees when I make the mistake of trying to wobble upright. "Of course. We shall be more than happy to provide such a small favour to such an important—"

The snap of his fingers splits my hearing like a thunderclap. My world fills with white light, and I feel a lurching in the pit of my stomach, pulling me up this time. Yan Wang's final words dissipate into a thrash of static, meaningless, all-consuming. The wrenching sharpens into rippling nausea as I, centuries or seconds later, plunge back into my meat suit.

Something stinks. Me, most likely. I roll over onto my back and groan. There's plastic under my skin, and the glare of the noon sky above my head. I think I smell durian, so completely rotted that not even its most ardent proponents would defend it. Carefully, I stretch out my arms and wince at my protesting muscles. I crinkle my nose. Definitely in a dumpster.

And that smell is definitely me.

(One of the sad realities of life, ang moh. No one will change the underpants of a presumed corpse.)

"Hey, boss. I've got a question."

I shouldn't have taken the bus. I shouldn't have taken the bus. Especially not the cheapest ride I could find. Gasoline fumes tangle with the stench of unwashed armpits, rust, and vomit. The seats, a sliver of fabric over creaking metal, rattle loudly, even as the passengers rock and sway in place, trying in vain to keep from spilling into one another's laps. I crane my head as far as it will go as my aisle mates, an obese man and his shih tzu hybrid, fall on me. Neither of them appear particularly acquainted with soap.

On the bright side, no one has commented on my aromatic presence either.

"Rupert! Ahahahaha," the boss chimes down the phone, pitch-perfect. In the background, I catch the silvery murmur of opulent dining: jazz music, a delicate tinkle of silverware, voices pitched low but confident. "If you're calling to ask about my favorite way to prepare a Fury, the answer would be: whatever way you impress me with."

I carefully slant my legs away from the dog. There's a look in its eyes that suggests the owner should have probably taken the mutt to the toilet before they got on the bus. "Actually, it's something else."

"Yes?" His voice doesn't so much harden as arch; bright and attentive. "I am completely free and at your service."

"Why are you trying to kill your foreign guests?"

A beat. The answer unfurls, brimming with plasticky cheer. "Sorry?"

"Why are you trying to bread and fry the Furies? You invited them here. The least you could do is offer them amnesty from your appetites." The bus lurches across a speed bump and I barely avoid severing my tongue as I jolt upwards, nearly tumbling into the walkaway as I crash back into the so-thin-it-might-as-well-be-skipped cushion.

The boss doesn't answer. I can hear furniture being pushed back and the sounds of fine dining (ghouls have bottomless appetites and varied tastes; it isn't sustenance they pursue, so much as consumption) recede into the snarl of traffic. It isn't until there is absolute silence on the line that the boss, charm unruffled, begins to speak again. "Because it is sadly *necessary.*"

"To eat... a goddess?"

"Why, yes." Surprise knots around an edge of malice. "Do you really think I'd give up the opportunity to sample such a delectable delicacy?"

"That's not what I meant." Guan Yin save me, the dog is actually peeing on its owner. Despite the warm, acidic puddle spreading over his leg, the man remains, astonishingly, dead to the world. In a fit of morbid curiosity, I raise a palm over his nostrils. Still breathing. "You *know* what I meant."

"Absolutely not, Rupert. Why don't you outline the situation clearly for me? Careful with what you say, though. I don't want to have to sue you for libelous conduct. Ahahaha." He is absolutely not joking, I'm sure.

I swallow and glance out of the window. Oil palm trees as far as the eye can see, an endless stretch of serrated bark and yellow-green leaves. "You called the Furies to Malaysia. You sponsored their stay. You want them dead so the Greeks will attack."

"You are a smart one, Rupert. I keep telling my wife, but she wouldn't believe me. She thinks you're a talented chimp." The boss laughs musically, the reverberations overflowing with calculated amounts of goodwill. "But, yes. You're right. I did. It's—I don't know if you can understand it. But I am so *very* sick of the power disparity in this country."

My eyes travel the bus. Power disparity, especially in monetary terms, is something I understand exceedingly well. I clamp down on the impulse for unnecessary witticism. "Mhm."

"Sick of it. I was here when your first ancestors landed on the soil, you know? And I watched as they gained the advantage. Your grubby little pantheon grew with them. *Miserable* stuff, all and all."

"Uh-huh."

"Look at you, Rupert. Always so scintillatingly polite. It's why we keep you around. Anyway, without going too much into ancient history, I decided it was time for a change."

Evening swaddles the horizon in blues and shadows. The dog has finally gone back to sleep atop the fat man's lap; his owner, in turn, has finally slouched against the window instead of my shoulder. "Why now?"

"You should *really* keep up with the world news." A dangerous note of coyness, as the boss chuckles to himself. "Find out yourself. I'll tell you this much: it's an excellent season for new ideas."

I nod, realise he can't see it, and make more affirmative noises. If I'm lucky, he'll talk himself into a confession.

"Anyway. Yes. I want to dethrone the Chinese. Take them down a few notches, or possibly get rid of them entirely. I'm nowhere near fussy about the matter. I just want to see justice where justice is due."

"Sure. Fair." I can never leave anything well and alone. "But what about me? Why am I—what's with the whole 'cook us a Fury' deal?"

"I want conflict. It doesn't matter who instigates it. You or Ao Qin. It's all the same to me. Except I'm slightly more confident of one party's survival than the other's. No offense. You understand."

"None taken."

"Coincidentally, since we're on the topic of betrayals and callous manipulation, I'm going to take this moment to point out that Minah belongs to us."

I freeze.

"She is, officially, the property of our wonderful little tribe. George too, if you recall. Now, had you been a better employee, she might have already acquired her freedom. But you're not. She's still ours, and officially, we can do anything we want. Including pulp her for serunding, should a certain Dragon King come knocking on our doors. Are we clear?"

My voice emerges as a croak. "Crystal."

"Perfect. Enjoy your trip to Port Dickson. Send Ao Qin our regards."

THIRTEEN

"TYPE O NEGATIVE! You remembered!"

"Only the best." I incline my head and try to feign indifference as The God of Missing People suckles on the blood bag like a juice pouch. It helps, of course, that the deity has provided phenomenally effective discretion.

The ghost of Xiao Quan is precisely as I imagined: decorous, elegant, beautiful in the way only dangerous predators can be, and very slightly translucent. Her eyes are large and sad within the sharp-jawed frame. As I study at her, the Dragon King's daughter flows into a low bow, every inch a model of sinuous grace.

"Forgive this one for all of the trouble she has caused." Her manner of speech is appropriately archaic, several centuries too formal for this irreverent millennium.

"No sweat!" The word pulses free. I rub the back of my neck, awkwardness heating my cheeks. I like respectful people as much as the next person, but you can feel unqualified for the attention. If she knew what I'd been up to, she'd likely have choicer words. "I'm, I mean. I'm very honoured you could make an appearance."

"This one did not intend to cause trouble. This one had her own desires, her own... agenda. This one wanted to die." No drama colors that proclamation, only wistful frankness. *This one wanted to die.* The words seep through my bones. Minah has never so openly articulated her desires, but she had always desired escape. Instinctively, I run my fingertips over my phone, hoping for the buzz of an incoming message. Nothing. "This one also knew her father would not accept—"

So, feeling rather like a sexist heel, I talk over her, and over the thoughts extricating themselves from the morass of my memory. "Couldn't you have just told your father about what was happening?"

Xiao Quan's laugh is hollow. "And what? This one's sire would have simply told this one to go home, and preserve face. One cannot abandon the fate they've made for themselves."

Waves smash into the rocks of Port Dickson. We've found a secluded corner in spite of the area's popularity among the country's overworked and underpaid middle-class. I probably didn't need to be adjacent to an ocean to summon Ao Qin, but the idea had romantic appeal. Sort of. Up until the point I discovered one of my fellow passengers suffered from explosive bowel troubles. Of course, by then, there was nothing to do but grin and bear it.

Anyway.

I swallow, glance over to the sea, a muddied brown that inspires no desire to wade into its depths. I suppose I could have found a more inspiring spot. "I see."

"This one meant no harm. At least not to anyone other than her beloved spouse. The Furies seemed like the perfect option. Certainly, the local nobility trusted them."

"I—" I falter. Murder victims usually aren't quite so apologetic about the violent crimes, but normal employers rarely participate in grandiose chess matches, utilizing ancient spirits and domestic dissatisfaction as game pieces. There's no template for me to pin a response, really, so I shove that line of thought aside. "Why did the Furies off you too?"

"It was mariticide," Xiao Quan explains, edges shimmering. She collects her hands over her belly. I don't recognize her garments from her corpse. They're simpler than what I would picture; cotton rather than silk, pale oceanic colors bare of complicated embroidery. "The Kindly Ones could not allow for it. This one had to die, if they were to fulfill this one's request." She hesitates. "But they were kind. It did not hurt for long."

I nod. The God of Missing People has wandered off towards the shore, still clutching its sacrificial plastic sack. Flashing us both a curious stare, it drops to its knees and begins listlessly scooping at the beach with its fingers.

"Will you tell this one's father she is sorry? This one was tired. After so many thousands of years, this one simply desired to cease."

"I—" I purse my mouth, but incline my head. There's nothing more to be said here. At this point, any criticism about her life's decisions feels unfortunately moot. Lacking the right words, I delay my answer by looking over towards the God of Missing People, who is locking fingers with a spectral hand it had just unearthed. "Yes. But, don't you think it would be better to tell him yourself?"

"No," Xiao Quan replies, fading into intangibility. "Not at all."

I almost let her go. Almost. The exhaustion in her gaze digs like a hook. I know that look far too well. But even as Xiao Quan diffuses, fading into the pale curve of a smile, I chatter another incantation, an ugly barrage of consonants. Her outline snaps back into hard focus.

"What?"

"I'm sorry." I fold into a half-hearted shrug, feeling somewhat like an adult challenging a toddler to a test of arms. "I sympathize. I do. But you're going to tell your father about what happened so he'll call this whole thing off. And please, *please* can we avoid mentioning the bit with the ghouls? I don't want to be a bastard, but if you tell, I will make sure it goes just as badly for you as it will go for me."

THE ENCOUNTER IS less dramatic than I expected it to be, less a meeting between two reptilian divinities, more a pow-wow between father and daughter. Ao Qin wears his human shape throughout the muted conversation as they stand with their foreheads pressed together, the Dragon King's forearms rested on his daughter's shoulders, Xiao Quan's fingers loose about his wrists.

My daughter my daughter my daughter his memories have lightened to hazy watercolour figments in my head, barely distinguishable from a dream. But I feel the afterimage of his agony, his guilt still twinges like an old injury.

Hours later, or maybe minutes, the two separate. Xiao Quan bows low as, shooting a hurt look in my direction, she finally dissolves into air, leaving Ao Qin to goggle at the space she occupied. Three long breaths later, he marches up to me, carrying the smell of salt and death.

"Thank you."

I nod.

He pauses. You can almost see the words hanging suspended in the air: the apologies, the reassurances, the vocabulary of comfort. But I'm just a man, and he's a god with a questionable grasp of the value of a human life. Such limitations prohibit wanton brotherly love. "We need to know: was anyone else involved?"

"No."

His lamplight stare burns molten. "Are you certain?"

"We are. I mean, I am. One hundred percent."

Ao Qin's expression remains placid, although his skin does not. Patterns writhe with unverbalized emotion. I glance away just as it reaches his eyes. The God of Missing People is wisely keeping its distance, more preoccupied with the ghost it found in the sand than my predicament. Typical.

"Your daughter had her reasons. Bad ones, definitely, but this is something she wanted. No foul. You have your evidence. You have a confession. *I* have a confession. Bring it to... to god court, or whatever you call it. I did my job. Now"—the words catch as I hold out the tape recorder for his inspection—"let Minah go."

The Dragon King says nothing, only regards the device in my palm with what appears to be mild befuddlement. I'm briefly wracked by concern. What if he—

"Thank you." The gratitude comes stiff, unpracticed. He takes the machine, pockets it, then snags my hand in a rough handshake. "We will have a word with the Furies and their masters. This is more than sufficient for what we require."

Not trusting myself to speak, I respond with an equally graceless nod. It's not every day that you catalyze a war for a woman's sake.

Ao Qin glides sidelong, taking a step back towards the ocean. "Are you certain there's nothing else you wish to tell us? No further details?"

Karma feels like the weight of the world compressed into a single pin, its point impaled upon the middle of my forehead. I suck in a breath. The universe is watching. This is one of those moments that you clearly recognize as instrumental in the charting of history. One of those decisions that divide reality into parallel dimensions, that defines centuries to come. I clutch that breath like a lifeline. The *right* thing to do would be to prevent the risk of global conflict.

"No."

You know what they say. Love makes fools and warmongers out of all of us.

"How DID IT go, Rupert?" the boss queries, effervescently delighted.

"Wonderful. I started a war for you."

He laughs. "Excellent, excellent. *Excellent.*"

I meander up the hill side, back onto the road. Several metres away, a black sedan sits purring, its driver nonchalantly reclining against its frame. "You sent a ride?"

"Of course. And a change of clothing. We're told you absolutely reek." He laughs quietly. "Make sure to change before you come in today. We already have to deduct your pay for your absences. We'd rather not have to cut it any further because of your inability to maintain personal hygiene."

I don't ask how he knows, or even why he cares. The boss isn't exactly someone who should complain about offal, given his predilections. I nod towards the driver, yet another Aryan bombshell. "Sure, boss."

"We have lamia in stock today, by the way. I hope you're prepared for the challenge."

"Sure, boss." Just another day in paradise for Rupert Wong, cannibal chef.

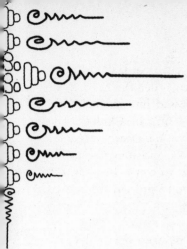

PART TWO
RUPERT WONG
AND THE ENDS
OF THE EARTH

FOURTEEN

"CAN I CALL you back? Cooking for dear life here. I—yes, no—yes, I guess it's an euphemism. No? Yes. I—"

Oil fountains through the air as my new iPhone performs a ten-point dive into the wok, slipping from where it was wedged between cheek and shoulder to bury itself in a hell of pumpkin croquettes. I jerk back away from the splatter and sizzle of a few thousand ringgit gone the way of good bacon.

There is no time to curse, though, or even think. I'm on a tight schedule here. I toss the pan a few more times, drop it on the counter, and then spin about to slice up slivers of large intestine. It's definitely not the best prepared length of meat my knife has seen. Bits of decomposing waste material blink at me from between puckered folds, shot through with dying tapeworms like fistfuls of wanton noodles. But the boss says the detritus of the human digestive system gives *character* to a meal. Who am I to argue with the monster who pays my rent?

(He has *ghoulish* tastes, ang moh. Get it? Get—anyway.)

Across the stage, my opponent is in trouble. He's standing impaled in the spotlights like a Scandinavian Jesus before a Roman tribunal, fishmouthing all the while. In front of him, set in a bed of wilting roses, are the remains of a Brazilian pornstar, megawatt grin sutured in place, final million-dollar erection jutting proudly from a death-bruised pelvis.

The crowd is chanting, pounding its feet. They want him to do something with that colossal penis. Suck it, cut it, flay it, pickle it in chocolate syrup and make it into a meat eclair—anything, so long as he does it *dramatically*. But language barriers and terror keep the Swede from capitulation. Instead of putting on a show, he clumsily saws off a leg and scuttles off to the oven. Bad move there, Thor. Briefly, I contemplate volleying advice in his direction, but it's do-or-die here.

Literally.

I turn back to my own counter. I've got my own porn star neatly split into eight portions. There's barely any blood on the wood. Most of it's been drained into separate containers for later use in my sambal-laced black pudding and the rosewater popsicles I've got planned for dessert. The ghouls of Kuala Lumpur might be sophisticated by the standards of their species, but they're still bloodthirsty predators. No gore, no talk.

I cut the epidermis from the stomach with a scalpel, before carefully smearing the exposed muscle with salted egg yolk, mango extract, and a glazing of soy. Then I replace the skin, sew it together at the ends, drizzle the surface with caramel and put the amputated torso in the oven. If this was any other situation, I'd have marinated the meat for at least a day, but c'est la vie, as the Europeans say.

Or something.

The gong booms. Two hours. Behind me, I hear the Swede swear, hear a pan clatter onto the floor, and something *sizzle* through the air. Another yelp, louder, pain-whetted. Guan Yin help me, this isn't going to end well for our blond friend.

I peek quickly at the audience as I go for the peeler and the bone saw. Our spectators are gathered in concentric rings around the stage, identities concealed in the penumbra, craning forward like dogs on a leash. They've stopped talking entirely now, and it's *disconcerting*, I tell you. You never really notice the sound of breathing until it is gone.

Of course, I probably shouldn't be listening for it. I should be hacking— carefully—through this perfectly-shaped cranium. And maybe doing something with the scalp, even if the whole concept is ethically questionable.

What am I saying? *Everything* I'm doing is ethically questionable.

IT GOES BETTER than I expected.

Not only do I extract the brain intact, I am ameliorated of some of my lingering existential guilt. The porn star's gray matter is a road map of early-death risks: brain lesions, abscesses, even a tumor, no larger than a small child's tooth. He was going to go, anyway, right? Right.

The slurry of neural tissue goes into a pan with ghee and caramelized onions, turmeric and chilli and garlic paste. Almost instantly, the fat begins to crackle, and I watch it like a hawk, pulling the pan away the instant the meat begins to smoke. Too much time on the fire, and you get charcoal. Too little, and it's just an unappetizing mush. (Don't ask how I know these things. We all sacrifice something different for our careers.)

A quick glance at the clock informs me that I've about half an hour left, and I spend it injecting globs of lime-laced honey into chilled eyeballs before plating it carefully amid passion fruit foam and clots of lemon curd.

The minutes slip by.

"*Time.*"

I drop my utensils with a clatter of iron, jumping back a heartbeat before a lithe, black shape bumps against the back of my knees. The Swede does not and I hear a whine of pain, sharp, quickly cut down to ragged gasps. I glance sideways: someone's split his palm open and blood is pooling on the stage. I lick my lips nervously. Not good.

The spotlight comes back on, the phosphorescent blaze drawing all eyes up to an alcove in the walls. Like everything else with the ghouls, the ornate balcony is strange, a bizarro arrangement of whatever might have interested the maker at the time: Parisian balustrades, Roman columns, a patchwork of Banksy paintings redone in polished sea glass.

There's a figure staked in the light, his silhouette haloed against a revisionist nightmare of the *Water Margin*, intimating a saintliness that I *know* is undeserved. If there's anyone in this spectacle of murderers that's a proper bastard, it's the Boss. He grins, all teeth, slicked-back hair and arrogant posture, the Armani-armed image of Malaysian patriarchy. He's power and he *know*s it.

"Two contestants walk in. One walks out."

A murmur of appreciative laughter slithers through the crowd.

"The winner will receive all he desires"—liar—"and the loser will regret his inadequacy."

The audience chuckles again. Terror batters against my temples. No matter how many times I've been conscripted into this horror show, it still gets to me. I think it's the theatrics, the aping of normalcy, the pantomime of reality talk show innocence. I wipe my fingertips along my gore-streaked apron and straighten my back, bladder clenched against the escalating dread.

"Our judges"—more polyps of light break against the murk, and three new faces become illuminated: blandly attractive, utterly forgettable—"will now sample the meals. The participants will be judged on taste, timeliness, versatility, and command of ingredients."

Another susurrus of noises, now with an undercurrent of savage. The Swede's eyes are glazed, his forehead slick with sweat, although in retrospect that could be blood loss rather than terror.

I walk my gaze over his flotilla of food: only seven dishes, not the prescribed nine. No desserts, either. Around the ledge of his shoulder, I spot his biggest error: he's amputated the penis but done nothing significant with it, leaving the organ to lay deflated in a puddle of congealing cranberry sauce. You'd think he'd be wise enough to make it the centerpiece.

Yeah, I can't see this ending well.

"Will the contestants bring their dishes forward?"

I WIN.

Of course I win.

I've never *not* won. We wouldn't be having a conversation if I'd ever lost. The terms of the tournament are simple if never advertised, a *de facto* knowledge secured through survival.

The winner acquires employment. The loser gets served on a plate.

*   *   *

THERE'S PLENTY THAT I dislike about Chee Seng. His haircut, his voice, his indifferent hygiene, his penchant for public earwax excavations. But I can't fault his professional technique.

Chee Seng is fast and very, *very* discreet. The Swede barely notices his exsanguination. He surrenders the barest expulsion of air, almost a sigh but infinitely more ephemeral, before he sags onto his knees, Chee Seng's arm suddenly crossed over his breastbone. And then carefully, with more strength than you'd anticipate from a chubby Chinese man in a wife-beater, he guides the giant down. Blood tendrils across the stage, an abattoir masterpiece.

The Scandinavian spasms—once, twice—before he begins to thrash, bellowing like a cow, but no matter how hard he struggles, his bulk stays pinned under an expertly positioned knee. Chee Seng drones scriptures with a practiced flippancy; the ghouls demand halal treatment of their meats, even if their preferred cuisine itself is sacrilegious in every Abrahamic faith. I make eye contact with Chee Seng, who shrugs. The air colors with the stink of urine. The crowd roars.

Eventually his quarry's convulsions subside, muscles slackening. The odour of piss picks up a fecal undertone, and I grimace. Hopefully, they'll have Chee Seng prepare the carcass as well, an ordeal that he tolerates but I flat-out loathe.

As the last of the Swede's life bubbles away, Chee Seng and I raise our gazes, like Dobermans trained to a nod. His smile is patronizing, calculated. I tense.

"Thank you for the assistance, Chee Seng."

Motherfucking chee bye chui.

"Rupert." And here, the Boss's grin *spreads*. The seams at the corners of his lips undo, widening, revealing jaws that span his head. "If you'd like to do the follow up..."

No. No, I don't. "Y-yes, boss. But Chee Seng's way better than—"

"We prefer the *personal* touch of a chef." His voice is an oratory wet dream, the baritone of a radio announcer or a successful politician, and it booms across the auditorium without enhancement. Despite the honeyed enunciation, the subtext is clear: there's no room for negotiation here.

"Of course, boss." Asshole.

He maintains his grin. Ghouls aren't telepathic, but I'm putting no effort into disguising my revulsion. The boss loves dissatisfaction in his employees, though, especially since he knows mutiny is an empirical impossibility. So, for now, we're cohabiting a page.

Irradiated by halogen, the last breathing human in an ocean of the dead, I grab the tools of office—bone saw, cleaver, a toolbelt of kitchen knives in different sizes—and march towards the fallen behemoth. If anyone ever tells you that the life of a cannibal chef is glamorous, punch them in the scrotum for me.

FIFTEEN

BEACH CLUB IS as cavernous as memory supplies, an altar to ringgit-driven debauchery and piss-poor, pricy alcohol, the first ill-advised port of call for gullible sex tourists. I push between two rotund Australians, their skinny legs sunburnt and bowed under monumental bellies, then duck from under the arm of a malignantly smiling drunk, phenotype largely unidentifiable. A pair of gorgeous women, palm-sized skirts tasselled and moderately see-through, blink impassively from under heavy, artificial lashes.

The thing about Beach Club, really, is that it's stratas upon interlocking stratas of accidental subversion. On the surface, it's a place to mingle and drink, a venue for predator and prey and play, ostensibly indistinguishable from any other club. Here, flabby Caucasians court SPGs aka Sarong Party Girls aka 'women who allegedly covet white dick,' a misnomer in many instances because at least half are escorts, prowling for an easy mark. Not that the men ever seem to realize, pickled in their own ethnic supremacy, blithely sure that Asian damsels are obsessed with melanin-free meat.

(Some of that is true, but I'd advise you against judgment. There's a kink for everyone, big and small, strange or stranger.)

Peel through the obvious and, like an onion, you'll find even more layers, maybe even realize that some of the women aren't just out for cash or the prospect of foreign nookie, they're gunning to secure lucrative pre-nups, international visas, a comfortable lifestyle for the next three generations. (Don't let the media fool you, ang moh. An absent education often only exacerbates a fierce intelligence, and lipstick's the woad of the modern Amazon.)

But I'm not here for those ladies, no. Mixed within their esteemed ranks is a smaller, more secretive demographic, no less potent but more tangibly dangerous. For reasons I haven't quite figured out yet, Beach Club is a haunt (get it?) for the country's most well-to-do penanggalans: an entirely matriarchal and very progressive line of vampires who are most famous for their ability to detach their own heads, spines, and digestive tracts.

They're also *violently* territorial, which is partially why I'm visiting to discuss matters with Beach Club's latest manager.

"Ah Siong!" I bellow as I hurdle a conga line, slide between extraordinarily bad dancers, and park myself at the bar. It's crowded here. Only nine pm, and the counter is already an elbow room exclusive. A massive Scandinavian, blonde and bearded, his arms wreathed with eager women, steps on my foot, and I bite back a snarl as I tilt a scowl upwards. My stomach flip-flops. It could just be that I have no facility with Caucasian features, but there's something of the chef from today in his mien. Vomit sours my tastebuds.

But I don't move away, reciprocating his aggression, wedging my shoulder between his ribs. Too drunk to take offense, he reels off a line about small men and bigger people and staggers away. By the time I look back to the bar, Ah Siong's right there, ugly mug made uglier by the strobing neon lights.

He beams at me. "Rupert, how you doing? You want whiskey? I can get you whiskey—"

"I'm not—" I slouch onto a stool.

"Tequila!" He announces, incandescent with inspiration, plucking a bottle from a spectrum of colored glass. "I know how much you like tequila. Girls also like tequila, am I right? You drink. They drink—"

"Ah Siong, seriously—"

"You got heartache, is it? Miss Minah again? Tell you what. Vodka will fix it. I just import smores flavor from overseas. You try. I—"

"That's not—"

"No? What about—"

"Are you—"

"—going to make you a cocktail? Can also!" His unctuousness nearly propels me into another objection before the offer connects and I hesitate, an argument dangling from the tip of my tongue. Ah Siong might be a detestable louse, a tick on the unkempt coat of Jalan P. Ramlee, but he's very much the Wayne Rooney of cocktails. "What kind you want?"

"Paloma Hermosa?" I read about it once in a magazine, a concoction sandwiched between drinks that demand gold leaf and drinks that *need* garnishes of opium, if you know what I'm saying.

Ah Siong doesn't miss a beat. "Okay!"

I count out the seconds as the bar manager trots between booze and juice station, swilling together tequila, St. Germain Elderflower liqueur and fresh grapefruit, dousing it with lime and agave, before adding egg whites and finally crowning it with an unnaturally phosphorescent blue lotus.

"What's this?"

"Straight from Greece. Very fresh." His answering smile is a miasma of rotten enamel, gold teeth and missing gaps. "Got power, you know?"

"Yes? No? That doesn't answer my question! Seriously, man, we've got to—"

He glides the brew across the syrup-mottled bar, and I'm struck by the intensity of the fumes, and a sly whiff of something even more insidious. "Nymphea caerula are *contraband*."

"Not if you got the right license," comes the response, coy.

"*Do* you have the right license?" I stare longingly at the drink nonetheless, already feeling it dismantling the stress of the afternoon. Realization hits: I'm tired. Bone-tired. Drooping-meat, saggy-knee exhausted, the kind that makes you sleep for forty-eight hours straight. I breathe and the lotus teases a sigh from my lungs, a grin from Ah Siong.

Bastard. He knew exactly what he was doing.

"Aiya, what you say la, Rupert. We're old friends, right? Old friends don't ask difficult questions."

Wincing, full of loathing for the decision, I nudge the glass away with a finger, my smile collapsing into a professional scowl. Around me, Beach Club heaves and writhes, the music switching from Soul Train to Skrillex. A German spills his beer on a tattooed Indian man and a fight attempts to break loose, only to be stymied by poor reflexes and worse balance.

"I wish I could," I begin, slow, letting menace leak in my words, or at least a dollop of measured direness. "But I'm here on official business."

"Fine." The greasy charm slides off Ah Siong's face as he sighs, relaxing into a subtly more intimidating posture. He signals an underling with the barest crook of a finger before swivelling back to slouch, elbows rudely propped up, at the bar top. "What you want, then?"

"To tell you that the penanggalans are not happy with you."

Eyebrows go up. "Unhappy? Why unhappy? I do everything they want. I give their boytoy special discounts. I got Sabtu Special. I even pay their protection fee. I am a hard-working businessman. What more do they want from me?"

"You really don't know?"

"No. Honestly, no. Cross my heart and hope to—"

"So, you're not giving the pontianaks a happy-hour discount if they promise to keep the floor clean and to buy at least one bottle of vodka per five-woman group?"

"—call my lawyer before you can make any more slanderous accusations."

It's hard not to be impressed. He slicks effortlessly from put-upon innocence to educated insolence, nose arched slightly higher than before, as though my words nauseate him.

I snarl. "You're fucking kidding."

We hold each other's stares, with all caution you'd use with a loaded gun. Neither of us speak, both of us all teeth and tension, both of us teetering on the brink of fight-or-flee. For Ah Siong's sake, I hope it's the former; if he makes me run after six cardio-free weeks, I will pummel him with his own leg.

He breaks first, slumping. "What do you want me to do la? You really going to take away my rice bowl? You really going to make me suffer? I'm just a man lah, Rupert. A man with children—"

"No, you're not."

"—from another mother. A man with responsibilities, a man with cats—"

"You're allergic."

"—dogs—"

"You hate dogs."

"—plants that needs to be water—"

"You killed the cactus we gave you last year!"

Ah Siong, fist held against his sternum, manages to look profoundly injured, mouth pinched tight. Clearly, he wants more time for melodramatics, but he's run my patience into the mud. I slap both palms on the counter and force out an amiable smile, even though my forehead is pleated like an accordion.

"Stop," I say and as I do, I feel the start of a migraine congregate behind my right eye socket. "Not another word. You know exactly the problem. You know what you have to do. And you know you're going to have to say 'yes,' because if you don't, we'll need to have worse words and I don't want to do that. You were Minah's friend. I—"

I lose the plot of my own soliloquy, trip over a tongue abruptly clumsy with pain. Invoking Minah's name was a mistake, a knife in the ribs I hadn't anticipated. Even now, it hurts to think about her. Six months ago I sold the world to buy her a one-time pass straight to the wheel of reincarnation, and right out of my life forever.

I haven't stopped missing her. I'm still listening to her voicemails, still listening to her reminders to eat, sleep, and cultivate a healthy existence.

"—help me out, okay? Follow the rules. The penanggalan don't *care* about competition; the competition just need to be policed."

Maybe, it's the look on my face, maybe, it's mention of the finally departed, but something empties Ah Siong of his chatter. His expression loses its frantic gleam and he palms a hand over the back of his neck, sheepish. "Okay. I see how."

"No. No 'see how,' Siong. You know how this is done. You got to sign it in blood."

A sigh wheezes out of him. "Okay lah, okay lah."

Blood. Everything starts and ends with blood. Ah Siong rolls up a sleeve and extends his forearm, a faint disdain marking his features, his eyes narrowed against the oncoming ceremony. There was a point in my life where I'd have hesitated, thought twice about doing what I'm about to do next, but those are ten years gone, dead and buried under a decade of bureaucracy-led bloodshed.

I don't waste time. I extract a pocket knife, split an artery on Ah Siong's arm. Blood wells inhumanly black. A customer, rotund and badly stuffed into a gaudy Hawaiian shirt, gasps and mumbles something loudly about gay men and their predilections. I roll my eyes and count the gaps between Ah Siong's heartbeats, tying the rhythm to a simple spell of binding. The enchantment is standard-issue, nothing fancy, an agreement to play by the rules or risk having his license revoked.

(What, ang moh? Did you think our Hells are as gratuitously vicious as yours?)

A second slips by. Two. Six. When I'm done, I blot the wound, swab it with iodine, and delicately tape a bit of cotton in place. Years in this job teaches you a few tricks, including basic first-aid. "There. Kau tim. See? Not so bad."

My patois buys me a judgmental stare. Ah Siong huffs like a winded horse, breath shaking in his chest, the noise interlaced with small profanities. I ignore them. I'm done here. I have, at the very least, delayed interspecies warfare, a key function of my underpaid station. As I move to stand, a hand, large and impassively strong, shoves me back down.

A hasty glance reveals an unfortunate development.

"Horse-face!" I shout. "Ox-head! Buddies! How *are* you doing?"

Two monolithic figures, human skins practically smoking from contact with hellion flesh, glower silently. Ox-head is the more attractive of the two, with a linebacker's silhouette draped in vaguely fashion-conscious attire. Horse-face, on the other hand, can barely give a fuck. He grins, and the epidermis pulls back against distinctively equine bones, warping the shadows of his borrowed countenance into a glue merchant's worst nightmare.

"Ao Qin is on trial." Ox-head has a voice like the last call on your last night in the last bar on earth: a notice of execution, sonorous and grim.

This won't end well.

"That's unfortunate," I reply, groping behind me for the cocktail that Ah Siong had tried to bribe me with. Unsurprisingly, my fingers only find empty space. "What did he do?"

"Treason," says Horse-face and *his* voice bubbles like the fat of his tongue is being deep-fried. There's a kind of *pleasure* in his proclamation, drawn out into a hiss where appropriate, that makes my skin recoil from its fat.

"I see." This definitely won't end well. In hindsight, I really, *really* wish I had accepted that bribe. "Um, I'll send him a gift card, I guess. A hamper? They don't really do extravagant Hell offerings in the store this season, but I'm certain—"

"He's *named* you in the trial," one of them says. I don't register which because, frankly, it doesn't matter.

My blood congeals into ice. "Oh."

A smile flutters at my mouth, the corners twitching, but it doesn't take hold. There's no further explanation, and none is needed. All three of us know what's coming next. Sulphur coats my tongue as the two move closer, the air growing molten, every motion executed in absent lockstep, their physiques eclipsing the writhing mass of inebriated humanity. I don't try to escape. You don't escape the guardians of Diyu.

You could try, I suppose, but it'd likely end in *dismem*-barassment.

I manage to suck a breath between my teeth before the dagger punches between my ribs. It's a testament to Ox-head's skill that I feel nothing, at first, only the tiniest filament of pain, red-streaked as it tendrils between failing neurons and misfiring electrical impulses.

A gasp slides loose, an involuntary error that jolts my lungs into agony. The taste of copper bubbles from the back of my throat, vomit-stained, astringent. Balance dissolves. Muscles grow jellied, impotent, and before I know it, I'm oozing off my stool. My last thought before consciousness fades is this:

I hope I get back here before I shit myself.

SIXTEEN

THE CHINESE HELL isn't such a bad place if you're just visiting.

Unpleasantly warm, sure. Cacophonous, definitely. But the denizens are cultured, fastidious about personal hygiene, and too practical for blanket judgments. If you can get over the idea that the *entire* dimension pivots on an industry of deserved torture, Diyu, while hardly a top vacation spot, is rather like a more sanitary Kuala Lumpur.

That's once you *get* there. The path in, at least the one I've been consigned to, is outright agony. Boiling air whistles between my bones as I plummet through dimensions, cooking viscera that won't cease regenerating, heat scorching the shrieks from my lungs, the thoughts from my synapses. For an endless interval, I'm anguish incarnate, and then I am not.

Colors adjust. The phantasmagoric blur resolves into extravagant architecture, archaic in a way that feels entirely purposeful, gabled roofs and an abundance of dragons, some of which are very much alive, lidded eyes burning like embers against sandalwood columns. What isn't inspired by ancient China is very much neo-futuristic: endless glass, endless steel, intimidatingly cold and monochromatic against the infernal landscape.

(Fun fact: *The Matrix* was a hit down here. Don't ask me why.)

I hack a bloody wad of phlegm, spit it out on the pavement. Beside me, Ox-head and Horse-face loom, colossal in their natural guise. The former's got his human self on the flat of a palm, neatly folded, the creases smoothed out. Horse-face, on the other hand, didn't bother changing. Translucent ribbons of skin trail from the slats of his armor. There's bits of brain and bone snarled in his mane, a loop of intestine tangled around the pommel of a sword bigger than I'm tall, some sinews in his sleeves.

Good old Horse-face. You can always trust him to be a traumatic influence.

"Aaah," he says with a gusty sigh. "*Much* better."

I probe my mouth with my tongue and find a loose tooth, which I extract with a quizzical frown. The morphogenetic properties of the human soul remain a mystery to me. Technically, I'm just a soul here, but that hasn't ever stopped my discorporeal form from being hurt. Of course, that's not always the case. Sometimes, I get through being boiled alive without a scratch. This time? I lose a tooth. Go figure.

"Hate to seem like a country idiot, but where's the party?" I scan the desolation, frowning, the hairs on the back of my arms prickling. Diyu loves its parties, you see. Loves them. They'll use any excuse to throw a festival. Marriages, divine birth, civil uprisings, executions. *Anything.*

But right now? There's nothing.

"Everyone is inside," supplies Ox-head, already lumbering forward. "Ao Qin's trial is a thing of gravity."

"So's a mass beheading, but that didn't stop anyone from borrowing Freddie Mercury—"

Horse-face whickers into the side of my head, his breath a fetid marriage of rotting meat and moldering hay, the worst of all worlds. I gag. It takes me about a minute to realize he's laughing at me. "The little one is afraid."

Damn straight. But I'd rather cut off my own balls than let him know that. "You're conflating curiosity with fear, man. I just wanted to know if I could get a beer. Not sure if *you* register it, being foaled and raised in these brimstone pastures, but it's *hot* here. Can't blame a guy—"

"Walk."

"Okay."

We march silently into the gargantuan structure, three abreast, footsteps completely silent. Even when we traverse a long corridor of glass, which arches over concentric tiers of suffering, each a different climate from the last. I don't look down. Eventually, the glass transitions to volcanic rock, blackened in the kiln of the metaphorical earth itself, and the ceiling itself begins to rise. Higher, higher, until there is nothing but darkness uninterrupted. But my concerns don't belong there.

A low chatter snags my attention, sweeps it through an auditorium recently rebuilt in the style of Grecian coliseums. I scan the crowd as Horse-face and Ox-head march me towards the witness stands. *Everyone's* in attendance. Every Buddha ever put to paper, every bureaucrat ever consecrated as a saint, every yaoguai ever disemboweled on the altar of misplaced blame. Even Guan Yin is present, colossal and impossibly effulgent, her expression veiled beneath white silk. The Yellow Emperor's absent, of course, but I hear he doesn't get out of bed for anything but a gastronomical miracle, like a style of *xiao long bao* he hasn't tasted before (i.e. never).

I flash a cloud-maiden a grin as we pass, and she crinkles her nose, eyes rolling back to the two-tailed cat beside her. It laughs at me, mouth razored, muzzle practically human. A phoenix empties its bowels on a nearby balustrade, eliciting an outraged scream from a retinue of kitchen gods. Business as usual.

No one else takes notice. And besides, the crowd has eyes for one thing and one thing only:

Ao Qin.

The Dragon King stands speared in a column of orange light, fully bipedal, questionably human, hands loosely folded behind his back. For someone accused of high treason, he appears remarkably composed, a half-smile balanced on the line of his jaw.

I keep my mouth shut as I'm wedged into the witness box. A magistrate strolls into the middle of the floor, unbottling and unrolling a vast scroll. As the parchment ribbons across the white sand, the official begins reciting a litany of names, none of which I recognize. The droning persists and I'm just about to beg for recess, when he says *my* name.

Uh oh.

"*You.*" Ao Qin hisses, head whipping in my direction. Frills balloon through the flesh of his cheeks and his throat, tearing it apart even as his body spasms and shakes, mammalian anatomy bending under the momentum of divine rage. He snarls, mouth distending too far, skin peeling to reveal oversized teeth, the bone straining as though it might launch itself from its imperfect meat. "You."

I raise Ao Qin the Vulcan salute. "Yo."

He screams then. And it is a hurricane gale, a tsunami, a psychic blow so potent that it should have atomized my very essence. But I only feel the damp echoes of the assault, a whiff of salt and death. Ao Qin's lamplight stare widens.

"Do that again and we will hold you in contempt of the court, Ao Qin." A new voice. We both turn to its source: a man in the bright robes of a magistrate, unremarkable save for the pitch-black skin and the red tongue lolling from between his lips. Despite the magnitude of the organ, he doesn't lisp.

"Fan Wujiu, you would take his side over ours? He is vermin. He is mortal. He is dirt. He is nothing. He is—"

"—not the one on trial," Fan Wujiu interrupts, tone bland. "Rupert Wong attends this court as a witness, not as traitor."

The word is a gunshot. It culls all conversation, leaves the auditorium haunted by a terrible silence. Ao Qin glares at Fan Wujiu, chest already split open, reptilian breast heaving within a frame of broken ribs. A noise warbles in Ao Qin's throat, wordless but unmistakable, a vow of violence. If the Dragon King lives, there will be a reckoning.

"All rise for the venerable Yan Luo." Another voice this time, similar in tenor but lower in pitch: Xie Bi'an, Fan Wujiu's bone-colored counterpart.

A different silence. Reverent. Everyone who is not already standing clambers onto their feet, and we bow in perfect synchronicity, a ripple of motion to follow the ingress of the massive figure. The King of Hell has arrived.

"Sit," he says, ascending to the bench, and the court complies. "Begin."

*　　*　　*

THE NEXT FEW hours writhe together, bizarre ritual and labyrinthian legal processes, a thousand rites plucked from a hundred cultures, a hundred dynasties. The charges filed against Ao Qin are horrific: perfidy, intent to incite, murder of foreign dignitaries, and more. I throw up when Xie Bi'ian gluts my vision with panoramas of the Erinyes' death. Ao Qin is unmistakably a proponent of the old adage: an eye for an eye, a hideously disemboweled torso for a hideously disemboweled torso.

Every now and then, I'm poked and prodded, sometimes figuratively, sometimes literally. They make me repeat my testimony so many times that the meaning of the words corrode, leaving only a stammer of syllables. But it's nothing compared to Ao Qin's torture.

There's a downside to immortality, one that polite company rarely discusses. What you can't kill, you can infinitely hurt. So, they burn him. Over and over. They cook him to the marrow and then pull apart the charred skeleton like a wishbone in a Hollywood Thanksgiving dinner, before waiting until he has reassembled and doing it all again. Through it all, Ao Qin keeps to his story, keeps to his conviction that I'm the patsy responsible for interpantheon war.

"Ask him," He croaks, eyeballs roasted to a cloudy white. Smoke drools between his teeth. His cheeks are yarn, tangles of scorched tissue haphazardly threaded between slack jaws. "Ask-k-k-k-k him."

"Rupert," Yan Luo studies me, gray and sad, like a forgotten geriatric. "What do you have to say?"

"I don't know what he's talking about, Your Majesty."

"*Liar—*" Ao Qin's accusation crests into a screech as the flames roar up again, liquefying what little fat and sinew remain. The air sweetens with the smell of crisping bacon, then becomes choking with ash.

Minah. I roll her name in my head, clasp it near.

IN THE END, Ao Qin submits.

In the end, he confesses.

Because, dragon or monkey, that's what you do when someone won't stop roasting you alive.

I know what you're thinking, ang moh. And you're right. I should have said something, should have halved his punishment by admitting my involvement. That would have been the honorable thing to do. But here's the rub: damned men don't get tax breaks.

Besides, the asshole did cost me my deposit.

"RUPERT."

I raise my head at Yan Luo's voice, and turn to find the King of Hell looming behind me, no longer sixty feet tall but a more reserved seven-feet-eight. He looks more human now too, his official raiments supplanted by cotton robes and threadbare slippers. A doughy gut rests comfortably along his middle, complementing a bulbous nose and pleasantly round cheeks, creating an utterly unthreatening silhouette. "Yes, Your Majesty?"

"We need to talk."

I try a smile, teeth and battered bravado. "Nothing good ever comes out of anyone saying—"

"No more jokes, Rupert." Yan Luo arranges himself into one of the pews, expression mild. "We have to talk about your future."

Fear creeps into the curve of my spine. "Your Majesty."

"There is no easy way of saying this. Heaven thinks you're a traitor. At least half of the pantheon has petitioned to send you to the Greeks along with Ao Qin. Or worse."

I swallow. "I had nothing to do with this."

Yan Luo laughs, the sound reverberating through the auditorium, now hollowed of gods and hanger-ons. "You've always been a brave one, haven't you? Do you remember when you called on us?"

A wincing smear of memories. Those were not happy days. "Yes, Your Majesty."

"You were so adamant about employment. You kept calling and calling, wheedling and scheming. You had an answer to everything and you wouldn't *shut up*. Most people would have begged for their lives."

"I knew better than to ask." I hold my place, uncertain if I should sit or bow or grovel.

The King of Hell flashes an easy grin, removing a flask from his shirt. He uncorks it, and the scent of plum wine uncoils like an old lie told so many times, it's become truth. "You did. And I trust you know better than to keep pretenses around me."

"Your Majesty."

"Was she worth it, Rupert?" Here, a flicker of sorrow over his voice, the first indication of real emotion. "That girl of yours? She was a monster."

"I don't know what you're talking about—"

The ghost of something not unlike a smile, as Yan Luo drains a long mouthful from the bottle. "Oh, please, Rupert. I can see inside your head. Any god who has seen a few millennia can see inside your head. The only reason you weren't dragged onto the floor is because you weren't the one on trial and because— well, because I didn't allow it. But you haven't answered me yet. Was she worth it, Rupert? That Minah of yours."

Yes. The word throbs in my head before I can strangle it. *Yes. A thousand fucking times.* Yan Luo's smile broadens, his expression bordering on paternal. He chuckles and then eases into silence. The King of Hell sips his wine again and frowns. "The choices she made in life. Those were hers, you understand? The murders, her... expulsion from the cycle. None of it was forced onto her. She made those decisions. She made herself what she is."

I say nothing.

"And yet, you would sacrifice a *king* for her."

"Your Majesty—"

"This might be difficult to believe, but I regard you as a friend, Rupert." Yan Luo massages circles into the bridge of his nose, pinching the wrinkled skin. "Not just an employee. A *friend*. I've always appreciated your irreverence, your ingenuity, your willingness to play Xiangqi even though I know you loathe the game."

"I keep telling you. A PlayStation 4 will change your world. I—"

"So, I hope you understand that I'm speaking as a friend when I say: you need to leave Kuala Lumpur."

"I—" The words knot in my throat. "Your Majesty? I—go where?"

"Anywhere. You're a wanted man, Rupert. Get out of here before you become a dead one."

SEVENTEEN

"This isn't Beach Club."

The Boss wedges a sliver of bone between his teeth, begins picking at a thread of pink meat. "No."

I sit up. "This isn't a dumpster either."

"No. No, it's not."

"Or my apartment."

"If that's what you call that wasteland." The Boss flicks his toothpick aside and steeples his fingers, leans forward in his chair to stare. Just. *Stare.* His spouses trade amused looks; a husband reaches across the table to daub at his counterpart's blood-stained countenance. "And no, it isn't."

I knuckle at an eye, taking the interlude to examine my surroundings. Definitely not home. Definitely not in a safe place. And I have definitely—I glance down—had my personal space compromised. My original getup is gone. Instead, I'm dressed like one of the Boss's help: black tie, black loafers, black pants, and a black shirt, of course. Black goes with everything, especially blood stains. I swing my feet from the table and hop onto the ground, fight the urge to pop my collar, a last-ditch fumble for personal identity.

"Nice threads."

The Boss tips his head.

"So, to what do I owe the honor, boss?" I keep my gaze from the table, keep it fixed on my employer's face, even as one of his wives spools a strip of muscle around a fork, unwinding it from the thing trussed up between them. It—I don't check what it is, I'm too exhausted for it—thrashes in place and screams into its gag, a long, ragged gurgle, full of blind, animal desperation; leg kicking, the gnawed remnants of a foot scrabbling against expensive wood. I ignore it. Not my problem, not my place.

"We heard there was a complication."

"I didn't mention any of you, if that's what you're asking." My response is immediate, guarded.

"Yes." He beams. "We know."

Crack. Their dinner screeches again.

I cough into a fist and take a meaningful step backwards, hear the slither of silk against steel. I don't look; there's no need. My imagination populates the gaps with demurely garbed valkyries, vacant-eyed, unsmiling, bodies and lives committed to the fulfilment of their master's impulses. "Glad everyone's on the same page, then. And since we all know that there was no foul and no harm, I'm going to—"

"I never said you could leave, Rupert." The Boss removes his bib, an ostentatious flurry of white ruffles branded with a bright red lobster, and stands. Even without stage lighting, the man's an impressive specimen: Olympian silhouette, custom-tailored Desmond Merrion in the most expensive shade of too-damn-much, a patina of make-up so expertly applied that you'd almost believe it's his own skin. "We need to talk."

"I've been hearing that a lot lately." I don't quite keep the whine from my words but I have an excuse, damn it.

There's something fundamentally uncomfortable about watching a ghoul walk towards you. Call it a lizard brain thing, if you want. It probably relates. The ghouls *wrench* at their limbs, dragging them on axes too wide by half, joints twisting and *crunching* through a boneless imitation of human locomotion, infinitely sleeker, exponentially more unsettling.

The Boss stops about three inches away, a distance best described as 'unnecessarily personal.' I can smell the carrion on him, a dull stink of rot and metal. He grins. I wish they'd all stop *grinning* so much. "Do you have a passport, Rupert?"

"What? I mean, yes. Yes, I do. But also, what?"

Crack. Then: *crack* again, but a flimsier sound the second time around, like eggshells being splintered, or a skull being opened.

"Excellent. Go home and pack up. You'll be going to London."

"What?"

His eyebrows rise. Behind him, a team of Amazonian blondes scurry to replace the carcass on the table, swapping the mangled detritus for a fresh entrée. I hear a whisper of silverware, before the muffled wailing renews. Female, this time. Healthy. Marathon runner, judging from that lung capacity.

"You're going to London."

"I heard that part."

"And?"

I press my tongue against the roof of my mouth. "And I—well, I guess I'd like to know why exactly I'm going to London?"

The Boss rolls his eyes to the ceiling, where a blasphemous fresco of the Prophet straddles the dining space, lovingly uplit in gold. "*Rupert.* I'm disappointed. What happened to the snivelling yes-man that wouldn't think twice about putting a foot through a man's throat? What happened to your people-pleasing skills? Because I'm. Not. Pleased. With this. Oh, no. What happened to your understanding of our roles in this existence? Mine is to command. Yours is to roll over and *beg*."

The Boss is fast. Faster than I remember, faster than human reflex can accommodate. He rams me into a wall, hand around my windpipe, elevates me so that my feet dangle over the floor. And *squeeeezes*. I twitch, impotent, every breath now a choking wheeze, saliva singeing tear ducts. "Boss."

"Meat," He spits. "You're *meat*. Do not ever forget what you are. *Meat*. Food for the worms, food for the ghouls. Walking, talking, shitting *food*. And food, Rupert—food doesn't talk back to its betters. Do you understand that? Do you *get* where I'm coming from?"

"Yes, boss," I burble.

"If I tell you to jump, you ask how high; if I tell you to eat dog shit, you ask me for cutlery. If I tell you to gut yourself, you ask if I'd like to have your intestines braised, broiled or beer-battered and airfried—"

"But it's *really* hard to cook when you're disemboweled, boss."

Unexpectedly, the boss laughs, airy and pleasant, a businessman on a cruise. He releases his grip and I plummet onto the ground, hacking convulsively, the air scraping my throat like the flat of a knife. I stroke fingers across my neck: the flesh is puffy, raw to the touch. Yeah, that will *definitely* bruise in the morning.

"Oh, that wit of yours, Rupert. I'd miss it if it were gone. Don't ever lose it. We'd have to eat you otherwise."

"I don't doubt it, boss," I rasp.

The Boss crouches down, his long limbs uncannily arthropodal, surreal. "But to answer your *previous* question, we're loaning you to the Greeks. They've recently lost their cook and are dying to have some decent cuisine."

"Wait, wait—"

"Quiet, Rupert. Before I make you eat your tongue."

I clamp my mouth shut.

"It'll be fun, I'm sure. Brisk English air. Terrible people, terrible traffic. Terrible fish and chips. An entire history of imperialist arrogance built into shit-colored walls and pretentious accents. You'll absolutely love it." The Boss unfolds, smoothing a crease in his shirt as he glides away, circling the rim of the banquet table to trace long fingers around his spouses' silent, adoring visages, before finally reseating himself at the head of the charnel spectacle.

"Boss. You know I live for your enjoyment, but—but this is going to get me killed," I blurt, staggering back onto my feet, without any consideration for the magnitude of my objection. "The Greeks have to know what we've done. And if they don't, I'm—"

"What did we just discuss, *meat*?"

"Just tell me why. I'm practically on the way to the airport already. Context. That's all I'm asking from you."

The ghoul, older than his lineless countenance claims, cocks a playful smirk; a husband carves him a chunk of muscle from their dinner's well-defined thigh. The nub of a tongue protrudes from the boss's mouth, a sign of rumination; for a second, I'm optimistic.

"No."

"Yes, boss."

DESPITE THE URGENCY of his command, the Boss keeps me in the manor until well after midnight, entertaining a cadre of drunken penanggalans. It could be worse, to be fair. The kitchens that are my fiefdom have actual ventilation, albeit only in select sections (notably those unoccupied by squirming, sniffling *ingredients*). And the penanggalans rarely demand anything more strenuous than a Bloody Mary.

I make them finger foods, anyway. Not actual fingers—that'd be crass—but stacks of black pudding, accompanied by a fan of wafers, processed bone meal fried to a crisp; miniature char siew baus; nang kai tort, complete with edible bottles of homemade sriracha, sugar-glass glimmering copper in the dim. The penanggalans shrill over my offerings, gobbling hors d'oeuvres in between outbursts of gossip, intestines flailing wetly in the crepuscular light of the living room.

"*Aiya*, if you ask me, Muhammad has no idea what he's getting into. America's such a dangerous place, these days. Why lah they want to go there?" chirps one of the decapitated heads, finally exhausted of kittenish energy, hair and entrails delicately arranged along velvet bedding.

"Because very fashionable mah. Los Angeles, New York. All the big movie stars suka, you know. Some more, they say you can meet the new gods there!" replies a more matronly monstrosity. Her tresses have been clipped into a loose bun, skewered in place with enamelled chopsticks.

"Got meh? Like who ah?"

"Aiya, I don't know. Like someone they call Big Money."

A crooning chorus of admiring voices, blending into a single word.

"Seriously?"

The matron glances at me and juts her nose at the platter in my grip, intoning in a strained accent she probably thought of as 'posh.' "Do you have any more of those little cracker things?"

"Er." I set the tray down, allowing the penanggalans to squelch closer, like birds descending on breadcrumbs. "The wafers?"

They assault the tray by way of answer, ropes of viscera pulsating, gleaming pink-gray. I retreat to the kitchen, double-doors opening with a plume of spiced air. Heat undulates against my skin, humid, comforting. But not untenanted. A male figure stands drooped over a pot of broth—tomorrow's tonkotsu, brewed with genuine-article *sarariman*.

"Fariz! Dude! What you doing here?"

He peers up and beams, squirrelly cheeks emphasised by his wide smile, eyes vanishing into a cloud of wrinkles. Physically, Fariz is nothing like the other ghouls, skin sallow instead of brown, accent revealing his private school breeding. Innocuous and cherubic, he wears his station lightly, his shirts looser, preferring geek-chic to six-hundred-dollar suits. Case in point: today's faded Ghibli T-shirt.

"I just wanted to see how the soup's coming along."

I veer closer, inspect the pot. A dessicated face, mostly bled of collagen, glares up. The soup itself looks fantastic: syrupy yellow, gelatinous, the steam silky with the promise of flavor. Absently, I scoop more Marmite into the seething cauldron; a dash of anchovies, another helping of shiitake extract. Almost perfect. If it wasn't against six kinds of humanitarian laws, I'd put the recipe online. I grab the lid and close off the view, before smiling desperately at Fariz. "It's going great. Better than I am, at any rate."

Truth be said, I actually like the ghoul. Ignoring the dietary predilections, the unfortunate need to develop shisha blends from flavored man-rind, Fariz could almost pass for normal.

He scratches at the back of his scalp, nails only fractionally too long. "I know! I know. I'm sorry. We weren't expecting the company. Uncle's extremely big on courtesy—"

A lie, but I take it. He always means well. "Yeah, it's fine. That isn't my problem. I—"

"I know." Fariz winces, retreating behind a rack of condiments, looking uncomfortable. "I know about the, uhm, London trip. It's sudden. But there's a point to it. It's to keep you safe."

"Are you serious?" I cross my arms. "That's what you're going with?"

"And Uncle, he—I—" Fariz deflates, palms fanned out. "Look, it's meant to be a test. Do well and we give you a get-out-of-jail-free card. Do superbly, and Uncle might even consider a raise, or a place on the family property. You know. *Stuff*."

"Stuff."

"Stuff," he repeats, hangdog, begging for a break.

I sigh, relenting, and sigh again when Fariz brightens. "You sure this isn't some kind of double-crossing whatever-you-want-to-call-it?"

Exhaustion has clearly minced my capacity for language.

"I'm sure." A beat. "Well, no. I'm not sure. But I'm sure Uncle likes your food, which counts for something. Cannibal chefs are in short supply." Another pause, longer, more thoughtful. Fariz shrugs, meek, stoop-shouldered. "You know how it is with him. He schemes. Something is always up, but it's not like he's going to spend that much money just to get you shot, right?"

"I know you say that to make me feel better, but somehow it's not working."

"Best I've got."

I consider needling him further, but there's no point. I dig two fingers into my shoulder blade and rotate the adjacent arm, wincing as muscles realign and ligaments click into place. "I thought the Greeks were in Vegas? The Olympus?"

He shrugs. "They're everywhere, but the big bosses are in London since, like, forever."

"Fair enough. Mamak?"

"I guess Man Utd is playing tonight."

"Liverpool's going to win."

"Hah. Sure. Let's go. I'll get the shisha."

EIGHTEEN

"WAH, THIRTY-SIX-HOUR FLIGHT ah?"

I examine my boarding passes—four in total: two printed on crumpled A4 sheets, two freshly minted and official—and flip them over in my hands a few times. "Yes? No? I'd like to buy a vowel?"

The flight attendant titters obligingly, hand over mouth. She's a cherubic, aggressively cheerful figure, with silvering hair worn in defiant Princess-Leia buns and a throat glittering with bronze necklaces. "Just saying. Most people will not fly such long distances for their first trip overseas."

A question dangles in her last remark: how could a thirty-nine-year-old man have avoided travel for so long? I ignore it, slot a tired smile into place and balance an elbow on the counter. "My boss is special."

I wink. She laughs, the sound richer, less restrained. "Cheap, you mean." A lidding of kohl-sharpened eyes, a hint of disdain. "I hate bosses like that. I *bet* you he's using air miles for your trip. That's why he's making you fly for such a long time."

Somewhere, between the dim clatter of four-a.m. thoughts and the hunger scratching at my belly, a light bulb coughs into life. "How long's a trip to London normally?"

The flight attendant glances slightly away and waggles a hand. "Twelve, fourteen hours? Depends on the weather."

Click. "Oh."

Professionalism yields to compassion and she stretches up to pat me on the arm, smiling kindly. For one hysterical moment, I consider telling her that I cook people for a living, just to see if she can keep acting the saint.

"It's fine," I declare at last, folding my travel documents into my pockets, the unhealthy impulse drowned. "Trust me, he's done worse."

Another laugh, marginally less unrestrained, fishing for an explanation. I pull away, muttering appreciation, hoping to escape before she gets it into her head to interrogate me further. When it comes to topics associated with the Boss, the phrase 'if I tell you, I'd have to kill you' is pretty much literal.

Kuala Lumpur International Airport swallows me in seconds. It's big, too big. Not labyrinthine, in the way some places are, but just unconscionably *vast*, acres of wasted space pockmarked by overpriced stores, gray tiling and dull steel, a shrine consecrated to the small man's need to compensate for small things.

Getting through customs is easier than I expected. The bored security officers don't waste time asking questions, barely glancing over my papers. Immigration is even faster: a quick two-step with a machine before I'm plunged into the departure hall. I glance at my cracked Seiko, minute hand wobbling dangerously. Two hours to go.

ONE SIXTEEN-RINGGIT *MEE goreng*—a too-salty plate of noodly styrofoam that almost made me storm the kitchen in protest—later, I'm at my gate, clutching my bag to my chest and self-conscious in the face of the stares. Ang mohs in crisp navy suits glance over occasionally, gazing critically at my knock-off Levis and no-name hoodie.

Or maybe the tattoos.

Probably the tattoos.

Hopefully not the tattoos.

I glance at my forearms. The flesh is brindled with scars and ink, veins crawling in between, still decently muscular even if the skin's already beginning to wear thin. Not that many ever notice, too riveted by the tattoos that line me from throat to toe. I inspect them carefully, every nightmarish polyp, every painted eye, every elongated limb, nails twining in double helixes, fingers crossed against every misfortune. Stillness, silence.

So far, so good.

I look up into the eyes of a tow-headed toddler, nauseatingly adorable and utterly fearless, mouth and eyes spherical with wonder. I flash the start of a smile, but his mother darts forward, ushering him away with a hiss of a warning.

"I wasn't going to give him candy, I promise!" I call to their retreating backs, slightly too loud. The kid turns, waves exuberantly, before his parent grips his arm and forces it down. *She* doesn't turn, but the rest of the passengers do, scowling and shaking their heads, contempt in their expressions.

With a shrug, I hunch into my chair and don earphones, play one of the podcasts that Minah had loved, a bizarre radio show about a town that doesn't exist. My eyes shutter and I stretch out like a lump of dough kneaded flat. Then time skips, and somehow consciousness is returning, dispensed in increments by an obnoxious *tap-tap-tap*ping on my shoulder.

"Sir?"

I dislodge an earphone, let it fall, Metallica blaring tinnily from the tiny bud. The world can stay on the other side of my eyelids just for a minute longer. "Yes?"

"I'm sorry, sir, but we are boarding." A quaver of stress.

I bolt up, startling the gangly flight attendant, and push the heel of a palm against my eyes. The world swims with halogen light, silhouettes and shapes muddling into a confused haze. Slowly, it resolves into milling bodies, clumped up between aisles, cattle being led to the roast, bags and children at ready. Up front, a plump woman shouts for all remaining passengers to board.

"Sorry. Early flight. First flight. You know how it is," I offer, gathering my luggage.

His quizzical stare says otherwise, but he holds his smile nonetheless, too well-trained to object. "I hope you enjoy your flight, sir."

"Me too, buddy. Me too."

You know what they say about the best laid *optimism* of mice and men?

Nothing.

But they should say something. Because my obstinate hope for a decent voyage is quickly annihilated. Hell isn't a place where horse-faced demons keep wardrobes of fraying human skin; Hell is twelve hours with no place to go. Hell is the endless drone of colossal engines. Hell is a middle seat in a row of four, with a single mother and her airsick son on one side, a screeching teenager on the other.

It really should have occurred to me that something was amiss when the flight attendants shook their heads and apologized for the full flight. No free seats, they said, in funereal tones. I shrugged. Of course, I shrugged. I had *no* idea what they meant. But now? Now, I do.

"Sorry," the mother says for the fifteenth time, dabbing at her progeny's lips. The boy beams queasily up at me. The paper bag in his grip sloshes.

"It's fine." I pull my elbows closer, knees throbbing from repeated collisions with the seat in front. "Everything's fine."

The teenager is the worse of two evils, I decide, patience slimming to nothing. I glance over to see him craning over the aisle, iPad brandished like a trophy, one leg jabbed into *my* square of space *again*. Briefly, I consider stomping his foot, partly because he's encroaching on my territory, but mostly because I don't like his attitude.

High school preppiness and I have never agreed. Not when I was a teenager, and certainly not now, especially when it comes served in an ugly cardigan. I study the kid. He's got the kind of jaw that didn't start out pretty, but has since been tweezed and pulled into some kind of acceptability, the skin rubbery and bright from the cosmetic surgeon's care. The perpetual scowl doesn't help, minor underbite adding a caveman quality to his petulance. Probably never had anyone tell him 'no' in his life.

A sigh escapes when his friends stampede from adjacent seats, pouring across the corridor to gawk at the tablet, its surface emblazoned with a close-up of tanned breasts. And all this would be okay, really, if he would *just move his fucking leg.*

"Hey, if you could—" I prod the adolescent's ankle with a toe.

He ignores me.

"Kid. Seriously." Another push, more empathic than the last. *"Kid."*

That gets his attention. He rotates and we make eye contact, and I balance a thank-you on the tip of my tongue, prepared to gush over the kindness of youth. But nothing follows, no sorry, no quip, no belligerent comeback. *Nothing.* Only a continued stare of increasing awkwardness. Twenty seconds later, with enough pageantry to incite a round of laughter among his cohorts, he looks very deliberately *away.*

Fuck it.

I put my foot down. Literally.

The teenager yelps like an injured Pomeranian, recoiling into a ball of limbs, knee pressed to his concave chest. "What the actual fuck, man?" he roars, pure upper-crust snobbery matching the crest hand-stitched onto his rumpled blazer.

"Sorry." I peer down at my feet, tone as mild as I can make it. "I didn't see *your* foot in *my* spot."

"What the fuck—" he repeats, as though I said nothing at all, spinning about to address his peers, jabbing a finger at me. "Did you see? Did you see what he *fockin'* did? I'm going to kick your arse. I'm going—"

Feigning deafness, I lace my fingers over my belly and gaze forward. Unreasonable behaviour is a tango for two.

"Did you *see?!* Did you—"

"Sir," a new voice interrupts, and we all look up as a stewardess sways down the aisle, the picture of concern. "Could we ask that you lower the volume? Other passengers are trying to sleep."

"He *fucking* stepped on my foot."

I shrug. "I'd been sleeping. How was I to know that he'd moved his foot there? I'm very sorry—"

"Sorry? *Sorry?* You did that on purpose." A gleam of teeth in the corner of my vision, the stink of whiskey adding character to the kid's halitosis. "You fucking did that on *purpose.*"

"Sir." The stewardess again, her billboard-ready smile slipping, just a fraction. Nine hours is enough to unravel anyone's facade, especially if it's been picked at, one stitch at a time, by people like us. "There are children on board. I don't think their parents would appreciate the use of foul language. And"—her voice drops, conspiratorial, even as she sinks to a crouch—"*I* don't think you should be using that kind of language either."

The boy opens his mouth but shuts it again when a friend—smaller, somehow blonder—squeezes his shoulder and shakes his head no. Grudgingly, he capitulates, mouthing an insincere apology before flopping back in his seat.

The stewardess flicks a glance at me. I nod, trying hard not to seem too gleeful, and don the airplane-issued headphones, pointedly cycling through a list of available media. Me? An accomplice to noise pollution? Perish the thought. I eventually settle on an inane sitcom about two first-world girls with too little problems and too many complaints, and stretch as far as it is socially acceptable, which is about two inches in each direction.

Peace at last.

Thump.

Maybe not.

I jolt up as the back of my seat is kicked again and peer into the divide between chairs. There's just enough space to see the culprit: another teenager, this one less-obviously Caucasian, gelled-back hair streaked with green. His smile is acid, knife-thin and eager. And to no one's surprise at all, he extends the one-fingered salute.

I sigh. Swivel. Stare at the kid beside me who is now sitting with knees spread, fingers steepled and head slightly cocked, a warlord on a winning streak, Kublai Khan gone melanin-free. His sneer broadens.

"Really."

Thump.

"Don't know what you're talking about."

"Yes, you do."

Thump.

"No, I don't."

Thump.

"Yes, you do."

Thump.

"No, I don't."

"Yes, you *do*."

"God"—he throws his hands up, sneer twisting into incredulous disgust—"what is *wrong* with you?"

"I'm very good at taking vicious pleasure in what few small triumphs I can enjoy?"

He gawks at me, silent, disbelieving. "You're a fucker."

"No, I'm just exhausted. Can we please just call it a day? I haven't slept in—I don't remember the last time I've slept. That's more a case of my life being what it is, rather than anything to do with this plane, but that's beside the issue." I flap a hand dismissively. "I'm tired. We're all tired. Can we please be tired together and fall asleep?"

"You a fag, then? You like being fucked in the—"

I lash a hand out and twist his arm, exposing the veins. "*Manners.*"

"What—"

"Sssh." It takes a single thought to sieve through the knot of somnambulant spirits and I rouse it with a reminder of overdue rent. (Don't look at me that way. We all sell a part of ourselves to make ends meet, ang moh: integrity or epidermal housing or access to an orifice, it's all the same.) The imp—a parasite worm, really, barely cognizant of ideas like punctual payment—squirms across my skin, exiting through a recent scar. At its first gasp of air, the newborn shrieks, acquiring depth and weight, sloughing off the flesh it fought so hard to borrow.

"The fuck—"

"Sssh," I repeat, rotating his arm further until I feel the joint resist. And then I push harder, leaning my weight into the movement. "You *don't* want to make a scene."

The worm is free now, carapace gleaming slickly in the dim cabin lights, and we both watch as it creeps up and onto the teenager's arm. Before he can voice another complaint, it burrows into his flesh, sliding between muscle fibers like a ghost.

"Sssh."

Every pretense of bravado vanishes, replaced by a high-pitched, hiccuping whine.

"Now. Now, here's how it's going to go," I murmur, as the worm investigates the breadth of his arm. Every now and then, the kid convulses in his seat, like he's been plugged into an instrument of capital punishment. "You're going to sit very, very quietly in this chair until the end of the flight. If you fuck this up, Bob Junior's going to eat his way into your brain and ride you like the cuddliest pony in a carnival. Do you get me?"

"Y-yes."

"Good."

I TAKE THE worm out when we land, of course.

Honestly, what kind of monster do you think I am?

NINETEEN

"Business or pleasure?"

"Um. Neither?"

The immigration officer—a sullen, toadish, disconcertingly *pink* creature with a nose that's more nostril than structured cartilage—glares. "Business or *pleasure*."

"Contractual obligation?"

"Mister"—he flips a page in my passport—"Wong, was it? I'm not sure if you understand, but you're treading on dangerous territory. If you insist on this absurdity, we may have to take action."

"Sorry. Wisecracking's a bit of a coping mechanism." I sweep a palm over my head and tack on a smile. "No harm, no foul, right?"

"Business. Or. *Pleasure*." Apparently no more chicanery is to be tolerated.

"Business. I guess?" Behind me, the crowd rumble its displeasure, a long shuffle of scuffed sneakers and rolling luggage, the miasma of unwashed bodies drifting overhead. "I don't actually know?"

That proved a worse answer than misplaced wordplay. Instantly, the man's body language shifts, transitioning from irritation to outright aggression. He bloats with self-importance, and raises a scowl. "You don't know."

"See, my boss asked me to—"

A snort cuts my excuses short. Blatantly disinterested in whatever I have to say, the man begins rifling through my scant papers again, attention shuttling between passport and landing card and back. Occasionally, he raises one or the other up to the light, as though the cold fluorescence might reveal an incriminating truth. He purses his lips, disapproval vibrating in his chest. *Hmmmm.* Flashbacks to Hao Wen, a sak yant master that had wanted to see me resting in pieces, clenches my ribs. "You didn't put in a length of stay either."

I can hear a threat gliding through the remark, a shark in the water. "Two weeks."

"Do you have a return ticket?"

"Um. No. But"—I jab at my supine passport, a desperate smile at the corner of my lips—"look there. It's a Malaysian passport. I get six months here, right?"

"And I get to tell people like you that such privilege is at the discretion of the government and if you don't comply with the rules, I can send you *home*." He waves his hand as he speaks, the movement steadily angrier and more emphatic. At the final word, he closes his fingers into a fist and bangs the counter.

"Okay."

My acquiescence, however deferential, seems to infuriate him. He splutters, half-formed obscenities melting together, every syllable tripping over the one that came before. It takes a moment, but he regains his composure, smoothing his expression into one of bland distaste. "Follow me."

A door in his glass-walled roost swings open, and the immigration officer waddles out, righteous importance in every heavy-footed step. I follow meekly, dragging my duffle across the floor by a handle. One of these days, I'll learn to keep my mouth shut.

"MR. WONG, I presume?"

I look up, parched of conversation, throat raw from six hours without a sip to drink. The voice is beautiful. Like holy-holy-angels-on-high *gorgeous*, a celestial tenor, the kind to bring entire auditoriums to their knees. I shiver.

"Master of Universes Wong, actually, but otherwise, yeah."

The new arrival framed in the doorway is lithe and self-assured, thin frame dwarfed by his colossal wheelchair. Dark curls spiral across a jaw honed sharp as an arrowhead, while blue, sunken eyes rest in otherwise Mediterranean features. He smiles, indulgent.

The youth glances down at the bulky creature that pushes up beside him and I tense immediately, reptilian brain shrieking. The dog is *massive*, a Rottweiler on steroids; broad angles, absolutely no poetry whatsoever, just power. This isn't a killing machine. This is the End Times with a stubby little tail. Muscles strain under short charcoal fur as the dog dips its breed-agnostic head beneath my rescuer's fingertips.

It luxuriates in the scratching, eyes rolling up, but only for a few seconds before it returns to duty, fixing me with its brimstone-golden glare. Growls. I feel my bladder seize.

"I was afraid you'd say that. I'd have hoped that our new chef would be able to keep himself out of trouble for at least a day." A beleaguered sigh, too theatrical to be entirely sincere, as he scratches between the hellhound's ears. "My name is Orpheus."

"I—" I clench a fist. The syllables gnaw like rats' teeth, but they're too small, too weak to eat through my fatigue. I *know* I know that name, but I can't map it to a reason. "Nice to meet you."

Orpheus smirked, eyes dancing. "And you."

He wheels himself out without another word. The dog follows, cocking a quizzical look at me before padding noiselessly away. A few minutes' meaningless waiting later, I get up and follow suit.

I FIND ORPHEUS and his hound holed up in a coffee shop outside of the arrival gates, the former delicately sipping a chemical orange drink, the latter huddled under the table. Orpheus glances up as I shamble closer, lips flexing into something like a smile.

"Drink?" The table is arrayed with six neon-colored beverages, each less appetizing than the last.

"Sure." I slump into a chair opposite, swiping one of the counterfeit slushies. Surprisingly, it doesn't taste as vile as it looks: ginger-orange syrup with an aftertaste of iced tap water. "So, I'm guessing you're the welcome committee."

"In a sense. We drew the short straw." A noisy slurp, and he leans forward. "You're not very good with Greek mythology, are you?"

Below us, the dog makes a whuffling snort, halfway to a human laugh.

"I wasn't a very good student." I shrug, trying not to seem too self-conscious, distracted by the clamor of Gatwick. It's more cramped here than I'd have expected. Not that I've been to many airports. Not for legal reasons, at least. But the contrast is difficult to ignore. Unlike KLIA, Gatwick feels like a pit stop rather than a destination; noisy and utilitarian. "People here look a bit... *pink*."

"It's the national color."

I can't tell if he's serious.

"*His* name's Cerberus, by the way." Orpheus wafts airily over the rim of the table. The dog thumps against the table as he scuttles onto his feet, head sliding into view, eyes still a reproachful brimstone-gold. "You *have* to know who Cerberus is."

"I just met—oooooh. *Oh*. Hm. Yeah. I know who he is. Hello, Cerberus. Please don't eat me." I lean away, fighting the urge to go into a fetal position. The dog laughs again and there's a look in his eyes that says one day, it'd eat me alive. "Why doesn't he have more heads, though?"

Orpheus clicks his tongue, a headmaster noise, sharp with disdain. "Because it would scare the normal people, wouldn't it?"

"Hrm. Yes. I suppose." I rub the back of my skull, pushing a fingertip into the top of my spine. "Sorry. It's the jetlag. It wasn't exactly the best flight. I—I should shut up. Quit while you're ahead and all that."

A glacial silence envelops our small table. Boy and dog glare, expressions somewhere between incredulity and indignity.

"Yes," Orpheus deadpans. "A *head*."

Energy glissades through the air, synesthetic, sea-salt and clean grass, a taste and a smell and a sensation. It's old magic, precise as an operatic solo. Reality peels back, and glamour recedes to reveal—

Oh.

Oh, that's awkward.

Orpheus is a literal *head* on the seat of his wheelchair, the stump of his throat putrid, purple-blotched. A tangle of nerves worm from beneath the flaps of his skin, knotting in the wheels, crawling over the armrests. I suspect that's how he moves around but I'm not going to ask because frankly, I think I've hit my daily foot-in-mouth quota.

As for Cerberus, the only thing I have to say about him is: *eep.*

"If I openly confess to being an idiot, would that help to make things less awkward?"

"Mr. Wong, has anyone told you that you talk entirely too much?"

"Funny you should say that."

"Shut. Up."

"Shutting up now."

The illusion reasserts itself and Orpheus levels another smile, taut and cold. "Are there subways in Malaysia?"

Flummoxed by the change of topic, I bob my head. "Yes?"

"Good," He scribbles onto a scrap of receipt, slides it across the table. "Here's the address. You can get there on your own."

TWENTY

As it turns out, elevators are serious business in the London underground. They're not mere conveniences, expected variables in the infrastructure, a service to the slothful. They're always there for a reason.

I wheeze up and down stairs, broken and dispirited, too many hours from the memory of sleep; ravenous, constipated, whittled to the bone, a husk of a man, no more human than the pipes and the tiles and the scream of the trains.

"Sorry. Do you mind not sitting on the stairs?" A portly woman taps me on the shoulder, moments after I crumple onto a step. I look up into her wide face, framed by corkscrew curls, think about my answer, and say:

"Yes. Yes, I mind a lot."

Disapproving glances follow me to the next station. I ignore them. There are bigger problems to deal with. Twice, I take the wrong line, find myself halfway to something called the Tobacco Docks, and then Kensington, before finally being turned around and pointed in the current direction. (You're wondering why my sense of direction is so terrible, ang moh, but I'm about to get there.)

'The dead' is a phrase that gets bantered around a lot and often, and the image that it evokes is one replete with diaphanous apparitions, poltergeists; things that go boo in the night. But the dead aren't always in high-definition. For the most part, London's deceased lack faces; a miasma of ambiguous silhouettes, drifting through commuters, forever drifting towards home, too old, too forgotten to hold onto any self.

Here and there, I catch glimpses of younger deaths: wide-open mouths, shocked eyes, jellied viscera trickling down crushed skeletons. I keep my head down, pretend ignorance as they whisper endlessly, repeating the histories of their demises.

Eventually, after a few false starts and a non-violent altercation with an incontinent corgi, I find Croydon, and step out into the omnipresent drizzle.

The borough proves a surprise: grittier, more *ethnic* than the rest of London's been, closer to Kuala Lumpur than the intersection in Canada Water, but at the same time, also much *shorter*. And colder, but that I expected. The absence of skyscrapers, however, has me completely perplexed. There's something bizarrely *scenic* about London, almost like they stole buildings from the Harry Potter movies and staggered office blocks in between, just for variety, a peculiarity that permeates even this part of town.

Filing away the observation, I pull my hoodie tighter about my shoulders, the chill pushing against my bones like a cat, and scan the road for an accommodating face. No one official; I've had enough of that for the time being. The businesspeople seem too harried, and the women too purposeful. A pair of men, slickly dressed in bargain-bin suits, the fabric worn and the ties slightly askew, look up at my confused approach. They smile like sharks, eyes black, dead. One lifts a handful of crumpled fliers with unnecessary enthusiasm, mouth straining even wider, and I babble an objection before scampering away. I throw a quick glance back as I hustle around a corner: they're still watching, mannequin-still, heads cocked at perfect right angles.

Mental note: avoid this part of town.

Serendipity distracts from all fevered contemplations of the strange encounter, however. My trajectory puts me into earshot of a gaggle of smoking teenagers loitering just outside of the station, twee uniforms balanced by a shared look of insouciance.

"Hi."

They stare.

"Do you know where"—I uncrumple the sweat-stained, balled-up wad of disintegrating paper and frown at the mosaic of ink—"Peregrine Yard Mews is?"

"He actually mewled!" A convulsion of giggling escapes an Asian girl to infect her peers, where it develops into a full-blown epidemic.

Damp, dog-tired, and filled with despair, I blink: "Excuse me?"

"Sorry. My mate 'ere's got a fing for cats and accents," one of the boys replies, gangly and brown-skinned, hair impressively circular. His body language suggests considerable standing in the adolescent social hierarchy. "Wot can I 'elp you with?"

"Yeah, um. I need to get to Peregrine Yard Mews?"

"Ooh. Rough neighbourhood, that one. I s'ppose you do look like you're from ends." He looks me over, before jutting his chin at an intersection. "It's not far. Walkable, if you're feeling up to it. Tram could get you ha'fway there, but it'd add ten minutes—actually, you got Citymapper? Signal?"

"I—"

"Oy, guys! What's the best route?"

Phones are brandished in unison, battered clamshells and sequin-sheathed iPhones, a Samsung cozied into the spine of a Totoro, and suddenly, everyone's frantically thumbing through their devices. No one's invited me under their overhang yet, but I suppose that might be asking too much. Their patois shifts, accents deepening, quickening. I register about four words in twelve, just enough to understand that they're not simply toying with me, although at least a few seem unreasonably amused at my predicament.

Finally:

"It's pretty easy," declares their beaming spokesperson.

It isn't. I listen and nod at the fusillade of instructions. No one seems willing to let him speak in peace, interjecting whenever possible, introducing food recommendations, words of caution, advice on how best to save another two minutes, every remark leading the argument onto a new tangent entirely.

The wind drags ribbons of cold water across the street. Above, the clouds clot asphalt-black. I sigh. I've gone from soggy to squelching in my sneakers. "Actually, I think I'd just try to find—"

"Mate! Stop!" The afroed boy grabs me by the wrist. I tense, and my household of tattoo-spirits stir, a susurrus of power that licks across the youth's skin. He flinches away. "What was—"

"Static." I rub my arm, slide the sleeve over my bony wrist. "What were you saying?"

"Yeah." He stares at me, cagey, eyes narrowed. He knows something happened. His flesh knows it. His bones know it. His lizard brain, frothing with terror, knows it. But his tongue and his thoughts? They've lost the language for that subcutaneous dread. "Anyway. Hope you find wha' you're looking for."

Nod and smile. Nod and smile. I retreat, take a corner, plunge into a ripple of people, freshly discharged from the train lines, all power-walking in the wrong direction, and zip in front of an encroaching bus to emerge into slightly ramshackle suburbia.

The walk doesn't take long, at least not compared with the voyage here. Thirty minutes later, I'm in the courtyard of an oppressively functional building complex. There's no art to the three-flat arrangement, no suggestion of a legacy built on unethically acquired tea. It is brown brick and gray concrete, pure practical geometry; a place to exist, rather than to showcase alongside mentions of six-figure incomes.

A geriatric woman, possibly Russian, white-haired and armed in floral print, a headscarf tied under her chin, glares at me from the stoop. "Who you?"

I gawk at her, bewildered but mostly impressed. I've never seen anyone smoke so *aggressively*. It's as though the cigarette is a grievous affront, a thing to be attacked, to be fellated into sobbing penitence.

Her eyes slit. "Who you?" she repeats

"My name's Rupert, I was wondering—"

"Wrong flats. Get out."

"But—"

"Out."

I grapple the Asian instinct to obey matriarchal authority, and force myself a step forward. "Lady—"

"Out!" Suddenly, she's on her feet and charging at me, screeching wildly, arms flapping with unreasonable zeal.

I backpedal, surprised. I've seen a lot of shit over the years, argued semantics with nightmares beyond labelling, defused rallies of demonic fetuses, but I've never, ever had to contend with an outraged grandmother. Do I run away? Do I brace for a hard pinch? I—

"Alina." A cold, bored voice cuts through the pandemonium. "*Sit.*"

She sits. She actually *sits.* The old battleaxe drops to an unmistakably canine squat, palms on the pavement, head raised, manner attentive.

"*Heel.*"

I avert my gaze as the babushka prances away, inexplicably embarrassed, and look up at the woman slouched against a doorframe. I almost swallow my tongue. Power oozes from her. Not the raw stuff of any old god, but *militarized*, locked and loaded and cocked at my sense of autonomy.

She pushes her will on me, and I push back. "I'm guessing you're one of the Greek—"

A dismissive sniff. "This is incorrect."

"Excuse me?"

She scratches the old woman beneath her chin before easing herself forward, dragging her godhead like a cloak of lies. The air shimmers where she touches it. She's beautiful, of course, but it isn't a *concrete* beauty, nothing nailed into marrow and meat, but a shifting glamour cycling subtly between every definition of the idea. Certain features hold true, however. The brown curls, freefalling over muscled shoulders; the maple-gold eyes; the slinking, serpentine walk. Contrary to Disney, it seems, the Greek Pantheon isn't cobbled from Aryan idolatry, but a more Mediterranean stock.

"You're not on your knees."

"No." Bizarrely, I find myself feeling somewhat sheepish. Her tone is accusatory, more petulant than righteously aggrieved, and weirdly more distressing for that reason. I fight the urge to pat her head, despite the six inches she has on me in sandals. "I'm not."

"Kneel." Another shudder of deific energy.

"No."

"*Kneel.*" This time, it's a snarl, a whipcrack; the metaphorical gun fires, and I feel the impact. I feel her will unfurl, chittering locust-loud. *Bow. Beg. Bear worship to the altar of her being.*

The tattoo-spirits gobble the payload up before Diyu's wards even begin to itch.

"What—"

"Long story, but it starts with 'I belong to another pantheon entirely,' and from what I can tell, to people above your paygrade." I start forward again, a hand extended, ready to nudge the goddess aside if that's what it takes to get through the door.

Her eyes burn gold. "How dare you?"

"Ananke. He is a guest."

We both turn. The new arrival is another woman, earthier, more voluptuous, hips and curves and softness. Tiny flowers are threaded through the expanse of her hair, which she keeps in complex braids. There's a humanity in her that's absent in her counterpart, manifested in the wrinkles indenting her eyes, her mouth.

"Demeter—" The sound that Ananke makes isn't anything a human throat should produce.

"Do you want to explain to the others why we'll be short a chef, then? He's been *invited*, Ananke. Leave him be." Demeter fixes me with an evaluating stare, mouth puckering. "Though you're a bit *thin*, aren't you? Unusual for a cook."

Click. Epiphany A into Slot B, tagged with a nervous chuckle: this is Demeter, goddess of agriculture and maternal affairs. Ostensibly sweet, but you can never tell with these icons of fertility, what with their affection for ritual sacrifice. Ananke, though, I can't place. I keep silent as she storms back into the building. A hint of scales glimmers across the skin of her back before she is swallowed by the gloom.

Demeter tuts loudly. "Sorry. Ananke can be so *shrewish*, sometimes. She still expects everyone to bend their knee to her, but that's just—" She crouches down, corrects the placement of the old Russian woman's scarf, strokes the back of a hand across the dessicated cheek. It'd all be quite sweet, if the unfortunate senior weren't still on all fours. "Anyway. Don't judge us for the actions of our predecessors. The primordials are not as well socialized."

"Uh-huh." I gulp, steady myself, close the distance between us and hold out a hand in greeting.

She stares at my outstretched digits, silent, a smile coagulating. Finally, she rises, fabric billowing across plump limbs, more obedient to aesthetics than physics, as if moved by a non-existent breeze. In all fairness, as an exhibition of power, it's far less gauche than the norm.

"Demeter." She holds out a supple palm, fingers slightly crooked.

I stare back, conflicted. What's proper protocol? After some deliberation, I go with excessive obsequiousness; slavish respect is rarely out of vogue. I dip forward, press a kiss to the ball of her wrist, half-bowing, half-something, a bending of the knees that might, in certain circles, be construed as a curtsey. The ridiculousness elicits a warm laugh, one that soon transcends into sensation, and it washes over me and it is—*not sticky equatorial heat, but something continental, laced with a breeze that tastes of the sea. Summer. Smell of the harvest and human sweat, the—*

"Lady." Her name aches in my chest, a benediction. But reverence quickly gives way to shock when the realization hits, the knowledge that I've been surprised into exaltation. It hooks into my gut, drags out the words, hoarse: "Lady, what are you *doing*?"

"Sorry about that. It's… automatic, sometimes. Like breathing." Demeter's contrition would almost be believable if it weren't for that smile, hanging like a corpse from the trees. She withdraws her hand, pivots to enter the flat, gazing over the bridge of a shoulder. "Come. We'll make it up to you."

I bite down the impulse to explain that isn't the *point*; that an apology, especially one so flippant, is hardly compensation. *She shouldn't have done that*. At least, I don't think so. Doubt dogs me as I pad along behind Demeter. The inside of the building is musty, damp, white halogen casting hard shadows across a space that isn't so much dilapidated as it is *old*, worn gray by generations of living.

A light strobes as we pass underneath, a warning. Smells tendril from behind closed doors. Marijuana. Tobacco-smoke, six different brands, clove and menthol intertwining. Indian food, unctuously rich, not spiced in the way I remember, not pungent with chilli oil, but still enticing. And underneath that, old beer and human urine, underpinning the acrid, decade-deep stink of cleaning bleach.

Human smells, all of it. Nothing supernatural whatsoever.

"We keep a low profile," Demeter remarks, as though she's been reading my thoughts on a board. "Life has not been easy for us in this country."

I don't reply, my attention focused inward; an auction is begun, a channel for negotiation opened. Room on the wet curve of a ventricle for whichever demon is willing to take on the Greek gods. Bob—his name is not actually Bob, but call a demon a duck and you bring him to your level—wins, of course, committing the entirety of his self to the effort, and I wince as he seeps through muscle fibers and abdominal cavity to write himself on cardiovascular tissue.

I breathe, feel his teeth behind mine, feel his power compound the wards that I knit under every intake of air. Rudimentary safeguards, sure, but still another layer of protection, another minute I can use to buy an excuse out of whatever hell might visit. Bob strains against my skin, stitches his essence through my cells, laces himself in *tight*. I feel him grin. I might regret this one day, but that supposes I *get* another day.

If Demeter notices any of it, she says nothing.

We skip the mold-spangled elevator, rust crusting its hinges, and walk up several flights of stairs instead. The floor that we turn off is indistinguishable from its peers, maybe even rattier. Demeter supplies no further conversation, just strolls up to a door and raps on the wood. (Her knuckles don't actually come into contact with the wood. My eyes water, even as visual cortices argue with the sliver of cerebrum familiar with everything eldritch; the world writhing between two interpretations of material truth.)

I knuckle tears away and squint, Demeter already blithely gliding through the crumbling timber like it's not even there. I wade in after her. *Mana* hits, rich and old, not cut with modern-day apathy. Pure. I bite down on the tip of my tongue, hoping to offset the dose, which snarls like a straight shot of LSD to the brain.

"Rupert." A new voice; male, this time, deep baritone rolling across my ears. "What took you so long?"

I blink, and blink again. My vision acclimatises, mana-warped imagery coalescing into familiar shapes. Blink. If I expected to be impressed, I'm disappointed: the domicile of the Greek gods, or at least whatever waystation this represents, is dingy and slightly moist, with low ceilings and questionable lighting. The walls, peculiarly, are draped with paintings in bronze baroque frames, poorly maintained.

"I"—probably not the best idea to roll Orpheus under the bus—"decided to take the scenic route, I suppose. Get to know London, and all that. Enjoy the sights. Things."

"I see," the man resumes, disapproval weighing down the words. He's taller than I am, barrel-chested, with a beard to embarrass entire lineages of Chinese men. "Could you perhaps have done it on someone else's time? We are on a schedule—"

"I'm sorry. I just got off a thirty-six-hour flight. I barely even know which way is up. Could we just do this tomorrow? Also, I didn't catch your name—"

He reaches me quickly, too quickly, spatial physics obliterated in a wink of his will. Before I can react, he clasps my hand and forearm, shakes the limb with unnerving gusto. "I am Poseidon," he booms. "God of the sea. And—"

A tickle of power, frothing up like sea foam. Bob screams an objection inside my skull, pressing up, *up*, even as the wards heat.

"Proprietor of the worst fish and chip shop in Croydon," drawls yet another voice, older, gnarled with cynicism. "Hephaestus. So glad that you could join us. I hope you weren't anticipating any sort of fanciness, because there's none—"

"Watch. Your. Tongue." Poseidon releases me to spin about and glare at his brother-god. "Who do you think you are?"

"The only god with any relevance in this forsaken country we've been piled into. This cold, wet, terrible place." Hephaestus hobbles forward. He's the ugliest god I've seen, face warped by the fire; skin red-veined, smoke wisping out between the cracks.

"*Enough.*"

Darkness, still and heavy. Like the drape of a pall, like the caress of a mourning veil. It is not an onslaught, not the thundercrack of a broken skull, not a blade between the ribs, not the heart tortured into a final rictus. But quieter, more insidious, the last hours before dying, that muffled grief that comes as you memorize the planes of your beloved's arm, hoping, hoping you'd be able to hold that moment, keep it safe, keep it whole, even though you know she asked for this, and this is not a death but a release, but you need her to stay anyway, need this piece of her, this scrap of time to tell you that you had something beautiful once and—

Minah. I drown her name, halfway nauseous from memory, and look up as Hades make his appearance. He is tall, gaunt, unmistakable, saturnine and regal, black hair framing cadaverously lean features. Unlike the others, he is pallid, albeit less like a Caucasian than a corpse, waxy and cold. All in all, a fearsome sight, were he not wearing crocs, shorts and a floral batik shirt.

"*Must* we always fight?" Hades' accent is, bafflingly, crisp and disdainfully British, the kind prevalent in bad adaptations of Jane Austen's works.

"There's no fighting, brother. It's not my fault that Poseidon cannot stomach the truth of his predicament."

"I'll have you know that shop is—"

Hephaestus rasps a wet, choking laugh and I wince. He sounds like he's gargling razors. "So he says. So he says." Another tortured paroxysm. "How do your subjects feel about your use of them, I wonder?"

Another horrifying laugh. This time, he almost hits the floor, and I drop my duffle, to go to his aid, only to be waved off by the irate deity. The other gods watch in silence as Hephaestus heaves himself upright, glassy-eyed, lip flecked with rust-streaked spit. He glowers at us, dragging an arm across his mouth, before retreating into one of the rooms.

"Petty," Hades spits the word like something profane. Then, he says: "Welcome, Rupert. I hope that my brothers have not been cruel."

"Your sister"—I glance across the hall; Demeter is suspiciously absent—"was pretty hospitable. Can't say the same for Ananke."

"Tonight, you rest." Hades continues as though he had not heard me at all, arms held out in an expression of patrician grace, absurdly clashing with the crocs. "Tomorrow, you shall join our brethren in transforming this wretched borough into a place of plenty. We are honored by your presence. We shall see you tomorrow."

"R-right."

Calling it now: I'm dead.

(Well, not literally. But you'll see, ang moh.)

TWENTY-ONE

MORNING ARRIVES SLATE-GRAY and appallingly cold. I'm awake long before the sun clambers above the cityline, a sickly radiance behind the smog, largely useless except as an indication that the day has begun.

Sleeping, to put it delicately, has been difficult. Jet lag alone might not have been insurmountable, but it came escorted by the deep autumn chill. Of course, that wouldn't have been a problem either if this thrice-damned flat had any concept of heating—or, hell, if the Greek pantheon understood that a blanket needs to be more substantial than a square of tissue.

Groaning, I force myself upright, lose balance, and collapse back onto the creaking, wire-thin mattress. The impact startles a few moths from hiding. *Lovely.* I stare at the ceiling. My arms and legs, strangulated by seventeen layers of fabric, tingle alarmingly, as though warning of impending necrosis. I clench a fist and watch as the blood drains from my fingertips before draining sluggishly back into place.

I should probably fix this.

I swing my feet onto the ground, touch bare toes to the wooden flooring and immediately jump back. Maybe later. Maybe never, in fact. A wild idea rouses itself. Would it be possible to engage in tele-cooking? If someone rigged up a camera in whatever kitchen I'm meant to occupy, would it be possible for me to just delegate to an army of sous chefs? It could happen.

Even as my sleep-addled mind dwells on the possibilities, creating a daisy-chain of command that could be transposed onto a multinational culinary business, the door swings open to reveal Demeter. In the pale of morning, she appears younger, unsettlingly vulnerable, the lines of her face gentled. Her curls fall in vine-tangled rivulets, eclipsing the hunched shoulders, the folded arms. As I study her, she drops her hands to her sides, revealing a mottling of fresh bruises, like newborn scales.

I swallow. A memory of Minah unfurls: angles and spindles of bone, mouth pearled with gore, a history of hurt soaked into her skin.

It isn't my place to ask.

"What happened to you?" The question comes anyway, pursued by ghosts.

Demeter's expression does not change, her eyes haunted, old as the soil. She slips from the door to seat herself on my bed, a leg crossed beneath her hips, hands latticed about the curve of a knee. "Did you sleep well?"

"I... slept. I guess." I'm not used to having an unfamiliar woman on my bed. I'm barely used to Minah's absence, to the knowledge that I won't find her in the kitchen, a song on her lips. I clear my throat, scoot back. "Can I help you with anything? You need someone beaten up?"

Demeter doesn't smile, arching forward to drape fingertips on my thigh. I wince. "Who was she?"

"Minah." Her name is a bright, sharp pain.

Demeter's expression flickers. A muscle in her cheek judders, stills. I pin my breath to the roof of my mouth, the stem of my spine broken into spasms. I fight the memories down: her smile, her hands; her walk, like music is running through her spine; the jut of her cheekbones and the sweep of her lashes; a gold-limned vision of Minah, bracing against the dawn, exultant, embers in that black river of hair. She laughed as I pulled her inside, beating out the flames. I have never seen anyone look so happy.

The goddess retrieves her hand and curls her fingers around the crook of an elbow. It takes another moment before she raises her gaze, mouth pinched with rue. "I'm sorry."

"Don't ever fucking do that again. Don't you ever fucking dare. Don't— don't—" The words burst in fits and starts, and I choke on them as anger metastasizes into an infinitely more complicated emotion. "Don't ever fucking do that again. Just. Don't."

"I won't." No platitudes, no exaggerated contrition. And for a moment, I love her and the way she perches at the rim of my bed, silvered by the morning, like she has salvation to spare and all I have to do is reach out and ask.

"So what are you doing here? Somehow, I don't see you as the femme-fatale kind of goddess, seducing acolytes with a saucy wiggle of your hips." My voice stays raw, a chain smoker's husk.

"Good eye." A genuine smile, this time, inlaid with something cynical. "I wanted a chance to see what you are up close."

What. Not who. "You mean the tattoos."

"Yes."

"They'll behave."

Demeter says nothing, holds my stare for a moment or six, before she dips her head in acknowledgment. In a voice almost too soft to be heard, she says: "You'll need them, I suppose."

"Anyway, you going to—wait. What did you just say?"

She doesn't reply, rising instead, silks trailing across brown skin, suddenly inaccessible as the Mother Mary. "Get ready. We leave in twenty minutes."

* * *

WE LEFT IN eight.

Why? Because nothing is funnier than towing a Chinese man, hair foamy with shampoo, mouth frothing with toothpaste, out of the shower, I suppose. I'm crammed into a white shirt and black pants, both grease-streaked and reeking of burnt fat; tied into an apron that might have once been merely filthy, and then strapped into shoes that stink of someone else's feet. After that, I'm hoisted into the back of a van and left to puzzle at my half-washed condition.

A panel in the bulkhead slides open about ten minutes into our teeth-rattling journey, and Poseidon's voice booms through the slit. "How are you doing?"

I drill a finger into a still-soapy ear. "Probably worse than you."

He laughs gustily, and the world swerves into *a hard* right. I ram a shoulder into the wall and drag a hiss between my teeth, moments before I'm flung to the other side. *Thump.* This time, cranium connects with aluminum, and my vision sparks white. But the good thing about being a reformed criminal, a fairweather thug who occasionally still muscles for a living, is that this really isn't that unfamiliar.

Head spinning, I crawl up to the bulkhead and hook my hands through the opening, peer through the divide. To my surprise, Demeter's driving, fingers barely grazing the wheel, a cigarette between bared teeth. The window is open; as I watch, she leans out, slaps a hand against the door and screeches something in Greek.

"Time of the month?" The van jolts to the right before she recovers, correcting our trajectory.

I need to learn to keep my mouth shut.

Poseidon takes a long look over a shoulder and laughs again, teeth flashing white. "She doesn't like yoking our son to the road."

"Son?" I run my eyes over the inside of the van. To all outward appearances, it is a vehicle, and nothing but a vehicle, so help me traffic department, empty except for a few taped-down boxes and a disgruntled Chinese man.

"Areion." Poseidon's reply is almost off-hand, summoning a twitch in Demeter. Whatever's going on, she disapproves of this, of him, of his nonchalance, his disinterest in their two-ton offspring.

I think about the purple-black marks flowering on Demeter's skin, the stories of the Grecian pantheon. I don't ask; I don't want to know. But even as I cozy myself with the delusion of indifference, the image continues to cycle, eventually blending with a memory of Minah.

We don't stop. Demeter's a competent driver if a reckless one, taking corners like a stuntwoman. Cars beep, slam their brakes; Demeter slices between red buses, a knife through hot butter. I rack up more concussions, but we survive the trip. She parks and the two disembark before Poseidon releases me from my cage. I wobble out, jelly-kneed, squinting against the gray sun.

"Here we are!" Poseidon announces, scooping an arm about my shoulders.

I blink and take in the vista: another consortium of shophouses cobbled from brown brick, unattractive and dull (except, perhaps, for the graffiti spray-painted across one wall); a woman with a warning grin, not quite human, not quite nightmare. School children dart past, laughing, oblivious to the old man urinating in the corner, the piss forking and lacing across the pavement.

"Where's *here*, exactly?" I look away as the geriatric zips up and scratches his nuts.

"Your"—Poseidon, dressed today in a straight-cut black sweater and expensive jeans, bobs an awkward bow—"new kingdom! Your castle of condiments, your bastion of basil."

"This is the soup kitchen that you'll be working at," Demeter slinks up from behind, cat-silent, tense. She makes eye contact with Poseidon before looking away, the ghost of a sneer mauling her face. "And don't worry. Poseidon isn't in charge."

"Oh, come now, Demeter. Is that how you treat your husband?" He reaches for her, only to have the goddess yank her shoulder away.

"*Don't.*"

The faintest crackle of power, earth and ocean, soil and sea, before the two separate, smiles on their faces, tension in their spines, actors who've played out the same conversation six million times. I clench my fists, and Bob wakes the legion. We wait. But nothing happens. Demeter prowls forward, enters a door unmarked by signage and bracketed by cloudy windows. Poseidon shrugs and follows, his grin effortless, confident, patriarchal.

We go in. The premises are large, larger than I expected: roomy enough to hold at least sixty men. More, if they're willing to squeeze into the corners and cram like sardines. Tables and benches are arranged like ribs, bracketed by food stations; the kitchen is partitioned away by a low wall. Sequestered in a narrow corridor, a door with the universal symbol for a defecation-safe zone.

"Impressed?" asks Poseidon.

"That depends. Which answer gets me a bed without bed bugs?"

On cue, he roars his amusement and smashes a hand between my shoulderblades, a blow that nearly crumples me in half. I straighten as he struts away, already indifferent to my existence, his eyes on a new prize: a pair of young women, fawn-like in their restless, leggy beauty. I pick my composure up, walk myself to where Demeter stands in front of a colossal fridge, arguing feverishly with a pale, unsmiling man.

"Hi?"

Demeter doesn't turn, raises a finger. "One minute."

The tempo of the conversation accelerates. Demeter and the man dance between languages, slinging English and Greek and something unidentifiable with a liquid, angry grace.

"Um."

Hand gestures are being mobilized.

"Um."

"*One moment—*"

"There's a roach in the pot."

The lie achieves its desired outcome. Both Demeter and the man leap, argument discarded in the wake of a common adversary, and I stand quietly until the two figure out my ruse. It doesn't take long. They glare. I smile. "It kills me to have to interrupt such an important conversation, but someone decided it was very important to have me take a thirty-six-hour flight and then make me go to work the very next day. I feel like there are earth-shattering issues at work here, and I'd hate to cause the end of the world because I was too shy to ask what I'm supposed to do."

More glaring.

"Too much? I'll stop."

To my mild surprise, the pale man laughs; a hacking, machine-gun noise that borders on drugged hysteria. He grins, and like everyone else in my life, his dentition is much too sharp. "I like new toy, Demeter."

"Employee," the goddess corrects.

"A mortal?" His gasp is as theatrical as the hand that twitches up to shield his mouth. The man looks me over again. He's tall. And *shaggy*. Black hair, threaded into a map of braids, flows from a widow's peak, carpeting him like a pelt. A musk clings to him, not immediately unpleasant, but I recognize the base notes, an abattoir palette that makes me stiffen instantly. "I thought we only *serve* mortals."

He chortles at his joke. No one else laughs. I give Demeter a quizzical look, and she reciprocates with a stare that announces in block letters *I'M NOT DOING THIS WITH YOU*.

"Veles," she sighs, clearly unimpressed.

"Come on! Is clever joke. You people need sense of laughter," he declares, shaking his head, reaching back to tighten the strings of his apron. Forearms bulge below his rolled-up sleeves, the weathered skin tattooed with wolves.

"Humour," I blurt out.

"What?"

"It's 'sense of humour.' Not 'sense of—'"

Veles flaps a massive hand. "Same thing. Don't be pedant."

I clack my mouth shut. Demeter, too old to roll her eyes, nonetheless displays a hint of churlishness, jabbing a finger at the fridge, mouthing a warning at Veles and gesturing at me to follow. I fall into step behind her, hesitantly returning the man-mountain's ebullient thumbs-up.

"So, who's Veles? My Greek mythology isn't up to snuff, but—"

"Nobody of any significance anymore," Demeter says, almost sadly. "Once, the Slavic people knew Veles as a god of dark, growing things. The earth and the water, the forest and its wolves. But Christianity tore his worship to shreds. He became their saint, and then their devil, and then nothing at all."

I have nothing to say to that. Demeter takes the scenic route, lazily winding around food stations, periodically stopping to pop open lids and inspect contents. The buffet, from the little I can see, is unexpectedly wholesome. Roasted aubergines and brie-drizzled asparagus; mushrooms steeped in rich brown stew, a hint of anise and peppercorn wafting in the steam; golden buttered corn, char-grilled cauliflower, thick slabs of herb-crusted lamb, perfectly roasted. There's even stuffing. And *gravy*.

"Rich fare for a soup kitchen."

A sidelong glance and a small smile. "I try to make it worth it for them."

I shiver.

I'm silent as she points out stove and microwave, oven and freezer, the location of every utensil and pot and article of crockware, my head bobbing in time with every pause. The idea of divine charity is as incomprehensible as thermonuclear physics. What agenda could they have? What are they doing with so much good food? Demeter might be the embodiment of agriculture, but this cornucopia of exquisitely seasoned excess had to have cost her, had to have cost *them*. Yet at the same time—

"You got everything?"

"Crystal."

We both pause.

"I'll just assume that you just said 'yes,'" she announces drily, then walks away, no goodbye offered, cold again.

Finally unchaperoned, I scan the kitchen, make eye contact with the other staff, a coterie of uniformed men and women, no more memorable than the proverbial man on the street, their plain-faced humanity only slightly too flawless to be authentic. They stare at me in return, silent, their eyes refracting the amber sunlight.

I'm on the verge of salutations when the front door swings open again and everyone swivels, Demeter's voice pouring out in warm contralto welcome. The people who shamble in are old, young, male, female; every ethnicity you can name and every shade of lost. They're received without prejudice, however, with Poseidon himself escorting each new arrival into the ever-expanding queue.

And soon, there's no time for nurturing suspicion, just work, just doling out food and replenishing empty tureens, just good, clean labor. To my surprise, I enjoy it. It's *possible* that Demeter watered her harvest with the blood of one-armed orphans, but I can't see any evidence of foul play, nothing bloodier than fresh-plucked poultry and shelves packed with raw beef. For once, my kitchen isn't a place of murder, and I'm not going through the motions, perpetually careful to not speculate on the origin of the meat I'm marinating. For once, for the first time in as long as I can remember, I feel human.

Thump. The door opens, but it doesn't shut. I look up. Men in suits pour through the front door, grim-faced, straight-backed, an army of Agent Smiths equipped with briefcases. They assemble in two lines, one on each side of the exit. Stop. Wait.

"Shit"—Demeter's voice, from the corridor that leads to the bathrooms— "*get the fuck down!*"

As one, the men snap open their briefcases and extract SMGs, beetle-black and gleaming. There is no posturing, no overture to violence, no commanding the innocent to move out of the way. Before the last syllable of Demeter's warning can die, they open fire and the world frags into gore and muzzle flash.

TWENTY-TWO

DESPITE THE MEDIA's hard-on for it, death isn't glamorous. It isn't blood in the water, or curds of brain dribbling from a neat round hole, still wisping smoke, or a clean red sickle opening like a smile under your chin. It's piss and shit and screaming and bodies in hypovolemic shock. It is spluttering gut wounds and grown men crying. It is the smell of compromised intestines, still processing the junk crammed down the gullet that morning. It is fecal matter and bile and so much vomit because it is *hard* to hold your lunch when your stomach's honeycombed with fresh holes, and you've plugged fingers into every opening, hoping it'll stop the blood that pisses out with every whimpering breath, but *it won't fucking stop.*

The suits are relentless. Theirs is a death by number, eschewing efficiency for quantity, proselytising the idea that if you put enough rounds in something, it will eventually die. They're not wrong. In the last two minutes, we've lost at least twenty-five people: mostly patrons, but also a handful of the staff. The rest of us are holed up behind kitchen equipment, all bashed up with no place to go.

"Who the *fuck* are they?" I scream as more bullets bang against the food station.

Veles, jaw hanging by a twist of muscle, laughs uproariously. "High-interest credit card company!" I'm not sure how I'm hearing him speak.

With that, he vaults over the barricade, skin tearing where it fails to keep up with the sudden multiplication of muscle tissue, frayed hide trailing like gauze. Veles' body ripples like a column of tumors developing in fast-forward, and he *laughs* as he rolls his shoulders, cartilage popping even as his spine sprouts another two feet of vertebrae.

"Come! Vanquis! Veles is not scared of you." He pounds a fist into an open palm, guffaws as his face warps into a muzzle, blood drooling from newly wolf-yellow eyes.

The intruders pause, just for a heartbeat, as though silently conferring;

twitching and rocking on their heels, mouths palpitating, Adam's apples bobbing in concert. A consensus is reached, and the air splits with the sound of twenty-six high-power firearms unloading in unision.

The rounds punch deep into Veles' neo-nightmare mass. Ordinarily, the bullets would simply bed down in the vitals, pinpoints of metal lodged in a slurry of liquefied meat. But this is a numbers game, and volume's an ace up its own sleeve. Wounds iris wider with every new perforation, exposing punctured, oozing viscera.

And still Veles keeps laughing, keeps stalking through a sea of chewed-up corpses, arms held wide.

A lucky shot takes his jaw off completely. Veles screams in rapture.

Shit.

"Ham kha—are we really going to sit here while he gets himself killed?" I demand, scrabbling across the floor for a knife. If this is the best that the Greek gods can do, I'd best start evaluating contingencies.

"No."

Demeter rises, power steaming from her skin, evaporating into filaments of possibility. Reality dithers like an old television set. And for one infinitesimally brief moment, the universe peels open, and I can see *everything*—how physics and velocity and time intersects with the idea of a heaven above, how meta co-exist with the fundamental truth of their non-existence, how the sun can be a star can be a ball of dung rolled across the galaxy by a gargantuan beetle. Suddenly, it is all so *clear.*

And then Demeter pulls on the strings of what-is and what-can-be, and the room goes white.

"*Fight*, Rupert!" Her voice, a command that spears through my breastbone, anchors itself in my ribs and drags me forward through the all-encompassing light. Not a compulsion, but a call to arms, an entreaty to put down fear and arm myself with vengeance. It is the last thing I hear before another detonation— gunshots clipping too close—removes my hearing.

Before I know it, I've cut deep into a vein. Blood gushes and with every drop, I pay out another microsecond of my lifespan, another unoccupied neuron. My tattoo-spirits lap it up, drink it down, and regurgitate raw power into my soul. Buoyed by the surplus, Bob drags himself to the surface, wreaths my face in bone, and with a curse between my teeth, I leap over the food station.

Hell unravels in silent, flashing vignettes.

Bang. Veles kneeling atop an agent, fingers on the man's chest. Pulling until the seams of his skin give out, and breastbone gleams red-slick in the light.

Bang. Demeter, not-Demeter, a thing that could have been Demeter, bearing down on a pair of vacant-eyed men, screaming something that I can't hear.

Bang. Poseidon, his arm held high, fingers curled. Beatific as he stares at a man floating in the air, legs kicking, water burbling out of his mouth.

Bang. The kitchen staff, shimmering between guises. Swarming. Teeth and talon, threads of black hair, constricting about wrist and throat and—

Bang.

A weight slams into my side and I go down, hand already whipping around to bring the knife on my assailant. The blade cuts cleanly through his chest—a boy, maybe eighteen, hollow but still so achingly young—to emerge the other side, and even though he's starting to hiccup blood, he doesn't stop. The youth wedges the muzzle of his SMG under my sternum, pins his weight over the machine, depresses the trigger.

I'd be dead ten times over if it weren't for Bob, who howls up to swallow the bullets, to swallow the kid's arm, amputating the limb at the elbow. The suit doesn't scream, just falls back, more baffled than anything else. He gawks at the stump of his arm, brow rucked, looks up at me, eyes clearing.

I see a jitter of confused terror but it's too late to stop Bob. United, we twist onto all fours and lunge, landing with our teeth in his throat and our hand cupped around his heart, which spasms in my grip like a terrified hummingbird.

And. I. *Squeeze.*

Pop.

Or, maybe, *splorge.*

It's all the same when you're elbow-deep (both literally and figuratively, ang moh) in the fight. Regardless, the fighting ends almost as quickly as it begins.

"So, Veles get share of money, yes?"

The words clatter into the gory silence, innocent, too loud. I've an arm around a pudgy man with a flamboyant hat, glasses cracked but somehow still in position. Ropes of dark hair cling to his face in bloodied loops. His name's either Weasel or Ferrett, or something else that is sleek and deceptively cute. I can't remember exactly. But he is *remarkably* ebullient despite his injuries, radiant despite a face bleached of its natural pinkness.

"Money?" I ask as I usher the man out of the soup kitchen. Wobbling, he doffs his hat at me, and shambles away.

"Money. From dead pool."

"Like in the movie?"

"Veles—" Demeter's voice again, thick with warning.

"Da. Just like in movie." Veles resumes, oblivious, once again topically human. "We make bets on who survive each evening. Win big, sometimes. Ariadne won flat-screen television that way."

I toe at a corpse flipped on his face, arms splayed, face pillowed by a plate of mash. From a distance, congealing blood—especially blood with extraneous bits—could be mistaken for lingonberry sauce. It is not a pleasant revelation.

"That is *morbid.*"

"Da. But Greek gods don't pay, and homeless people don't tip." Veles shrugs, hefting a body onto each shoulder. He beams. "So, we do what we can. On bright side, Veles get loads of money on main gamble. Thirty-two dead! Right on the cash!"

"I—*what?*"

"Had to wait for necessary casualties, but was worth it." Veles thumps his chest with someone else's foot, the leg itself broken at the knee, white bone jutting from the ruined joint.

I consider the ramifications of his words, and chew out a question that I already know I don't want an answer to. "You mean we could have saved some of these people?"

"Da. Easy." Veles begins to stroll towards the kitchen, where he offloads his burden of bullet-torn carcasses. "Vanquis goons are pushovers."

"Wait. *Wait* right there. So, you're telling *me*"—my voice trembles towards an octave it can't quite reach, and I ball my hands into fists, wincing—"that we could have saved *aaall* these people, but instead we—"

"I don't think you're approaching this correctly," Poseidon intrudes. I turn to find the god sweeping bodies towards the kitchen like so many hairballs, limp arms and legs flopping everywhere. A hysterical laugh saws through my chest. Ragdoll physics; they get you even in the real world. "You could have gone out there all on your own. You never needed a 'we' behind you."

"But—"

"But what? Exactly?" Poseidon is relentless. "But you were afraid? But you weren't prepared to go out there alone? To risk your life for unwashed strangers? Is that what you were going to say?"

"Poseidon, that's enough." Demeter finally stepping in, too late.

His grin is salt-white, cold as the deep. "Before you pass judgment, perhaps spend some time meditating on the fact that you are a dyed-in-the-wool coward."

"I said, enough."

That was unfair. Three small words. They hang stillborn from the tip of my tongue. I want so badly to tell him that he's being unfair, that he was mistaken about my intentions, that the hail of bullets was a perfectly legitimate thing to be afraid of, that the desire to survive is practically constitutional.

But he's right.

He's right.

"If it helps, it wasn't as though they were destined for a long life rich in grandchildren." Poseidon shrugs and returns to his labour, smile feline. "Cheap fuel for the divine fire."

Another frisson of dread, echoing my earlier unease, but I swallow it down and tug on the straps of my apron, flattening the cloth.

"It's fine." I clear my throat and straighten my spine, head held stiffly, an old line twisting in my thoughts: *Fake it until you make it.* I can do that. I can feign dignity. I've done so before. "Everything's. *Fine.* So, what are we going to do with all these bodies?"

Two triangles of corpses lie stacked in the kitchen, one on the counter and one on the floor, limbs still comically splayed. Gore dribbles and drips like so much discolored treacle, while blank eyes gaze up at blood-speckled staff, standing silent as statues. I stare at them, stare at the two piles, breath twitching in second-long intervals, an uncomfortable epiphany skittering multi-legged up my bones.

"Blood and meat is the oldest communion," Demeter announces, tone inscrutable.

"Waste not, want not," Poseidon says. "Get to work."

IT'S EASIER WHEN you don't think of them as people.

We start with dismemberment, the team of kitchen staff and I, separating limbs from torsos, heads from shoulders. Legs and arms are divided from hands and feet, fingers and toes amputated, breaded, and fried to a crisp.

Next: we skin the bodies, strip them down to the muscle. Ram-horned kitchen boys, now pared of glamour, scour the vast sheets of epidermis, plucking hair and draining abscesses, anything that might dilute texture and taste. After that, the skins are either cured, or baked, or fried as the individual sous chef desires.

When it's just bone and meat, unidentifiable from any other slab of raw muscle, we suspend the decapitated torsos from hooks in the freezer, drain out the blood into freshly scrubbed buckets. Then the carving knives come out.

Just ingredients now: tripe and sirloin, drumstick and heart.

I don't waste anything. Not even the gallbladders, which I spice and saute, before slicing them thin and plating them with creamy globs of yoghurt. The small intestines are rinsed, over and over, until only the faintest stink of decomposition remains, then poured into the food processor with garlic, layers of caramelized onion, pepper, and a glazing of white wine. At some point, after they've been sewn up into their casings and left to smoke for weeks, we'll turn them into proper andouille.

Everything else, I play by ear, too dazed to consider the slaughter. Easier to be a function, easier to pretend that this is nothing but marrow and tissue, a carnivore banquet to salt, season, and stir-fry. No thinking about the why, or the who it's from. That's how I've always gotten along.

I make bowls of pho, bake powdered calcium into bread, roast bone-in calves with nothing but sea salt and black pepper, a hint of thyme at the end. Nothing ostentatious, though, no feats of molecular gastronomy. I can't manage that. Not today.

"It makes no *sense*," I slam the butcher's knife on the cutting board, straightening. Around me, kitchen staff jump, stare, cat-eyed and eerily silent.

"What doesn't make sense..." A woman tiptoes closer, unguligrade feet making for a syncopated walk. She cocks her head about twelve degrees too far, a reptilian grin held up uncertainly, as though the purpose of the expression confused her to no end. "...*sir?*"

"Everything." I snap. "Nothing. I—"

I've been at peace with being a coward. Heroism kills, after all. But there was just... *something* to Poseidon's sneering dismissal. Or maybe it was losing everything I've loved, or becoming a political fugitive. Or both. Probably both. Probably all the events of the last six months, meeting up with the psychic repercussions of every bad decision I've ever made.

Or maybe, just maybe, it's my stomach disagreeing with personal responsibility.

"Nothing," I say again.

The woman nods. Hunger, or some unfortunate circumstance of genetics, has cooked the softness from her face, laying bare an alien framework. The cheeks are built too high, the mouth—a teeth-riddled slit—pulled too close to the chin. A tail whips free from under her pinafore, a tuft of brown fur slaps against the counter and sways away.

"What is your name?"

I wipe my hands on my apron and smooth a hand over my skull. The buzzcut is beginning to grow out; I make a mental note to do something about it. "I'm sorry. What did you say?"

"What..." Like the old song goes, the words don't come easy. The syllables sound unpracticed on her tongue, unnatural, like a parrot's caricature of a conversation. "...is your name?"

"Rupert. Obviously. I'm sure you'd been briefed." Now the entire kitchen is listening to us, every pretense of decorum dropped along with their glamour. From the corner of my eyes, I see fur and coiling tails, scales arranged in rainbow gradients, and even stranger appendages.

"What is your name?" she repeats, a frown creasing her eggshell brow.

Oh. The texture of the air alters. Curiosity becomes airless anticipation, thick enough to fillet and grill. A prickle of fear travels my spine. *That* kind of name. I feel the collective lean in, hungry, but I'll be damned before I give up something like that so easily. (Technically, I'm already damned, but that's hardly relevant to the story, is it?)

I flick a glance around me. The staff has me circled. Not exactly lynch-mob-in-waiting levels of surrounded, but definitely in the you're-staying-right-here-buddy genus. Nothing to do but procrastinate. So I do. I wash up. I scrub down the knives, disinfect the cleaning board, whisk peeled fingernails into the bin. Under my breath, I reel off most of a warding spell—the last vocable, the trigger, I keep tied up in my throat—and feed the loop of sounds to Bob, who picks it up and repeats it in a droning subvocal circuit.

The chanting does little to alleviate the pressure of the kitchen help's scrutiny. I keep my eyes on the prize, though. Hygiene first, difficult answers later. Pot and pan are plunged into a hot storm of suds, even as the help eddies about me, clearly impatient. The ring of bodies spasms tighter, shoes and talons scuffing at the floor, tacit demand for acknowledgement. I reply by taking a rag to the counter. One of us *will* break, but it won't be me.

"Ach, can we give up on this standstill already? I don't even know what the point in this fucking madness is. The dens are gonna close in a few hours, and I, for one, would like to cash in on the bloody prize."

At least, I *think* that's what the voice said. The suet-thick brogue borders on impenetrable.

Something leaps onto the tap, and I see hands—fingers fat, meaty, pink as raw chicken—close around the steel pipe, even as a tail dips into my field of vision. The entity continues: "Seriously, laddie, all the huldra wants is to know your real name. Not your human-name. You can't lie to us. It's obvious you're not human. We can smell your kin on ya. All nine hundred and seventy-two o'em."

"Actually, there are only nine hundred tenants and believe me, I'd know if there were squatters in—" I wring out my sponge, make the mistake of looking up. "Aggwaghhhh."

Bright, sea-glass eyes glare at me. "Wot."

"Agggh."

"Bit of a rude one, ain't cha?"

"You're a cat"—I pause, affirming the visceral reality of the next words—"with *hand*s!"

"I suppose I am!" The scraggly tom, banded in scars and black stripes, one ear chewed into a necrotic stub, lifts a wrist to daintily lick the back of his hand. "Ooohwee. Such wit you've got there. Wouldn't know I was a cat with hands if you hadn't told me the now. Now, what great revelation will you surprise us with next, laddie boy?"

"What the *fuck* are you?"

He hunkers down, hindquarters arched. The cat touches his forefingers together and grins like the devil on the dismount. "Like ye said. A cat with hands. I suppose it would have been nicer if I was *the* cat with hands, but we cannae have everything now, can we? Now. Like the nice huldra asked, *what's your name*? Give us a bone, and we'll give you the whole rack of lamb."

"*Fine.*"

This won't work. This can't work. This had better damn well work. A smile in place, I let inspiration ricochet into a recitation of Bob's true name, a polysyllabic maze of stridulations and guttural consonant clusters, like a cicada singing racist epitaphs. It's a gamble, but if I'm right, they'll take it at face value, what with Bob's recent monopoly of the dermal real estate.

Note to self: talk to Bob about said monopoly.

I chew at my tongue, breath caged behind clenched molars. To my surprise, it does work: the group bobs in unison, hivemind in concert, and take up Bob's name like a hymn. Only the cat is silent, grinning, body dangling off the tap by its plump pinkies.

"*Such* a pretty name. Who'd thought that a dam'd be so kind to a wee runt like you? I'd almost think it belonged to someone else."

His expression turns sly, but I've played enough Big Two with Horse-face and Ox-head. He'll need to try harder if he wants me to fold. "Don't I know it."

The cat yowls a laugh. "I suppose it's our turn then, eh? He showed us his, and we should show him ours."

A flush of power in the air replies, seismic, dizzying, sweet from mythos older than entire civilizations, and a rawer energy, static discharge tingling in the hairs on the back of my neck. Like being baptized in electrified gin. "Sounds good."

"Glad ya think so, but you..." The cat jumps onto the counter, head rotated one hundred and seventy-nine degrees, so that he's staring at me upside down as he haunch-swings along the metallic surface, tail curled into a question. He pricks an ear—the healthy one, not the rotted stub—in the direction of the outside world. On cue, something roars, jangling metal and mammalian anguish, a ceaseless ululation that invokes the image of a machine being vivisected without anesthetic.

"...are going to have to wait till later. The Body Train calls."

TWENTY-THREE

THE BODY TRAIN, as it turns out, is both an actual train *and* a myth. According to the Cat, it is operated by the London Necropolis Railway, which was very much a real entity, but one which was interred along with the city's plagues. This paradox has, naturally, done nothing to slow services. In fact, I'm told that the Necropolis Railway is considerably more reliable than any of the subterranean lines known to the general populace.

"But does it play funky tunes?" I ask as the group promenades through the tunnels of Waterloo. Getting here has been an adventure unto itself. As far as I can tell, the process is as much ritual as it is movement: sixteen steps to the left, four to the right, open a door thrice, shut it twice. Ceaseless, senseless gestures that my companions—alfar, huldufólk, whatever the politically correct description might be—assure me are completely necessary.

I wonder how many of them were responsible for keeping the dead at bay. For all that ghosts unsettle me, their absence worries me more. Since we began this journey, I've not seen a single apparition, not a wraith or a tremor of ectoplasm, nothing to suggest that this place once bred tragedy—which is, I guess, code for a place that once was alive.

"Wot?" The Cat scrapes enthusiastically at the underside of his jaw. As a human, he's less phantasmagorical, more standard-issue menacing, a wire-thin skinhead collared with equal amounts of gristle and fat. His face is a transcript of every fight he's ever lost, scarred where it isn't knife-marked with runes. The hands remain repulsive, yellow-nailed and gangrene-black, the fingertips swollen, soft.

"Body train. *Soul Train.* Vehicles of mass melodies? The popular '70s TV show? No?"

"No." The Cat wipes his knuckles over an eye and then laps obscenely at each bloated finger. "Don't know if you realized, but I'm a cat. An *unneutered* tom, I might add. I got better things to be doin' with my time."

Oh, that conjures imagery I'd rather not have suffered. I flinch from the thought of the Cat groping at a sleek little Persian, discolored fingers scrabbling in her fur, stroking her ears as he positions himself. "Like licking your asshole?"

He yowls a discordant laugh. Three round-faced women, all blonde, all feigning adolescence, dart curious glances in our direction. The Cat tips an imaginary hat at them as we cross longitudes on the moving walkways, them going in one direction, us going in another, strangers in a nowhere place. One blows the Cat an unsteady kiss, before the trio burst into screeching laughter.

The huldra—I call her Hilda, which isn't her real name, but as close as I come to pronouncing the real thing—rolls her eyes and slouches an elbow over the handrail. Her seeming, freshly reinvented, now includes mile-long legs and pitch-dark hair, a waist small enough to trap between your fingers, a latex dress that barely skims propriety. Guilty spouses and hoodie-armored teens, skinny as alleycats, flash her yearning stares, but she ignores them. To be fair, I'd gawk too, but she's shown me her hollow back, her graceful spine and the splines of wetly glistening rib.

"Don't play with your food," she rumbles, voice too low for her elegant face.

"Have a heart, ye black-hearted *sow*. Can't a cat take what few pleasures he has left in life? The Greeks barely feed us scrap from their tables."

"That isn't his problem to hear." Hildra exposes unsettling dentition: baby teeth packed in flat rows, too many and much too small, all the more disconcerting for their roundedness. Supernatural anatomy is defined by spikiness, and any variation from the norm is, like all deviance, deeply alarming.

"And who made you judge? Ain't he one of us now?"

Of the six in accompaniment, the huldra and the Cat seem most invested in my company. The others—a rusalka, a fox, a feldgeist, a man who proclaims himself to be the first Jack, or so sayeth the huldra—seem content to share in my cordial, nameless indifference.

"I suppose," the huldra drawls, eyes lidded. "You can answer his questions, if you like."

The Cat revolves his head like a demonic owl, skull rotated two hundred and seventy-five degrees. "You got any questions then, laddie?"

"What are *you?*"

The huldra laughs, a bark of wry, astringent pleasure. She loops a curl of charcoal hair around a long, long finger and gazes deep into the encroaching crepuscule. "What an excellent question."

The walkway ends, and we spill onto the platform, seven in a row. The rusalka and the feldgeist intertwine fingers, touch shoulders. The fox, one side of his head artfully shaved of crimson hair, exchanges a grin with a young mother, while Jack continues to loom in foreboding silence, a man out of his era. Fortunately, since it *is* London, land of endless theatre, no one questions the waist-coated giant in Victorian regalia.

Even if his shadow is convulsing in desperate, soundless torment, nailed in place by a polished boot heel.

"A thing like Jack is a good place to start, I suppose," the Cat drawls, coming to stand beside the towering character. "Jack came from the nightmares of the Big Smoke, from all those stories of a man who could kill and nae be found. He was a fantasy that people brought alive. Like a god, but better, 'cause ye dinnae have to listen to anyone pray."

I examine the two, who could not appear more different, between the Cat's industrial savagery and Jack's urbanity. The killer stares at the two of us, head tipped just so, as though to say he is, at the very least, nominally intrigued by the lecture.

"And you're"—I give the Cat a once over—"an urban legend as well?"

"Nah, mate. I'm a YouTube video."

"What?"

Another train, orange-banded white like a coral snake, roars past. I fidget as it disgorges passengers and foetid air, halitosis and body odor mixing with the warm damp of the dark, soil and steel and scurrying things.

"Well, I suppose that's not fair," the Cat muses, scratching at his jowls. "I'm more of a short film than a YouTube video. A man named Robert Morgan spun me out of his sister's nightmare and then the Internet gave me some meat to my bones. And ever since then, I've been a real boy, sustained by page views and retweets, gorged on every ten-minute twitch of human horror."

His grin is ghastly. "Don't look so surprised, now. I'm just like yer gods. Only hipper."

The thought of Yan Luo or Guan Yin participating in modern trends, trading phrases from MTV videos or donning hipster-glasses, elicits a strangled laugh. The Cat grins wider. "You heard it here first: churches are dead; YouTube and Snapchat and Facebook are the new houses of worship."

To my surprise, I find I have nothing to say to that.

The platform empties. We continue to haunt our corner, waiting, no one speaking. The fox yawns and levels a bright, cold eye at me. Two more trains come and go, and then reality stutters. If Demeter had unstitched the natural world in a blaze of numinous authority, the Body Train simply steals between the seams, a maggot squirming through cuts in the skin.

It doesn't scream its arrival. It rumbles and growls, an exhausted beast of burden, shaking as it worms up to the platform. The carriages are metal and meat, strung together with cartilage, the windows membranous. A moment later, reality flickers again, and the grotesquery eases into something more palatable: oxidized steel, metallic rivets, clouded glass, a faint twinge of ammonia.

For once, I don't ask any stupid questions. This is clearly the ride we've been waiting for. I follow as the group piles through an orifice and scatters across the plump, velvet-tasselled seats. Before I can take my spot, the air fritzes. Fabric becomes skin, becomes sinew dyed an inoffensive periwinkle blue. Another heave of the air, and everything skews up, strobes to black.

I spend the fraction of a heartbeat concerned I'd accidentally died. But normal comes back the way it left: quickly, without rhythm. By the time vision returns, it is mundanity all the way down. No overstuffed seats, no gilded tables, no sandalwood paneling on the walls, and no evidence of intestinal furnishing. Just regulation-compliant blandness: slightly grimy, typical of any piece of public transportation.

The doors dilate. More commuters enter, and I glance to the Cat, who shrugs, leans back, ankle hooked over a knee. His reflection grins from the window.

"They're normal people." The feldgeist has a little-girl voice, sweet and trembling and high.

I glance over. This close, she's almost ordinary, coltish and lanky, maybe seventeen at a stretch, but likely older. Blonde dreadlocks, woven with pearlescent beads, clatter as she fidgets and shifts, half-squatting on her seat.

"I figured. What are they doing *here,* though?"

The rusalka strokes her companion's back in wide circles, leaning forward as she does. She works fingers into the feldgeist's hair and begins scratching her like a churlish pet. "I thought education in Asia was exemplary. You should know this."

There's a schoolmarm's bite to her voice, the accent crisply Eastern European. She smiles truculently, but I don't smile back, drumming fingers against the back of my seat. The feldgeist pops a knuckle between her teeth, begins to gnaw, eyes flitting nervously between us.

The rusalka sighs. "Isn't it obvious? The Body Train loves its snacks."

I'M IN TROUBLE.

Again.

The lights have been going out periodically during our journey. Each time they do, they return with one less passenger, one less drunk in a three-piece business suit, one less teenager with a thousand-dollar phone.

Nothing for us to worry about, said the rusalka, plaiting the feldgeist's maize-yellow hair. *We're* invited. Despite her tart reassurances, however, everything's gone belly up. The last electrical malfunction didn't just pinch a commuter, it took everyone. Everyone except me, and the guy at the tail of the carriage.

I watch him as the halogen bulbs stammer, a *Silent Hill* standoff. Horror movies always begin with 'hello.' If I say nothing, maybe this will *stay* nothing, a rush-hour purgatory in the belly of a literal beast.

A smile crawls onto the man's lips. He cards his fingers through dense curls before heaving himself onto his feet. He is lanky, slightly stooped, furtive in the way of the habitual criminal. The lines of his face are simple, and unnaturally sharp. Not unhandsome, but not quite human either; a sketch of a man, an idea.

He saunters up to me, smell of tobacco and synthetic leather, skull tipped to one side. He digs his hands into his pockets and lets the smile creep up one side of his face. When he speaks, it's with the rolling accent of Croydon, consonants kept to a minimum.

"Hey."

I glance at the window. No reflection, just a distortion in the glass about the width and length of a six-foot man. "Hi."

"I suppose that was a bit dramatic."

"You could say that."

"Mm." His quiet unsettles, for reasons I can't yet put in words; it *scratches* at the inside of my cranium. My head is a casket full of fog, thoughts eating themselves, looping into incoherence, and I feel like a senile old man trying to recite his own last rites. "I needed to get your attention. Sorry."

He isn't. We both know it. But I let the insincerity of the apology slide, rap fingers along my thigh. Itch, itch. *Itch*. A crawling pressure develops behind my right eyeball, presses down. Something is wrong, a degree of *nope* that surpasses even the inherent stickiness of the whole situation.

"That's fine. I'm fine."

The conversation, stilted from the beginning, shudders to an uneasy halt. I palm my neck, while he watches on, not breathing, not moving. My apprehension grows, and I'm quickly reminded that the fight-or-flee response is actually closer to fight-or-pee. Again, the man smiles. I'm now convinced that he's tuned to my internal monologue, one more god with a finger on my psyche.

"No," he says, lips peeling back over gray-pink gums, his eyebrows scrunched together, expression marginally pained.

"No, what?"

"I'm not a god, bruv. You couldn't get me to be a god even if you paid me." He plops himself beside me. His presence contracts further, a comma of projected self, so small that it might as well be hypothetical.

And maybe, that's what gets me: the silent insistence he's indistinguishable from the everyman, a chump, a pal, a man of the people. Because clearly, Guan Yin help me, clearly, he's not.

His smile twitches. Right, he's still listening.

"I'm better than a god," he says, drawling the second word, *be'ah* rather than better. He sheds his humour as he leans forward, an intensity sieving into the vacancy. The train eels on, preternaturally noiseless, and as it takes a corner, I find myself wondering if it's eavesdropping.

"Okay." The safest of all answers. I tilt back. "Better how?"

"*Better*," he repeats, listless, eyes now tracking the darkness beyond the glass. A faint smile appears. I don't follow his gaze. I'm afraid of what I'd find. "Because I believe in due compensation for services rendered."

"There's always fine print."

His grin is crooked, all jagged teeth. "Of course there is. But the difference is I'll let you read it first."

It feels a little like coming home, that announcement, that subtle challenge, slid under the door like an envelope stuffed with news. And in a way, it is. In an ideal world, I wouldn't work, would just laze in off-season Ibiza, a Singha in hand, and never worry about bagging bloodied bones again. But if I had to choose a labour, it'd be something with paper.

Clerical work is alluring in its austerity. No moral quandaries, no risk of existential self-reflection, no opportunity for compound fractures. A minefield of possibilities, sure, but the threat is reactionary, dormant until invoked. More importantly, it doesn't get you killed. Sepsis by papercut; a lie.

I percolate the idea through my head.

"Do we have—"

"No."

That brings him up short. "What?"

"I said no."

"But I hadn't finished."

"Answer's still a no."

To my delight, a strand of whining petulance creeps into his next answer. I've fazed him. I gazed deep into the abyss, and the abyss *blinked*. "You're going off-script."

"Aren't you supposed to stamp your foot and disappear in a cloud of sulphur when I refute you three times?" I cross my arms. If he expected me to come racing at the prospect of a challenge, well, he's wrong. Slothfulness is healthy. Enthusiasm is not.

Another turn, another halogen seizure. The man rolls his eyes up, stares at the ceiling, and I observe with glee as he counts down from ten, teeth grinding over every number. At last, he sighs. Loudly. Sharply. When he lowers his gaze again, something gives. His veneer of humanity pops like a soap bubble, and the color leaches from his hair, his skin, his eyes, even the various grays of his attire.

He opens his mouth, and it's not words that disentangle themselves from his larynx, but *meaning* itself, multimedia synesthesia. He hijacks the parietal lobe, pumps nuance straight into the cerebrum. It doesn't all show up right. I catch snatches of memory, mine, his—*its*.

Cosmic anecdotes that dissolve neuronal pathways as quickly as they find them. Gusts of childhood aromas, a first encounter with sambal. Ambition, alien in its scope, seven-dimensional scheming to make my mind shrivel. Minah's smile.

The dissonance doesn't last. Eventually, it germinates structure. There is no language that can adequately encompass what he shares, no trick of storytelling that can convey the multi-sensory soliloquy. It is a montage of recollections and augurings, quick cuts of destruction: my apartment exploding, smoke and glass geysering from the duct-taped windows; documents shredded; every living relative, gutted, split open from ear to ear; Ao Qin, charred and grinning, drooling black, rising from a bank of black fog—

The universe creaks as an immeasurable weight leans down, presses on the caul that separates matter from metaphor, an analogical pseudopod extended through the gulf of time, a supplication to obey: carrot and stick, held up like weapons. And for a moment, everything holds its breath, history itself pausing to ruminate on the narrative. I grin, the world swimming between colors, a fugue of almost-shapes, and say what every action hero should say in a climactic scene.

"I need to talk to a lawyer first."

PART THREE
MEAT, BONE, TEA

TWENTY-FOUR

"IF YOU'RE GOING to throw good money down the drain, laddie, why not just give *me* the proceeds? Laywers won't save your wallet. Besides, it's not like the Boulder isn't stinking with them."

I blink. "Wha—*aaaggggh*."

The Body Train is gone. In its place, a raucous basement pub that looks like it was built in a crypt, capitalism gleefully feasting on architectural carrion. It teems with people and pustules of furniture, radial tables and high bar chairs. Thick stone pillars merge into the vaulted ceiling. Flatscreen televisions sprout between the joints, blaring sports commentary and beer adverts, both of which are indiscriminately booed by the patrons.

Somewhere in the crowd, glass smashes on someone's skull and the mob roars its approval.

"'Aaagh' what?" the Cat asks, still too close, his arm slung proprietarily around my shoulders.

I shrug myself free and shake my head, scanning the chaos for a glimpse of the bar. No luck. More crucially, no explanation for whatever had happened. The encounter with the nameless man feels so unreal now, a trick of alcohol poisoning. But I know better. Reality has a flavor, a metallic aftertaste, like a film of blood over your tongue, and it is unique to each individual world. Diyu, for example, is spiced with sulfur, and Banbudo—the in-between place, a marketplace for the myth-born—is pungent with odors that the piriform cortex can't translate.

The place where I'd been taken to was dry ice, old water, salt and time, like nothing I'd ever sampled. It lingers in my throat, a stillborn laugh, and I swallow again as I fight down the questions itching beneath the recollection. Later, I promise. For now, there are more immediate concerns. Like how we'd gone from public transportation to pub, and why my left forearm is dripping with cider.

"What's this?" I jab a finger at the damp limb, nearly dropping the beer stein I didn't realize I was holding.

"Your arm," the Cat offers unhelpfully, taking a swig from a martini glass, pinky extended in some blasphemy of courtesy.

"I know it's my arm. But why is it wet?" In times of doubt, I find it best to cling to irreverence. A second glance around the pub reveals the rest of our company, holed up in a side room, flinging dice across a table, aggressively entertained.

"Because you spilled cider on it, obviously."

"Yes, but how?"

The Cat lets fly a wailing laugh. "Wasn't me, laddie. But it might have been yon lad, who disagreed with you hitting on his lass."

"Really?" Slowly, I put together a map of the property. Chambers bud from the main space, cleverly obscured by angles of architecture. Every alcove is occupied by games of chance, some more identifiable than others. In some stand roulettes and blackjack tables, dealers in pinstriped uniform. In others, more esoteric paraphernalia, equipment that could be mistaken for sex apparatus if it wasn't for the bookies and the blackboards, surfaces chalked with odds.

Actually, who knows?

"Aye. You were on a kissing spree, you were." The Cat finishes his drink, his grin now spreading from ear to ear, teeth yellow and chipped. A single incisor is capped with gold, surface brocaded with glyphs.

"Kissed a lot of girls, did I?"

"Plenty. And also a few men."

"What about children?" I sip the tepid cider. It tastes better than I'd expected; flat, dulled by exposure to the air, but still a sweet enough cocktail of passionfruit and lime. I smile, slightly artificially, eyes ticking across the room again. The third inspection reveals the towering Jack, haloed by negative space.

The Cat doesn't miss a beat. "Hadn't seen you accosting the wee ones, but there's a kitchen boy who sobs for his marm when ye get close."

I stare at the Cat. "Jackass."

His grin grows manic.

I take it as my cue to leave, patting the Cat on a chunky shoulder, before setting off towards the awkward emptiness that Jack'd built. Swollen though the crowd is, it's easy enough to navigate, largely congenial, apologizing even when I'm the one to bump foaming beer from hands, or tread on unlucky feet. I imagine the appropriate response would have been to retaliate with yet more profound contrition, possibly even prostration, but I swagger on. Stereotypes are there to be exploited.

Eventually, I arrive at Jack, who sits nested at the corner of the bar, top hat upturned on the counter like a begging bowl. His face, now divulged, is generically local. Pinkly English, perfectly forgettable, mediocrity in the flesh. Even his hair follows the pattern, thinning along the firmament of his skull, a widow's peak gentled by the short cut. Just an average Jack. I think I might be disappointed.

"Yo." I flash the Vulcan salute.

Jack scrunches his face, perplexed; replicates the gesture. Then he sighs gustily and tips the brim of his hat forward, a bizarre little motion that nearly has me putting a coin into the velvet cavity. But I don't get far with the thought. A figure lunges through the crowd, black-haired, braids flapping everywhere. Veles doesn't pause before scooping me into his arms, and crushes any objection I might have from my lungs.

"Rupert! Glad you made it. Wasn't expecting you to show your face." Veles swaps his grip, clasps a hand around each of my arms, still somehow keeping me aloft the whole time. "How are you?"

I grin at him, sickly, feeling rather like a bullied nephew. "Peachy."

He kisses me sloppily on each cheek, moist smacks that curdle my expression. Veles looks worse for wear; a new scar bridging socket and jaw, the flesh inflamed, glossy. Fresh deformities aside, he seems happy.

"Come. You meet Sisyphus. He will want to get to know man who helped Veles win big."

"Who's Sisyphus?" I gingerly begin prying at his fingers; it accomplishes nothing, but I feel better for trying. The thick slabs of Veles' extremities might as well have been hacked from stone. "Any chance you could put me down?"

"Yes." Veles releases his grip, and I plummet three inches to the floor, thoroughly mugged of any remaining dignity. As I rub sensation back into my arms, he presses on. "Sisyphus is Lord of Boulder, Master of the Ring, Gambler Ki—"

"Er." I consider his testimony. On the edge of my peripheral vision, I see Jack signalling a frightened bartender for more whiskey. She leaves, comes back with a bottle of smoky emerald, no tumbler in sight. "What?"

"Sisyphus is in charge of our bets."

"Sisyphus." The word hisses along my tongue, trailing memories. I don't like where this is going. "As in the damned bastard king? Sisyphus, as in the Sisyphus? Of the Sisyphean ordeal."

"Da."

Oh, dear.

"I"—I drag out the pronoun, scooting back a step—"don't think I want to meet him. I don't know what it's like where you're from, but where *I'm* from, people hate it when you make them lose money."

"Sisyphus understands fair play." Veles shrugs, leashing my shoulders with an arm. He doesn't push as much as he unthinkingly steamrolls me forward with his sheer momentum. In a fit of discontent, I endeavour to ping Bob but he, along with the other spirits, is unusually uncommunicative. How bizarre. I shelve away their silence for later introspection, too busy keeping tempo with Veles' long strides. He steers us towards one of the smaller rooms, the mob parting before us like a boozy, swaying sea.

Finally, we arrive. Two men, both about six feet tall and about six feet wide, freight trains gone vertical, stand on either side of the entrance, hand over fist over genitalia. Veles nods at them. They nod back.

Veles scruffs me like a misbehaving kitten, hand twisting into my collar, before ushering me inside. The room, similar to every other room in the Boulder, is packed beyond capacity. I breathe sweaty armpits and the sour, stinking aroma of human anxiety. Veles seems entirely unmoved by the rancidness. He resumes leading us through the throng, until at last we come face to face with a small-boned, smiling accountant of a man.

The only indication of Sisyphus' sovereignty is the crown that sits in his gray-stippled hair, a simple diadem of bronze, absurd in its plainness. His glasses are comparatively more interesting, magnifying pea-green eyes to give him the appearance of a Ren and Stimpy extra.

He doesn't acknowledge our arrival, focused instead on the floor. The tiles have been replaced by varnished pine, inlaid with a byzantine alphabet of pictographs, a syllabary that resembles nothing I've ever seen, all laminated with the faintest shimmer of gore.

At the heart of the board, a body—no, a living man, naked, penis a dessicated stub against a pale, bruised pelvis. Someone has opened him from throat to groin, *flayed* him, before pinning the skin to the wooden floor. His entrails glisten, frosted with gold ink, runes beyond counting. As I watch, Sisyphus creeps forward and pens another whorl, another character along the sinuous fold of an intestine.

The man moans, softly, orgasmically.

"What. The. Fuck."

Veles shrugs as he comes to stand beside me. "Just like normal man require motivation to work, prophet need motivation to see."

"Who is that?"

"That is Helenus," Veles explains, patient. "Cassandra's idiot brother. Several decades ago, we misplace his sister. So, Helenus must now serve in her place. Unfortunately, he's not as good. His spoken prophecies are *eh*. But Sisyphus discovered that blood cannot lie. What Helenus lacks in eloquence, his entrails make up for in effectiveness. So, we read the future in his offal."

"That is—" Sick? Repulsive? Coming from a cannibal chef, my revulsion would sound a bit rich; but bile coats the back of my mouth nonetheless. I swallow it back. Absently, I scratch at my neck, nails gouging into unexpectedly dry, scabrous skin. "Unusual."

Double entendres for every occasion.

"Da. But this millennium is unusual. We make do." Veles, as always, is disconcertingly chirpy. "Not long now. He is just auguring tomorrow's casualties. Few minutes. After that, Veles make introductions."

True enough, Sisyphus is done in a few minutes, rising to a ripple of respectful applause. A boy, maybe ten at most, scurries forward to proffer a steaming bowl, towel draped over an elbow. Sisyphus, with great care, dips his hands into the liquid. When he is done, he dabs a finger along the boy's forehead: a benediction of some variety, judging from the kid's radiant expression.

It is only after the ritual is concluded that Sisyphus strolls towards us, a peculiar moue balanced on a thin, almost lipless mouth.

"Huh." He announces, in place of a greeting, removing his glasses to wipe them with the hem of his shirt.

I blink, nonplussed, while Veles booms with laughter. "Well, hello to you, too."

"You're still alive."

"You say this like it's a bad thing."

His expression crystallises into a scowl, eyes ticking to Veles, less nonchalant now. Veles, for his part, seems jovially oblivious. "I hope you understand that I will be incredibly disappointed if he doesn't die tomorrow."

"Is unfortunate development." Veles pounds a fist on his sternum, grin feral. "Rupert is Veles' lucky rabbit. So he's going to stay alive."

I'm halfway through a nascent sense of camaraderie when Veles adds, broad palm clapping my shoulder. "But if he stops being lucky one day, eh. He can die then."

"How generous." I grouse and scratch at my arm, up through the sleeve. I find another encrustation, thicker, rougher than the first.

The two ignore me, Sisyphus tallying numbers or affronts under his breath, finally sighing as he taps a finger against his temple. "It'll cost me nine thousand ingots if he doesn't."

"Not Veles problem."

"You could have half of that, if you ensure he dies. Helenus saw room for your possible involvement."

"Tempting, but Veles can make bigger money the respectable way."

"Firstly, I don't know if any of this sounds respectable to me. And secondly, I don't know if either of you have noticed, but I'm..." Itch. *Scratch*. Had Veles passed on his lice? In exasperation, I begin to pick the rind gloving my forearm. Skin, or something similar, comes loose in a single sheet. I pull harder, more frantic, even as I snarl at the two men: "*Standing right here*. And I don't like the idea of dying unnecessarily."

I don't like the idea of dying for a reason either, but this isn't the occasion for semantics.

"What makes you think I'd let myself get murdered for a *bet*?" I wad the ribbon of dried blood into my palm, hands starved for a distraction, anything to divert from the enormity of what I'm likely to say.

Sisyphus widens his immense gaze, shucking indifference for something worse: piercing interest. "It's always about you, isn't it? In every timeline, in every reality, in every variation of now, you always make it go back to you. Aren't you ashamed, Rupert? You stand at the precipice of a maelstrom, a needle in the eye of time, a clot drifting through the veins of reality. With a single decision, you could change everything. Everything, in a world where reality doesn't care about you or me, or even the gods in and out of the machine. You, Rupert, could change everything, and yet: you make it about you."

There we go.

"Hate being that guy, if you know what I mean, but I have no idea what you're saying."

He sighs. Somewhere in the background, someone is spooning glutinous rice balls into Helenus' slack mouth. Peristalsis, much like many other bodily secrets, is something best kept behind whole skin. "What I'm saying is that your death is dependent on the temporal ecosystem. If you are fortunate and I am not, the timeline that keeps you alive will emerge triumphant. Inversely— *well*. Well."

"Look, seriously? You're still making no sense whatsoever. You—you're suggesting that I was some kind of chosen one, or something. An aneurysm of history, or whatever you want to call it. But now you're telling me that I have no choice but to hang around and see if I live or die? It really makes no fucking sense." I unroll the scab, review my find, finally conscious of what my hands had been doing. The air evicts itself from my lungs. I'd expected red-brown tissue, transparent flakes of epidermis, a few strands of hair, whatever you'd normally connect with an unnaturally cohesive scab—but there isn't any of that. Instead, it's one of the tattoo spirits, crumpled in my hand; eyes wide, lifeless, terrified.

"You are not the only playing piece on the board." Sisyphus tuts.

"Fuck you."

Shit.

My vitriol robs the room of its voice. Everyone stares. In a surprise twist, Sisyphus proves the most tolerant. Instead of enlisting the crowd in my evisceration, he takes off his glasses again, wipes them on the corner of his shirt. Squints. His expression spasms into a grimace, delicate. "What did you say?"

I consider everything that'd went down recently, every aggression, every confrontation, every use of power to befoul, belittle, and break down. The thoughts churn poison. *Coward.* Poseidon's voice again, bilious, so thick with disdain that I choke on the memory. But self-preservation swells like an ill-timed erection. (The mind can crave heroism, *ang moh*, but the body's a sucker for survival.) I wet my lips with a dab of my tongue and grin, earnest, hoping it comes across as pliantly amenable, rather than just pained.

"I said fuck you. With greater emphasis on the first word. *Fuck.* You." The words surprise me even as they abandon my mouth, falling, cold as coins. "There is always a choice."

Sisyphus restores his glasses to their roost, face smoothing, bland. He taps the frame to the bridge of his nose with a finger—the middle one, of course. Blink. Stare. Crocodile smile, no heat, nothing but swampwater cool. In that moment, Sisyphus transcends into everything we associate with kings, terrible and absurd and full-on, *fuck-you-peon* swagger. "If that helps you sleep at night."

Before I can grunt an objection, he discards me, discards our conversation like yesterday's crusty boxers. I'm speechless as he struts into the crowd, Veles' fingers gouging a warning into my clavicle.

"Stay," he rumbles, although he still sounds amused.

"Not a dog." I jerk my shoulder, hoping to dislodge him, but the motion only compels him to strengthen his grip, nails cutting through fabric and into skin.

I let the tattoo spirit fall from my hand, to be mashed into the floor by passing feet. The urge to claw out of my shirt, check out how many tattoos have gone the way of the first, is overwhelming. But I don't think I want to cash in on that suspicion. I know what I'll find: indecency charges, and a spine beaded with dead ghosts.

An image of the man from the train resurrects itself, smile mild, head cocked, the apocalypse skinned in banality, a kid standing on a mound of crawling ink.

"Da. But is rude to talk about someone's handicaps." He chortles at his own joke; a whuffing, thundering noise. "Don't make ruckus, Rupert. Sisyphus has big ball."

"Don't you mean balls?" I fumble for wit, discover schoolyard humour instead, a vaguely acceptable compromise. Sisyphus has gone back to doodling pictograms on Helenus' entrails, each fresh inscription eliciting another rapturous shudder from the prophet. I avert my eyes as Helenus' pleasure grows carnal, flaccid cock rousing from its matted bed.

"That too." Hand anchored in my flesh, Veles walks me towards the bar, shouldering aside anyone unfortunate enough to intersect with our route. "Come. Veles will buy his lucky bunny a graveyard."

"Er, that doesn't sound so—" The thought of escape stirs to life, and is expunged the next moment. I'm not winning this one, not this far out of my element, not with a cloak of corpses on my back.

His grin is the moon, the smile of a wolf on the cusp of a kill. "Is great. One drink, and you won't just see two Veles, you'll see twelve."

"I swear, Veles, that did not sound as good as you think it did in your head."

Now, listen, ang moh. Listen. Forget everything you've learned about getting drunk. That bottle of Chivas, cut with bottles of cheap Coke, might get you there, but graveyards are a one-way ticket on the fast train to Knockoutville.

A trifecta of whiskeys, triple sec, equal amounts of rum, vodka, gin, and tequila. Mix with beer *and* stout. Consume. You won't know what hit you.

Actually, you will. Because unless you've lived a truly unfortunate life, chances are that first sip will be the worst thing you've ever put in your mouth.

I can't believe I'm standing.

More slumping than standing, to be fair, most of my weight hanging off the crook of a stranger's arm. But there is still a degree of standing. Somewhere.

My toes scrabble for purchase on the rippling pavement. I push upright, tip sideways. Whoops. Someone catches me. I beam hazily, my world cottoned with daubs of orange fluorescence, and boxy shapes that only tangentially resemble a street.

It could be cold. I'm too numb to tell.

"Careful." Not Veles. Not Hildra, either. The voice is unfamiliar, bassy, straight from the gut.

I blink, blink again, crane my sight up and stare until the summit of a top hat comes into focus. "Jack!"

The glob of shadow crooks at its zenith, suggesting a nod. "Jack."

"Jack!" I repeat and totter in place, vinegary bile pushing against the underside of my tongue. The sliver of brain matter not otherwise committed to staying upright is racing with a hodgepodge of images, and impressions of tastes too vile to duplicate even in memory. I drank—*something*. Many instances of something. Pulped roadkill, most likely, left to ferment, essential oils reconstituted into a blasphemy of alcoholic reprieve.

"Jack," I announce again.

He pats my head, innocently paternalistic. "We will have you home soon. I just need to do one thing first—*ma'am*."

His voice cracks through the damp, piss-piquant silence. Out of the periphery of an eye, I catch movement, the lineament of a woman cosseted in dense, dark fabric. She stops, cigarette-cherry burning in the gloam.

"What." A French accent.

I feel a shimmer of power—asphalt, tar, alleyway-dust—as Jack gently deposits me in a corner and steps forward. The street empties. The air stills. And suddenly, it's just the three of us, strangled in sidewalks and silence, and something is not *right*. I reach out, snare the tail of his coat between my fingers.

Blood, arterial, boiling from a heart that refuses to quiet. Her pulse, a thunderstorm beneath its sheath of silken brown skin. If I made an incision here, I'd be able to—

"What the fu—" I bend over, throw up on his shoes.

Metal shaves through the air in a wide silver arc, nicking my skull, pares a curl of skin and hair from my scalp. Pain foams. My vision clarifies into a portrait of Jack, haloed in the street lamps, his face a slurry of nictitating meat. Flesh drools in gelatinous skeins, aligning into new jaws, fresh arrangements of teeth and eyebrow. Even the eyes saccade between colors, numbers, shapes and depths.

"Diu." It's amazing how quickly abject terror can burn through booze.

I fall backwards, hit the ground ass-first, scrabble across the cobblestones as Jack, Jack the Ripper, Jack the First, Jack the Trypophobe's Best Nightmare, advances. Lips extrude from swirling muscle fibers, wrap about the dentition, twist into a snarl. He blinks. Sixteen eyes. Four. Three hundred. Two.

Behind him, rooted in place, the girl, blank gaze refracting the light.

Then she winks.

She is on him before my brain stem can articulate a reaction, a blurring; her skin bunching, distorted, distended from a prize pack of auxiliary body features, barely elastic enough to hold under the rapid-fire mutations. A fan of mouths opens, bites down. Jack wheels, roars, claws at his back. He howls as she burrows deeper, chewing herself an access point between the span of his shoulders.

Slurping, audaciously loud. I see a tongue extend, snake across the gore dribbling from the planes of his back, see muscles half-masticated. The girl-thing nuzzles into his scapula. A crisp snapping follows, like twigs being halved, and Jack's right arm goes slack. He screeches, enamelled razor clattering to the ground.

In desperation, Jack flings himself backwards, crashing into the wall, maybe hoping it'd loosen her grip, but it doesn't. Draperies of wool animate, thrashing. Fabric attenuates into needlepoint; spears burst from his torso, six on each side.

Out of misguided loyalty, I stagger upright, shouting the first spell that wanders into the orbit of my consciousness. I shred my lip, spit blood into the incantation. It fizzles into confused life, quaking, as dubious of its existence as I am with its creation. On a whim, I extend an invitation to the tenants tattooed on my skin, only to find a rotting silence in my head. I forgot about that. Damn it.

"Let my, er..." Not 'friend.' Deranged, sustenance-starved chaperone, maybe? I pause, wilting with indecision, before finally concluding: "...coworker, who I have absolutely no personal ties to, go!"

She stares and she *smiles,* smiles with too many mouths and just enough teeth, alimentary canals snaking in the chilly air, a ruff of sinuous tubes and disembodied ligament. My stomach turns. One of her maws snaps forward, grabs my cantrip as it sings through the air. Swallows.

That's that, then.

"I tried. I'll be going now."

"No." *Her* voice is polyharmonic. As I watch, her mouths rear like cobras. I see Jack's features pulsate, consolidate into pure, animalistic fear. The air rankles with ammonia; he's pissing himself.

Then, just like that, it is over, and Jack's body is on the floor, face-down, throbbing periodically as the girl eats *into* his ribs, hollowing him out. It is only when she is done, when she's colonized the topology of his meat, when her eyes open behind his eyes, and she smiles *again,* that I wheeze out:

"I am very scrawny and would taste horrible, even if you fry me and dip me in ketchup."

She laughs at me, glides closer, and pins my chin in Jack's stolen fingers. Another tickle of power, an explanation transmitted through skin. And I think: *oh.*

If there can be a God of Missing People, scrapped together from a thousand parents begging *pleasepleasecomehomeplease*, there can be a God of *Being* Missing, a goddess of waiting for it to end, a deity of clenched teeth and knife wounds and prayers emptied into corners where no one will come, of a rage that holds on. All of the hurt in the world had to come together somewhere, didn't it? Makes sense that it'd coalesce here, gathering to gestate a killer of killers.

She pushes Jack's tongue into my unresisting mouth, and I hear her crooning, sleek and dark and gorged on his essence, coiled like an embryo in the womb of his bones. Of course she'd hunt things like Jack. Of course. Of course. *Of course.*

She breaks the kiss, a strand of saliva yawning between our mouths. I wipe it away, try not to think too deeply on what just transpired.

"Tell them they cannot prey on ours any longer. Tell them they are no longer wanted here. Tell—" A smile, incandescent and peculiarly girlish. The next words are sly, a joke hemmed between the pauses. "Tell them that we are coming for them."

And that is all she says before she walks away, wearing the body that Jack built, even as the world restarts in fits and London comes pouring through the cracks.

On the plus side, at least I'm sober.

TWENTY-FIVE

"RUPERT, OLD CHUM, old pal, old ball and chain. The mightiest of all Asian recruits, master of dumplings, sovereign of chopsticks. How are you doing? Good. Of course you're good. Why wouldn't you be good? Say, I was going to ask, are you going to make a bet today?"

I knot apron strings behind my back, sluggish despite the four cups of coffee I've already consumed. Sleep had been difficult, haunted by nightmares of Ao Qin grinning up at me from the shower drain. And then there were the actual morning ablutions, which became an exercise in funerary attrition. I spent an hour disentangling tattoos from my epidermis, and then another hour figuring out how to unclog the toilet.

All in all, not a pretty morning.

"Aren't you going to ask me about Jack?"

The fox flicks white-tipped ears forward, jaw hanging in a grin. A gray tongue laps over his nose. "No."

No one cares that Jack's gone. Then again, no one gave a damn when we lost the knockers in the first attack; their corpses were eventually crammed into black trash bags and left outside for collection.

The best the group ever musters is a threadbare sort of disgruntlement and even then, it's never entirely holistic, contaminated by self-absorption. Forget the dead men/women/anthropomorphizations/things. What about the *responsibilities* they left behind?

(A thing worth thinking about, I suppose: when we die, will people weep or whine?)

Still, it was enough to make me leave the breakfast table in disgust, allowing them to bicker over cups of tepid coffee and stale scones, the rusalka lazily devouring fat sticks of butter. There aren't many people that I like, fewer I trust, but I'd at least ponder a minute of silence, if one was serendipitously axed. Not rant on about bathroom duties.

Ang moh, am I right?

"I understand," drawls the fox, as though my thoughts were printed on the air above my head. He sucks in a breath through yellowed incisors. "Such things are important to you and surely, they're just as important to me. But Jack is Jack and Jack is dead, and Jack is a relic of older times. Poor, unfortunate Jack. Yes. So tragic. So terrible. But we can't help the dead, can we? We can *discuss* the dead, but that's hardly useful. What's useful, though, is you telling me: are you going to place a bet or not?"

"Sure." I pick up the mop, squeeze its tendrils dry of yesterday's brown foam, plant it back on the ground, and push. "What am I betting on?"

A gleam of sharp teeth. "The *bet*, obviously."

I sigh. Sunlight slants through grime-clouded windows, gray, cold, unbothered by the rain. No one has stepped in yet, despite the 'open' sign hanging skewed from the door, a nervous entreaty to benefit from our free food. Maybe word of the massacre has finally gotten out.

"That's not helpful, Reynard."

He stiffens. A frisson coughs up his spine, hackles pluming. His brows pucker. "My name is not—"

"I know." I stop him before he starts. "It's a joke. It's—"

Wood scrapes across linoleum. A squeal of hinges, caked in dried gore. The door opens and my head shoots up, alarm dinging in my ears. The soup kitchen no longer stinks of shit and offal, but there's a certain unmistakably *metallic* je-ne-sais-quoi loitering in the air.

A figure, gaunt even under its candy-striped parka and oversized cap, inches through. I open my mouth, ready to circumvent any signs of gibbering panic, but the rusalka makes a precipitous appearance, padding from bathroom to door. She seizes the new arrival by the crook of an arm and smiles. A wash of magic, faint, almost negligible. But enough. The stranger droops, docile, and the rusalka leads him triumphantly to a bench.

I watch as the rusalka cups the figure's face, fingers rested under the jut of the malnourished chin. Her chest inflates and the newcomer imitates her. A silvery mist twirls from the latter's nostrils, spiralling into the rusalka's open mouth. She breathes again, the rusalka does. Deep. And I can see something go out of her victim, see them grow smaller, shrunken, sapped of substance, the light in their eyes dimmed, decayed by the rusalka's appetite.

"Bet? Yes or no?" says the fox, barking each word, enunciating with elaborate care.

I glance back, disgusted. A soup kitchen, but not for the homeless, helpless people that wobble through the front door, convinced of altruism. *Those* people are just food. "So you eat these people—"

"Rupert! That is not important! That is not the hill that you should choose to die on!" The fox is almost shouting in his agitation. "I asked you a question! Are you playing! Will you place a bet! A bet! It is critical you tell me if you'd make a bet!"

"Sure. Fine. I—"

"Live." His tongue lolls from a muzzle halfway to humanity, bone already shrinking into a mannish skull. "Or die?"

"*What?* That is completely not ominous at—"

Boom.

No fucking warning, not really; the sound comes milliseconds after the fact. The shock front takes us all unaware, too fast, too close, searing through the air. It hits *hard*. I feel bone give, and ribs snap, and tendons sever, even as the softer components of the human body are pulped, windpipe and intestines and all manner of tubular offal collapsing onto themselves.

I breathe. Or, at least, the body endeavours to breathe. I heave air into lungs that won't inflate, pressure constricting around my chest, bones splintering through useless tissue. Every gasp sears through my nerve endings, agonizing. It takes a moment to develop a chronology of events: I've hit the wall, fallen over, and am now prone on the tiles, with a gut neatly bisected by a panel from the dishwasher, the dials somehow still ludicrously intact. A mass of exposed intestines slops over my apron, black with soot, or else burned.

"Shit."

With that, the ceiling comes down.

"Mr. Wong. Mr. Wong, are you alive yet?"

Yet. The first motes of consciousness string together around the word, an utterance that catalyzes curiosity. Muzzily, my brain concludes that 'yet' is a weird adverb to use in that sentence, something that should be expressed.

I gum the air, smack my lips over sounds that should have been words, but arise as dumb mewling. This is not good.

"Mr. Wong."

Something pries open my eyelids, fingernails scraping over corneal membrane. The world goes white. I flinch seconds after the fact, reflexes crippled by internal trauma, sensory ganglia still reviving. I lick blood from my mouth. My tongue strokes across a thread of dangling nerve. I snap it at the root. Hopefully, it didn't go anywhere important.

"Mr. Wong."

"Will you just fuck off. Ham kha chan."

Laughter, completely pleasant, disarmingly reminiscent of the Boss' frothy, friendly chuckle. "We'll take that as a 'yes.'"

More hands come, brace against my back and shoulders, propel me into a sitting position. And I scream. A long, wet note of anguish that goes on longer than I'd thought I had breath or dignity for. The blinding sunlight resolves into silhouettes, then placid, smiling faces. I blink through a bloodied film, take in the half-circle of observers.

"Don't tell me," I slur. "Mormon boy-band?"

Polite chortling all around. The men—no, not just men, but women too, with slicked-back hair and identical smiles, immaculately suited—exchange knowing expressions, before fixating on me afresh. "No. We are Vanquis."

"Oh." I rummage through myself for something more articulate to say. "*Oooooh.*"

"We have a proposition." One voice, twenty-six mouths. Not a choir of voices, or even one voice duplicated by twenty-six larynxes. Just one voice, emanating from the general vicinity of twenty-six mouths, all pantomiming the words in unison.

"Uh huh." I take inventory of the adjacent damage. The soup kitchen's gone, every profit margin buried in chunks of rubble like broken teeth. My legs are doing marginally better: one borders on functional, even if the other is nothing but cords of bleeding muscle, skewered by bone. I run fingers up my arm, find untattooed skin.

Right. I forgot about that.

"Join us."

"You're not selling this really well." I massage a thigh, finally coherent enough to register two important details. First, that I'm in the process of healing, as opposed to fully healed, an anomalous occurrence given past resurrections. The second is that I have no memory of being dead, no recollection of Diyu or the interstitial areas between: only emptiness, only dark.

Which means that something else had reached into the abyss and fished out my soul, something big enough, *powerful* enough, to supersede Diyu's authority. The thought rakes ice-water down my spine, freezing my tongue in its seat.

"Like the scars of old London, like the poverty of Hackney, the old pantheons cannot stand in the way of progress."

"Guys, I keep hearing variations of this. Tell me something new." If I keep them talking long enough, I might be able to get into a situation where I can, if not run, then at least hobble away with reasonable efficiency.

"The old pantheons will fall, *must* fall to make way for the new." A restless energy glissades from face to vapidly smiling face, never lingering long enough to be mapped or measured, only to be acknowledged. Whatever that force is, it *wants* me to know its watching. "Join us. We've loved you from the moment you first breathed data, and we'll love you until the world burns. We will never abandon you. We will never be like them."

"So I've heard." Trapping fingers around my knee, I brace myself, squeeze my face into an anticipatory grimace, and *wrench*. The joint torques into position, overshoots; I feel the splinters of my fibula grind into the muscle, feel bone gouge furrows through subcutaneous tissue. I howl into a closed fist, pain spasming in magnesium-white flashes.

Fortunately, the Vanquis agents are too preoccupied with their sales pitch to notice.

"—the Fathers have fled, they've shut the doors. It is only their children who linger, lost pups, starving—"

The air glistens, oily with new magic, fresh-minted power crackling with the smell of burnt wire. A rapid-fire rotation of images, flickering like a zoetrope: black cables, pregnant with data; families in cramped houses; moonlight oiling down the neck of a bottle; a sorcery of sub-clauses and subliminal marketing, credit cards piled up like a dragon's hoard.

I blink, and the hallucinations fade, a gauzy overlay, almost thin enough to ignore. Vanquis' cronies continue, voice plunging to hissing whispers. Their soliloquy fragments, alters in delivery; now relayed in pieces, first by one body and then another, each new conduit palsied by its passage.

"—a new order comes—"

"That's nice, guys. Any freebies? You know, any 'get in on the ground floor, and we'll throw in a prize' kinda thing." Again. I steel myself, suck three quick puffs of air, and pull at my knee. This time, I'm prepared for the momentum, but the pain still gets me, and a choirboy shriek wheezes between my teeth. But it works. Cartilage and ligament merge, accelerated by eldritch forces, and anchor the unmoored patella to the socket.

Three more breaths. I count to ten, an incantation against agony, my vision wavering.

"—a new order grows—"

"By grow, do you mean 'organically' or through paid—whatever the fuck social media calls it—" I pant, grinning through bloodied teeth. Wobbling, I knuckle into a squat, the heels of my palms digging into bitumen. No one has come out to gawk at the tableau yet, leaving me to wonder if we've been relocated into a discrete pustule of reality, only tangentially attached to normal.

Not that it matters.

Focus, Rupert. One. Two. Three deep breaths, and I'm up. Every molecule of my person immediately objects to the sudden machismo, pain denticulating through the capillaries, bullet-bitter on the tongue. I spit blood and stagger, but I don't fall. That's the important part. I don't fall.

A faraway roar, a warscream.

"—from the diseased pustulence of the old—"

"Yes, but tell me..." I shake like an old drunk, limbs jellied, every trembling step an Olympian triumph. The rain coagulates into silver, washes the London skyline away. I breathe pain, raw and hot and charnel. *God.* "Tell me how you *really* feel."

Their voices become a cascade.

"What we need—"

"—we need—"

"—we need—"

"—we need—"

An asphyxiating twitch of magic, like a noose drawn taut. I keep moving. It clips into a rhythm: three breaths, a few rickety steps diagonally, away from the crescent of possessed salespeople, cupped palms dripping threads of rain. One. Two. Three. *Step.*

Inefficient as it might be, the repetition hypnotizes, numbs awareness of the ambient hurt that clicks like a punctuation at the end of every motion. I'm halfway to convincing myself that it's just a trick of the gray matter when Vanquis' myriad voices consolidate, straight-salvo into the medulla oblongata. "—is your skin."

"Sorry. What?"

The air pulses, tightening. But Vanquis—a moment's inspiration tells me it's a single distributed entity, rather than a creche of brainwashed goons—never gets the opportunity to reply. A white van howls around a corner, and I see Demeter hanging from the window, *literally* blazing with glory.

Also, an assault rifle.

I throw myself onto the road, hands over my head, as she opens a cannonade, and gore, syrupy with pulped tissue, rains down. The artillery fire is relentless, explosive, precise. Fuck natural physics. Demeter's loaded her ammunition with godfire or whatever it is that deities cram inside the little lead cartridges, an apocalypse in every bullet.

Boom. One last time. I peer up in time to see a man *burst* into chunks, red offal and bits of spine. Brain flops through the air in spongy pieces. As his body, chewed-up and spat out by the patrons of ballistic trauma, sags onto the ground, the van comes to stop. Demeter slides from the window and into the driver's seat, kicking the door open in that same sharp motion.

"Get in."

I don't wait for her to ask twice.

TWENTY-SIX

"SOMETHING ISN'T RIGHT."

"Oh?"

"I can't stop thinking about it. How did they get a bomb into the kitchen? The doors were locked. The wards were untampered with. There were no signs of forced entry. I know; I *checked*. But they got in and they got out without a whisper. Someone has to be working with them. Also—"

I pause in my stride.

"Also, why are there so many grandmothers—"

Demeter marches me past a ludicrous diorama of geriatric women, thronging the courtyard like snoozing cats; eyes glazed, mouths slack. They knit and gossip, voices languid, play chess and read, perform all the rituals expected of old women. Except there's no sun and it is freezing, and they're clumped in the rain in flimsy gowns, newspapers melting from blueing fingers.

"Because Vanquis is still an infant, concerned with"—she weaves her fingers in a complicated motion—"patterns, the fiction of itself. Old people mean too much to the desperate. So much, in fact, that they are necessary to Vanquis' identity."

"And what's that?" I limp along beside her, arm held over freshly sutured ribs, mouth burning with the memory of her lips. She'd kissed me once during the trip. Lightly. Perfunctorily. A honeyed warmth that spread across my skin, piecing together whatever was left to fix. Not perfectly—Demeter lacked either the resources or the willingness to expend them—but she did enough.

"Vanquis is..." We enter the council building. Demeter's face, robed in shadow, is unearthly, eerie. A tinge of violence lingers, trails behind her like the smell of gunpowder and boiling steel, and I'm reminded again that gods of fertility only ever want blood sacrifices for Christmas. "I don't know. Like so many other things, it began with a desire, a need, if you will. In this case, a requirement for accessible short-term loans."

"You're *kidding*."

She pins me with a glare and I lapse into silence, cataloging the modifications that have been made to the interior instead. Every door we pass is bolted shut, strung with chains and padlocks, reinforced with thick wooden panels. *They're under siege*. The thought prickles, rust-edged, dangerous.

"You'd be amazed how many people pray for temporary salvation. Nothing lasting. Nothing that might require a lifetime of devotion. Something small. Something to get them by for the next day, the next week. And Vanquis grew swollen on that need." Demeter sighs, mounting the stairs to the Grecian lair. I hesitate for the sliver of a heartbeat, long enough to register the way the light follows her like a dog, and how the darkness, musty and absolute, slinks after.

I fall into formation, shadows nipping at my heels.

"It became a god. Not just a manifestation of the company, but a god of debt, a god of desperation." Demeter's brow pinches with distaste.

I trap my tongue against the ceiling of my mouth, consider the next words, the worth of a quip. A dull ache permeates my body still, pooling in the joints, where muscles were foreshortened and tendons stretched too far; nerves are fused into balls of hurt in the marrow, casualties of unfavorable circumstances. I miss Bob, and Joe, and Billie Jean, and every spirit to have etched a tenancy agreement into the ledger book of my soul. They might have been literally eating me out of house and bone, but they were a reassuring last resort. A stopgap.

Just like Vanquis.

Unsettled, I squelch down the epiphany, say nothing. Instead, I focus on placing one foot after another. We all need a few lies to get through the day, after all. Today, this is mine. Outside, the world pales, white and unfriendly, a cold reminder that I'm a long, long way from normal.

EVERYONE IS HERE.

Bizarrely, the apartment reeks of terror. Unwashed armpits, fear-sweat. Human odors, rancid, pheromone-laden, utterly incongruous against this spread of manifested myths.

Demeter says nothing as she vanishes into the clamor, leaving me to fend for myself. I mill slowly, ignoring the knots of conversation; the gods standing with glasses of water in shaking hands, Orpheus sitting illuminated at the window, Cerberus' head on his lap; the nymphs, the ram-horned satyrs, fornicating anxiously on a stretch of carpet.

Even Helenus is present, nailed to a wall, intestines drooling from the open cavity of his torso, pink and gray and pictograms of gold. He has a spigot jammed into his wrist. Someone—a squat, strange figure, broader along the shoulder than they are tall—is pouring themselves a drink.

I go past. Hades and Poseidon sit enthroned on two lazy chairs opposite each other, regal as kings, ridiculous as sauced-up uncles at Chinese New Year's. At my arrival, Hades tips his chin.

"Rupert—"

"Hades, you fucking asshole, you piece of shit—" Demeter's voice, thunderous.

The gods fall silent as she shoulders back into view, face white, lips peeled from the gums. It crackles from her, that rage of hers, singed-earth and lava, bubonic, all-encompassing, the end of the world clasped in the quiver of a choked syllable.

"How could you?" Under her anger, there's something else: a hurt that's entirely too familiar, lodged so deep that it might as well be budded from the marrow. Loss; singing like the last, lonely star at the end of time. Her voice drops to a hiss. "I—how could you?"

Poseidon is on his feet before Hades can concoct a reply, sinewy arms held out either in affection or to restrain. Demeter ignores him, tries to walk past, but he grabs her, traps her arms under a muscular limb.

As the goddess struggles, snarling, Hades finally speaks, his voice sanded down by repeated offense, unsurprised. "She is my wife. There is nothing untowards about how I treat her."

"You—" Demeter buries her nails in Poseidon's flesh. Blood weeps in luminous strands, honey-red, slightly gelatinous. "That is not how you treat anyone."

"Her body is mine." Hades, patient. "As mine is hers. And what takes place between spouse and spouse has nothing to do with you."

"I am her *mother*." A ragged expulsion of air, spittle. The vines in her hair come alive, barbed, needle-petalled flowers tearing at the square of Poseidon's chin. Injuries gape like mouths on his skin, healing as quickly as they appear. Despite the damage he sustains, Poseidon's expression stays cloyingly fond, like someone indulging a rambunctious kitten. He grins at her, his lips to an ear, crooning reassurances even as Demeter's rage devours him, again and again, tearing the divine meat from his skull.

"Yes," Hades replies, flat. "You are."

I glance around us. The other deities have returned to their conversations, their brittle chuckling; bodies angled ever-so-slightly away from the elephant in the room.

"You're *embarrassed*." I don't realize I'm the one who has spoken until I'm skewered by their attention, incredulous, distaste in their fine-boned faces. Someone laughs into a hand.

"It's a family affair," Ananke declares from an armrest, knee gathered to her chest, sleek frame scaled in kevlar. The loose curls are gone, shorn to fit her newly martial veneer. "Stay out of it."

"But you're—" I don't finish. Ananke isn't subtle. Her will is a violation, an assault, a demand supplied through the barrel of a gun. It burrows past Diyu's wards, comes out clean the other side, a hook threaded into a flap of skin. Without my tattoos complicating matters, I don't stand a chance. Ananke tugs and I gasp, staggering forward.

"Quiet." Her glee is disgusting.

Through it all, Demeter says nothing, watches through lidded eyes, hair suddenly stagnant. She sighs. The blossoms rot, browning petals falling soundless to the floor.

"Ananke's right. This is not your problem." Her voice is husked, guttural.

I'm not given a chance to riposte. Another contemptuous twitch of Ananke's mind, and suddenly, I'm lurching back to the broom closet I've been assigned to. I fight it, hard. I push back against the symphonic mutiny of limb and lung, twisting this way and that, upsetting my own centre of balance, forcing the compulsion to re-calibrate. I steal myself seconds of autonomy, gasping. "Don't you want to know about the soup kitchen?"

Hades doesn't miss a beat. "No."

"What about Jack? And"—a memory exhumes itself: Jack's stolen body, grinning, teeth pale as bird bones—"the thing that killed him. It said they were coming."

"There is *always* someone coming," Hades sighs, rummaging through his coat for a sodden cigar, which ignites itself without provocation, burning blue-white at the tip. "We are at war."

"No one told me that." I'm still being walked, stiff-legged and halting, to my claustrophobic accommodations. Poseidon has reseated himself, Demeter propped stiffly on his lap, her fists balled.

"You weren't conscripted to be a soldier," comes the even response. Hades stares at me through rectangles of smoke. The supernatural have such a thing against puffing carcinogens normally. "We hired you to be a cook."

"A cook? More like cannon fodder, am I right?"

Ananke exerts more pressure. Sweat rolls from the crown of my head, soaking into my blood-soaked wardrobe, beading on my lips and my nose. My teeth begin to rattle from the effort.

"Y-y-ou just like h-having m-meat shields."

Hades crooks a grin, the first I've seen on him. And it's ghastly. He twitches two fingers straight, a motion that loosens Ananke's hold, before leaning forward, cigar pushed to the corner of his mouth. "Do you know why gods don't answer prayers?"

"B-b-ecause you're c-cunts—*fuck*." I bite halfway through my tongue and wince, mouth filling with the raw-meat taste of iron.

"Because we don't need to."

"F-f-fuck you," I'm starting to feel light-headed, possibly because my brain's sustaining repeated impact trauma. Is it possible to give yourself a concussion doing absolutely nothing? I will probably find out.

"If you weren't so useful—" A sigh eases from his lips. The grin is gone, erased, replaced by the humorless flatness I'd come to know and be completely ambivalent about.

"S-s-say that again?"

Hades leans back into his chair, leather squeaking. He pulls on a lever and the foot rest bounces up. I almost manage to laugh. "Do what you want with him, Ananke. I am done."

She doesn't hesitate. This time, *this time* she comes at me full throttle, no holds barred, no safety equipment. Her essence overwhelms, pure torrential *need*, flensing away anything that isn't her desire, her want. What remains of my individuality is beaten into a twitching heap of misfiring synapses before it is boxed up and shipped off to wherever my sense of masculine pride now lives, tail permanently soldered between its legs.

I drool as I shamble down the corridor, barely more than an animal, eyes rolled up. Ananke's laughter fits around me, an amniotic sac, distorting all external sound. In place of a mother's heartbeat, I feel her scorn pulsate, a wonder-bloated disgust, like someone witnessing the live birth of the cockroach messiah.

And I give in, then, exhausted, drained of fight. Fuck it. I lurch along. Until the swaying pendulum of my throbbing skull puts me in view of an opened door. Inside, emaciated lines hemmed in gray sunlight, stands a girl.

She doesn't look good. She's thin, too thin. Not the calculated emaciation of a runway model, but a starved angularity, like skin wrapped around bone. The waxen skin is finger-marked, purple-black. Her legs—the calves are contourless, almost entirely bone—are scarred by bites, the imprint of human teeth demarcating the stretch of her femur. Around her throat, a necklace of bruises.

Worse than the evidence of hard use, worse than the ooze glistening along her hipbones, is the way her inert form's been arranged: hands demurely crossed at the pelvis. Legs together. A venerated corpse. Loved. Cherished. The incongruity makes my stomach crawl.

"Move." Ananke's voice, vibrating against my cochlea.

I plant my feet. "Who is that?"

"*Move.*"

"Is that—" The question loses itself in my throat and suddenly, I'm choking on the implications, on a vision of Minah after she'd walked out of the shower, wringing wet from long, black hair, her skin discolored by a system rigged from the beginning. "Is that *Persephone*?"

Ananke doesn't ask again. In that moment, I discover exactly how filthy some gods will play: she makes me wrench my own arm out of its socket, thumb buried into the glenohumeral joint, fingers hitched through cartilage. I scream, of course, until the sound is sandpaper, grating across my vocal chords, every other thought suspended in raw-veined agony. For a frictionless eternity, it is only pain and its every manifestation, only the excruciating awareness of muscles being unstitched, pulled apart, fiber by fiber.

Luckily for me, she doesn't force an amputation, content to simply separate the bone.

"Move," she repeats, smug.

Insert unpleasantly sexist word here.

TWENTY-SEVEN

"Rupert, how's it—*what happened to you?*"

I grin dully into the camera, a pinpoint of emerald against the black border of the laptop screen. "Life. Life happened."

Ghouls don't photograph well. Something about natural camouflage, a confluence of specialized cells, meant to refract and distract from their ongoing decay. Like chameleons except bigger, badder, and considerably hungrier. Naturally, this extends to video calls.

Fariz blurs around the edges, cheeks distended by a lag of pixels, features smudged to relative anonymity. In a police lineup, he'd only be identifiable as 'possibly Asian.' Or 'articulate chipmunk.'

"Your arm is—" He interrupts himself with a dose of a shisha, smoke leaking from his nostrils. Behind him, the sky is dark, orange-tinged by street lamps and pollution. I can see plastic tables staggered in the background. A projector screen emblazoned with a football match. Tropical vegetation. A man attending a charcoal grill. "Seriously, man. What did you do to yourself?"

I wipe my jaw with the back of my functional hand, the other piled uselessly on my lap, middle finger crooked for effect. The pain is almost manageable, enormous enough that my brain is beginning to fool itself into thinking it's always been there, the baseline of existence; that there was never a universe not saw-toothed with hurt.

"You wouldn't—it's not important. Seriously. I..." I hesitate, flicking a glance at the door. "I need to know what's going on."

"What do you mean, 'what's going on'?" Fariz says, guarded, a nervous rhythm drummed on the plastic table. He's never had a good poker face, whatever he says.

"Cut the bullshit. You know what I'm talking about. I haven't forgotten the thing about the Furies, or trying to drive the Chinese pantheon extinct. *What has he done?*"

A long pause. "What has *who* done?"

"Fuck you."

Fariz titters, gags on the noise. He takes another hit from his bong. A server drifts by to deposit a plate of fried noodles, the intestinal-looking mass topped with a fried egg, yolk running off the sides.

I wait until the waiter's gone before I bark, "Seriously. What the fuck is going on?"

"Rupert, I don't know where to start. It—I didn't want to alarm you."

"You knew." I squeeze the wrist of the broken arm, let pain blunt the spiking rage. "You. Fucking. Knew."

"Look. Not everything, okay? It isn't what you think it is. Not some great conspiracy to keep you in the dark. Well, a small conspiracy. It's just that Ao Qin got *out* and—"

"What."

"He's on the warpath. I—I don't really know how to say this, but he found your apartment."

"What."

"And your personal records."

"What."

"Possibly a few family members, if you even have those."

"*And?*"

"Ao Qin might have had a tantrum."

I lean back, away from the screen, as though it might ejaculate torrential saltwater at any moment. "Well. Shit."

Fariz winds a mouthful of noodles around his fork, almost embarrassed. I wait as he performs the necessary ceremony. Gulp. Chew. Swallow. Ghouls might not share our dietary requirements, but that doesn't mean they're not drawn by the allure of deep-fried saturated fats.

"'Shit' doesn't cover it."

A hollow laugh shakes itself loose, and I hiss as the movement uncoils a starburst of pain along my arm. My fingers feel worryingly numb. Reflexively, I clench my hand into a fist, massaging a thumb up the wrist, hoping to encourage circulation, keep the muscle from flirting with necrosis. A vision of the Cat's extremities, black and green and tumid as rotting berries, flits across my mind.

"This is well above your pay grade," Fariz declares sympathetically, eyes averted. He lances the egg and it belches yolk onto his noodles, a punctured blister bleeding pus. "The best thing you can do now—and I'm saying this as your best friend—is to lay low and wait. Let the Greeks and the Chinese fight it out. When they finally collide, they won't even remember who you—"

I let myself buy into the fantasy, just a moment. I rub my eyelids as Fariz wheels out a future of blessed mundanity, bought by the deaths of legends. A simple life. A new home, a cat, an illegal subscription to Netflix. I could have it all. A pawn's paradise.

"Where does Vanquis fit into this picture?"

"Come again?"

"Vanquis. The—" *The man on the train.* The phrase drapes over the tip of my tongue, but I swallow it down. Fariz, for all his mealy camaraderie, his sheepish demureness, is—has *always* been, in fact—clued into this. No need to show him the entirety of my hand, when he's got his closed around the knife in my back. "Gods of desperation and debt. London is swimming in these new deities, and they've clearly got a vendetta against the Greek Gods."

"Well, no one likes those—"

"They also know who I am."

"Ah! Yes. Erm. About *that.*"

I can't keep the irritation from my voice. "*Fariz.*"

The door clicks open, saving him from whatever facsimile of a confession he might have been contemplating. I slam the laptop shut at the sight of Ananke, her eyes trailing over the beaten machine, a slow smile turning up the corners of her mouth. (And nowhere else: the eyes stay mirror-flat, inscrutable.) She folds an arm under her breasts, hip sloped against the doorframe.

"I could have been masturbating."

Ananke chimes a short, unpleasant laugh, but otherwise says nothing, head cocked to a bird-like tilt. We stare at each other, mouse and god, daring the other to commit the sin of the first move.

In the end, I break. I feel her triumph effervesce briefly through my veins, a reminder that I'm still hers; even if the leash has gone momentarily slack, it's still chained to my throat. "What do you want?"

A tug on my psyche, as though she heard every last thought. "People are hungry. You should make us lunch."

COOKING FOR NINETY-FIVE is hard when you're short-handed.

It's even worse when you're also *one*-handed.

But at least the chore amounts to a measure of privacy. The gods ignore me as I bustle through the kitchen, a crawlspace turned massive by some devilry of spatial readjustment. Ananke's orders were simple: make food. More specifically, make *good* food. Or else.

Not that any of it bothers me. For all my magical inadequacies and questionable driving, I've always been able to *cook*. Out of deference to the situation, I go Mediterranean, in part because it's all I have to work with. The larder brims with staples of Greek cuisine. Olives in every format. Slabs of cheese. Aubergines, courgettes, tomatoes, wild amaranth, produce so fresh that they're practically glowing with a Hollywood sheen. Fish, glassy-eyed. Lemons. Eggs. Haunches of lamb and wild boar in the freezer, still furred, ice crystals glittering in the rough hairs.

There is honey in small earthen jars, pistachios in the cupboard, all the ingredients to make baklava. Glass vases hold rosemary, dried bay leaves, green sprigs of oregano, thyme, and basil. I catch myself leaning in, breathing the aromas, delighting in the excess—and slam the broken arm against the edge of a cupboard.

Right. Right. Anyway.

The fish—plump seabream and silvery mackerel, a few sardines—are prepared first. I descale and debone with reasonable success, only slicing my thumb once throughout the ordeal. Some, I grill whole (the fish, not the thumb; besides, I only have two), to be served with a dressing of lemon juice, olive oil and spices. Others, I layer into roasting tins, together with tomatoes and potatoes, cubes of garlic and messily sliced onions, parsley leaves and oregano torn up by hand. (*You* try chopping with one arm, ang moh.)

Occasionally, Ananke appears to inspect my labors, never actually speaking, using small jerks of her will to drag answers from me. I make faces at her behind her back, my one rebellion.

In between her visits, I crush lemon zest and garlic into a paste along with olive oil and even more oregano; slice cuts into the lamb and work the mixture through the lacerations; fill tins with potatoes, drizzle them with duck fat and black pepper, and set the meat into the oven to roast. I make Greek salad—ruby-red tomatoes, cucumbers, crumbled feta—with a flicker of trepidation, concerned that it might be in the same category as Asian-American cuisine, a bastardization of local traditions.

But whatever, it's not like they have me holed up in the Ritz. They can dine on political incorrectness.

"They're hungry." Ananke again, about four hours into my task.

I roll out another sheet of filo dough, glaze it with melted butter. Baklava is harder to make than I thought. A pyre of burnt confections sits in the trash, testament to this truth. "They can come in and help me cook, then."

The goddess slinks up beside me, smelling of cracked earth and jasmine, desert-scent, serpent-musk. I ignore the unnatural warmth of her, focus instead on spreading a mixture of nuts, chopped pistachio and crushed walnuts accented by cinnamon and clove.

"You're doing it wrong," Ananke announces, tone furtive, slightly puzzled, like a woman who'd woken up to find all the clocks in her house ticking backwards. She dips a finger into the honey syrup, drags free a tendon of gold. Sniffs. Licks. "It needs orange extract."

"Be my guest."

"You'd have to do it all over." Confusion metamorphoses into a kind of agony, despair over a job poorly done. "The cloves need to be toasted. *Whole.* Not powdered—"

"You do it." I thrust my brush at her and stalk back to the ovens, where the lamb and boar are roasting, skin crisping beautifully, caramel-bronze. Despite my bravado, I'm braced for Ananke's command to heel. It never comes. I hear a clatter instead and swivel to see the goddess scraping my efforts into the rubbish, fork screeching against the pan.

"What are you doing?"

Screeech. Strips of metal peel from the surface. Ananke absently picks the shavings free, then begins to unwind a fresh stretch of dough, movements enviably deft. "Fixing your mistakes."

"Oh. Okay."

Silence, awkward.

"You know that you probably shouldn't use that pan any—" Ananke glares, dusting her fingers with flour, terrifying in her domestic competence. The phrase 'a goddess in the kitchen' shouldn't be as literal as it is here. "Er, nevermind."

More silence, equally awkward. I take the opportunity to plate the fish, eschewing fanciness for a light dressing, a handful of parsley. When I turn, they're gone, which suggests two things. Either Ananke's a *very* quick and very *greedy* eater, or I'm under intense surveillance. Again, don't like my options.

"Hey, you."

Ananke rears up from the baklava. "What."

"Why—" I gesture at the food with a spatula before scooping myself a mouthful of the boar stifado. The taste is alright, flatter that I'd have preferred; the meat is too chewy, too gamy, the shallots too mild. But passable. Briefly, I consider leaving the stew to its mediocrity, only to have pride kick like a mule. A professional never compromises on his art.

"You were saying something?"

I snap to attention, suddenly aware that I'd become transfixed, hypnotised by the act of measuring out a portion of dusky, golden honey. I dip the spoon into the stifado, let the truffle-infused sweetness spread into the stock. "Oh. Uh. Yeah."

"Well?" Impatience knifes through the syllable, accompanying a warning fizz in my gray matter, my vision strobing white in the corners.

I screw my eyes half close and take a steadying breath. "I appreciate that you're absolutely terrifying, but you don't have to keep rubbing it in."

"Talk."

"What's with you and syllables? Do you hate them? Do they offend you? I—" Neck muscles spontaneously clench over the esophagus. I gurgle obligingly for about ten seconds, before beating my palm against the counter, hoping that Ananke understands tap-outs.

The pressure eases. Maybe we'll bond over MMA one day. Probably not. I flick a glance at Ananke, who is glaring at me as she trims dough from her creation. Most likely not. Hand to my throat, I wheeze out the rest of my thought. "Why this? Why the soup kitchen? All of it seems so *pointless*. You could just—I don't know, kill people and take their whatever. More importantly, why am I cooking for you all? You don't even need to eat."

Ananke's face strains under its expressions, cycling from modest dislike to bafflement to indulgent, gosh-the-dumb-animal-tries-so-hard amusement. Finally, as she sets the baklava in a spare oven, she says: "Why not?"

I consider the response. "Point."

"Quality. It is about quality," Ananke declares, abruptly, thoughtfully. "You humans have an aphorism about atheists and foxholes, do you not? A belief that death can make believers of the faithless? There is some truth to that."

I arrange braised artichokes on an armada of plates. "Christopher Hit—"

"You're complicating things unnecessarily."

"I'm told I'm very good at that."

"Do you ever stop talking?"

"Well, I'm frequently told—"

"Shut up." Ananke leans against the counter, head canted towards the window, skin coruscating with the idea of scales. In the distance, an ambulance screams. "It is simpler than that. At the precipice of death, the body will *fight* for one more moment, one more taste of war, one last second of soiling itself, straining to eke out another heartbeat in this miserable world. And that need, that desperate hope to live, that hunger to *be*—we can sustain ourselves on it. It is just another flavor of faith, if not a particularly palatable one."

"Like spam versus steak?"

Her lips shape a grin. "Yes."

Nodding, I add melt-on-your-fork slabs of lamb and steamed asparagus to my little dioramas, balance poached egg yolks on the long green stems. A crumble of feta and black pepper follow, just for texture. "That doesn't explain the soup kitchen."

"The desperate will pray to anything for a warm bed and a hot meal. And they will *do* anything when you take it away."

"But the point of a"—realization sets in—"are you actually *pushing* basic amenities? Like heroin? You're—"

"I'd like to think of it more like cultivating foie gras."

"*We're not geese.*"

Circumstances rob Ananke of the final word, as a killing-chute scream guts the air. Ananke doesn't wait. She's out of the door in three fluid strides and I charge after her, poking my head out of the kitchen to see—

Smoke.

Garlands of black smoke rippling from a burning figure in the hallway, its hands cupped in limp supplication, arms trembling from the weight of the flames. Oil pours from its nose, its eyes, its mouth, like colorless blood, filmed with bluish-white fire. Poseidon is trying to quench the inferno, conjuring acres of water from nothing, the air clouding with steam and the smell of brine. But nothing works.

The silhouette continues to burn, to crisp, the fat in its arms popping under the spray. Everything smells of bacon and burning fabric. Someone is screaming, telling Poseidon to stop, even as the form sags—*finally*—to one knee, face charred beyond—no. That's not right. Recognition coaxes bile from the pit of my stomach, even as it gives a name to the squat build, the mountainous shoulders.

Hephaestus.

The irony is spectacular, rhapsodic. A statement piece. To set a god of fire on fire is to *create* a point, rather than merely proving one. Hephaestus coughs once, hands moving to his throat, fingers fusing in place as the flames keep rolling. Coughs again, vomits fire down his front, and *now*, hell breaks loose. The blaze sears across the surface of the kerosene swamp, up the walls, along the ceiling. Alive, almost. Ravenous. It licks its way up to the feet of the crowd and then, all at once, reality fast-forwards into a horror show.

Gods and mythological bipeds go up in literal smoke, transfiguring into columns of phosphorescent white heat. Mouths and eyes gape black, tissues and humors cooked in a flash. Seven go down this way before the rest of them collect themselves enough to organize a stampede towards the front door.

Eight. Ten. *Twelve.*

In the commotion, someone crashes into Orpheus' wheelchair, sending his disembodied head rolling straight into a pool of fire. I stare, rooted in place, in horror at the flame lapping up his screaming features, his eyes boiling trout-white before they sizzle to ash.

"Crap."

As far as last words go, I suppose I could have done worse.

TWENTY-EIGHT

THE FIRST RULE of dealing with a burning building is—actually, I have no idea. I should have stayed in school. Filled with post-public-education blues, I paddle through the fumes into my room at the back of the apartment. The smoke rolls into the corridor behind me, surging in waves, as though propelled by some unseen heart.

"Crap," I announce to the spare, shirt-strewn space, as I shoulder the door close. Black fumes glissade through the cracks. "Crap. Crap. Crap. Crap—"

Coughing, I grab an unwashed hoodie from my bed, try to swaddle my uninjured arm and fail. I stare at the puddle of black cloth, forlorn.

"Crap."

One deep breath. One enormous regret. Wheezing smoke, eyes watering furiously, I charge the window, elbow first. Glass explodes in a shimmer of hard edges, sunlight turning the shrapnel into diamond. Like a lonely paramour finally come home, gravity hauls me into her embrace, dragging me over the window frame, down onto the balcony a storey below.

Whumph. The impact jolts the air from my lungs, and the world judders into watery smears of color, indistinguishable from whatever fiction my brain constructs in its flirtation with unconsciousness. I think I scream. I'm not sure. Pain ignites in bright blinding pops, skating between cuts and fresh-broken bones, expanding, crescendoing in a vivid fastigium of hurts.

But I'm alive.

I guess.

In the periphery of my hearing, I catch the sound of a balcony door opening, feet picking a shuffling path through a mosaic of glass. A silhouette looms over me, blocking out the smudged heavens. "Holy shit."

I shakily raise a pair of devil horns. "Rock on."

And with that, I finally pass out.

*   *   *

"WHAT AM I supposed to do with you, Rupert?" A man's voice, two octaves too close to pre-pubescence, yet cold and slow, like a long death in ice.

I crack open an eye, see a landscape of plaster and bandages, my appendages dangling from straps in the ceiling. An itch of indeterminable size stirs, somewhere inaccessible, as sunlight fissures through ragged curtains. I twitch my fingers. Six respond; four spasm in bafflement.

I'd say that everything hurts, but that's a lie. The world is cotton and clouds on a crinoline of gauze, so fluffy that I could, if you'll excuse the reference, die. Truth be told, I've a nagging suspicion that this fuzzy, furry patina of morphine is the *only* thing keeping me from expiring of circulatory shock. I wiggle my digits again and try to raise the middle finger. It comes up half-mast. Good enough.

Sisyphus sits spread-kneed on the edge of a chair at the side of my bed, hands steepled against his lipless maw. His stare has the weight of court orders. The silence lengthens into awkwardness.

"I'm sorry?" Grudgingly, I fit words into the waiting quiet.

The damned king grins briefly, stroking the fleecy jut of his chin. Rubbing beard hairs between thumb and index finger, he looks at me appraisingly. I writhe away, propping myself up as best I'm able, which entails resting part of my weight on a sling and slouching the rest against a rickety headboard.

It is then that I realize that there's a cat on my belly. Specifically, *the* Cat, a heap of mange and black-whipped fur, gray and white at unplanned intervals. He scratches at the stub of an ear, and opens lime-green eyes. I wriggle fingers at him, hoping the motion would communicate both my desire to scritch and my inability to do so.

"You don't die. You don't listen. You don't do what you were meant to do. When destiny comes calling, you run away every single time. What am I supposed to *do?*"

"Man, if I had a dollar every time someone said that to me, I'd have enough to pay off the world." The Cat nuzzles under my palm, and I scratch at the stiff hairs of his hackles. "Wait. What do you mean—are you the one working with Vanquis?"

That actually makes Sisyphus crack up, slight frame twitching with laughter. He leans back, stares out of the door as a nurse, dark and slim, black hair corkscrewing from a sharp-edged face, saunters past. The Cat rattles with sub-aural growling, walking a tight circle across my chest, and Sisyphus continues ignoring him. "Oh, please. If it helps, I'm not complicit in your suffering. I have no more reason to hate you than to hate the man on the streets. Sure, your torment generates revenue, but this world pivots on suffering; it isn't *personal*. I am not your enemy. But I am unhappy. You stand at the fulcrum of change, but you don't see how it works."

"How what works? Cutting some random idiot open and rooting through his stomach to decide what's going to happen? Trusting in the Ghost of Entrails

Past Expiry? Hey, you know what would be an absolutely novel idea? Telling me things straight instead of jumping through wordplay. It'd get all of us where you want to go a lot faster."

"No." He sighs, rises from his seat to narrow the distance between us. From his pocket, Sisyphus extracts two coins, verdigris-coated and old. Very old. The centuries reverberate within the discs, histories so sociopathically abhorrent that they refuse to lay down and die. He sets them between my collar bones, the metal chill. The Cat hisses, but Sisyphus ignores him. "I can't. You must make this choice independent of outside intervention. This must be your decision, your choosing."

"Again, if I had a dollar—"

"How I envy you. How I envy the things that Helenus had forseen for you."

"I'm beginning to get very concerned here."

"If only we still had his sister, things would be so very clear." With a *schwink* of metal unfolding, a switchblade pops into view. I tense, straining between the urge to survive and the desire to have it all over with, to give this wretched carcass up, reboot the game and come back, shit-stained but whole. "But we do what we can. We play the cards we've been dealt."

"Tell me. Was all that drama really necessary? Does it make you happy, Your Highness? Does it?"

Sisyphus carries on like I've said nothing at all, bending down to cut my face, but the Cat intervenes, slashing at the blade with a paw. Snarling at the impudence, faster than I could imagine possible, he pins the thrashing Cat against my broken ribs and slices the feline's throat.

"Fuck—"

Calmly, Sisyphus wipes his blade through the geysering blood, the Cat twitching, his gaze emptying of animation. I gape, shellshocked, as Sisyphus strokes the flat of his knife over the coins, awakening whatever slumbers within them. A pale wash of impressions, like the dregs of a nightmare; eager, grotesqueries too vague to fully comprehend, full of hungry life.

"Collateral," he announces, the Cat's only eulogy.

"You cannot fucking perform an animal sacrifice in a hospital—"

Sisyphus rambles on, indifferent to my sentiments on the matter, bored of me: "Helenus made another prediction before it all went to shit, by the way."

"And?" I'm sodden and sticky with blood. My uncovered ass, I realize, with a paroxysm of hysteria, is the only place still cold.

"You're going to do great things. You're going to change the tide of the world. You will win this war for—"

"You?" A laugh wrenches my lungs, a coyote's wobbling giggle. "I"m going to win the war for you. Is that what you're going to tell me? After randomly murdering a cat and god knows what else. Look, you understand the fundamental error in listening to a gibbering madman you've turned inside-out, right? The fact you take bets on his fortunes suggests that he's not very good at them, so how are you even—what was I saying again?"

(Ang mohs, don't do drugs at home. In fact, don't do drugs at all. Unless it's a matter of life-or-death, and as a general rule of thumb, you should avoid matters of life-or-death too.)

Sisyphus, a frown pinched between prodigious eyebrows, shakes his head. "It doesn't matter. What matters is that you will be responsible for changing the—"

I spin a fingertip in a tiny circle around my temple. "You are fucking *nuts*."

"And you are an insolent little cow. If it weren't for Demeter—" His scowl deepens.

"Excuse me? *Excuse* me? Now, I don't know if you realize, but I'm not the one who walked up to an injured man to start cutting up his face. Because seriously, if you don't get why this is a crazy thing to do, I— wait. What did you say about Demeter?"

Shoes clack over linoleum and we look over to see a silhouette in the doorway, clipboard tucked into the crook of an arm. A doctor, judging from the rumpled coat and the stethoscope dangling from his throat, the shadows hanging heavy from puppydog eyes. "Sorry. Am I interrupting?"

Statement masquerading as perfunctory apology. Sisyphus raps a chord against my rib, holding the physician's gaze, neither backing down. But my doctor has the advantage of actual authority and they both know it. The undead monarch eventually capitulates, although not before migrating the coins to my eyes, a ferryman's wages pre-paid in full, the Cat's body dangled by its scruff. "This is not your story."

"Fuck you. Wait. Come back here. You still haven't answered me yet."

He leaves, sandals slapping a sullen beat across the floor. I contort my face, hoping to dislodge the coins; one falls, the other does not, pulsing someone's misery across my skin. The young medic walks up beside me and plucks the remaining doubloon from my eye, mouth undecided between a grimace and an encouraging smile. It flickers fully to the latter, even as he rings up Security, his manner efficient and terse, composed to minimize the risk of alarm.

"Did you know that man?" His accent is glass-cut, prim, predominantly British except for an inflection of the exotic, a liquidness that suggests time on other continents. He raises the coin to the light, inspects the surfaces but neither numbers nor insignias reveal themselves, no clue as to a beginning, all legibility eaten away by green-blue rust.

"Nope. Some random crazy."

We clinch stares. I wait for him to call my bluff, but he doesn't.

"How are you feeling..." He sets the coins on my bedside table and scans his sheaf of papers, tongue poked from the corner of his lips. "Mr. Wong? That was a bit of a fall."

"You could say that." I stiffen, cagey as a pet-shelter feral, acutely and abruptly conscious that I'm alone, incapacitated, and in the presence of Schrödinger's threat.

"Multiple fractures, two broken ribs, some thoracic spinal lesions, a concussion—and that's just the current inventory. Still, nothing irrecoverable.

Bed rest, physical therapy, and good life decisions should have you up and running in no time." He skims a finger along my IV drip and examines the bag of clear fluids, before fumbling through a dresser for supplies.

Rubber gloves go on. With enviable dexterity, he carves me from my bandages, begins the cleanup process, all the while maintaining a conversational lightness to his chatter. "You've led quite the life, Mr. Wong."

"Led?" I wince as he paints antibacterial fluids over my stitches. "I don't know if I appreciate the use of past tense."

"Mr. Wong, I understand that things may still be confusing, but you can trust me, I promise you. I'm only here to help." He swaddles me in fresh bandages, manner still calm.

"Yeah. That's what they all say."

He sighs. "Okay. So what can I do to change your mind?"

I don't miss a beat. "Yorkshire pudding with Cumberland sausages, onion gravy. A side of biscuits. Fried bacon. Properly fried. Like, unhealthily crispy."

"How about something from Tesco and I'll see if the cafeteria will fry you some bacon?"

"Deal."

HE COMES BACK.

He actually comes back. With onion mash and sausages dripping in hot gravy, Yorkshire pudding stuffed with crumbled bacon. No biscuits, unfortunately, but he substitutes a slice of lemon tart, lumpy with white chocolate. I don't know why he didn't return with Security, and how I'm not swimming in policemen, but I am not about to look a gift horse in the mouth.

"Isn't this against terms and conditions?" Gingerly, I clamp trembling fingers around the spoon, losing my captive twice, cutlery falling onto my blue woolen blanket.

"Probably." The doctor—Sunil, according to a discreet nametag—shrugs a shoulder, grinning, fingers raking through prematurely gray hair. "But hey."

"Hey." I grin back and dig in.

OBJECTIVELY SPEAKING, THE meal wasn't great. Store-bought sausages are always criminally overstuffed and woefully under-spiced, porcine detritus given a last shake at self-worth. And the gravy is invariably a watery, one-note disappointment.

The bacon was chewier than it was crispy and the tart too sweet, but the fact it was there, steam lacing the air, savory and rich and resplendently greasy, made all the difference.

Subjectively speaking, it was the best meal of my life.

I'm pretty sure that means I'm about to die.

Permanently.

* * *

IT'S LATE AND I'm still awake, walking one of Sisyphus' coins along my knuckles, counting as I go. Metacarpals and phalanges twinge from the exercise, but I press on, coercing joints to flex, to bend. Twenty-five. Twenty-six. Twenty-seven. Twenty—

The disc slips between my fingers, hits the floor with a decisive *clink*.

Bracing, I lean down, ignore the pain shooting across my oblique as I twist to collect the fallen coin. There has to be a secret here, some metallurgic cantrip leavened into the gold, something useful. But the coins relinquish no answers. In frustration, I thread a schoolyard charm together under my breath, the magic flickering limply, an unflattering mirror of my health. It gutters out before I can even breathe it into being, and I sigh.

I don't remember ever being so heartsick, so ill with someone else's sin. I'm exhausted, I realize. Whittled down to an ache. And every time I shut my eyes, there are bodies laid out like plates on a table, dead because someone thought it was amusing—or worse, because no one noticed they were there. Used, abused, ground down into food, or raw material. An entire charnel house steeped in pointless casualties. At least the ghouls—

No. Fuck.

The lie unlaces itself from my thoughts, presents itself as what it is: a crude excuse for my complicity, just another way to get through the day. I run the coin over my knuckles, metal glimmering in sinuous waves, hoping to find absolution in repetition. A muscle in my cheek twangs. I don't like how guilt feels.

The coin tumbles through another circuit.

Silence, but for the sound of the patient in the other bed, wheezing through an uneasy sleep, an orchestra of acute pneumonia. No answers there.

"Like you're even real gold." I bite down on the coin.

It isn't. Or, at least, it no longer is, the material altered by the metaphysical. Memories, until now an indistinct aftertaste, burst across my tongue. The alloy foams and fizzes, dissolving; a stink of lye whirlpooling into my lungs, chemical burn that swells the throat, pricks at my eyes until they water. I spit phlegm over the side of my bed, globs of green-yellow infection; scrape the roof of my mouth with my tongue, again and again, but the flavor *sticks*.

Briefly, the amygdala coquets with the idea of panic. Genetic memory is clear: that taste is *poison*. But common sense counters with a quick rebuttal, gleefully highlighting the fact I'm too well and truly fucked to do anything except stay horizontal and accept the inevitable. And besides, why did I bite something covered in someone else's blood?

The bitterness continues to funnel down my throat, a metallic warmth invading capillaries and digestive tract. Fuck it. At least I had a last meal. People have died under worse circumstances. *I've* died under worse circumstances. As far as these things go, everything's coming up slightly-better-than-everyday-Rupert.

Feeling dramatically better, I flick my attention up to the ceiling and map animal shapes to water stains.

But the end never comes. Instead, its antipode swaggers up, a truly *phenomenal* itch, one that spiders across my sinews and rappels down my spine and sides, worming into fractures and misaligned muscles: cellular repair sped-up into an exquisite torture. I buck as my ribs slot together. It hurts like a bad marriage, a slow death exacerbated by the faith that the end goal is axiomatically better than any alternative.

I miss morphine.

Still, what goes up must come down, and even eternity has an expiry date. My torment ends, somewhere between the past and I'm-going-to-pee-myself-screaming. I inhale shuddering gouts of air, soaked to the molecule with sweat; trembling bone and skin so raw that the fibers of my hospital gown grate like razorwire. The fact that I'm whole again, fresh-fleshed and fully functional, feels like a participation trophy, rather than any miracle of royal mercy.

I swing my legs from the bed, picking the IV drip from my arm. Air-conditioning billows noisily, a death rattle not dissimilar from the respiration of my bedmate, glacial against my bare calves.

"I guess it's something," I tell the indifferent quiet as I waddle stiff-legged between cupboards and drawers, rummaging for my passport, wallet. I find both. I also find someone else's clothes, a stash of fresh twenties, and car keys.

Everything gets requisitioned, of course. You can't save a universe without stealing a few cars.

TWENTY-NINE

"Sorry, friend."

I stroke a hand along the lithe lines of the car, moonlight flashing silver across the gunmetal chassis, feeling like I'm saying goodbye to the woman of my dreams all over again. I'm not generally a vehicle guy, but there are exceptions to everything. The RX-7 I've commandeered is *exquisite*, better than new, almond-pale leather and voice controls, a stereo system with an operatic bass, an engine that *croons*.

Unfortunately, where I intend to go, it's just a useless chunk of gorgeous metal. I keep at the ruse for a while nonetheless, driving in aimless patterns around Waterloo station until the fuel light winks a warning. Only then do I park and step out into the time-honored existential dilemma: to keep the car or to not keep the car? That is the fucking question.

I keep the keys, just in case. I pat the hood one last time, forlorn, and slink out of the alley. Central London is beautiful at four thirty in the morning: buildings glazed silver by the omnipresent drizzle; street lamps pooling golden on the glistening cobblestones; the dark waters of the Thames, jewelled, strange; no drunken milieu to mar the composition of glass and old Georgian architecture. Just me and the overly affectionate chill.

I pull my hood over my head, zip up the coat and shake a frisson from my spine. My new clothes are too big around the shoulders, too tight around the waist: business-casual with a touch of consensus-developed street, a middle-class fantasy of criminal cool. Poor funerary clothes, but thieves aren't allowed to whine, are they?

Brain churning with worst-case hypotheses, I lumber into the station, palming exhaustion from the crevices of my eyes. To say that I have a plan of action would be like saying that the human species is born with foreknowledge of its trajectory through this strange, savage existence, every shining accomplishment and humiliating failure prenatally selected from a cosmic brochure. That said, I do have the barest framework of a plan; which is, depressingly, more than I ordinarily have.

I trot into the mouth of the station. It's eerie at this time of the morning. Waterloo was obviously constructed to house the masses, and their absence rings like a scream. There is too much space and not enough personality, a hostile sterility that brings to the imagination old horror movies, hospital corridors with nowhere to hide.

What I should be doing right now is putting together a ward, a failsafe, some measure of protection against the shoals of dead dithering through the underground. If London's spectral demographic follows the same conventions as the rest of the world, they'll likely be feeling quite rambunctious (adjective: feisty, ferocious, ravenous, man-murdering, inclined towards inflicting eternal torture) right now. But instead, I go on a hunt for a coffee.

"Hello! Welcome to"—yawn—"Costa. What can"—yawn again—"I get you?"

"Flat white for me, and could I buy *you* a coffee?" I count out coins from a stylish wallet, pausing to flip through a rainbow of cards. Anthony Sebastian Lions, you had a good life.

"Haha! Good one." My barista, a local named Tom Pritchard, is bearded and squishy, infectiously cheery, with a tuft of aqua-green hair combed into a flaccid fauxhawk. His eyes keep hidden behind massive aviator glasses. "It's the whole 'opening the store'"—jazz hands are executed—"'at four-bloody-a.m. in the morning.' I'll be fine. Honest."

"Sure?" I slide over an inexact amount of money and slot a cautious smile into place, not entirely sure what to do with his exuberance.

"I mean, I probably shouldn't have stayed up for that premiere, but it was *so* good. My mates and I were, we were like, *whoaaaaah*. Marvel movies are fucking awesome. You a comic fan?"

"Sometimes?" I scan the empty café, disoriented. No one is allowed to be this ebullient at this time of day. It's unnatural.

"Don't tell me..." He palms his forehead, extends the other hand forward in perfect imitation of your dollar-store psychic. "You're a Dark Horse guy."

I guffaw. Probably harder than expected or even should have, body folding, arm over my waist. An espresso machine hisses steam in the background, and the ambient soundtrack changes, switching from elevator music to a syrupy pop song about someone vapid. By the time I recover, Tom's laving hot milk over a styrofoam cup, grooving in place, head gyrating in rhythm with the command to *shake it off, shake it off.*

"Here you go, mate. Sure I can't get you a stroopwafel to—"

"A what now?"

"Stroopwafel."

"Excuse you?"

"Str-ooo-p waffle," He repeats, teasing out the syllables like ropes of taffy. "It's Dutch for 'small, delicious waffle.'"

I square an incredulous look and Tom chortles merrily, perfectly on beat, so impeccably good-natured that he probably bleeds confetti. I twirl my fingers in three quick circles, a smile crooked at his beaming countenance. "Fine. You win. I'll take your waffles."

And then the light *flickers,* the tiniest aberration, as though every source of illumination breathed in together and held the air caged while something flitted unseen into the room.

"Shit."

"You okay, mate?"

I unscrunch my eyes, open them to find Tom's soft face riveted in concern, a bag of miniature waffles held out. My mouth seizes into a rictus before it rearranges into a wincing smile. Just my imagination. Surely. I reach out a palm.

A seam opens in the center of Tom's forehead, a fine line of claret. It divides his mouth, throat; runs along his tan-colored shirt, past the white apron. I watch, silent, tongue swollen to silence. Gingerly, I pluck the stroopwafels from his grip and take a step back.

The two halves of the late Tom Pritchard shudder once and his eyes roll up as he sighs, long and gustily, somehow serene. The release complicates into a moist, *slorping* cacophony, like viscera in operation. Something arches beneath his skin, bulging against the side of his neck, the dermis turning rubbery. Briefly, I see the contours of knuckles, a flattened palm.

I chew my fist as *he* finally wriggles loose, shedding Tom Pritchard like a bad habit, skin puddling onto the ground. The man from the train is exactly as I remember: black leather, brown curls, knife-jawed smile.

"I'm sorry. Did you still want your coffee?"

"I think today might actually be a good day to quit coffee. And coffee shops." I glance at the stroopwafels and let them fall to the tiles. "Also sugar. And maybe even today."

The man shrugs. Despite his recent ecdysis, his attire is pristine, artisanally rumpled, not a drop of gore in sight. Tom's face, slack without its bones, teardrops from the bend of the man's wrist. Skin tears. The sack of tissue falls, ignored. "Your loss."

He plucks my flat white from the counter and sips at the surface, painting his upper lip with a foam mustache. I *almost* laugh at the banality, hysteria bubbling close to the surface, but I bite down on a knuckle again, harder this time, skin pinned between my teeth, and gnaw. "You know? You could have just waited," I manage not to wail.

"I get impatient."

"I completely understand that." T-Swift is effervescing softly about something else now, voice wound slow: cherry lips, a door opening in a beast, breath distilled into a silvery drink. "But I was looking for you. I was *literally* in the process of going to find you. Did we really have to kill an innocent bystander?"

The man takes another drink of my coffee. "Probably not."

"Then why do it?"

He doesn't answer, only props a slim elbow alongside a case lush with confections, condensation dewing in the glass. As I watch, the moisture crystallises into patterns. He grins, his teeth white, a cigarette abruptly smoldering between them. "What did you want from me, Rupert?"

I slip a hand into a pocket, close a grip over Sisyphus' orphaned coin, the metal scalding in palm. "I want to make a deal."

A WARM, HUMID smell of urine rises from the underground. Animated billboards fritz like malfunctioning televisions as we go past, and I feel the hairs on my neck rise, the borders of my vision flooding with horrors: wide, white bodies, maggot-soft; a noose of eyeless faces; fingers, spiralling like ferns.

I keep my gaze forward.

"She's gone, you know?" His voice comes sympathetic, paternal.

I don't answer. But anyone with eyes could see it's a gut punch, anyway, the thought smashing my ribs to kindling. When I breathe, all I get is a lungful of shrapnel.

"Your ghoul." Smoke tendrils indolently from his joint, a blend of marijuana and something sweeter, a suggestion of citrus.

"Minah was a langsuir, thank—"

"They lied to you. We are the shape that we inhabit, an actualization of an idea of self-awareness. The moment we give that up, we disappear."

"I hate to be *that* guy, but I should probably point out that we're currently swimming in ghosts." Nails trace the back of my arms, the slope of my shoulders.

"But they haven't given up their identity, have they? Ghosts are concentrated passion. Their very existences pivot on desire. As the madman Descartes might have said, 'They hunger, therefore they are.' In contrast, those content enough to surrender to the idea of an idyllic afterlife—"

"They vanish?"

He says nothing. Skeins of cannabis-fueled vapors trek through the air, writing secrets in an alphabet of forgetting. In between the warping curlicues, apparitions convulse and squirm, defying active scrutiny.

"So, basically, you're telling me that Hell exists and Heaven actually represents a complete dissolution of self, and we're all lying to each other?"

The silence textures with smugness.

"You know what? I really didn't need the exposition. Pass the fucking joint. *Please.*"

He does. I swallow a toke, clutch the heat as long as I'm able, hoping it'd burn through the grief rising in my ventricles, before I let the smoke leech away. To my vast disappointment, the weed reveals no precocious properties, no ability to instantly elevate my mind, send me soaring into a state of higher numbness. It simply *is*.

"Well, fuck."

The man retrieves his blunt and begins to take deep, ruminative puffs. "Sorry."

"I don't know if I believe you."

"That's entirely fair."

"I'm pretty certain that I don't, at any rate."

"You do you, man."

I flinch at the colloquial terminology, the ease with which he uses it, the wrongness of the juxtaposition. Entities like him, whatever he actually *is*, have no right engaging in popular culture, although I suppose it could be argued that, by that logic, they have no right to *any* form of communication native to sapient life. But then again, does mortal philosophy matter at all in the face of world-shattering consciousnesses?

Minah. Her name repeats beneath my pulse, a knot of sounds like a noose around my throat. It's hard to breathe.

"So what are you?"

He exhales a single pearlescent word. A locus of glittering syllables, both terrible and haunting, inaccessible by the human larynx, sound and shape and undiluted sensation. The utterance expands into visions: a writhing nebula of tentacles in the center of the universe, suspended among galaxies, singing dumbly to a court of protean dancers; a man at a gate, his shadow crawling with nightmare forms; a worship that will not die; a name, a name, a—

I tear myself from the frenzying hallucinations, images of unnatural architecture seeping from my neurons like sand between my fingers. "That absolutely isn't an answer."

He sighs. "Nyarlathotep."

"Who?"

"Me." He passes me the joint. "That's who I am. I am the Crawling Chaos, the God of a Thousand Forms, the Stalker among the Stars, the Faceless God. I am the son of Azathoth, the Blind Idiot God. I am the voice of the Outer Gods, the destruction of humanity, and a happy fabrication of H. P. Lovecraft."

"You're a figment of someone else's imagination?"

"More like an analogy for an irrational fear of the foreign." His mouth rises in passable mimicry of a smile. Trails of lacy smoke ribbon around his face.

"I guess that makes some amount of sense." I pause. "Does this mean you're actually an octopus, then?"

"I—what are you talking about?"

"Lovecraft made Cthulhu, didn't he? And Cthulhu, if I recall, was a gargantuan beast with a squid for a head. And you can't deny that he had a marine theme to his works, what with Innsmouth and—" I smack my lips thoughtfully. Maybe the weed was more potent than I thought.

"Exactly how much Lovecraft have you read?"

"About two animes, six movies, and several graphic novels."

We hit the bottom of the escalator. Taking another drag, I risk a gander behind us, discover a flight of steps practically short enough to jump. About what I'd expected, I suppose. That conversation had far too much time to percolate. I flick the joint against a wall and trot after Nyarlathotep, who is already halfway to the gates, the barrier swinging open before him.

"How does that work, anyway?" I ask after he leads us onto the lip of a darkened platform. The dead keep their distance, eeling restlessly just outside of view. "Being a literary construct and—and whatever you are?"

"Priorities, Rupert." In the penumbra, his face is garish, a chiaroscuro of flat lines and shadow, a drawing that occasionally stirs to three-dimensionality. His cigarette flickers blue. "You were here to make a deal."

"*Right.* Right, I—"

The Necropolis Railway saves me from gibbering my way into an untenable contract with what is either a metaphor for the existential terrors that plague men of relative leisure, or possibly an actual divinity of unthinkable hideousness. The Body Train roars into position, excreting steam, moisture beading on its shuddering flanks. A noxious musk washes over the platform, exhaust and sweat and steel and assorted glandular secretions.

Polyps in its dermis flower into eyes, pupils rolling in my direction. Strangely, the train's attention doesn't come across malevolent, only distantly curious, an arthropod's insouciant interest in the world outside its lifespan.

"Step into my office." Nyarlathotep gestures at a door, his smile cranked up to used car salesman, all teeth and no authenticity.

"Classy." I make a face and step through.

"Dɪᴜ—"

The epithet slips before I can stop myself. There's someone else in the train. *Many* someone elses, in fact, if they're all ostensibly piloted by a single consciousness. Men and women in three-piece suits litter the carriage, some propped up against the walls, others strewn loose-limbed over the seats, marionettes abandoned after a disastrous comedy act.

"What the fuck is Vanquis doing—"

Nyarlathotep flicks a disinterested look at the scattered bodies, their million-dollar smiles still soldered in place. "No idea. You can ask them if they make an appearance."

"I don't know if I'm comfortable with this."

"Tough." He drapes himself across a plastic seat, elegant as a lord, ankle perched on a knee. His foot begins to wag, the shoe branded with an anime girl's puzzled face. "Enough procrastination, Rupert. Present your terms."

The train jolts into motion. I steady myself against a pole, free hand clasped around the dead king's gift, the orphaned coin hot against my palm. "So, are you working with Vanquis?"

"Rupert." A warning skims across his friendly South London voice.

"No. I got to know. Background research, you know what I'm saying? You don't pick jobs at random. You figure out if you're capable of jiving with their corporate culture. Vanquis tried to kill me."

"They did not."

"They brought"—I enunciate each word slowly, deliberately, and with rising emphasis—"a *building* down on my head."

"Collateral."

Memory strobes: ash in my lungs, intestines smeared across my apron, the ceiling collapsing. "Collateral is a very nice word for what happened."

"But also an appropriate one, innit?" He twitches fingers and a bar cabinet materializes in the wall, lid popping open with a noise like cracked knuckles. "Whiskey?"

"Pass."

Nyarlathotep shrugs. He picks a clean tumbler from its casement and a sphere of ice from its box, plops one in the other. A bottle of Laphroaig is uncorked. The air glazes with the smell of kerosene-soaked oak and smoky peat, a faint moting of sea salt. He decants an unreasonable portion of alcohol into his glass.

The Body Train clacks around a corner, whistling to the endless void. "So, what's your connection to Vanquis?"

"You are a persistent *fuck*." Nyarlathotep swirls the whiskey, ice tinkling loudly against the sides; the sound is somehow louder than the noise of the tracks. "Honestly, you were never in any real—look, you can just ask them yourself."

"I—what—oh, fuck."

The darkness resolves into the cool, waxy glow of an encroaching platform. As the train begins to slow, the inert suits start to rise, first swaying like newborns, tottering this way and that, before accreting a kind of symphonic grace, every movement harmonized to the notations of a greater purpose.

"Vanquis." Nyarlathotep tips his head.

Ssh. Ssh. *Sssssh.* A shushing noise transfers between throats, white noise-jabbering which slowly crenellates into speech. Twenty pairs of eyes lock on. "You're heeeeeerrre."

"I'd really rather not be, if that helps." I scoot an involuntary step back. "So—"

The nearest vessel presses a finger to its lips, one tintless eye shuttering closed. Behind me, I hear another chink of glass, a splash of alcohol over melting ice. The doors to the Body Train yawn apart and a deluge of souls spumes into the carriage.

There are hundreds of them. Thousands. So many that there is not even standing room for the spirits. Faces overlap, silhouettes combine. Individual identity is pulped together into raw material, deleting any beginning or end, any distinguishing feature. Their fear gusts over me, dull, cow-like, not quite awake enough to process the enormity of the future.

"What's going on?"

No one replies, preoccupied with the fresh arrivals. Vanquis is, if nothing else, terrifyingly efficient. It segregates the souls along mysterious vectors. Agents queue in parallel lines to coax ghosts into neat configurations, while others box them into unmarked white packages, their motions thoughtlessly industrial. In minutes, Vanquis has organized the milling chaos into symmetrical cardboard stacks. The doors whoosh shut.

"And that makes eight thousand." Nyarlathotep declares, dusting his hands, as the Body Train jerks forward again. "Compliments to your employer for bringing us up to an even number."

I whip my head about, a chill attenuating into a knife between my ribs. Of course the Boss would be involved. Why wouldn't he be? "I'm afraid I didn't get the memo on that."

Nyarlathotep bares a grin, hunching forward to rest elbows on spread knees, glass loosely clutched in a hand. "That's *your* problem."

"Fair enough." A sidelong glance shows Vanquis obsessing again over the arrangement of boxes, moving containers seemingly at random, creating grand forts before disemboweling them to build stubbly hexagons. Isolated from their artillery, this god of low-income terrors seems almost *child-like*. "Okay."

"So." The tumbler vanishes without preamble, no dramatic deconstruction, no emission of diamondine light. Just—*poof*. "Are we going to deal?"

"Yes."

He nods once. And just like the glass, Vanquis, the boxes, the train, the transit-choked warrens under London—it all disappears.

THIRTY

STARLIGHT.

Galaxies unnumbered, nested within spiralling nebulas; constellations twisting in their death throes; a thousand comets fleeing. My breath hitches. The lambency of the universe dims to needlepoints, and Nyarlathotep molts from the gloam, skin slick with ice. The stars flatten into a glittering, glass-like lamina under our feet.

"Seven points for drama," I manage, my voice a croak.

He shrugs and reclines into the nothingness, an absence of existence that pulses blue-violet against the eye, like a ghost of the sun seared into the retina. "You were saying."

"Okay." I lick my lips. The air isn't cold as much as it is some unidentifiable variance of uncomfortable, dry, salt-tinged. "Firstly, I want to talk to you about what the terms of acquisition incur."

"Go on."

"Do you gain proprietorship over my soul? Do we share joint ownership of my body? If you buy over the entirety of my person, spirit and flesh, will you also take responsibility for all bodily functions?"

Nyarlathotep shrinks his brows into a confused frown. "What are you talking about?"

"Fecal elimination. Also, urine. You'd have to take care of all that. Similarly, if you want a monopoly, you're going to have to make sure I'm walked, fed three times a day, preferably with high-quality produce, as opposed to McDonalds, and—" I know I'm gabbling, but if I stop, hysteria will catch up.

"Wait."

"Yes?"

"When did it get so *complicated?*"

I pace the emptiness, footsteps marked by growing ripples of light. "When you decided you needed to procure my, uh, er, *me*. So, which is it? What do you want from me?"

His eyes color to gold; pupils become cephalopodic, black as eternity. Nyarlathotep sits forward, fingers steepled, and I catch an impression of tentacles in the valley of his cheeks, his features gaunter than I recall.

"We need all of you—"

"I miss hearing a living girl say that."

"—for three months. Tops."

I cross my arms. "And why?"

"To infiltrate the Chinese pantheon so that we can destroy it and be on our merry way." Nyarlathotep pauses. "That sounded rather super-villainly, didn't it? The flesh keeps its idiosyncrasies, I suppose."

"It—what—nevermind. I don't need to know. You understand that I don't have access to anything but Diyu, right? I can't go to Ti—heaven—whatever. I literally cannot. My soul—"

"And you understand that the idea of heaven is nothing more than a fantasy created to instill comfort in the dying, right?"

"You remind me of that Dawkins fellow. Only somehow less eloquent."

He glares.

"Right. Wisecracking. Got to keep that in check." I scratch at the back of my head and avert my eyes, take a step forward to learn that the landscape is apparently Escheresque. While I wasn't paying attention, I'd somehow wandered up, around, and behind Nyarlathotep's right shoulder. I halt. "Can't you just—can't you just, you know, go and beat up the Chinese pantheon without me?"

"Yes. But we'd rather borrow a Trojan Horse, if you will."

Something finally clicks. "'We'?"

"You can't mount an invasion with just one person. Although you can rest assured that I will be your principal contact in this agreement and will, in turn, take responsibility for the actions of my colleagues." Nyarlathotep flashes a thin, cold smile. "Three months. Full insurance coverage. All expenses taken care of. You don't even have to be switched on for the period."

"I've had my affair with recreational chemicals, thank you. Don't need to lose days like that ever again."

"Whatever you like." His tone grows clipped, impatient. "Rupert, I don't know where you got the impression that we're at odds, but we're not. We both want the same things."

"Truth, love, and minimum wages for everyone?"

"We both want the gods dead."

"I don't know if that's necessarily true."

"Shut up."

"Shutting up, sir."

"You've been lied to. You've been incarcerated. You've been forced into demeaning labour. You—you cook for their livestock. You are an ancillary function, unimportant. Most importantly, you've been disrespected. Instead of telling you the truth, instead of letting you know what would happen if you let Minah go, they chose to lie to you."

He breathes in. "If this were a dystopian movie, this moment would be where you rise up, hold your fist to the sky, and vow vengeance on those who had wronged you. But instead, you keep making excuses for these... monstrosities. We want to give you a chance to change that. One little pantheon at a time. Help us help you."

"And you."

Nyarlathotep breathes out slowly, mouthing the numbers from one to ten; it's an affectation I'm certain he doesn't actually need, but secretly pray that he does. "Tell you what. As a token of good faith, you can have a freebie."

"What kind of freebie?"

"Anything you want."

I sigh and rock on my heels, back and forth, before I bounce up, blowing out hard, hands waggled outspread, like an overeager boxer. This is it.

"How about: I want Vanquis *dead*."

"Done."

"Wait. Wha—"

Between one blink and the next, the landscape shifts, alters from nothing to something, geometries of inhuman construction, plastic seats, and ribs of greasy metal. The train sways, clips around a turn. Lights convulse, plunging the world in a stop-motion film, black and white and red and *oh*.

It takes me longer than I'd like to admit to register the smell. The carriage stinks of feces and ruptured organs, gunpowder and bile. A faint miasma of urine provides an astringent counterpoint to the blood clotting in the air. I cup my hand over my mouth.

The actual carnage is no less impressive, multi-tiered, a debauchery of slaughter to do *Pulp Fiction* proud. Vanquis agents lay spread over the carriage, decapitated, dismembered, disemboweled and, in some cases, deboned. I pick a route across the limbs and gray loops of intestines, discarded skins.

Even more disconcerting than the mayhem itself is, perhaps, the fact that the massacre appears mutually inflicted. None of the corpses evidence any sign of struggle, no bruises around throat or wrist to suggest they'd fought back. Instead, I find bodies with their arms looped together, pistols pressed into each other's mouths, the backs of the skulls split like melons, drooling curds of brain. Bodies in seeming embrace, hands dug below their ribs, fingers cupped about the hearts. The epiphany hits: this had been consensual.

It had been a suicide.

A sacrifice.

"Is Vanquis really—"

"Yes."

I kick a denuded skull across the way. "Aren't these just its—"

"No. More than anyone else, I imagine, Vanquis understood that we're merely components in a grand invention, cogs and wheels and bits of machinery. We're expendable in the name of the—I'm doing it again, aren't I?" Nyarlathotep squats over a mound of bodies, each corpse slitted from mouth to groin.

"Mm-hmm."

"I'll figure it out one day." He stands and opens his arms to encompass the space, a messianic figure, spotless despite the environment. His grin says everything. He doesn't believe the shit that he's hawking. "You've gotten your wish. Let's talk about mine."

"I could just run away."

He looks out the window with a smirk, even as we continue speeding through the void, traversing routes that only ever existed in an architect's delirium. "You wouldn't get very far."

"Probably not."

"Don't keep me waiting, Rupert."

"I have three more requests."

Impatience darts across Nyarlathotep's face, entirely too angular now to be mistaken for human, jaws and cheekbones extended to inhuman proportions. "Three. *Really.* Don't you think you're being—"

"Hear me out. First," I declare, very loudly, counting out my terms on my fingers. "You get me all-you-can-eat access to every restaurant in London. Second, you give me twenty-four hours to sort out my mortal affairs. And third, we start with the Greeks first."

His smile grows teeth. Not figuratively, literally. Dentition multiplies even as the smile extends past the normal capacity, lips stretching to accommodate the new coalition of pearly-whites. I count about twenty-five extra on each jaw.

"Deal."

I DAB PALE, fatty broth from the rim of my grimace. Shoryu wasn't anything like what the website had advised, but it was *tolerable,* which I suppose is good enough for an establishment in the middle of Piccadilly Circus.

Outside, tourists ripple across intersections, brandishing cameras in the encroaching twilight, while a lone busker plucks at his guitar, largely ignored by the crowds. A line of iconic red buses snake along the streets.

Twenty-three hours and counting.

I nibble at my last remaining slice of char siu, chase it down with another mouthful of soup. They've gotten the consistency mostly right, at least. My lips are oily from the rich decoction, the decadent porkiness underscored by garlic. But I'd have browned the aromatics longer, and I think there's *milk* in the mix.

"Can I get you anything else, sir?"

A do-over for my entire life. "More beer?"

The waitress nods and flounces away, leaving me to my study of central London. I glance down at the small black bowl beside my serving of tonkotsu. Once inhabited by a tea egg, it now iridesces with greenish-blue foam. When

I'm certain that no one is looking, I use my fork to pry out a spool of muscle from a fingertip, wincing as I disconnect the tissue and deposit the bloody pink lump into the bowl.

The froth consumes it. I press my thumb over the torn flesh, chant a quick summoning. Nothing grand, no conditional evocation; a rookie's mistake in stereo, presented on a bed of seismic power. More than enough incentive, I hope, to compel a brisk manifestation.

The light flickers.

"I didn't know we were friends."

The God of Being Missing is the quintessential girl next door: small-boned, attractively mousey, with a speckling of freckles and straight, dark hair, a smile like a feral thing. Her entrance is abrupt. One minute I'm alone and the next, she's there, curled primly into the chair opposite mine, my eating arrangement perfectly mirrored, down to the mostly drained pint of beer.

"We're not. But I needed your help."

"I don't *have* to help you."

I tense from the horrific memory of her prehensile maws, fanning from the stump of her throat. She'd eaten her way into Jack and then put him on like a jacket. "No, but I'm hoping to appeal to your incredible sense of generosity. By the way, how's the mister?"

"Digested." The deity scoops *her* black bowl into small palms and sips from the foam, the very picture of decorum. I don't need to check to know she has her ankles hooked together, knees welded shut. An angelic little girl dying for sexual emancipation; exactly the quarry her food need her to be.

"Good to know. I guess."

"What do you want, Rupert?"

The waitress returns with a fresh pint and a crystalline smile, deposits both without preamble and leaves again without casting a glance at my companion. I lap at the foam. "Information."

"On?"

"Persephone."

"I never pegged you for a homewrecker."

"Cut the crap." I put my glass down, and peck sullenly at the dregs of my ramen instead, gathering the noodles into a final, luxuriant heap. "Like you would care even if I was. I just need you to tell me: what's her story?"

"Millennia ago—"

"No. I read up on *that* story already. I need to know what's happening *now*. I think—I think I saw her body. At the Greeks' hide-out. Hades had hurt her. Demeter was furious. And obviously nothing is going right—"

"Why do you care?"

"I—" I hesitate. "I don't know. Because I'm tired of seeing the little guy get kicked around, maybe. Or, maybe, because I'd seen one innocent girl fucked by the system. If I could—I—look, that isn't important, is it? She's one of yours. *Help her.*"

That hits a nerve. The goddess sheds her playful demeanor, smile leeching into a hard line. She slopes her head to the right, the dusk etching light along the contours of her jaw. Fingers beat an irregular rhythm on the wooden table. I wait. Nothing about her softens, although stereotypical thinking would suggest that this is where she divests herself of her predatory mien, exchanges it for maternal concern, gauzy and edgeless. But it doesn't happen. If anything, she seems harder, brought into greater focus, accentuated. And in that moment, I'm reminded of Kali-ma, mother and murderess, not diametric sides of the same coin but a singular entity.

"It was a compromise." A sigh, deep. "When everything went catastrophically wrong, Hades realized that he had a problem. Persephone was bound to the underworld. Six months a year, she had to remain there. Oh, he tolerated it for an interval, but husbandly needs quickly overrode common sense. Hades wanted his wife available, so he took with him the only thing he can remove from the underworld: her body."

"And Demeter doesn't like how the necrophiliac abuses Persephone's corpse."

"Correct."

"Man, I always thought that Hades was one of the nice ones." I bury the clump of noodles in my mouth and begin to chew, slightly resentful. The tepid broth had congealed unpleasantly.

"Sexual fidelity isn't necessarily representative of character."

"Fair enough." I rest my cutlery. "And what about Demeter herself?"

"Domestic abuse is outside of my realm." She empties her bowl; a strand of tissue flashes momentarily into view, rat-tail whipping, before she slurps it down. *Clink.* A frown wrinkles her face, lips mashing into a moue. "You understand."

"I think I do."

A nuanced silence hovers between us, crammed with things unspoken, a hundred questions and arguments held at bay by a circumstance of allegiances. The waitress comes back after a few minutes, drawn, perhaps, by the lack of movement and the empty crockery. Space appears to be a premium in these London eateries.

"They were right about you," the God of Being Missing declares, softly, after I'd paid my bill with Lions' credit card. (You'd be amazed, ang moh, by the things that swagger can buy. No one questions you when you look like you belong. Actually, ignore me. You probably know everything about *that* already.)

"Who?"

Her fingers find mine, thumb stroking spirals across my knuckles. Each rotation triggers a flutter of memory, mine and hers: children's faces, frozen in monochrome; a thousand missing people posters, twisted into limbs and stretched across a birdcage torso. Ah. Of course. "What did they say, exactly?"

Another show of teeth. A near-smile. "That you're soft."

Somehow, it doesn't sound as much like an insult as I thought it would.

I smile faintly. "By the way, there's one more thing..."

*   *   *

WHAT BOON DOES Rupert Wong ask from the God of Being Missing? Can't tell you yet, ang moh. The story's not over.

THIRTY-ONE

"*Sick tats.*"

I squint at the teenager, wire-lean and pale, hair dyed mangosteen-purple, tips glowing yellow. Her eyes, swamped in black liner, are enormous in her face. "Thanks."

She reaches out a hand but recoils at the last instant, her smile uncertain, fingers wilting into loose fists. I appraise my forearms. The skin teems with star maps, indecipherable instructions to places I doubt any space program will reach; every coordinate is listed in an eye-watering alphabet, the sigils subtly protean, unmoving yet forever changing. It seems apt—poetic, almost; a replacement for the lives that Nyarlathotep flensed from my yearly income. I roll my sleeves down, smooth a bland smile into place.

The girl blinks and twitches her head, a delicate motion, pupils dilating to their natural size. She loops a strand of hair behind an ear and grimaces at me, shaken by whatever's fizzing through her brain, already bending away, turning towards the exit. I slouch in the opposite direction, only *slightly* concerned that someone might think I'd creeped on her or something and needed a rebuke.

Slightly.

God, I hope no one decides to be a good Samaritan.

Luckily, no one succumbs to charitable behaviour, and the train wheels uneventfully into my station. As I scoot up the walkway towards the exit, a plangent droning sound assumes tenancy in my ears. "What the—"

The noise clarifies into voices, whispers layered in strata, each half an octave above the last. They're *singing*, the cadence matched to the high, sweet serenade of a flute. What about I have no idea, but there's a chill slinking down my spine, and an itch kindling beneath my new skin, like muscles rebuilding in accelerando, or a cancer flowering. I could be wrong, but I suspect I don't want to know what the voices are saying.

Unnerved, I lengthen my gait and take the stairs two at a time.

The night is orange-lit, freezing. No rain this time, but a wind that chews through the skin. I zip up my hoodie, although it offers no protection from the chill. Old habits. I scan the road outside of West Croydon station. In retrospect, I should have been wise enough to ask someone about safety procedures, if there are any bolt holes, emergency contact numbers for when a rival faction sets everything on fire.

Oh, well.

I debate making an immediate beeline for the estate, see if anyone had survived the pandemonium. It's possible. They *are* gods, and I imagine Nyarlathotep would have indulged in at least some token gloating had the fire successfully consumed the lot. But it is also possible that the self-proclaimed Crawling Chaos is just a dick, preferring to let me nurture a dim hope for a little while before quenching it.

A pair of drunks totter out of a pub across the street, the exterior worn but magnificently twee; walls yellow, window frames green; gold font declaring *The Old Fox & Hounds*. I shrug at the vacant road. No harm in starting there.

I slip through the door, exchanging nods with a middle-aged white woman smoking furiously at the door, a Bluetooth speaker glowing at her ear. The pub inside is cozy despite the claustrophobic ceilings; a womb of dark wood and antiquated furniture patinaed by the dim light, run ragged by the decades, and softened with alcohol-induced camaraderie. No one glares at the stray Chinese man, although two women seated at a window—city types in skirt suits—stare at me blankly.

Feeling nonplussed, I stump up to the bartender, a large-figured fellow with a bald pate and overgrown sideburns. He wipes the counter down with a greasy rag and slings it over a broad arm. A walking stereotype if there ever was one, every trope neatly checkmarked. The moment that thought shelves itself in my consciousness, I tense up. Coincidences have never signalled good things in my world.

"Bit shit out there, innit?" He beams in welcome.

I shrug, torn between sitting down and getting out. I settle for palming the stool in front of me and keeping at arm's length, a decision that raises the barkeep's eyebrows. True to form, however, he does not question my eccentricity, only broadens his smile further.

"Quiet one. I can respect that." A calculated twinge of a brogue, lilting his words, precisely enough to make him sound quaint, amenable. No more, no less. "You look like a rum man, I think. Something rough, maybe. An overproof to burn away the blues."

Try as I may, I can't quarantine a snort.

"Wray and Nephew? Sixty-three percent. Like a house on fire." And it is the smile that gives it away, the slightest hint of a sneer.

Foresight, for a change, was as visionary as hindsight. I jolt from the bar, already reaching for a non-existent armament, fingers shutting over nothing. "Hey, man. If this is about—"

"Relax. I'm just fucking with you." The accent is gone and in its place: nothing. No impression of a motherland, no identifiable pronunciation, nothing that could tie the bartender to a country or a culture. His eyes glitter pale. "Wasn't sure you'd come back."

"Why the fuck wouldn't I come back? Also, with all due respect, who the fuck are you?"

"Sucellus, at your service." He twirls his paw to indicate the room. The two women decant from their seats and prowl forward. They're trembling slightly, but move with weird grace and unsettling purpose. One cocks her head like a hound that'd caught a forgotten scent. Now I notice the torn clothes, the blood under the nails, the wild hair. "Gaulish god of wine. And these lovely ladies are, of course, Maenads."

I reangle my stance. Crazy, flesh-eating celebrants of meat, mead, and mutilation are required to stay in my field of vision at all times; keep your arms and your legs firmly attached to your torso. "Maenads?" I asked. "Shouldn't they be with Dionysus?"

"Funny," Sucellus says, smile falling short of his eyes. "Funny fucking guy." He clocks my blank expression and cocks his head. "Wait, you didn't know about Dionysus?"

"Not so much."

"Vaporized in L.A. by the new outfit. Things have been hotting up recently." He shrugs. "These poor girls have found themselves without a patron, and I've kindly taken them under my wing." He winks and props an elbow on the counter, chin cradled in palm. "Anyway. Like I said, I wasn't sure you'd come back to us, what with that terrible run at the Boulder."

"What do you mean?" The Maenads fan out, crossing the bar with alarming speed, bare feet making no sound at all on the floorboards.

"The bet, of course." Sucellus clucks, expression shading to indulgence. "You lost."

"But I never even made the bet—" I mutter, focus bisected by the god and his women, smiles now dressing the latter, vague yet knowing, prophets drunk on the future.

"No, but Helenus foresaw your answer."

"Excuse me"—I wheel on Sucellus, so that I can behold him in his porcine entirety—"but doesn't anyone else think that it is deeply contradictory to build important decisions on the blubbering of a man who has been proven incapable of producing accurate—ah, shit."

No warning before cool metal wedges itself under my chin. A smell of wine, saccharine, slightly sickly. Hair against my skin, a storm of curls, tickling at the nape of my neck and the back of my ears. Close. Too close. I stop breathing. Those Maenads are fast.

"Just a precaution. You understand." Sucellus seems borderline embarrassed, waving a hand vaguely.

"Mm. Easy for *you* to say." The flat of an unseen blade presses harder against my throat, instructive of its bearer's opinion of my sass. "Okay, okay, sorry"—the compression of my Adam's apple reverses, and I wince as airflow is restored—"can't a man get a few good non-sequiturs in?"

No one laughs. No one even rolls their eyes. Cursing inwardly, I realize, too late again, that I've lost track of the second Maenad, although it could be argued that there's nothing that she can do that her counterpart can't. Still, her disappearance limits my options, and I grit my teeth against the route my life has taken.

"Anyway," Sucellus says again, with mounting exasperation. He levers up a section of the counter and glides through, graceful despite his bulk. A smile breaks his face again, while his hair piles up on his head, joined by a huge, bristling beard. "Like I was saying."

"Uh-huh?"

"I'm surprised you came back. But not *displeased* about it. Every goblet of wine demands its accompanying dish, every portion of liquor its partner in veal."

"I'd laugh at your joke, but I think she'd cut—ow! Stop it. Ha. Ha. There. Happy? Fuck you."

They march me deeper into the interior, past saloon-style doors into a better appointed space, the accoutrements appropriate to the decade. Even the paint job is reflective of the change, seamless, unmarked by gravy stains.

Not many of the gods remain, and those who do wear guarded expressions, bodies brocaded by the conflagration, injuries weeping pus. Hephaestus is gone, of course, deconstructed into ash. Demeter sits alone at an unattended bar, largely vegetal, skin whorled with bark. Poseidon and Hades conference in a corner, their bravado still intact, the air surrounding them cycling between hallucinatory content; a glimmer of the deep ocean, black, riddled with monsters; a suggestion of the underworld, similarly attended by abominations.

No sign of the feldgeist or Hildra, no trace of Veles. Despite everything that had happened, grief clenches at my lungs, resolving into a memory of the Cat, drooping like a comma from Sisyphus' grip. They'd been friends, all of them.

Ananke, right arm terminating at the elbow, the flesh grown over and smooth, is the only one to acknowledge my arrival. "The prodigal cook returns."

"That's one way to put it." The empyrean throbbing in the rear of my mind magnifies into obtrusiveness, as though titillated by proximity with the pantheon. "How's tricks?"

She doesn't answer. Sucellus allots another minute of silence, and then gestures me forward, the Maenad releasing her hold. I glance backwards, find her propped against a wall; fingers laced behind the small of her back, foot drawn up, face shadowed by a banner of unruly hair. She winks. I nod.

Sucellus leads me to a table inhabited by poker players, its axis domed with entrails: kidney, cuts of liver, the plumbings of a heart. Everything is meticulously packed into transparent tupperware.

"What the—"

"Helenus."

"*Ooooooooh.*"

Sisyphus, leading with most of a stomach, peers up at me over the rim of his glasses. "Welcome back."

"So I hear I've lost big, somehow."

"All in." Sisyphus shovels his cache of viscera into the central pile. "You did."

"See, I'd have thought that this was the kind of thing you'd bring up when you're visiting someone in the hospital. I mean, you had a lot to say about everything else."

"Straights," mumbles a wan-looking woman with feathers for hair, elbows tufting into vestigial wings, fingers scaled with keratin.

"*Better* straights," counters another woman, similarly plumed but built on a more intimidating scale.

A rumbling from the minotaur in the third seat. He stretches forward to harvest the assorted offal, a grin dragging horrifically at its bovine face. "*Three* of a kind."

"Hold on, there." A girl, an elfin thing cobbled from sticks and bone, places her tiny hand on his, head shaken slowly. "I've got a flush."

"And *I* have a full house," Sisyphus clucks, waving both of his adversaries away. Everyone groans, graceless in defeat. The air bristles with profanities, Greek and English, woven between dialects more guttural yet. "What were you talking about? Oh. Yes. That was a social visit. This is business."

"Of course. *Obviously.*"

Asshole.

I glance at Sucellus. He looks more himself now, cheeks red and eyes bloodshot. A tunic hugs his colossal bulk. No deity of excessive drinking is complete without alcohol, however, and as such, he's also inexplicably holding a clay pot of wine. Noticing my attention, he shrugs.

I grab a chair and spin it around, straddle the seat, one arm flung over the back. With any luck, Sisyphus will believe that some measure of cocksure, don't-mess-with-me machismo is lodged in my chest—something other than this gnawing, gristly, growing certainty that they're going to call my ruse, and this will all end in tears.

Having said that, whole species are built on this model of dominance, ours included. So it might work. I hope it works. More importantly, I hope it works well enough to divert them from the crucial questions. Like 'Do you have a doorway to the outside of our universe carved onto your arms?' (Which I do.)

"Far be it for me to comment on how you run your operation, but is it actually possible to force someone to pay for something that didn't actually agree to do?"

"You told the fox you would play."

"Yes, but I never actually said what I was betting on."

A dismissive flap of the hand. "We have that covered. Helenus informed us of your most likely decision, so we ran with that."

"Seriously."

"Seriously." The light slicks gold across his glasses as he grins.

"Asshole." I grind the words between my molars, restless, gaze running circuits around the hall. "So what do I owe you?"

"Everything."

At the word, a barb threads itself through my soul; the smallest tug, evaluating defenses, gauging weakness. I spin out a negatory charm, pure reflex, and Nyarlathotep's blessing, if you can call it that, secures itself about the spell, adding weight, power. We fling Sisyphus' probe out. He notices immediately, and I wait for him to question me, but he does nothing of the sort, only observes me cautiously.

"Even though I took down Vanquis?"

A silence froths across the numinous crowd, and the song of the Outer Gods crests. For all their pretenses at indifference, the Greek divinities have apparently been eavesdropping. I gather my eyebrows into an expression of mock surprise and then waggle them. Got to keep to the spirit of things.

"What?"

"Oh, was I mumbling?" I scratch under my jaw, teeth bared in pleasure. "I said I took down Vanquis."

Whispers skitter, rat-like, across the room. They merge into low-pitched conversations, every word swollen with urgency. It's all Greek to me (hah!), but their consternation is unmistakable, rising in pitch, spitting and stammering.

Chairs move. A glass breaks, and someone laughs, loud and frantic.

Let us in. Let us in. Let us in. Words, *actual* words, not the unholy bedlam I'd become accustomed to, but actual words, unstitch from the song pulsating in my skull, a single phrase repeated ad infinitum, growing steadily more urgent.

"You can't have taken down Vanquis." Hades, his voice changed: glass-cut accent withering in the advent of genuine emotion, subsumed by older cadences, likely derived from the dreams of an ancient civilization.

Let.

He does not walk towards the table; he floats. Feet skimming the floor, a perfunctory acknowledgment of gravity's omnipresence. A literal darkness follows close behind: a carpet of tendriling ink, as though someone had seized the shadow of a strangling vine and coerced it into animation. Poseidon takes the more quotidian approach and walks up to me, swaggering behind his brother-god.

Hades holds out his palm at hip level. The gloom stills.

"I can and I did."

"And what proof do you have of this grandiose claim?" Disdain greases every word. His contempt is magnificent to see, so complete, so thorough that it is practically impregnable, no longer an opinion but a state of being, the idea of something like *me* succeeding where he has failed so alien to his world view that he cannot allow even for its possibility.

Us.

Tough luck, I guess.

"Don't need any. Just give it another week and see if any desk monkeys show up to kill you in your sleep." I shrug again.

"Hermes, find out if he's telling the truth."

A slender man, with gelled blond hair and wraparound shades, flickers out of the gloom. He snaps a crisp salute, vanishes as quickly as he appears, not so much dematerializing as stuttering away rapidly, a carousel of key frames incorrectly played.

"And now we wait."

I study Sisyphus, endlessly shuffling his cards, their backs frescoed with depictions of infernal torture. On one, a spiky, stained-glass-looking image of a man rolling a boulder up a red mountain. There's a look on his face that I know too well. He *loathes* Hades, despises him in that special way that only service staff and the subjugated (I suppose they're both the same) can muster, and it inspires a pang of short-lived empathy.

In.

"How about we talk about what I get out of this?"

"What *you* get out of this?" A laugh, choked off when Hades realizes that I'm actually serious, horror briskly supplanting his gaiety. "I wasn't aware that this was a business transaction."

Let.

"Well, it is." I grip the back of my chair with both hands. "And I've got a long list of things that I want and have had far too little sleep, so let's just get this started—"

"I don't think you understand." Hades clenches a fist and the darkness corkscrews up from the floor, spooling around his knuckles, laddering into rings. "That was sarcasm. No-one's actually inviting your input, Rupert."

Us.

Another shrug. "Oh. I know. Similarly, I'm not really giving you a choice in the matter"—I hope this works I hope this works I hope this works I hope this works—"because you are all fucked up pieces of shit."

The atmosphere accrues a decidedly hostile tint.

In.

"I mean," I sweep an arm to indicate the celestial masses as they unknot into combative poses, power crackling through the air, salt and sinuous rage. "I guess you're slightly ahead of the curve, what with Zeus not being around. But the misogyny, and the whole dehumanization-of-the-human race?" I jab a finger at Ananke. "The pet grandmothers. Don't think I haven't forgotten your pet grandmothers. That's just cruel and unusual—"

Let.

Poseidon, through his signpost smile, all big teeth. "Rupert, watch yourself."

Us.

"No." I kick up from my chair, glowering, finger waggled with as much ferocity as I can devote. I'm dizzied from input. Nauseous, almost. There is too much going on, too much sound, too many angles, too many voices. *letusinletusinletusinletusin* "I will not stop. Least of all for *you*, because seriously, beating up your wife—"

In.

"Hah! I told you, Demeter. Everyone understands our relationship as wonderfully matrimonial."

"—and claiming weird things. *Stop* that. Honestly." I can hear the hysteria notched into my voice, and it is frankly unflattering. But it achieves its purpose. The manic irreverence seems to have the gods fazed, which is exactly where I need them to be. I chew open my tongue, consecrate the blood to the myriad divinities of Lovecraft, and feel my skin go warm.

let us in let us in let us in

The gibbering climaxes into a howl. A sensation of knives, spreading in reticular fashion, tracing the atlas engraved on my back. Anticipation. Pressure beneath my skin, as though of bodies heaving in excitement, thousand-strong, clamoring at the seam of my spine.

Hades: "I've had enough."

let us in let us in

"Me too." I grin.

let us in let us—

The doorway splits opens.

THIRTY-TWO

IT ALWAYS COMES down to tentacles, doesn't it?

Muscular, omni-directional and impervious to osteological injury, they provide a kind of three-hundred-and-sixty-degree functionality unmatched by rival appendages. As such, it's unsurprising that tentacles are favored by those capable of restructuring their physiognomy. It's arguably just good practice.

Maybe. I might just be trying to justify this cephalopodic nightmare.

Tentacles. *Everywhere.* Evanescing between dimensions, so proliferate that I can almost pretend it's something like foliage: ferns and vines, rapacious shrubbery, the wind scruffing its fronds like the short hairs on the back of an alleycat. Innocent, innocuous.

A tendril secures itself around a screaming satyr's waist, whips the unfortunate beast back and forth against the walls, each impact flattening the skull a little more. The air flickers; the young man from earlier—Hermes—is plucked from the air and dragged shrieking through the bar. Gargantuan cilia rise from the floor to grab the minotaur, four to a limb, and *rip.*

The Greeks are slightly more on top of the situation this time; or, at least, they're not immediately being steamrolled. The strobic, multi-planar quality of the battle, however, makes it hard to tell exactly who's winning, or even what's happening. One minute, men and women are clinched in battle, snarling, gouging holes in one another with knife and nail and gun and more exotic utensils. The next, it's all flickering light and the sense that my brain is being turned inside out, and introduced to new planes of horrified consciousness.

Needless to say, the experience is excruciating, and it's serendipitous that I've yet to be targeted. In part, I imagine, because I'm curled beneath a table, from which oceans of blood are pouring across the floor. Too late, I discovered that Nyarlathotep and his cohorts are unable to queue in an orderly fashion. Where they can't access the portal, they extrude from my pores, individual strands of pus constituting into many-eyed nightmares.

All things taken into consideration, however, things could be worse. I could be dead.

Wait. That would probably be better.

Despite the injuries, despite everything, I find enough cogence to crawl across the floor, dodging bodies and individual conflagrations, towards Demeter and Poseidon. The two are pinned in a corner, with Poseidon brandishing his trident, holding back what looks like a farm animal fused with a creche of juvenile squids, beaks clacking dumbly at the air.

Demeter, on her part, stands passively, exhibiting neither interest nor apprehension, seemingly disconnected from the furor. I scuttle into her field of vision and gesture for her attention, only to recoil as a *thing* of unspeakable grotesquerie smashes through the table I've taken shelter under and vanishes through the floor, its writhing prey pinioned between teeth.

It's Sucellus, entrails glistening through the air, intestines taut between two grinning maws. Eye contact is made, for a single frenzied moment, and he is gone.

"Demeter!" I hiss from the detritus, poking my head out again. "Demeter! Come here! I'm trying to save you!"

That sounded considerably less impressive than I hoped it would.

She blinks from her ennui and a smile roots itself in her face, the goddess of agriculture once again all the way flesh, her skin a rich loam. There is a fierce, abstruse delight in her eyes. Demeter does not accept my invitation. Instead, she presses a fingertip to her mouth and turns to Poseidon, who has just incinerated one of those calamari-goats.

"Poseidon."

Behind him, more of the—*Thousand Young*, chitters a voice in my head, unsolicited—gather, grinning, their mouths turned human, fringed by plush lips.

"Good, I need you to—"

No glimmer of steel. The weapon is older: dull, pitted bronze with a hilt of jaundiced bone. Demeter betrays no emotion as she brings both hands to bear on the pommel, weight thrown into the motion. The sword twitches deeper under Poseidon's diaphragm and blood oozes in lucent droplets. His expression is one of absolute mystification as he lowers one broad palm to cup her cheek.

"I've been waiting to do that for *so* long." The blade digs two inches deeper. "You have no idea. The hours. The waiting. The *planning*. But it is so, so good to finally be able to gut you like a fish."

The light discards his eyes, and Poseidon topples backwards into the gibbering maws of the Thousand Young, who immediately set upon him. Loud *slorping* ensues.

"*What the fuck was that?*"

Barometric pressure plunges sharply, tailspinning to breathlessness, and my vision throbs as I begin to cough for dribbles of air. Something important definitely just happened, and I'm willing to put money on it having to do with the fact that the Greek pantheon is now missing two of its integral patriarchal figures.

Through the deoxygenated haze, I watch as Demeter saunters away, hand curled around her curving blade, gait jaunty. She is *happy*. No, not happy; overjoyed. *Ecstatic.*

It was her all along.

How had I not realized?

Oh. *Right.*

Because I was busy being maimed, murdered, and otherwise mashed into puree.

For a scatter of moments, less than the time it takes a thought to bridge neurons, I contemplate scrabbling onto my feet and joining her in combat. But common sense coupled with a honed instinct for self-preservation argue another course of action: evasion. After all, Demeter just stabbed Poseidon in the chest and is, even now, walking into the throes of a tentacular apocalypse without so much as a sidelong glance at the gridlock of villi infesting the bar.

This is a damsel clearly capable of distressing her opponents without masculine intervention.

But then that *stupid* mutt skulks from the pandemonium on silent paws, fumes clawing from its soot-black pelt, heads low and muscles gathered, grins bared in glittering triplicate. And Demeter doesn't notice. Demeter *doesn't fucking notice*. Even as the air crisps with ozone, with the raw charnel stink of mana, with the sound of history pirouetting on the needle of Now, Cerberus creeps closer yet, headlight stare bearing down like a quick death on a dark highway.

"Shit. Shit. Shit. Shit." I jump to my feet and stumble after him, the word concatenating into a single desperate whine. If this is what heroism feels like, the virtuous can keep it to themselves.

THIS IS ONE of those moments that you remember in staccato, flash-bang vignettes manacled together by a blurred recollection of mortal dread, like the afterimage of the sun baked into your retina. I couldn't tell you if I shout first or if I lunge for Cerberus, or even if I do the intelligent thing and alert Demeter from a cautious distance.

Similarly, I couldn't say for sure if there's a smile on Demeter's face as she turns just so, just enough so that the glimmering parabola of a blade misses her hip, slams instead into the wall. If Hades' eyes go wide, if he sighs or screams as Demeter reciprocates, no magic on her lips, only bronze and flesh and a mother's hate counted in eternities—well, those are secrets the walls will keep.

What I remember is this:

Doggy breath, no matter the species, is excruciatingly *bad*.

*   *   *

"N-NICE PUPPY—*FFRRRAGGHEERK.*"

A giant three-headed dog is a complication that I wouldn't wish on my worst enemy, and that isn't just because I can't imagine the volume of shit it would produce. The end of the sentence drowns itself in a shriek as fangs clamp down on my upper arm, catching on the division between bicep and tricep. With a twitch of Cerberus' leftmost head, the connective tissue separates into a cat's cradle of bloodied strings.

I scream as the strength winks out of the limb, and again when I thrust the appendage into the hellhound's middlemost maw, its jaws crashing shut in a storm of halitosis. *Crunch.* Teeth crack through the bones of my forearm, slicing nerves to tufts, and I thrash under its bulk, keening with every exhalation.

Taking my ululations as encouragement, the rightmost head, till now an indifferent party, mobilizes. It jolts forward with a yelp of excitement and begins worrying at my side, gobbling chunks of skin and meat. Blood spurts messily, dribbling from its muzzle.

With a howl, I let go one of Cerberus' central snouts and twist, hand gliding up its muzzle. Momentum carries the canine forward and it buries its teeth into my shoulder, about the same time I drive fingers into its eyes. The cornea doesn't hold; aqueous humor bursts over my knuckles as I dig for the optic nerves.

And *pull.*

Cerberus convulses, screams as one beast.

I use the opportunity to scramble away, arm hanging uselessly—*again*—from the maimed shoulder, the clavicle snapped into pieces. Blood loss is doing a number on me. The light circulates in uneasy currents, adding an attractive soft focus to the carnage. I stagger, one knee going weak.

Growling. A warning, intended to be heard, a declaration in sub-aural vibrations. Cerberus takes his time. He oils forward. The middle head twitches, nothing but jerks and hard stops, a broken war machine. It laps at the air. Lips peel back over gray-pink gums and the hackles on the other heads bristle to spines.

"Nice doggy." I slip on an oil slick of my own blood and land on my ass, the impact rattling from tailbone to skull. "N-nice doggy."

Possibly too late, I curl my thoughts about the first protection spell I can think of, daubing runes in frantic shorthand across the floorboards. Tentacles lash overhead, tessellate into a ceiling of not-quite-meat. I can hear something in the ambient background. Not screaming, per se; lower in volume but no less high-pitched, a terrified whine that ripples without the need for air, practically seamless as it eases from one trembling sob to the next.

There's also chewing.

Let's not think about the chewing.

Cerberus keeps advancing. I throw up my magic, and he smashes it aside with a flap of a heavy paw; the air fractalizes, mana disintegrating in patterns of scintillant nacre. I kick away a little further, skidding back, red palmprints undulating from the point of retreat.

"You want a treat? I could totally make you a treat if you leave me long enough to go to the supermarket, buy ingredients at a competitive rate, and—"

Cerberus hunches, ears wicking back, shoulders and spine cocked. There is no warning. The hellhound saccades into motion, quicker than plausible, and all at once, I am out of time.

So I do the only thing I can: I ball up. Knees to chest, arms over head, head scrunched into the canyon of my shoulders, a decision that tangles into a locus of tortured nociceptors. (You say coward, I say pragmatist. Po-tay-to, po-tah-to. Screw you.)

But no heavy weight drives itself into my supine form, no teeth fasten onto my limbs.

"Heel."

Salt and earth, funeral smells. An overlay of ozone, golden with the dry, earthy, cut-grass sweetness of the harvest. I unclench to stare up at Demeter, magnificent in her mundanity, a wry smile worn like a badge of office. Her sundress is polka-dotted with green, her feet sandalled, and her silhouette is fringed with a corona of *yes*, of unspun possibility, invisible, immaterial, but entirely unmistakable.

Cerberus prostrates his bulk at her feet, central head lolling, eyes rolled up to its whites. Spittle foams from its mouth, blood-brindled.

"That's a good trick," I rasp, licking rust from dry lips. "Would have appreciated you getting to it sooner, though. By the way, good job. Whatever you just did. I think."

Her smirk is not unkind, but it is trimmed with warning. Demeter offers no answer, merely stoops to scratch behind one of Cerberus' myriad ears.

Ignored, I peer over her shoulder. The room quieted: not jungle-silent, where microfauna chitter and chirrup, a million noises coagulating into a kind of stillness, but silent. *Dead* silent.

On the bright side, there aren't any actual bodies. Entrails, sure, and in abundance; the walls are a holocaust starscape, notched with the marks of desperate hands. The floors are black.

"So, you going to tell me what is going—"

"Not yet." A gleam of an indulgent smile as Demeter rises, stretching her arms. The survivors cower, maggot-colored, identities pared into sexless uniformity: lumpless bodies, noseless faces, eyes hollowed into bruises. They huddle behind the detritus of the fight, crooning in nonsensical whalesong voices. All except for Sisyphus, who twists in place, bound by loops of muscle, his eyes pried open by millimeter-long hooks. Demeter ignores them. Her arms slowly rise, fingertips bleeding light. Her palms clap shut.

And reality spasms.

A slit divides the air and a moment is tipped out of time, heaped high with chthonic sights: lakes of pitch, fringed with glass-forests; a ribbon of black water haunted by a boatman; fields of eternal wheat, whispering to itself, bright as sunlight. An Ouroborosian debauchery of sinners tormenting sinners, sustained by the guilt of their collective subconscious. One vision stands out: a woman on an alabaster throne, her skin the color of limestone, head drooping over a skinny chest, ribs bladed against her skin. The eyes are gray, sightless, focused on nothing.

"Persephone." Demeter's voice rings out, strong and rich, like the call to prayer, and with her daughter's name, she rewrites the universe.

The world disembowels itself, reconstitutes with Persephone trembling in the center of the room, dripping silks of white. Still pallid, still alien, more ghost than girl, tottering on bite-blackened legs, but here at last. Here finally. Demeter runs to her daughter, catches her as she falls, Persephone's pellucid hair floating like a funeral veil. The goddess sinks to her knees, pressing kisses to her child's brow.

Something loosens inside me, like a rib shifting on its axis.

I swallow; claw my way to the nearest wall; prop myself up, an arm flung around the seat of an upturned chair.

The urge for a cigarette twitches under dulled strata of pain. That's what heroes do, right? Light up a smoke after the explosions have cleared. Maybe even strike a dramatic pose as the sunset paints them in orange gradients. Except that I'm not certain I was anything but the comic relief. Whatever the case, I have neither the energy nor a supply of nicotine, so I sit and hurt instead, and observe the reunion.

No tears from either of them; Demeter whispering in a language I don't understand, the words falling liquid; Persephone watching the walls, watching, watching for something that no one else can see. After an indefinite span, the mother looks up, brushing wisps of pale hair from the knife-wedge of her daughter's face.

"You're still here," Demeter declares, almost affronted.

I shrug around the weight in my chest and swallow, extremities now pleasantly numb. The world is a tide of softness, suffocated by gauze and cotton. "Not out of choice, if that helps at all."

She nods, rising, leaving Persephone to her strange vigil. Demeter flows across the floor, feet barely grazing the gore-crusted floorboards; the air seethes with her new power. When she reaches me, she cups both hands around my cheeks. A smile like the moonlight in coils of black hair.

Hurt tightens around my lungs. "You going to tell me what was all that about?"

"Rupert. You should know better by now. I don't believe in unnecessary exposition."

"But do you believe in collateral damage, though? I mean, you could have told me that you're working with these squids—" My tongue thickens as mana flows into my veins, needlepoints tracing the topology of my wounds, a cauterizing heat. I pant into the healing, grimacing. "Guan Yin stuff a peach up your ass, haven't you gods heard of morphine?"

No reply, even as Demeter withdraws, hands clustered at her base of her stomach.

"Thank you." A corner of her mouth twitches. "Minah would have been proud."

"Don't." The word jerks in my throat. "I thought I told you that you needed to stay out of my head. Don't bring Minah into it. You're not allowed to fucking talk about her."

"I'm just saying—"

"I don't want to hear it. I don't want you to tell me I'm a hero, or—" I'm losing my grip. Hysteria pounds against each syllable, demanding egress. I shudder from the effort of maintaining coherence, even as I palm tears from my eyes, gabbling erratically between sentences. "Get out of my head. I don't want—"

My argument buckles into an undignified whimper. I swallow the sobs. Swallow again and again, despair lumping viscous in my throat. "The only reason I did *anything* is because I know what it's like to scrape the bottom of the barrel, and you, and Persephone, and I don't know, but—"

"Honestly, Rupert, in all the millennia of my existence, you're the first to reject divine accolade." Demeter seats herself beside me, scoops a warm arm around my shoulder.

I shiver again. A sound tears itself out of my lungs, neither laugh nor cry. "Because I don't deserve any of it. I—fucking hell, I was a selfish son of a bitch. I'm still a selfish son of a bitch. Do you know why I tried to save you? Why I gave a shit? I think—I think it's because I'm a selfish fucking asshole who wants nothing more than to see his girl again. And I was hoping, praying, that if I did this for you, you'd make it happen. Or at least—"

Salt and snot mix in rivulets as I begin to cry in huge, ugly bursts, no longer able to withhold the wracking grief. "At least you'd tell me that she's still there in the universe somewhere. That she is alive. That there is some way that our atoms might meet in the future, perfect strangers tied together by a syllable of memory. I need—I need—I—"

"I think I owe you enough to not lie to you."

I inhale, trembling. "Fuck your honesty."

"Honestly, Rupert. I wasn't lying when I said she would have been proud—"

"Don't. Don't say that. I don't want any of that. Not your platitudes, not— fuck. I—I know that she would have been proud of me! Fuck you! That's *why* I tried to save Persephone, that's why I tried to help you. Because I wanted to do *something* that she'd have approved of, something she'd have agreed with. God."

Silence.

And then, into the trembling quiet:

"You're a good person, Rupert."

"You're such a liar," I look up, a laugh strangling itself in my voice, and wipe my tears on the back of my palm, gulping air. "But thanks. I guess."

Another deep breath, and I push myself to my feet. Demeter makes no endeavour to stop me or to coax me back into her arms. Her interest in my wellbeing is vestigial, contingent on the structures of courtesy. I expedited her revenge on her own pantheon and then broke down on her watch. Of course she had to supply platitudes. That's just how it's done.

But having performed the obligatory formalities, Demeter returns her attention to her daughter. Persephone, for all of the minutes she has spent corporealized, could be a ghost still, her hair colorless, her skin gray and dusted with starlight. Chalk-filmed eyes regard the abyss, impassive, blind. When her mother palms her shoulder, however, she startles, animal-quick, and something like recognition crosses the china-bone face.

"I'll leave you to it," I mumble, rising to my feet. The Outer Gods call out as I do, seeping from the walls, their incomprehensible warbling glissading into meaning, into non-Euclidean visions, glimpses of paradises sandpapered from nightmares, knowledge beyond mathematical probability, beyond three-dimensional perception.

I turn, and there Nyarlathotep stands in his borrowed skin, curls haloed in silver, the light sleeting through his bones, smiling like he is about to offer me the best damn mortgage plan in real estate history.

Crack.

Sisyphus' neck is briskly snapped.

"And our side of the bargain is complete."

Their song rises to devour my world.

THIRTY-THREE

The assimilation is violent.

Thoughtless. Instinct-propelled. Performed without concern for my comfort. Cilia of alien consciousness bifurcate into embryonic personalities, not quite theirs, not quite mine, but *hungry* chimerical amalgamations. Prose, turgid, tumescent with invention, translate themselves into Hokkien, Teochew, Malay, Cantonese; recreate themselves in a manner authentic to the associate culture. The words interlace with images of sanctified ground, of a titanic figure slumbering beneath the water, of eyes, of a sunken-eyed man staring raptly at a filigreed mirror.

More. A demand, eager. They pry at my memories, divest the amygdala of secrets, the hippocampus of truth. *More.* My brain ignites with fireworks. The glut of electrical impulses threatens to short-circuit what self remains under the weight of their curiosity. Desperate, I withdraw, building metaphorical walls, a fortress of nothing-to-see-here. The gods—the *whatever* they are—clamber past my shelter, too ravenous to multitask.

Possession, I discover, is not unlike digestion: a two-way street beginning with consumption. My new tenants excrete data; name and anecdotes and locations, a chronology of progressively more bizarre occurrences, ending with an aerial shot of a magician refereeing a fist fight in Egypt. A thousand novels, a hundred secret scriptures built in the bones of fiction. Television shows and radio dramas, more short stories than stars dying in the abyss.

Worship doesn't require *belief*. Worship simply needs to *be*. And a million books and a million fantasies and a million conversations about piscine hybrids and a city buried in the black of the ocean, terrors unimaginable and dream lands unfathomable, is more than enough to gorge a pantheon.

I wait and wait and wait until at last Nyarlathotep's presence reveals itself, rapturous, his form oscillating frantically. When he finally burrows himself between his siblings, identity latticed with theirs, with mine, I strike.

"See you in Hell."

The God of Being Missing had not lied. For once, dying is quick and painless.

"RUPERT?" YAN LUO in his celestial aspect, bigger than worlds; a disc of engraved jade caged in fingers. A pot of tea sits on an adjacent table. Steam ribbons from a bone-china cup. "What are you—"

"What's up, chief?"

"What have you done?" Nyarlathotep is on his feet before I can construct a lie, shimmering between forms, simultaneously the leather-jacketed man in the train and something *other*, a monstrosity that strangles every description in its crib. "Rupert, *what have you done?*"

The last is a shriek that shreds the last pretense of mortality, pulping his larynx as it climbs into an inhuman register. He does not lunge, but *something* does. A circle of greasily lucent pink flesh rises from around his feet and volleys forward. Seamless, faceless. A hodgepodge of extremities, teeth and talon and terrible things, wound into filaments of muscle and laced together in a grand blasphemy of terrestrial design.

I dance backwards, but I'm a human spirit stripped from his coat of meat and these are gods, for all the vulgarity of their origin, their pedestrian birth in the mind of a frightened American. They slam me into the ground. The impact is cataclysmic: screams and keratin raking across my face, tendrils puncturing my sides. Something catches in the nerves and I spasm in its grip, retinas misfiring in paroxysms of white. Intestines bulge ropily against the skin of my stomach. Lungs compress; my abdominal cavity inflates with the intruding bio-mass.

And all the while, something is *howling*, rage pumping hot through the noise.

Snap.

With a click of colossal fingers, existence rewinds. I'm on my feet again and Nyarlathotep is a glistening imago, scrabbling in his cocoon: a clump of pink flesh pimpled with slack mouths and staring eyes, his brethren squirming in polyps.

He charges again.

Snap.

This time, they don't even reach me. Reality winks its massive eye, and we zip back to where we began. There is no third attempt. Nyarlathotep extends a long-fingered hand, staying them. He trails his gaze up to Yan Luo's mountainous silhouette.

"This is not your house."

The King of Diyu sets his chess piece down and rises to his full height, bulk eclipsing the effulgence of his fireplace, which burns eternally, fed by dead men's hair. The fire gilds him in bronze, casts shadows on his face. "You are both guests and I will not tolerate violence between you."

"Suits me." I spit a tooth.

Nyarlathotep glowers, features teased into a semblance of humanity. Black curls and snug jeans replace tentacles and ramified limbs. His face smooths into inoffensive handsomeness, enough to appeal but not to dazzle, mouth wrenched back into a coyote's grin.

"I apologize for the outburst. But we had a deal, Rupert and I. And I did not expect him to renege on his side of our agreement. I did not expect him to murder."

"You obviously don't know me very well." I scoot behind Yan Luo.

Admonishing looks, in duplicate.

"Shutting up now."

Yan Luo inclines his titanic head and squats to our level, thoughtfully grabbing at his beard. "I understand your concern and I appreciate how upset you must be"—extending his palm placatingly—"but I promise you that we will reprimand Rupert as per regulation guidelines."

Nyarlathotep's smile freezes. "I'm sorry. What did you say?"

"Rupert is our employee," Yan Luo replies, inflection subtly modulated, timbre imbued with quiet authority. "As such, he will be punished according to our rules."

"*Your* rules?" Ice seeps into the smaller god's voice. "We had an agreement. Rupert belongs to us."

"As a subcontractor, certainly," Yan Luo counters. "He has every right to offer his services as a freelancer, so long as none of those responsibilities conflict with his employment in Diyu. If such conditions arise, I'm afraid that our arrangements supersede all other deals he may have signed. It is in the fine print."

The last words are spoken in staccato, every sound weighted with funerary gravitas, an end-of-the-world finality. The subtext is simple: *fuck right off.*

But Nyarlatotep won't be dissuaded. A growl escapes his throat before he composes himself, sickle-moon smile returning in force. "And *our* standard agreement includes a clause that states that the signee voids all former contractual obligations upon accepting our terms."

"Again." Yan Luo picks a clump of lint from his robes and rubs it between his fingers. "I think you're confused. Even if *your* contract states as such, you'll find that *our* contract has right of precedence. Furthermore, since Rupert is, in fact, an incorporated entity, all decisions regarding takeovers must be put through the committee and voted upon."

Nyarlathotep catches his temples between the thumb and index finger of his right hand. "I think we need to take this to court."

"I think so too."

"Yes." A flash of teeth. "Let's."

Yan Luo sighs, and as the echoes of the sound fade from the massive chamber, the walls themselves begin to melt, swapping Yan Luo's abode for the colosseum that had witnessed Ao Qin's sentencing.

Except there is no one else here this time. Just the three of us. The white sand remains distorted, warped by heat, alternatively soot-black or glimmering with contortions of glass. I ignore the blood stains; it's only polite.

Yan Luo lumbers towards his judicial stand and clambers into his seat, an excruciating process bookended by old-man grunts and the crackle of disgruntled cartilage. *Thump*. He steeples fingers over the ledge of his perch and glares.

"Present your case."

A *fwhump* of air, woollen, like the gust of wind from a closing door, flutters across the standards. Candle-wicks flare in the audience, attenuating into identifiable shapes: gods and spirits unnumbered, drawn to the promise of drama. When you live forever, I suppose, any cause for diversion is coveted.

EVERYTHING INEVITABLY GETS more complicated when lawyers become involved.

Of course, Nyarlathotep argues against Yan Luo's impartiality, citing personal bias. And of course, Yan Luo will not be persuaded to accept a candidate of the former's choosing. Naturally, it all becomes quite apocalyptic when I introduce a third variable: my contractual obligations to the ghouls, which states that they acquire full ownership the moment that Diyu's ability to maintain market share—whatever *that* means—is brought into question.

Let's not even get into what happens when they try to fill the jury.

How does it all end, you ask? It hasn't, yet. According to Yan Luo, there's no telling *when* it will reach a resolution. For now, I'm confiscated property, alienated from all my masters, protected by interpantheon law, and incapable of being forced into any new legislative activities until this debacle settles itself. Conditionally free, as the case might be.

Did I plan this? No. Definitely not. Do I really look like the kind of man who would carefully sign portions of his life away, fully aware that some sub-clauses might contradict others, leading to a legal gridlock of Herculean proportions? All the while waiting, just waiting, for the perfect piece to slot into a perpetual motion machine of complications in order to buy himself indefinite liberty?

Of course I don't.

AN ENDING

"Hey, Fariz. How are you doing?" I rest my forehead on the polymer frame of the phone booth, and try to ignore the man masturbating frantically on a bench five feet away. Even the most middle-of-the-road milquetoast has a breaking point, I suppose. And that man is embracing his with orgasmic abandon.

"Dude," Fariz hisses into the phone, sleep-slurred. "Where are you calling from? What time is it there? Are you even allowed to be awake?"

The frantic onanism is reaching a crescendo; the man's breathing labors through his moans; his noises deepen to bull-like lowing. I inch a few steps away, cup a hand over the phone. "Honestly, I don't know. I couldn't even tell you what day it is."

"Thursday?"

"Real helpful, man. Real helpful."

A gaggle of drunken women, hair bleached sunlight-pale, totter unsteadily onto the platform, heels clacking. Their chatter quickly rises to screeching horror. Out of the periphery of an eye I see the masturbator giving them a thumbs-up as the group clatters away.

"You're the one that's calling me out of the blue after I told you—"

"Yeah. About that." I push my tongue against the top of my mouth and stare at the ceiling. "What if I told you that you *might* want to consider, maybe, getting out of the house for a while and laying low? Because there is, and I'm not saying that this is *definitely* the case, the small chance that a bunch of angry people are about to come visit the manor."

"What did you do, Rupert—"

"People keep asking me that. I never know why. No one ever seems to like it when I tell them the truth. The short answer is: stuff. I did *stuff*. Stuff that your Uncle and a lot of people in power deserve. But maybe not you, because you didn't actively fuck me over."

"Rupert—"

A cadre of policemen materialize at the climax of the masturbator's performance, bright buttons gleaming like headlights in the navy of their uniforms. They escort him away without resorting to unnecessary mockery.

"I have to go. Good luck. Remember what I said. Get out. And if you're feeling generous, you know my bank account details. I'm really, really broke."

ANOTHER ENDING

"YOU'RE ALIVE!"

Veles shrugs, daintily abashed, disarmingly *normal* in his penguin suit, the shirt slightly too small for his ursine frame. He beams at me. His braids are gathered into a dense ponytail, and he smells corrosively of aftershave.

"And cleaned up," I add with a nod. "And working for a proper restaurant?"

The air is steeped with smells: caramelized onion and fresh pol sambal; cumin and cinnamon, black pepper and fenugreek, turmeric and curry leaves; a complex decoction of stews; meats crisping in their own fats, rich as kings. Sri Lankan high cuisine. You have to love it.

"New job has dress code." Another easy shrug. "So Veles comply. Only seem polite. And beside, owners had nice things to say about Veles' experiences in 'charitable service.'"

"I—" A rich pang of happiness, shapeless, wine-sweet. "*How?*"

He waves at the empty tables, eyebrows raised. The restaurant is small but well-appointed, if a little cramped. I take his hint and let him lead me towards an unoccupied seat by the window. Bracketed by residential streets, this corner of Croydon is a stolen quiet, unique in its stillness.

Veles sets a menu in my hands.

"New gods not so bad," he remarks, still beaming. "Like children, sometimes. Or angry puppies. Both things that Veles has experience with."

"I thought they would have tried to, you know, kill you or—"

"Here is thing that Veles learned. Thousand of years ago, man was too busy staying alive to understand social topics like wage parity, inequality, xenophobia. Now, there is language for it. There is knowledge. And there are gods to watch over the little ones, gods with voices that cannot be silenced any longer."

"So they took you in?" I pick out a simple course: egg appam and duck curry, sweet tea to counter any excessive spice.

"Something like that." His smile, bright, brilliant with a yearning hope, is something I know I'll always carry with me to dark places.

"I—what about everyone else? Hildra—"

"Modelling now."

"—and—and the feldgeist?" My voice staggers to a pause as a memory surfaces: the explosion in the soup kitchen. The rusalka and the fox were in there with me.

"Safe," Veles says, to my surprise. "She and Adriana are two sides of coin, da? They will always find each other, always save each other. Elsa brought her home. They live on farm now outside of London."

"And the fox?"

The god-turned-waiter spreads his palms. "Who knows? Tricksters don't die. They only get bored. Any more questions? Or should Veles go get Rupert food?"

"I—" A drizzle springs into life outside. "No. I'm good."

Veles walks away to fulfill my order, leaves me to contemplate the rain as it tinsels London in silver.

ALSO AN ENDING

THE LAST TIME I see them is in the garden of a elegant café, its wall bedecked with illustrations of Parisian leisure. Flowers tangle in black-steel trellises, starbursts of vivid purple. People ramble over coffee and buttery croissants, curled on plain wooden benches. A golden retriever, snuggled under a table, watches as two tow-headed children race between tables.

I almost miss them in the halcyon bustle, too preoccupied with the dissection of a duck confit. But then the sunlight catches on Persephone's hair just so and I raise my gaze to lose myself in her smile. She's still pale, still possessed by that otherworldly pallor, still unhealthily gaunt, but her eyes are alive, and she's laughing at something someone just said and the sight of it eases the weight of a hurt I didn't even know I had.

Her companion tilts a glance over her shoulder, lips crooking a wry little smile: Demeter. She daubs clotted cream from her mouth and winks an eye before rising to her feet, sundress falling in ripples of paisley. Persephone remains seated, attention transfixed by the butterfly that had deigned to perch on a raised hand.

A breeze carries an unseasonal warmth across the space, a promise of summer gone but not forgotten. Demeter tucks a curl behind an ear as she draws close. I'm mesmerized by the simple gesture, by the power that washes from her: golden wheat, a lungful of love and the headiness of a good harvest. She sits and I can hardly breathe through the impulse to offer worship. For once, it isn't a desire coerced, but something purer.

I'm marvelling over the implications when Demeter speaks, voice soft. "So."

"So."

"How are you doing?"

"Not bad, all things taken into consideration." The golden retriever is finally coaxed into entertaining the kids. It gambols around them in circles, accelerating with every orbit. "How are the two of you doing?"

"We're good. Persephone is talking. Eating. She's *damaged*—" Demeter's lips vanish into a line. The butterfly spreads its wings: iridescent blues and cyans, like stained-glass windows pieced from sapphires. "But it will be alright. We have eternity."

I pop a slice of fried potato into my mouth. The flavor is perfect: salty, steeped in garlic, soaked in the juices from the duck. "What are you going to do now with all that cosmic power?"

She makes a moue. "That might be slightly too generous a description for what I've inherited. But to answer the question: I don't know. We'll see. Perhaps, we will begin by seeing how we can make up for what we've broken. I have a lot to make up for."

I nod. "Seems like a good place to start."

Demeter leans over and touches her lips to my forehead. "Be well, Rupert. I hope you find the peace you need."

And with that, she sashays out of my life.

SIMILARLY, ANOTHER ENDING

"WHO ARE THESE women?"

I shrug and jab a finger at random geriatrics, elbows propped on the lip of the counter, legs stretched long. It had been an ordeal, corralling all the old ladies. "That's Nan. That's Grandma. That's Popo, Ah Ma, Grandmother, Granny. I think that's—"

"Those aren't names!"

"Those are absolutely things hypothetical grandchildren would call them."

The orderly gesticulates at my ensemble of pensioners, reduced to sputtering. Around us, a crowd kindles. I grin at him. Poor kid. He looks about nineteen, or a baby-faced twenty-two, gangly and unused to the length of his limbs. No one that should have to navigate such a bizarre encounter. But I have a flight to catch.

"Sir. *Sir.*" He clears his throat. "I understand your desire to be a good Samaritan. But you can't just check in twelve old women who you clearly are not related to."

"Can't I? You could just pretend they were anonymously donated. Call the newspapers or something. Everyone loves a weird story."

"Sir, *please.*"

I push myself away from the counter and wedge a hand in a pocket. The other, I flutter above my head in a grandiose gesture of farewell. "Enjoy the publicity, kid. And be careful of the Russian one. She's scary."

AN EPILOGUE

THE MAN STUMBLING through the labyrinth of plastic tables looks like he hasn't bathed in weeks. His trenchcoat is sodden, armpits discolored by black stains. Not that anyone could blame him. That attire is hardly appropriate for tropical weather. His backpack, large enough to store a whole life, is a menace. Every time he turns, he crashes into another plate, spills another mug of ice-cold Milo. Fried noodles erupt through the air, even as shouting chases him onward.

He gets closer. There is a frightening purpose communicated in his motions, and a clarity in his gaze that unnerves me, despite its drug-soaked intensity. We make eye contact. Instantly, he barrels in my direction, shouldering aside half-hearted endeavors to impede his approach.

I'm on my feet before he hits my table.

"You're Rupert." That glow in his eyes; it isn't meth or madness. If anything, it's *mythological*, divine power throbbing through the conduit of his mind. "Right?"

"Depends on who is asking."

My fingers clench around the hilt of a switchblade. It's been a good few weeks. The ghouls, abruptly embroiled in a sticky legal case that they had definitely not been expecting to face, are now the subject of criminal investigations. An anonymous source, rumor insists, apparently revealed critical information pertinent to their involvement in certain political debacles. None of this, of course, affected me—except that they're now too busy to interrogate me about my activities in London.

To make matters sweeter, Fariz, somehow removed from the commotion, actually took the effort to secure me accommodations and plane tickets back home. I wouldn't call the hostel I'm holed up in 'luxurious.' 'Adequate' at best, and even that's a stretch. But there is air-conditioning and an absence of cockroaches, and I do have a room for the foreseeable future. Plus, there's a Mamak right outside.

Everything has been great, honestly. Except for one thing.

I haven't seen Ao Qin yet.

But I suspect that's about to change.

High above, lightning scrawls an ominous agreement between the clouds. I shade my eyes and look for scales in the sky. All said and done, I suppose I just wouldn't feel right without at least one life-threatening complication hovering in the firmament.

"My name is Fitz. I think you have to help me save the world."

The storm furls itself into coils, clouds thunder-lit from within. Customers rouse themselves from their plastic chairs and plunge towards shelter, unwilling to endure the encroaching deluge. I sigh and straighten, rolling the kinks out of my neck, even as I call up a well of power from the base of my belly.

"Only if you can help me kill a dragon first."

ABOUT THE AUTHOR

Cassandra Khaw writes a *lot*. Sometimes, she writes press releases and excited emails for Singaporean micropublisher Ysbryd Games. Sometimes, she writes for technology and video games outlets like *Eurogamer*, *Ars Technica*, *The Verge*, and *Engadget*. Mostly, though, she writes about the intersection between nightmares and truth, drawing inspiration from Southeast Asian mythology and stories from people she has met. She occasionally spends time in a Muay Thai gym punching people and pads.